INTO THE FIRE

Also by Gregg Hurwitz

INTO THE FIRE

Gregg Hurwitz

MINOTAUR
BOOKS
NEW YORK

First published in the United States by Minotaur Books, an imprint of St. Martin's Publishing Group

INTO THE FIRE. Copyright © 2019 by Gregg Hurwitz. All rights reserved. Printed in the United States of America. For information, address St. Martin's Publishing Group, 120 Broadway, New York, NY 10271.

www.minotaurbooks.com

The Library of Congress Cataloging-in-Publication Data is available upon request.

ISBN 978-1-250-12045-8 (hardcover)
ISBN 978-1-250-62368-3 (international, sold outside the U.S., subject to rights availability)
ISBN 978-1-250-12047-2 (ebook)

Our books may be purchased in bulk for promotional, educational, or business use. Please contact your local bookseller or the Macmillan Corporate and Premium Sales Department at 1-800-221-7945, extension 5442, or by email at MacmillanSpecialMarkets@macmillan.com.

First U.S. Edition: January 2020
First International Edition: January 2020

10 9 8 7 6 5 4 3 2 1

To my parents, Alfred and Marjorie Hurwitz

The older I get,
the more I appreciate
the depth of what they gave me.

INTO THE FIRE

1

The Terror

The industrial sliding doors heaved open to a burst of bitter alpine air, a dizzying flurry of snow, and a barrage of hoarse cries. "Hello—*goddamn it*—somebody help! He's bad. He's really— Oh, Jesus, wake up, Grant. Please, just— Someone help!"

From the blurry white, Terzian emerged, lugging his injured companion into the waiting room. Grant's head lolled to one side, and the arm slung over Terzian's neck was limp. The toes of his rubber boots dragged across the hospital tiles, squeaking at intervals.

The intake nurse bolted off her stool, already reaching for the intercom to rouse Dr. Patel from her cot in the on-call room. The urgent-care facility was a one-doc shop—six beds, two nurses, a single ER physician now at the midpoint of her forty-eight-hour shift. Strategically positioned on the steep mountain road between the lake resorts of Big Bear and Arrowhead, the skeleton-crew operation serviced adventuresome souls damaged by the vicissitudes of weather or their own basic human stupidity. Torn ACLs from unyielding skis, ulnas shattered by lost footing on black ice, collarbones obliterated against steering columns—these were the bread-and-butter afflictions mended within the facility's weather-battered walls.

Grant's injury looked much more severe.

The intake nurse flew out from behind her station, and Jenna, the staff nurse, was running up the hall toward them with a gurney. Dr. Patel jogged behind her, flattening her stethoscope to her chest with a palm to keep it from bouncing. Though her eyes were heavy with sleep, she looked ready to work, her teal scrub sleeves hiked up over her shoulders.

"Let's get him horizontal *now*," she said, digging in her breast pocket for a penlight.

The nurses stepped to the patient, and he slipped from Terzian's shoulder into their arms. They puddled him onto the gurney. Though the doors had slid closed again, November air still swirled in the lobby, tasting of pine.

Dr. Patel rapid-fired questions: "What's his name?"

"Grant. Grant Merriweather."

"And you are?"

"Terzian. His friend."

"What happened?"

"He was driving, lost control—the slush—and . . . and . . . next thing I knew, we were over the edge, right out there—" With a wobbly finger, he pointed through the wall. "We hit a tree, and he was like this. I had to pull him out. Thank God you were so close. It's like a miracle."

"Left pupil blown and unreactive." Patel clicked off her penlight. "Epidural hematoma."

"Wait—*what*? What's that mean?"

"He's got a bleed in his brain. There's too much pressure. We need to CT him—now."

"You have to save him. You *have to* save him."

The gurney wheels rattled as the three women, trailed by Terzian, sprinted into an adjoining room and fed Grant Merriweather's body into the massive white tunnel. He started posturing, his muscles stiffening, limbs straining. His dilated pupil looked un-human, the halved marble of a stuffed animal's eye.

As the machine whirred calmingly, Terzian tore off his jacket. Sweat darkened the cuffs of his long-sleeved T-shirt. He stomped from foot to foot, yanking at his sleeves, his untucked shirt sway-ing. Sweat filmed his forehead, and he was breathing hard, the air thin here at seven thousand feet above sea level.

Jenna placed a hand on his back. "We're gonna take good care of him."

Dr. Patel was over by the monitors, reading the images. "We got midline shift, the brain pushed to the right side. Sheila, call for a medical airlift. We have to get him to a brain center—Cedars or UCLA."

"Wait, you can't take him," Terzian said. "You can't just *take* him."

Patel ignored him. "Jenna, get me the surgical drill."

Jenna hesitated. "You're gonna drill a burr hole? Are we set up for that?"

"No. But if we don't get some of this pressure relieved, he's not gonna make it to the city." Patel's dark eyes darted to Terzian. "And get *him* outside. Sir, I need you outside."

But Jenna was already gone.

"Is this gonna wake him up?" Terzian asked.

"It might. Outside, please, sir. We have to take care of your friend."

Terzian backpedaled through the swinging door as Jenna rushed in with the surgical drill. She handed it off and then slid trauma shears up the front of Grant's sweatshirt, getting access to his chest in the event they'd have to jump him. She pulled up one leg of his jeans before Patel said, "Wait. It'll have to wait. Hold his head."

The doctor readied the cranial perforator, then placed the drill bit three centimeters above the left ear, revved up the motor, and punched a hole through the parietal bone.

Blood drooled out, and then Grant's eyelids fluttered. He moaned and moaned again. "P-please . . ." he mumbled.

Jenna peeled back Grant's shirt, and her hand went to her mouth. "Doctor? *Doctor?*"

Patel looked down at the wounds puckering Grant's chest and stomach. More knots of shiny, angry flesh dotted the visible part of his thigh.

They heard the rasp of the door, and then Sheila breezed in. "The medevac's en route from—" She read Patel's face, went up on tiptoes to peer at the patient, the words sucked from her mouth.

"This man wasn't in a car crash," Patel said slowly. "He was tortured."

"Please," Grant mumbled again. "M-make it stop."

The door rasped again.

A shadow darkened the air at Sheila's shoulder.

For a split second, the women remained frozen, afraid to move. Then they turned in concert.

Terzian's suppressed pistol pipped three times.

A hat trick of head shots.

The women collapsed, jerked down as if pulled by unseen hands. They hit the floor at once, clearing Terzian's view to Grant Merriweather.

Terzian's affect had changed entirely. Not a ripple of distress stirred the surface of his face. He held the barrel steady, sighted now at Grant's groin. Half-moons of sweat darkened his shirt beneath either arm; controlling a grown man while wrangling electrical cables and clamps required a fair amount of exertion.

Terzian's cuffs had ridden up past the bulges of his forearms, revealing where he'd carved patterns into his skin, the scarification process leaving his flesh textured elaborately. Rose-colored divots scalloped the rich brown skin where Old English lettering spelled out his nickname: THE TERROR.

He spoke now with his true voice, the accent seeping through, rounding the vowels, rolling the r's.

"Give me the name," he said calmly. "Or it begins all over again. But worse."

Grant cupped his hand to the side of his head with disbelief. He looked at his palm, sticky and dark.

"The name," Terzian said once more.

The Terror

Grant blinked against watering eyes. A shuddering breath left him, the sound of defeat. "My cousin," he said. "Max Merriweather."

Terzian put a round through the hole Dr. Patel had conveniently drilled for him.

Unscrewing the suppressor from the threaded barrel, he pocketed it. Then he stooped to pick his jacket off the floor. In the far distance, the sound of the medevac came barely audible over the moan of the wind.

Pulling on his jacket, he stepped over the bodies and shouldered out through the swinging door.

2

Puzzles He Didn't Know How to Solve

At the Fuller Street trailhead of Runyon Canyon, Max Merriweather stitched his hands together behind him and leaned forward to stretch out his lower back, where thirty-three years of wear and tear had taken roost. Hikers were out in force, gay couples and aggressively fit moms, dog walkers and the occasional celebrity in oversize sunglasses and a don't-notice-me slouch beanie. To the west the sun coasted down behind a bank of clouds, fuchsia embers warming up into a sunset.

The older he got, the more life seemed to present him with puzzles he didn't know how to solve. Holding down steady work. Stashing away money. And Violet.

Two years and seven months later and he still couldn't think of Violet without feeling it in his chest, a ping to the soft tissue.

He knew he wore the weight of it in his face, in the knots of his shoulders, in the stiffness of his back. These days people looked at him like they didn't want him to rub off on them. He couldn't blame them. He didn't want to rub off on *himself*.

Oh, well. As his old man said, *A whole lotta folks do better with worse.*

The breeze blew sage and chaparral, the dusty scent of the Santa Monica Mountains when you got away from the asphalt and car exhaust. Max started up the trail, nearing a homeless guy five layers deep in rags. The man seemed to grow out from the base of the fence, an organism composed of tattered cardboard, scraps of bedding, and dirt-caked flesh. Swollen legs protruded from a shabby blanket, the skin the same color as the fabric, the dirt. His feet were bare, the soles cracked like shattered plastic. A pit-bull mix was curled up beside him, his snout scarred like the hull of an old ship—probably a dogfight rescue.

The man rattled some coins in a chewed Fatburger cup. "Help a guy out?"

Max said, "We all got it rough, pal."

The man nodded sagely. "Ain't that the truth."

Max jogged up the trail, weaving through the post-workday rush. Designer mini-dogs trotted on bejeweled leashes. Rihanna blared from Beats headphones. A few young guys moved together like a pride of lions, their hair cut in *Mad Men* parts, negotiating deals too loudly on their phones. A silver-haired husband and wife held hands and looked as content as anyone Max had ever seen outside a TV commercial.

He reached Inspiration Point and took in the downtown skyline miles to the southeast. The scrubby trail brush in the foreground framed the urban sprawl beyond, a snapshot of Los Angeles in all its rangy glory.

Violet had always loved this view. And now this was the closest to her he could get.

A mom nudged up beside him with an off-road stroller rugged enough to have been designed by the United States Army. Behind dark mesh a baby cooed, and Max turned quickly away.

He ran back down even harder.

As he passed through the gate, he heard the homeless guy rattle his few coins and call out to the pride of young men.

The loudest of the bunch muted his phone against his chest. "Quit bugging everyone, dude. You're a joke."

The homeless guy said, "Then help me *not* be a joke."

The young man laughed, white teeth flashing, and pointed at him. "Nice try, bud. Nice try."

Max walked up the street to where he'd left his truck, a Trail-Blazer with rust patches eating through the wheel wells. He had to climb in across the passenger seat because a tap-and-run months back had dented in the driver's door.

He sat for a moment, hands on the steering wheel. He thought of the homeless guy back by the fence, those painful deep cracks running through the soles of his blackened feet. *Help me* not *be a joke.*

He turned the truck on but couldn't bring himself to tug the gearshift into drive.

A whole lotta folks do better with worse.

Defeated, he cut the engine and climbed out over the console. He headed back toward the trailhead.

Three minutes later he returned.

Barefoot.

From the truck bed, he pulled out a dirty pair of socks and his work boots, worn from his by-the-day construction gig. When he crawled back behind the wheel, his phone chimed in the glove box.

He popped open the antique clamshell he'd been using ever since he fell behind on the payments for his iPhone.

A text from his father waited: YOUR COUSIN GRANT WAS KILLED LAST NIGHT. FIGURED YOU SHOULD KNOW.

Max lowered his face, took a few deep breaths, his hand clammy around the phone. Then he shoved the truck into gear, the transmission complaining, and headed into whatever the day held.

As Max drove up to his apartment on the last street in Culver City still unclaimed by gentrification, he reminded himself: He didn't know anything about anything.

This seemed true in general. But specifically it meant that he didn't—shouldn't—have to worry about the nonsense that Grant had saddled him with two months ago.

Puzzles He Didn't Know How to Solve

He recalled the scene with the clarity reserved for painful memories. Golden Boy Grant, the pride and joy of the Merriweathers, paying his first visit to Max's shitty second-floor apartment, standing on the worn carpet in a thousand-dollar suit so he wouldn't have to sit on the stained couch. Grant, whose exploits and accomplishments Max heard about at every infrequent brush with a family member. Grant, the forensic accountant, certified in internal auditing, business evaluation, fraud examination, financial forensics, and God knew what else, the licensure initials appended to his signature even on the family fucking Christmas card. Grant, caped investigator of misfeasance, who scoured the books at the behest of insurance companies, police departments, attorneys, banks, courts, government regulatory bodies, and the occasional private citizen. Grant of the rugged good looks, the strong chin, of the spit-shined wingtips and high-precision haircut. "Exactitude is my business," he'd told Max on more than one occasion. And indeed, sprawled on his inferior couch, Max noted that he could probably cut himself on the crease of his cousin's slacks.

Grant had handed him a canary-yellow envelope and said, "If anything ever happens to me, call the number inside."

Max said, "You serious with this Hitchcock routine?"

"Dead serious."

Max swallowed dryly and said, "Whose number is it?"

"A reporter at the *L.A. Times*. Don't trust this to anyone but her. Promise me."

"What's up with you, Grant?"

Grant laughed. "Nothing. Nothing's gonna happen to me. Look, I deal with some heavy hitters. And I've taken down my share of shady characters. I just want to make sure I have . . ." He paused, no doubt selecting his next word with that legendary exactitude. "Insurance. In case one day I kick over the wrong rock. It's not the kind of thing you'd come across in your . . ." Another exactitudinous pause. "Line of work. But as you said, you've seen stuff like this before in the movies."

In the movies, Max thought, this shit always worked out. The hero prepares his in-the-event-of-my-death file to disincentivize anyone from whacking him in a dark alley. Then he wades brashly into the conspiracy and outs the bad guys, saving the day. And no one has to waste a single thought on the schmuck holding the insurance envelope.

But this wasn't the movies, and if Max had learned one thing from real life, it was that it didn't go as well as cinematic bullshit.

He looked down at the holes worn through the knees of his jeans, sawdust still caught in the white harp strings of denim. "I don't know, man. This cloak-and-dagger stuff isn't really my thing."

"Come on, Max," Grant said, like he was talking to a kid or a dense customer-service specialist. "For once in your life, maybe step up, shoulder some responsibility."

A stiletto to the gut. It took Max a few seconds to breathe again. He kept his eyes lowered, not wanting to let Grant see how devastatingly effective his neat little salvo had been. He imagined that Grant had rehearsed it a time or two in the mirror at his health club.

Max studied his hands. "What about Jill?"

"My wife's not exactly a safe distance removed from me. Or my family. The thing with you is, no one will ever know. I mean, no one would ever think of you."

Max said, "Right."

"You know what I mean. Now, please, Max." Grant considered his Breitling. "I have to get back to the office. Can I count on you?"

Max picked at a ragged edge of thumbnail where he'd nicked it in a band saw. Without looking up, he held out his hand. "I promise."

"Great. Thanks so much." Grant almost seemed sincere. "Thanks, Mighty Max."

That brought him back. Five years old at a family picnic at Point Dume, and Max had built the tallest sandcastle. Then he'd Godzilla-stomped his way through it, and everyone had laughed and pointed, even his old man, and Grant had bestowed on him the nickname. A brief, shining moment when he'd been the pride of the Merriweathers.

Grant stepped forward and slapped the stiff canary-yellow envelope into Max's palm. Something jangled inside, small but solid.

Puzzles He Didn't Know How to Solve

A waft of expensive cologne and Grant was gone.

Nothing's gonna happen to me.

Parked at the curb now, Max recalled how long he'd sat there holding the envelope. How he'd duct-taped it behind his toilet tank before leaving to line up with the hardworking Hispanic day laborers outside Home Depot, hoping to be picked.

He pulled out his clamshell phone and read the last text exchange once again in case it had magically rewritten itself in the past fifteen minutes.

ME: HOW'D HE DIE?

DAD: GUESS HE WAS SHOT. PROB'LY ONE OF THE BAD GUYS HE HAD UNDER THE MAGNIFYING GLASS. A DAMN SHAME. ALWAYS THE GOOD ONES WHO GO YOUNG.

Pocketing the phone, Max started to climb out of his truck, but then he looked up and halted on all fours on the passenger seat. Up on the second floor of his building, the perennially unshaven and surnameless Mr. Omar had just emerged from his apartment to head to Max's place next door. He shuffled through the jaundiced beams thrown from the outdoor hallway's overhead lights. When he reached Max's door, he knocked with considerable force.

"Max, Max, Max. You're late again. Max? I can hear you in there. Don't make me keep being a bother, my friend. I have more important matters to handle, believe me."

Mr. Omar rapped a few more times, sighed audibly, and returned to his apartment. Through the big front window, Max watched him settle back into his Barcalounger, bathed in the aquarium light of his television.

Tomorrow's shift would put Max over the top for this month's rent—he'd beeline straight from work to Mr. Omar and settle up then.

Crawling from the truck, he closed the door as quietly as he could manage. Rather than risk the stairs and walk past Mr. Omar's window, he headed for the telephone pole at the edge of the building. Convenient U-shaped steps studded the pole.

Up he went, getting one foot on the convenient gutter ledge, and then in through the bathroom window he kept unlocked for moments like this.

He stepped down off the closed toilet lid and reached for the door when he heard it in the bedroom.

A tearing sound.

Shush shush shush.

He paused, not trusting his ears.

There it was again, a trio of unsettling rasps.

His lips felt suddenly dry. When he reached for the doorknob, his hand trembled ever so slightly.

He turned the doorknob slowly. The hinges were mercifully silent. The apartment lights were turned off, but a two-inch strip of pale yellow from the outside hall fell across his eye when he put it to the crack.

A man.

In his bedroom.

Working in the dark.

Wife-beater T-shirt. Prominent arm muscles oiled with sweat and marked with something else: Tattoos? Henna ink? Scars? One of them at the triceps was swirled like a pinwheel. The man's back was turned, his shoulders rippling, his hands set to some unseen task. The smell of him hung heavily in the unvented air, a pungent musk like meat on the verge of turning.

Max's drawers had been emptied, his few possessions strewn across the floor, the bureau tipped away from the wall. The TV was upended, holes punched in the drywall.

The man straightened up and armed his brow, his fist coming clear, clenched around a combat knife with a serrated edge.

Letters on his forearm resolved from the shadows sufficiently for Max to piece them together: THE TERROR. Visible past the man's thighs, beneath the stripped-aside sheets, the mattress had been sawed open at intervals, the ticking bulged out intestinally.

The man spun the knife in his hand with a skilled proficiency, bent over the mattress once more, and punched the blade into a virgin spot. It made a thwack as if puncturing flesh.

And then the nightmare grating came once again: *shush shush shush.*

Puzzles He Didn't Know How to Solve

A thought blinked through Max's brain. If he hadn't walked back to the homeless guy at the trail, he would've been three minutes earlier, which meant he wouldn't have seen Mr. Omar, which meant he would have strolled right through his front door into the teeth of this nightmare.

The rising burn in his chest demanded he ease out a breath. Painstakingly, he inched the door back into the frame and rotated the doorknob to its resting place. The click when he released it might as well have been a clap of thunder.

He backed to the toilet, crinkling his eyes as the blistered linoleum compressed with a click. One room over he heard a throat-muffled grunt, another thwack, and then the *shush shush shush* of the blade.

Max couldn't help but imagine the knife working its way through sinew and tendons. His vision speckled, and a wave of light-headedness swept through him. He firmed his legs, blinked himself back from the edge.

Move, he told himself. *Quick and quiet. You can do this.*

He patted blindly behind the toilet tank, tore free the canary-yellow envelope, and wormed back out through the window.

3

Ordinary

On the twenty-first floor of the high-end but somewhat dated Castle Heights Residential Tower, there is a door.

It looks like an ordinary door, but it is not.

The thin wood façade, which resembles every other residential door in the building, disguises a steel interior, which in turn houses an elaborate network of security bars. The core is filled with water, a new measure designed to disperse heat from a battering ram. A ram will buckle before it will breach.

On the other side of the door is a penthouse.

It looks like an ordinary penthouse, but it is not.

If you wander the seven thousand square feet of gunmetal-gray floor, you will see a variety of workout pods, from heavy bags to racked kettlebells. You will see a freestanding fireplace, a few rarely used couches, a spiral staircase winding up to a reading loft. The open design gives you a clear view into the kitchen with its poured-concrete countertops and brushed-nickel fixtures. You will encounter a living wall from which sprout mint, chamomile,

Ordinary

and a potpourri of other culinary herbs. What you won't notice is that the panoramic glass walls that gaze east to downtown Los Angeles and south to Century City are composed of bullet-resistant polycarbonate thermoplastic resin. Or that the retractable sunscreens, shaded an innocuous periwinkle, are made of an exotic titanium composite woven tightly enough to stop any sniper rounds that might penetrate the bullet-resistant panes.

At the back of the clean, minimalist space, you can walk down the sole hall. You might enter a master bedroom suite. To the right is a bathroom.

It looks like an ordinary bathroom, but it is not.

If you nudge the frosted-glass shower door, it will roll back silently on barn-hanger carbon-steel wheels. The hot-water lever hides invisible sensors, keyed to the palm print of one person only. Concealed expertly in the tile pattern is a secret door.

The bedroom is as sparse spotless as the rest of the house—bureau, floor, bed.

It looks like an ordinary bed, but it is not.

At second glance you might notice it is floating in the air. The mattress sits on a slab that is repelled from the floor by neodymium rare-earth magnets strong enough to anchor a small ship. Steel cables hold the slab suspended three feet off the floor. Were they severed, the slab would fly up, smash through the ceiling, and go airborne above the Wilshire Corridor.

A man sits on the bed, legs crossed, spine straight, so still that he might be carved from marble. He lives by a set of Commandments, and this act of meditating embodies the Second: *How you do anything is how you do everything.* His eyes are closed, but not all the way. His open hands rest on his thighs. He is nowhere, but precisely here. He is nothing more than his breath. He is doing one thing and one thing only. This is the opposite of multitasking.

He looks like an ordinary man.

He is not.

Within the top echelon of intel circles in nations of influence and instability, Evan Smoak was known as Orphan X.

At the age of twelve, he'd been pulled out of a foster home in East Baltimore and raised in a full black covert operation buried so deep inside the U.S. government that virtually no one knew it existed. His upbringing consisted of relentless physical, emotional, cultural, and psychological training, a grinding wheel that honed him into a razor-sharp implement. His handler, Jack Johns, raised him not merely to be a top-tier assassin but also a human being—two reactive elements that, if put under enough pressure, might combust.

And then Jack had taught him to integrate those pieces. To balance on the tightrope dividing yin from yang. To not combust.

It was a lifelong challenge.

When Evan had gone rogue from the Orphan Program, he'd kept his other alias—the Nowhere Man—and devoted himself to helping people in dire circumstances who had no one to turn to. His clients reached him by calling a little-known number that had become the stuff of urban legend: 1-855-2-NOWHERE. Each digitized call traveled over the Internet through a maze of encrypted virtual-private-network tunnels, circling the planet before reaching Evan's RoamZone phone.

He answered the same way every time: *Do you need my help?*

And then he stepped in to protect the innocent because no one else would, to shield them from those who would do them harm. To hunt a monster, the shopworn proverb went, you must become one. But to Evan's ear the saying had always rung hollow.

He had been monstrous once, a weapon sharpened to a singular point. His role as the Nowhere Man was an undoing of that. Every time he helped someone, he regained some tiny part of his soul.

And when he was done, he asked his clients to pass the favor along. To empower themselves by finding someone else in untenable circumstances.

Evan had last helped a young man with a gentle demeanor and a special brain, who had been terrorized by an entire criminal enterprise. Like every client before him, Trevon Gaines had his assignment—to find Evan the next person in desperate need. To give the Nowhere Man's phone number to that person. And Evan would be waiting once more on the other end of the line, ready to pick up and do it all over again.

Ordinary

"Redemption" was an imperfect word for what he was seeking. Confronting the world with his own code, illuminating the darkness with the guttering light of his own morality—that was a process of becoming.

Becoming less sharp. More human.

The more life he let in, the more he could sense the dawn of a different existence shimmering miragelike in the distance. He'd been on a single trajectory since the age of twelve, launched from a slingshot into all the menace mankind had to offer. As the Nowhere Man, he'd shifted his bearings, sure, but not his fundamental direction.

In the past year, he'd resected the cancer of his past. He'd vanquished the corrupt Orphans pursuing him. And the man at whose direction they'd been acting—the president of the United States. The plan to wipe out the innocent Orphans had been stopped and the survivors scattered to the wind.

Now that Evan was no longer running *from* something, he'd started to wonder where he was running *to*. Lately he felt worn down, bone-tired. More and more, questions were arising from some deep-buried place.

How much atonement was enough?

How much longer could he forge through the refuse-choked alleys of cities, staring down eyes as black as the abyss, souls clouded with sick intentions?

Would he just keep going until he was holding down a slab at the morgue?

At some point had he earned enough of himself back to deserve something better?

He didn't know. But he'd decided nonetheless.

The next adventure would be his last.

One more ring of the durable black phone that he kept on his person at all times. One more time he'd shatter through into the underworld and—if he could make it back alive—carry someone out of damnation. One more time sacrificing a pound of his flesh to win a piece of his soul.

One last mission and he was out.

4

A Healthy Touch of Paranoia

Parked in an alley behind a grocery store in West L.A., Max took a deep breath and tore open the cheery yellow envelope Grant had given him.

It contained a folded piece of Grant's letterhead with a name and phone number scrawled on it. Lorraine Lennox, who Max took to be the reporter at the *Los Angeles Times* who Grant told him he could trust. As he unfolded the bottom flap of the letter, a smaller yellow envelope tumbled into his lap. Three words written boldly across the front: *"DO NOT OPEN."* It had some heft to it, as if it contained a silver dollar.

Max tossed the smaller envelope onto the passenger seat. Stared at the number on the letter.

"If anything ever happens to me, call the number inside."

Max wasn't worth much, but he was worth his word.

He dialed.

Four rings to voice mail. Lorraine Lennox, asking him to leave a message, sounded trustworthy enough. At the beep he said, "Yeah, hi, it's . . . uh, Max Merriweather. I need . . . I really need to talk to you as soon as possible. So call me back. Like now." He heard the intensity rising in his voice and took a breath. "I'm sorry if that sounds all stalkery. It's just— Look, I'm in a super weird situation— dangerous, even—and I need to . . . Uh, you're the only person I'm supposed to talk to. Because I promised, and . . ." He rubbed at his bleary eyes, unsure how to explain. "Please call me back. Okay. Thanks."

He rattled off his phone number and hung up.

He blew out a shaky breath and reminded himself that a whole lotta folks do better with worse, that he could be in Aleppo or Fallujah right now.

That he wasn't absolutely fucking terrified.

He was down to a quarter tank of gas, and he had no clothes, no money, no clue what to do next. He debated for the fifth time or the fiftieth whether he should go to the cops, but Grant had told him to trust nobody except Lorraine Lennox. Max had given his word, and now Grant's request had upgraded itself into a dying wish. Plus, encountering a bowie knife–wielding psychopath nicknamed "The Terror" had inspired a healthy touch of paranoia.

The air coming in through the vents carried the sickly-sweet smell of rotting produce, which didn't help the acid roiling in his gut.

He put his hands on the steering wheel as if he were going somewhere, but he had nowhere to go. He cursed Grant, himself, the whole untenable situation, and then he lost an internal struggle and reached for the phone once again.

This time a prerecorded message announced Ms. Lennox's office mailbox as full.

He hung up and glared over at the *DO NOT OPEN* envelope.

It glared back.

He reached for it and then withdrew his hand.

Grant inspired a kind of compliance. The oldest of the cousins, he'd always been the patriarch of this generation of Merriweathers. For his fiftieth birthday last March, he'd rented a yacht and hosted a champagne-and-starlight party on the marina. Max had heard all about it from his old man—crab claws and Perrier-Jouët, a string quartet and iPad party favors, each luxury recounted with a kind of accusation.

Max had entered the world a disappointment to his father. His mother had died from complications giving birth to him, a cardio-respiratory arrest from an amniotic-fluid embolism, big words he'd learned very young. His father, from a close-knit family of five brothers, had raised him stoically, pretending not to resent the fact that his only kid had robbed him of his shot at the future he'd imagined. Terry had seen through his paternal duties with joyless competence, providing the basics and little more.

The best defense, Max had quickly figured out, was to keep his head down, to be unseen, the squeakless wheel. After all, he already had enough to apologize for. Not wanting to intrude on his father, he'd GED'd his way out of Culver City High and gone to work. As long as he had his freedom, he was content to be the least robust apple on the family tree.

Until Violet.

The summer of his twenty-sixth birthday, he'd met her after a George Thorogood concert at the Morongo Casino near Palm Springs. His buddy scored tickets, and Max bought the overpriced beers, and they'd spilled out onto the casino floor afterward with "Bad to the Bone" ringing in their ears and an unearned sense of optimism for what the night could hold.

He'd spotted her in front of a quarter slot machine, twisting a strand of silken black hair around her finger, a near-empty bucket of quarters in her lap. She'd left her sandals on the floor, one bare foot propped on the base of the empty stool beside her. Dark eyes and red lips against pale-as-milk skin. She looked like an artist's sketch, alluring and complicated, deep waters moving beneath that tranquil façade.

Max's friend was lost to a roulette wheel, so Max had rushed over to change in a fiver, casting glances over his shoulder all the while, worried she was a vision that might vanish. For the first time since junior high, he had to work up his nerve to approach a member of the opposite sex.

"Can I sit here?" he asked, jingling his bucket.

A Healthy Touch of Paranoia

"I'm having an unlucky run," she said, not looking up. "If you're smart, you'll get as far away from me as possible."

"Don't worry," he said, "I'm not that smart."

At this she favored him with a wry smile.

And right on cue his first pull of the one-armed bandit hit triple cherries, coins sheeting clamorously from the chute. Two hundred twenty bucks paid out in quarters felt like a million.

Along with a half dozen onlookers, she'd congratulated him. He'd gathered up his money and his courage and said, "I'd really like to buy you dinner."

They were close enough then that he could breathe in her perfume, orange blossom and vanilla. He didn't know much about fragrances, but it smelled expensive.

She regarded him with a dark gaze. "So you got a bunch of money and now you want to ask me out?"

"In fairness," he said, "I wanted to ask you out *before* I got a bunch of money. But now I can afford to." He shrugged. "I was just looking for an excuse to sit next to you."

She bunched her lips and studied him, but he could see the amused grooves at the edges of her eyes, and that optimism he'd felt earlier swelled in his chest.

"Okay," she said, "but we're splitting the bill."

She came from money, a lot of money, her parents owning a thousand or so housing units in less savory neighborhoods around Greater Los Angeles. They had used the purse strings to control her for so long that, she confessed reluctantly over surf 'n' turf, she'd thought that was just how families worked.

As promised, she insisted on going dutch, but she let him buy dinner the next night back in Los Angeles and the night after that. "No strings attached," he said when he reached for the bill.

"You mean I don't have to sleep with you?" she said.

"You don't even have to make eye contact with me."

"Thank *God*," she said, leaning into him.

It wasn't a fast and furious courtship, but their lives had slowly vined together. Texts during the day. A change of clothes left in a bottom drawer. Grocery shopping together.

And then more.

They'd been together almost a year when, after a midnight screening of *Alien* at the Hollywood Forever Cemetery, she'd snuggled into him on the picnic blanket and quoted one of their favorite songs: "'Let's grow old together and die at the same time.'"

He looked into her eyes and saw what she was really asking. "Prop plane going down over the Serengeti?"

She smiled. "I was thinking tragic scuba accident whilst on geriatric travel tour."

In the flickering light of the projector there among the cinephiles and tombstones, he'd felt a surge of gratitude so intense it brought tears to his eyes. "Violet McKenna," he said, finding a knee. "Will you?"

"Hell yeah I will."

They kissed, and the folks around them, shushing them violently moments before, had burst into applause.

After that, in their occasional overlaps, the Merriweather clan took to Violet. How could they not? In her, it seemed, they'd finally found something to recommend Max. They started inviting him—them—around more, folding him back into the family with Waffle Sundays and Taco Tuesdays. "Don't screw it up," his father told him at every parting, nodding at Violet and wearing a smile that wasn't a smile at all.

On the other hand, Violet's parents, old money at least by California standards, disliked the idea of the relationship. That meant little to Violet. Between her kindergarten-teacher's salary and Max's construction work, they were getting by just fine, freeing her to cut the strings by which her parents had controlled her. If anything, their disapproval lent a *Romeo and Juliet* sheen to the courtship.

When they'd asked Max to the inevitable brunch at the Sierra Madre Four Seasons, Max agreed, hoping for a fresh start. Once the twelve-dollar orange juice was poured, Clark cleared his throat. "So, Maxwell. What exactly is your angle?"

Sensing now that it would be a short meal, Max folded the starched napkin back along its ironed lines and rested it on his place setting. "My angle is I love your daughter."

A Healthy Touch of Paranoia

Gwendolyn blinked a few times through the amber-tinted sunglasses that she wore day and night. "If you saw fit to move on, we'd certainly be willing to ease the transition. Maybe buy you a car."

"A car," Max repeated, unsure that he'd heard correctly.

"I know it feels quite romantic between the two of you," she said, sipping her Arnold Palmer, "but we're from different worlds. Violet's a complicated girl. How are you going to take care of her? By *loving* her?"

She snorted as if that were the most naïve thing in the world.

Which of course it was.

Max took it not as an insult but a challenge. He worked extra shifts, put in overtime every chance he got. After a brief ceremony at the Van Nuys courthouse, they took a couple of friends to lunch at Chili's to celebrate. They didn't need anything more than that.

With Violet's encouragement, Max used what little they'd socked away to pay for night classes at Cal State Northridge. His twelve-hour days stretched to sixteen. He was going to get a B.A. and then maybe go to law school from there. With her at his side, he could be the person he'd always been afraid to be.

When she came out of the bathroom one morning, hopping up and down with excitement and holding a purple wand with a plus sign for positive, he actually broke down and cried like a baby. They bought plastic plugs to cover the outlets, started reading about sleep training and homemade baby food, cleared out the walk-in closet, and painted the walls lavender.

Those first notes of optimism, stirred into being by George Thorogood and a few lukewarm Bud Lights, had become a melody and now a symphony. They had become the soundtrack of his life.

Little did he know he had only three more months of bliss before it would all go to hell.

Max came out of his reverie there in his truck, parked between two grocery store dumpsters, breathing in the smell of garbage.

The alley walls rose up, crowding his windows, and the air pressed in on him, claustrophobic and thick.

The one contact Grant had given him had a voice mail that was no longer taking messages. He had an envelope he wasn't supposed to open. And a guy named "The Terror" on his tail.

Max gripped the wheel again and then slumped forward and rested his forehead on his knuckles. He hadn't been terribly fond of his cousin, but he owed it to Grant to figure something out as much as he owed it to himself to not get killed.

He needed answers.

Which meant going to the last place he wanted to be right now.

5

Social Environment

Evan sat in the darkness of the subterranean parking garage under his residential high-rise, grocery bag on the passenger seat next to him. Line-caught salmon, lemon, dill, capers, butter, cracked black pepper, sparkling water. He caught a whiff of the meal to come, savory and rich. It would pair nicely with a smooth vodka, something grape-based.

It was delightful here in his truck, a Ford F-150 pickup reinforced with as many discreet security measures as his penthouse. Right now, snugged into a parking slot between two pillars, he could be anyone else in the world coming back to the comforts of home, the evening ahead promising nothing but a well-cooked meal and a warm flush from a touch of alcohol.

But he couldn't be anyone else in the world.

At least not yet.

Grocery bag clutched in his arm, Evan started across the parking garage beneath the Castle Heights Residential Tower. At the top of the brief run of stairs, he hesitated at the door to the lobby, readying himself to switch personas. Among the building's residents, he was known as a tenant who led a bland life as an importer of industrial cleaning supplies. He had an average build, the better to blend in, and kept his muscles toned but not bulky. Just another ordinary guy in his thirties, not too handsome.

As he took a moment to seat himself firmly in his alias, he realized that he was on edge. Entering the humdrum world of Castle Heights could do that to him. Compensating for the wind drift of a sniper round was second nature to Evan. But engaging in small talk by the mail slots was torture.

He stepped inside.

The highly active and highly invasive homeowners' association had recently voted to upgrade the lobby furniture in an effort to create a more social environment.

Evan didn't like social environments.

Sure enough, a clot of residents had formed on the armless love seats by the Nespresso machine. Ida Rosenbaum of 6G, a wizened turtle of a woman, exhibited a vintage marcasite and amethyst necklace to cooing onlookers. "I finally got to the safe-deposit box to haul this stuff out," she was saying. "I mean, I'm not getting any younger. Say what you will about my Herb, may he rest in peace, but he had an eye for fashion."

Evan slipped inside, easing the door shut with tactical precision. There were only two people in the building of interest to him— Mia Hall and her nine-year-old son, Peter. Mia and Evan had engaged in something more than a dalliance but less than a relationship. He found her mind and her body unreasonably appealing, and it seemed she had found some appeal in him, too. Unfortunately, their rapport was complicated by the fact that—as a DA—if she ever uncovered who he really was, she would have to have him arrested. After she'd gleaned the contours of his extra-curriculars, they'd settled on an uneasy don't-ask, don't-tell policy that had worked out about as well as the Clintonian original. Their non-dalliance non-relationship had not ended harmoniously.

Evan was relieved to see that Mia was not among the crew roosting on the new lobby furniture now. Lowering his head, he beelined for the elevator.

Social Environment

"*Evan!* What's the big rush, chief?"

Evan froze, a prey instinct, as if he could blend into the background.

Johnny Middleton, who lived in 8E with his retiree father, spread his arms, a salesman greeting a customer on the showroom floor. His trademark sweat suit, which sported the logo of a mixed-martial-arts studio, was hiked up at the midline to reveal a middle-aged paunch. "Ida here was just showing off some of her old-school bling."

"Oh, don't bother *him*," Ida said with a dismissive wave of her liver-spotted hand. "He's not interested in anyone but himself. Isn't that right? You're rushing up to your penthouse. No time to kibitz."

"Yes, ma'am," Evan said.

The haze of her potent lilac perfume permeated the lobby. "Too good for the rest of us."

"No, ma'am."

Lorilee Smithson, 3F, slipped a yoga-toned arm around Evan's biceps. She'd been plastic-surgeried into a simulacrum of an attractive fifty-year-old, which might very well have been her age. She could also have been eighty.

"Ev," she said, "I'm charged with paper goods for Wednesday night's HOA meeting, and as such I need to volunt-ask you to bring some nibbles, okay?"

Ev? Volunt-ask? Nibbles?

Deciphering Castle Heights argot was harder than figuring out Cantonese inflection. Enduring it was worse than being waterboarded.

Evan cleared his throat, an uncharacteristic nonverbal tell, and said, "What?"

She repeated the request. Then added, "Something simple. Ya know, homemade cookies, maybe a crudités platter."

"Crudités platter," he repeated.

He looked at all those faces looking at him. Living outside the mainstream had left him ill-equipped for everyday interactions, but he knew that some kind of nicety was required. He cleared his throat, summoned the words. "Good to see you all."

Mrs. Rosenbaum snorted.

Evan backed away, offering a little wave that he instantly regretted. He turned around in front of the elevators and found himself nose to nose with Mia.

She was brought up short as well, phone pressed to her cheek, bulging satchel briefcase in hand. Inexplicably, she was carrying a plaster of paris rendering of California in a pie tin.

After they weathered the awkward hitch and stepped into the elevator together, Evan said, "I'm told GPS is more reliable."

Mia looked at him blankly. He gestured at the state sculpture. She looked down at it and then at him. She did not smile.

Instead she returned to her phone call with renewed vigor. "I don't care if he has brunch with the mayor every Sunday at the Bel-Air Country Club. I don't care if he *owns* the Bel-Air Country Club. I have a detective who's not afraid to request a search warrant of his place of residence. It'd be nice if my own boss weren't more skittish about blowback than I am."

Her tone confirmed what he already knew: Mia was not a DA he'd want to tangle with.

"Look, Don," she continued, "we don't know how far the tentacles reach on this thing. I'm busting my ass every night. I have Peter in math lab after school and the sitter picking him up from there. I've been running around all day with a friggin' state replica because the plaster of paris didn't have time to set this morning, and am I complaining? . . . Okay. But I mean *before* this? . . . Right. All I'm asking is that you let me do my job."

There was a time that she might have gotten off the phone when she saw Evan. There was a time when she might have smiled at him. Made direct eye contact, even.

Instead they stood side by side, eyes on the floor-indicator lights above. He could smell her lemongrass lotion and the clean scent of her shampoo. Her lush, wavy chestnut hair was clipped up messily, escaped strands falling across her left eye. The highlights showed through, blond and burgundy.

Not that he paid attention.

As Mia shifted under her load, the backs of their knuckles brushed.

They both tensed, and she took a half step away.

Evan could hear her boss talking through the phone, not the words but the drone of his voice.

She looked across at Evan, and for an instant emotion flickered through her eyes—something like wistfulness.

Then she focused on the call again. "I understand," she said. "But I only have so much patience."

Indeed, Evan thought.

The elevator reached the twelfth floor.

She gave Evan a cursory nod and stepped out. He listened to her walking away, the firm insistence of her voice. She'd head into 12B with a big grin. Her condo would smell of Play-Doh, some scented candle, and a trace of whatever the sitter had made Peter for dinner—probably chicken nuggets shaped like dinosaurs. There'd be laundry on the couch, dishes in the sink, at least one crayon stomped into the carpet. To Mia's dismay and secret delight, Peter would still be up, wired on sugar, waiting for a bedtime story, a glass of water, an under-the-bed check. She'd kiss him on the forehead beneath the cowlick swirl of his lank bangs and tuck him into his race-car bed. Then she'd shower off the workday, listen to some jazz, maybe the Oscar Peterson Trio.

Slide into bed.

How odd life was to bring him and Mia so close to something they could never have.

He rose to the twenty-first floor, the smell of lemongrass lingering, and strode down the hall. When he closed his front door behind him, it met the frame with a weighty thud, sealing him in.

The dark penthouse yawned before him, hard surfaces, high ceilings, and glass. Not a crumb on the counters. Not a smudge marring the windows. Not a drawer left open an inch or a millimeter.

It was immensely comforting. And bereft of human warmth.

How odd that both things could be true at once.

After this mission was over, he'd have plenty of time to figure out how to integrate those opposites. Until then it was a waiting game, leaving him frozen between one chapter and the next.

His footsteps echoed as if off the walls of a crypt. He reached the kitchen island and pulled out one of the barstools. It screeched on the concrete floor. He sat in the darkness.

After a time he checked the RoamZone, but it showed no missed calls.

He put it away and folded his hands.

He would have liked something to do.

6

So Much More to Wreck

The Spanish-style mansion, set behind a front lawn big enough to host a polo match, had a 1920s glamour. Through countless renovations Max had heard about countless times, Grant and Jill had maintained the original integrity of the house, whatever the hell that meant. All Max knew was that he'd gotten lost once trying to find the powder room.

Crickets sawed away in the lush landscape rimming the grass, an ominous trill vibrating the night air. Behind the curtains of the big front room, Max could see shadows moving around, the bustle of a household fresh in mourning. He heard the voice of Michelle, the oldest, home from Tufts law school. She was a second-year now. She appeared to be comforting her mother. Even over the crickets, Max could hear Jill's choked sobs.

He couldn't imagine her without her husband, and he doubted she could either.

Pausing on the walk, Max checked the street behind him once more in case he'd been followed. An image flashed through his mind—the Terror savaging his mattress with that big knife—and he had to remind himself to take long, even breaths.

Stepping up onto the broad porch, he rang the bell.

Chimes sounded musically in the vast foyer, ringing off the high ceiling.

A moment later Michelle pulled open the architectural door, her face red and puffy. She wore a fluttery sweater the length of a duster, clipped at the front. At the sight of him, she lightened. "Mighty Max," she said, her breath hitching, and then she hugged him. "I'm glad you're here. Mom's losing her shit over the funeral arrangements. Like, who cares if we have a lily wreath on the coffin? And no one wants to talk about just being sad. And, like, missing him, you know? I mean, given everything, I know I'm super emotional, but that doesn't mean I'm not right."

He shot another glance at the dark street and closed the door behind them. Then he looked her in the eye. "Don't let anyone else tell you how you're supposed to feel, okay?"

Her voice came out little-girl small. "Okay."

Jill's voice echoed in crisply from the other room. "Who's that?"

Max walked past the grand staircase and into the immense front room. He wasn't sure what it was called—a sitting room? a parlor?—but there Jill was, propped on one of the immense couches, her nose rimmed red, a cluster of broken blood vessels etching a fragile pattern beneath one eye. To her side a crystal vase the size of a trash can was home to a clutch of curly willow branches that resembled fingernails.

One of the house staff passed through the swinging door into the kitchen. As it waved open, Max heard voices—a family get-together he'd not been told about. Michelle hovered at the edge of the big room, arms crossed, nibbling her bottom lip.

Before he could offer his condolences, Jill waved a wrung-out tissue in his direction. "Why can't anyone *do* anything? I mean, he was scared for *days*. And you know Grant—he didn't get scared."

Max felt as though he'd walked in mid-monologue. From what Michelle had told him, maybe he had.

"That's why he was heading to the cabin in Big Bear," Jill continued. "To keep us safe. Because someone was after him."

Max's throat felt suddenly parched. "Who?"

"He didn't tell *me*. He'd never discuss specifics like that with us." Jill eyed Max pointedly. "He always put his family first."

An accusation.

Even so, she was right. Max knew that Grant would never bring anything explosive near his home, and it seemed the Terror had surmised the same.

"Yes, he did." Max took in a breath. "So you think it was a work thing?"

"Of course it was work-related." She snatched up a notepad, scribbled something else on her to-do list, and tossed it back onto the glass coffee table.

"Why didn't he go to the cops?"

At this she gave a nasty little laugh. "The cops. Right. You'd think they'd be some help. I mean, you'd imagine that they could swing in and . . . and . . . But it's amazing how helpless we actually are. When there's a *real* threat? The police are useless. Can you imagine, what with who Grant was in the community? Think of everything he did over the years for *their* investigations, for *their* cases. But he said they only offered the usual bureaucratic nonsense. Fill out a report. A cruiser by the house twice a night." She rubbed her eyes hard, smearing the lids in circles. "It's not like I expected them to whisk him off into witness protection, but *something*. And then this. Jesus God. I mean, they said it was a professional hit. A professional hit. On Grant. *Our* Grant. And they don't know. . . . They still don't know anything."

She sobbed quietly for a time.

Dread had taken up residence in Max's belly, lead-heavy and dense. If the cops weren't willing to help Grant Merriweather, what recourse would *he* have?

He took an awkward step toward her. "Jill, listen, is there anything I can do?"

Stifling a sob, she snatched up the notepad again. "There's really not. I mean, who's gonna know who to put on the guest list? And how many passed plates at the reception? And which suit . . . which suit of his . . ."

She dipped her face again into her tissue-wielding fist, her chin wrinkled above her knuckles, freckles pronounced on her blanched face. From the kitchen Max heard one of the high-schoolers—Terel or Ross—crack a joke and then the sound of muffled laughter. He wondered who else was in there.

He put his hand in his pocket, felt his fingertips brush against the folded *DO NOT OPEN* envelope. "Jill, I need to know if Grant . . . um, if he might have left any instructions for me."

She froze, her features hardening. When she looked up, her eyes held such intense disdain that he flinched. "You mean like in a *will*?"

"No," Max said. "No, that's not what I mean at all."

But she kept on. "As in, did he *leave you* anything? Not a good time to ask for money, Maxwell. I mean, the body's not even cold."

He wilted. "How could you think I'd . . . ?"

"Because *everyone* is, Max. You should see them crawling out of the woodwork already."

"I understand," he said. "But I'm not."

Michelle rushed forward. "Mom," she said. "Stop it. Just stop it."

But Jill ignored her, her glare boring through Max. "Then what *are* you asking for, Max? Why would Grant leave instructions for *you*?" And then, abruptly, her brow furled and she snapped to her feet. "Wait a minute. Is this something *you* got him into?"

"*What?*"

"Of course, that's why you're here. You needed his help, dragged him into something shady. You were always the fuckup, Max. What did you do?"

"No, Jill. Listen—" His voice had risen. Realizing he was arguing with a woman who'd been widowed for less than twenty-four hours, he clamped his mouth shut.

But she drove toward him, her face a mask of aggression. "How *dare* you. How dare you come here."

Frustration rushed through his blood, congealing into anger. His next words were just taking shape when he caught sight of Michelle. She was standing behind her mother, eyes welling, the flanges of her nostrils red. Her sweater had come unclasped in the front, swaying open, revealing a soft gray T-shirt rounded over her belly. Her words came back to Max: *Given everything, I know I'm super emotional.*

She saw him notice her pregnant bulge, gave a soft smile, and clipped her sweater again over it.

"So tell me, Max," Jill sneered. "Tell me the *real* story of why you're here."

He heard Grant's voice, edged with worry: *My wife's not exactly a safe distance removed from me. Or my family. The thing with you is, no one will ever know. I mean, no one would ever think of you.*

The minute Grant handed Max that envelope, he'd put a target on his head. And now Max had to choose whether he wanted to put Jill into the crosshairs with him. He looked at Michelle, still verging on tears, the slope of her stomach. He thought about the boys in the other room. This well-built house and all the life in it, such a contrast with his run-down apartment. There was so much more to wreck here.

"Forget it," Max said. "You're right. I'm an asshole. Sorry."

She studied him a moment, her features slack with disgust. Then she tensed.

He couldn't process what was happening in real time, not until she plowed into him, hammering at his chest with her fists, clawing at his face. "Get out! Right now! *Get out of my house!*"

He wrangled her arms as best he could. Michelle was shouting. The kitchen door swung open, and a stream of people poured through, both boys, all four uncles, a slew of cousins, his grandmother, the chef and the cleaning lady, and an assortment of well-heeled neighbors clutching plastic hors d'oeuvre plates.

Jill was twisting in Max's grip now, cursing and sobbing, and he let her go and stepped back. Before she could launch herself at him again, Michelle wrapped her up from behind. "Stop it, Mom! Calm down. Max didn't do anything. Just *calm down*."

Jill finally stopped struggling. She shook her daughter off, snatched up her notepad, and strode out of sight down the rear hall.

All eyes shifted to Max. In the rear of the pack, he caught sight of his father, his rugged face flushed. He seemed to be caught off guard as much as Max was.

Max felt a familiar gravity pulling him toward a familiar hope—that his dad might step up and say something in his defense.

But Terry just looked ashamed. In his pained expression, Max saw a reflection of his own original sin. That he'd come into the world a disappointment and would be one so long as his father was alive to lay eyes on him. That had it not been for Max, his mother would be around, laughing and pretty, warming every room.

That he wasn't worth the terrible cost that had been paid to create him.

Max was unable to find what words should come next. And unable to look away from his father. At last Terry broke off eye contact.

"Omigod," Michelle said, cutting in on the muddle of Max's thoughts. "You're bleeding."

His left cheek burned even over the heat that had risen beneath his face. He touched his fingertips to the spot, and they came away red. "It's okay," he said. "I'm sorry."

His grandmother edged forward. Dementia had made her fragmented and erratic, though she'd been none too pleasant before. She jabbed a crooked finger at him, her mottled face twisted. "It should've been *you*."

The words arrowed straight through him—clean entry, clean exit—leaving him winded. Once again his stare found his father, but Terry just took another swig of beer and looked away. Pouches had risen beneath his eyes, where emotion gathered for his dad and where it stopped.

Michelle said, "Fuck you, Grandma."

A few gasps. The ring of keen silence. The boys glanced at each other, suppressing grins. Only Grandma looked unfazed, picking at the edge of an empanada on her plate.

"It's okay, Michelle," Max said. "Show Nona respect."

Terry squeezed Ross's and Terel's necks, steering them toward the kitchen. "C'mon, boys. You don't need to see this."

The door flapped, and then silence reasserted itself once more.

One of the neighbors cleared his throat. "Perhaps you should go."

Max nodded. As he turned for the door, the envelope crinkled in his pocket. Feeling it dig into his thigh, he hesitated.

The others were already drifting back into the kitchen, but he called after Michelle. "Do you mind if I just clean this up a little before I go?" He touched his cheek.

"Of course, Uncle Max." She pointed to the hall opposite the one her mom had vanished down. "Third door on the left."

He started up the tile corridor for the powder room, glancing through the open doorways on either side as he passed. Guest room. Library. And then—as he vaguely remembered—Grant's office.

He ducked in, his shoes sinking into the plush carpet, and scanned the oak furnishings. A laptop was open on the leather blotter, family photos bouncing around on a screen saver. Max nudged the mouse pad, and the desktop came up.

He hovered the cursor over Contacts and clicked.

The "A" surnames sprang up first, important city officials and heads of industry, personal numbers and addresses listed alongside their work info. In the Notes section, Grant or his assistant had even typed in the names of spouses and children.

Holding his breath, Max scrolled down the alphabet, searching for Lorraine Lennox. Sure enough, there was her card, featuring the phone number at the *Los Angeles Times* he'd been calling. Her office address was listed and there—*bingo*—a cell number and home address as well.

Max had hoped for as much. That given whatever explosive information was at stake, Grant and Lennox had worked out unofficial channels of communication.

The sound of movement deep in the house straightened Max's spine. Several sets of footsteps tapped into the foyer, voices carrying up the hall.

Max jotted down Lennox's info on a pad featuring the Merriweather Accountancy logo, tore off the sheet, and crossed to the doorway. Peering out, he saw Michelle edge into view, seeing the neighbors out. Her gaze swept in his direction, and he jerked back out of sight.

When he heard the front door close, he swung out into the hall and walked toward the foyer.

Michelle turned as he neared. "I'm sorry. Like I said, she's out of her head right now."

Max said, "How could she not be?"

Michelle gave a sad smile. She caught him noticing her belly again, took his hand, and moved to rest it on her bump. He pulled his hand back more sharply than he intended, an instinctive recoil he instantly regretted. "Shit. I'm sorry."

"I get it," she said. "Just . . . don't be a stranger. You're the only one in this family I actually like."

He felt his breath tangle in his throat. He blinked hard and turned quickly away.

She shut the door behind him, ratcheting out the bright light of the foyer. He stepped off the porch, enfolded by the darkness, with an address in his pocket and little else.

7

Like Torn Rubber

Lorraine Lennox lived in an Elysian Park bungalow at the lip of a canyon fold, a loud street in a neighborhood lively with music and front-yard barbecues. In the distance the stadium was uplit for a concert, the grandstand glowing Dodger blue.

Standing on the cracked doorstep, Max double-checked the address. After calling Lennox's cell a handful of times and getting dumped into voice mail, he'd worked up his courage and driven over.

He rang the doorbell, waited, rang it again.

A clacking drew his attention to the side of the house. A gate, loose in the breeze. He walked over to it.

The latch slapped against the catch nervously. Through the fence he could hear people talking in the backyard.

A shift in the wind sent the Boss's gravelly voice rolling across Chavez Ravine, blasting from the stadium speakers: *Everybody's got a secret, Sonny . . .*

Max knuckled the gate open. "Hello?"

He drifted up the alley, blading past recycling bins.

"Hi, there! I'm not a robber! I'm just Grant Merriweather's cousin."

He emerged onto the square of browning grass that passed for a backyard. A few lawn chairs with tattered straps were arrayed around a fire pit.

Empty.

Gas flames leapt through the lava rocks, a reverse waterfall of orange and pale blue. The rear sliding-glass door had been laid open, and he realized now that the voices he'd heard weren't voices at all but a too-loud television blaring from the living room.

As Max edged forward, he spotted the back of a woman's head poking up over an armchair facing the flat-screen.

The lights were off in the bungalow. The flicker of the screen and the strobing flames behind him had an unsettling effect, the walls fluid and alive, the foundation no longer fixed.

"Hello? Lorraine?"

Max stepped across the threshold into the chill of the house.

"Lorraine? I'm sorry to barge in—" The words died in his throat.

Her head was cocked at an odd angle. As he circled the chair, the noise of the television predominated—Pat Sajak smarmy in syndication, praying for that big money, big money. Max knew that something was terribly wrong, but his legs wouldn't stop carrying him onward. The game show was wanting for reception, the contestants' words fuzzed at the edges. Despite the chill, sweat trickled down his ribs.

The sight of Lorraine Lennox inched into view, her throat bared, her head tilted back from the violence of the gunshot. Her tight black hair gave way to a thumb-size hole in her crown, the ebony skin jagged at the edges like torn rubber.

It seemed to be pulsing, the hole, and then he realized that the TV reception wasn't weak at all, that the buzzing he was hearing was flies.

His stomach lurched. A few quick strides brought him to the kitchen sink barely in time. Gripping the Formica counter, he emptied his stomach.

He didn't remember backing out of the house, but his calves struck the fire pit and he felt the breath of the flames against his shoulder blades.

Another blip of lost time and then the sound of the gate latch clacking behind him.

Then he was driving out of the Ravine, making turn after turn, sweat running into his eyes. He skirted the edge of Chinatown, red lanterns bobbing on strings, diners pouring from restaurants. As he came up Alameda Street, his arms started shaking and his chest tightened up. His windpipe cinched until he was sure he'd die right there behind the wheel.

He tugged the truck to the curb and got out, the fresh night air sweeping some of the fog from his brain. His fingertips were tingling, his mouth bone dry.

Overhead a sign glowed in the night: PHILIPPE THE ORIGINAL, the words rendered in a baseball-pennant scroll. He staggered inside, sawdust kicking up around his shoes, the hum of conversation enveloping him. Along cafeteria-style tables, diners dug into French-dip sandwiches.

His knees buckled, his vision spotting, and he went for the nearest empty seat. He collapsed into a chair and placed his palms on the tabletop, wanting to feel something solid. He couldn't get the smell of the bungalow out of his nose.

To his side, someone was ordering at the counter. "I want a slice of cheesecake please and thank you but no cherry drizzle on it 'cuz cherries are red and I don't eat red stuff and a glass of orange juice but not with a blue straw just a clear one."

Max still couldn't look up from his hands, but he sensed the man's shadow beside him a moment later.

"Excuse me, sir . . . um . . . um, it's cafeteria-style here so the dining norms are different, and . . . um . . . um, it's supposed to be okay to ask, so can I sit with you?"

Max's throat was still spasming, so he nodded a few times fiercely without raising his head.

The man sat down and ate for a time, humming softly as he chewed. Max's hands trembled, the pads of his fingers rasping against the surface of the tabletop. He thought about the hole in Lennox's head, how it vibrated with movement. The buzzing. The stench.

The man's next words came at him as if from far away. "Are you upset, sir?"

"No, no." Max's voice sounded scratchy and detached even to him. "I'm . . . fine."

"'Cuz your breathing went from thirty-two breaths per minute to forty per minute, and your . . . um . . . um, your face is red, and that's a social cue that you're upset."

". . . not upset . . . 'kay?"

"Okay." The man leaned to take another slurp through his clear straw. "'Cuz if you *were,*" he said, "I know who'd be able to help you."

8

Complicated

Making a floating bed was a pain in the ass.

There were no wobbles—the electromagnetic-suspension technology was sufficiently powerful to fix the slab in place. But without a headboard or footboard to pin the sheets, addressing wrinkles became a challenge.

Evan hated wrinkles.

His Original S.W.A.T. boots added another variable. Given the protective steel shanks between the insoles and outsoles, he had to keep his feet well back from the bed's magnetic field or risk getting sucked into the void.

Leaning forward, he tugged down the top sheet only to see the faintest ridge lift on the far side, pronounced in the early-morning light. Grimacing, he circled the bed and smoothed the ridge with his palm. Now the faintest fan appeared in the fabric at the opposite corner.

He told himself to let it go.

He told himself that it wasn't life-or-death.

That it was just a fucking bedsheet.

Then he rounded the slab once more and yanked the sheet flat.

That caused the hem beneath the pillows to shift to a slight diagonal.

He glared at it with enmity.

Perfection had been ingrained in his bones, a mission-essential trait on which his survival depended. Knowing where it should stop was a challenge. That meant that his life hung in the balance of every last detail, that his very existence—

Suddenly he was airborne, his boot ripped out from under him. He slammed down on his back next to the bed, his right foot twisted up, the boot magnetically adhered to the bottom of the slab.

Embarrassing.

He tried to yank his foot free. Aside from an ache that bloomed in his thigh, nothing happened.

With a groan, he hunched forward awkwardly, untied his laces, and ripped his foot out.

Standing, he tried to work the boot loose. It spun in a full rotation but would not pull off.

Stupid protective steel shanks.

Stupid floating bed.

Plus, the sheets were wrinkled all to hell.

In order to reclaim his boot, he'd require an Ampco nonsparking, non-magnetic, aluminum-bronze crowbar. The flat rectangular truck vaults in the bed of his pickup held weaponry, body armor, climbing equipment—a full array of good-to-go load-out gear equipping him for a variety of contingencies. Like, say, a full-frontal assault on a wayward boot.

He walked down the hall, grabbed his keys, and stomped to the elevator.

Of course the car stopped on the twelfth floor.

And of course, even before the doors parted, it was her voice coming through: "—because bubble gum isn't a breakfast food, *Peter.*"

Peter looked up, spotted Evan, and transformed into a blur of flying nine-year-old. "Evan Smoak!"

He bulldozed into Evan's side, his Batman lunch box swinging dangerously close to Evan's groin. Evan patted his back in an awkward hug of sorts, using the diversion to avoid Mia's stare.

She was wearing her good-luck court-motion suit—midnight blue, subtle lapels. The California-in-a-pie-tin was balanced atop her briefcase, which she held horizontally like a server's tray.

"Hello," she said.

Evan said, "Hi."

Sensing the tension, Peter released Evan and stood beside his mom.

He glanced over at Evan and then over at him again. "You're missing a boot."

Evan looked down. "Yup."

"Where you going with one boot?"

"To get a crowbar."

"Why?"

"To get my other boot."

Peter said, "Oh."

Evan looked at Mia. She looked at the wall.

"Adulthood is complicated," he said.

Back in his bedroom, armed with a crowbar, Evan reapproached the boot. First he dug the forked end beneath the tread, then pried it up a few centimeters before it snapped back against the slab.

He wiped his brow, took a moment to regroup. Then he got after the boot again, hooking it and setting his full weight on the end of the bar. It was right on the verge. As he repositioned, he felt the drift of his left boot and had precisely enough time to say "Goddamn i—" before he hammered the floor once more, the crowbar clattering at his side, his left boot cemented in place beneath the lip of the slab next to its mate.

Lying flat, his leg raised as if in traction, he blew out a breath and let his head thunk against the concrete floor.

And then he heard it. A distinctive ring. His RoamZone.

He dug it out of his pocket. Staring at the ceiling, he lifted it to his face.

He said, "Do you need my help?"

9

Bedside Manner

Once Evan pried himself off the floor and free of the bed, the call followed the traditional course: *Do you need my help?*

A harried masculine voice, cracked with adrenaline: "Yes."

"Where did you get this number?"

"Some guy who . . . who . . . Trevon something. I think he's on the spectrum. He said . . . he said you could help me. What does that mean?"

"It means what it sounds like."

In his socks Evan crossed to the window, the subdued morning light washing over his face. Across Wilshire Boulevard the buildings gleamed with the promise of a new day. He was relieved to have gotten the call, his last mission finally put into motion.

The man was talking. "I spent the night, I guess, working up my courage. Trying to figure out if this is real or some kind of hoax. I mean, an untraceable number? You gotta admit, it sounds—"

"Where do you live?"

"Nowhere. Not anymore. I slept in my truck last night. They're after me, and—"

"Name."

"What?"

"Your name."

"Max Merriweather?"

"You're not sure if that's who you are?"

"No, I'm just a bit rattled. Um—"

"Two hours from now," Evan said, drawing back from the window. "Tram stop at the base of Universal Studios."

"Is that some kind of code?"

"It's where we'll meet."

"Uh, okay. Is that it?"

"No." Evan looked at his floating bed. Two boots rising from the edge. A scattering of wrinkles interrupting the rectangle of the top sheet, causing static across his mental field. He turned away from the mess of imperfection, closed his eyes to clear the mechanism, and pulled together the strands of his focus into a coherent whole. "First you need to tell me everything."

Max Merriweather arrived at the tram station, a flustered figurine through Evan's Steiner tactical binoculars. Evan had set up eight blocks to the north on the roof of a Mexican restaurant, gravel roof poking his belly, the scent of fresh tomatillo sauce rising through a vent to his side. Before Max could work himself into a frenzy, Evan called his cell. He watched the figurine hold a phone to his face and glance around nervously.

"Hello?"

"Walk down to Cahuenga and get on the first northbound bus."

"Wait— What? We're not meeting here?"

"Keep your phone on. Further directions to come."

Evan hung up but stayed put. Over the next half hour, he called Max at intervals, routing him through Studio City in a rambling loop that wound up where he'd started. Then, slipping off the roof, he told Max to cross the street and get on the Metro, taking the Red Line toward downtown.

Now Max sat on the molded white plastic seat cushioned with paint-spatter fabric straight out of the eighties. His hands were laced, his head hanging low, doubling his chin. His blinks were long and sluggish, and his face had the washed-out pallor of someone short on calories and high on cortisol.

This mission felt distinct to Evan because he didn't know who he was targeting. He had no sense of who the Terror was or what other enemies might be arrayed against him. How could he fight an invisible threat? How could he kill something without a face?

By giving it a face.

And then introducing that face to the notion of consequence.

The Metro car was humid and smelled of someone's overly exuberant application of musk body spray.

Evan cut through the midday crowd.

His ARES 1911 was a ghost gun, engineered by his armorer from a solid forging of aluminum. Eight 230-grain Speer Gold Dot hollow points in the mag, one in the spout. Though Evan was a lefty, he shot equally well with either hand, so he preferred an ambidextrous thumb safety. Simonich gunner grips practically adhered the weapon to his hand once drawn, and the front-frame checkering was an ambitious eighteen lines per inch. The high-profile straight-eight sights were designed for clear target acquisition even when a suppressor was screwed into the threaded barrel.

The pistol rode in a Kydex high-guard holster clipped to the belt of his cargo pants in the appendix carry position. Appendix carry had multiple advantages. Better for semi-deep concealment, it guarded against the bump-frisk, aided weapon retention during ground fighting or grappling, and made the weapon demonstrably faster to present.

His Woolrich shirt, too, had been selected for tactical considerations. Despite its dummy buttons, the front of the shirt was held together by magnets that parted easily, which meant that he could draw the pistol straight through his clothes, a shortest-distance-between-two-points movement of the hand that would have been useful in the Wild West and was occasionally useful now.

But to everyone else on the Metro car, Evan looked like an average commuter.

He sat down next to Max.

Max stayed hunched over, his hands joined in a float between his knees. His knuckles were white. He was, Evan realized, trying to keep his fingers from shaking.

The train juddered along. The background noise would be sufficient to drown out a hushed conversation.

Max rocked with the movement of the subway, oblivious to Evan. His face was lined not so much from age, it seemed, but from defeat. Deep grooves like scaffolding propped up dark brown eyes. Beneath the wear and tear were ruggedly handsome features that seemed to be waiting to reemerge.

He checked his phone wearily, awaiting the next instruction.

So Evan gave it to him. "Hand me the envelope."

Max did a double take. Then he looked around at the folks hanging from the poles. A family clustered by the doors, the boys taking turns kicking each other's shins while the parents tapped at their phones.

"Wait," Max said. *"You're—"*

Evan held out his hand.

Max took the envelope from his pocket. Just as he'd described, bright yellow with that scrawl—*DO NOT OPEN.*

"I've been super careful with it," Max said. "Wanting to respect Grant's wishes, like I said. I figure whatever's in there is too dangerous for me to—"

Evan tore the envelope open and tilted it into his palm.

"Hey!" Max hissed through his teeth. "What the hell!"

A key slid out, attached to a slender Swiss Army knife key chain.

Max had turned away, averting his eyes. "I don't want to know. I don't want to know anything."

"Seems they don't care whether you know anything or not," Evan said. "They don't seem willing to take the risk. They want to kill you regardless."

"Great. Thanks."

Evan turned the key over. Shiny gold, larger than a house key, the cuts oddly symmetrical. It seemed like a prop—a secret key that led to a doomsday cache or a treasure trove of hazardous materials.

Max was pinching the bridge of his nose. "Tell me when we get to the 'helping me' part."

"The first part of helping you is making you face reality."

Max lowered his hand from his eyes. Then he looked at the key resting on Evan's palm.

"What—" Max's voice cracked. "What reality?"

"Your fingerprints and DNA put you at Lorraine Lennox's house. With her corpse. Earlier in the evening, you showed up at Grant's place in Beverly Hills behaving erratically, got into a confrontation with his wife. Your apartment is torn up, which would lead any reasonable detective to conclude that you're into illicit business with bad people."

Max's lips looked cracked. His eyes were wide, bloodshot. "Well," he said. "If you frame it *that* way . . ."

The brakes ground, a metal-on-metal screech Evan could feel in his teeth.

"Look," Max said. "I don't want to drag Grant's family into this. They're going through it bad right now. And his oldest kid, she's pregnant. I don't really have . . . I don't have a lot to lose, you know? So I need your help, yeah. But it's more important that we keep them out of this." He leaned back in his seat and exhaled, puffing out his cheeks. "Why'd you make me run around like that? The tram stop to the bus to the Metro?"

Evan said, "I was deciding if you're worth saving."

"Am I worth saving?"

The doors hissed open at Union Station. Evan plucked the phone from Max's hand, snapped it in half, and slid the pieces across the floor. They disappeared through the gap, falling onto the tracks.

Before Max could react, Evan grabbed his arm, tugged him off the train, and hustled him across the platform and up the stairs. They blinked in the sudden light of day.

Evan steered him across the parking lot and dumped him into the passenger seat of a white Chevy Malibu, a backup vehicle he'd picked up at one of his safe houses.

Evan accelerated out of the parking lot, pressing Max back in the cloth seat, and shot north up Alameda.

Max said, "Things go pretty fast around you, huh?"

Evan zigzagged across the 110, and then they were forging upslope, weaving between parked cars on increasingly cramped streets. He stopped next to a construction dumpster brimming with detritus.

Evan pulled a tube of superglue from the glove box and used it to coat his fingertips.

Max said, "Mind if I ask . . . ?"

"Fingerprints."

Max craned to look through his window at the crumbling dirt rise of the hillside. "Why are we here?"

But Evan was already out of the car, digging in the trunk. He produced an eight-ounce bottle of Marianna Super Star Cream Peroxide Developer.

Max was next to him now, gawking. "So we're gonna dye my hair? Disguise me?"

Instead of answering, Evan hiked up the steep slope, boots slipping, releasing tumbles of dirt. Max made his way up behind him. They waded through knee-high weeds and came to the back of a fence.

Max said, "Would you mind just telling me—"

Evan vaulted the fence.

He waited. A moment later Max pulled himself over as well.

Max took in the postage-stamp backyard, his mouth popping open at the sight of Lorraine Lennox's house. A dry breeze wafted the heat of the fire pit across their faces, and a faint smell from the house. Something fetid. The flat-screen TV emitted steady pulses of canned laughter.

Evan cranked off the gas to the fire pit, the flames drowning in the lava stones.

He said, "Don't move."

He breezed into the house, weathering the smell, and did a quick spin through, safing each room and checking the front yard. He ignored the armchair and what it held.

When he returned to the backyard, Max remained rooted in place, his feet staked to the dead grass. His mouth pulsed a few times, as if he were holding his gorge in place. "Look," he said. "I appreciate this a ton, but your bedside manner isn't exactly—"

"What did you touch?" Evan said. "Start here."

Max blinked twice.

Evan said, "Focus. Every single thing you touched."

Max pointed. "Side gate."

Evan jogged over, removing a rag from one of his cargo pockets and dousing it with the hair product. He wiped down both sides of the gate.

From behind him, Max said, "It has bleach in it?"

"Bleach is overrated. A lot of them are reducing agents that leave behind intact hemoglobin," Evan said, giving extra attention to the handle. "Whereas hydrogen peroxide is an oxidizing agent— generates bubbles that degrade DNA." He headed back to wipe off the rear fence where Max had jumped over and then considered the dilapidated lawn furniture. "Where else did you touch? Or even go near?"

They worked their way inside, Max averting his eyes from Lorraine Lennox's body. The smell was thick all around them, pressing into their pores.

Evan said, "Don't touch *anything*."

He lathered down the counter and then poured the solution into the sink, running the water and the garbage disposal for a solid two minutes. When he shut it off, Max was standing over by a bookshelf, staring at photographs.

"Let's go," Evan said.

"We can't just leave her," Max said.

Evan paused halfway through the open sliding door. "She won't know the difference."

Max pointed at the framed pictures. "She has a brother. And looks like her parents are still alive." He wiped his mouth. "Her people deserve to know."

Bedside Manner

Evan's own mouth tensed. He leaned to look down the brief hall through the front window. No one visible on the street. Yet.

Then he strode inside, plucked the phone from the base station, and tapped out three digits with a superglue-tipped finger. He rested the cordless on the counter and ushered Max outside.

Behind them he could make out a tinny voice asking, "What's your emergency?"

10

Area of Expertise

Downtown Los Angeles stretched skyward around Evan and Max, a huddle of high-rises shot above an apron of urban sprawl, as if a few square blocks had snapped off the slab of Manhattan and floated to the wrong coast. On a clear day, the San Gabriel Mountains loomed with deceptive closeness to the east. Snow-capped Mount Baldy dominated the jagged tear line where earth met sky, and beyond, smothered in an ocean of pines, lay Arrowhead and Big Bear, where Grant Merriweather had been put down with a bullet to the head.

Here on the bustling city sidewalk, a wintry breeze rattled an empty Pressed Juicery bottle over the cracked concrete past Evan's and Max's shoes. On the corner a man sold roasted corn out of a food cart, his face weather-battered, his skin a rich shade of umber. The smell reminded Evan that he hadn't eaten since breakfast, and he stared longingly as the man rolled an ear through metal troughs of melted butter, Cotija cheese, and powdered chili. Along the cart's frame, freshly carved mango hung in clear bags, marinating in lime, salt, and sriracha.

Grant Merriweather's firm, the imaginatively titled Merriweather Accountancy, resided on the seventeenth floor of the black-glass rise before them. This was a convenient part of downtown for a forensic accountant, a few blocks from City Hall, LAPD headquarters, and the Criminal Courts Building.

Evan clenched the Swiss Army knife key chain, the key swaying beneath his fist.

Those oddly symmetrical cuts. The shiny gold finish, unworn by use, not a single scrape from tumbler pins.

"Are we ever actually going to, you know, go inside?" Max asked.

Dragging Max along, Evan had circuited the nearby blocks three times, checking parked cars, passing faces, and searching windows for glints thrown by binoculars or sniper rifles. They'd ridden up the elevators of surrounding buildings and watched the street from various vantages. Sipped espresso in the catty-corner Starbucks and studied the lobby.

The Third Commandment: *Master your surroundings.*

Evan slid the key chain into his pocket. Then headed for the entrance.

Max followed.

They slid through the weighty revolving doors, delivered onto a white granite floor scuffed from the tread of loafers and high heels. The elevator bank was to the left, set behind a directory shimmering with brass letters. Foot traffic was light. Cutting across the lobby, Evan circled his gaze from faces to hands to faces.

No one reaching. No one sweating. No one with THE TERROR scraped into the flesh of his forearm.

Keeping Max at his side, Evan moved straight past the elevator and a sextet of Le Corbusier lounge chairs scattered like dice cubes. They stepped into the stairwell, the door sucked shut behind them, and they stood a moment in the silence.

No one walks in Los Angeles. And no one takes the stairs.

They started up.

Floor after floor, accompanied only by the tapping of their

footsteps. Max seemed to be in good shape. Working construction will do that.

They emerged onto the seventeenth floor, Evan pressing the door open slowly with a flat palm. The empty hall fanned into view and, at the end, the sign for Merriweather Accountancy.

Corner office.

They exited the stairwell, Max picking up the pace.

Evan put the bar of his forearm across Max's chest, stopping him.

Max said, "What?"

Evan pointed down. White drywall dust sprinkled the carpet fibers by the baseboard, right at the seam where a vacuum couldn't reach.

Max said, "So?"

Evan pointed up.

Drilled into the ceiling, angled down the hall toward Grant's door, was a bullet security camera with the sticker still applied to its base: IRONKLAD KAM. Fresh from the company.

Grant had been scared, all right. Scared enough to install a new security system at the office.

"What do we do now?" Max whispered.

Evan reached up and swiveled the camera, moving to keep them both in its blind spot. A red light glowed at the bottom the whole time, the recording uninterrupted. They wound up on its far side, the lens aimed at the stairwell door through which they had just emerged.

They walked down the hall. Evan paused near the thick wooden door, peering around the corner up the intersecting corridor. Aside from a fire-extinguisher cabinet and an anachronistic ash-tray stand by the elevator, this hallway was also empty. Evan turned back to the door. Set his ear to the fine grain. No vibrations from within. The knob turned readily in his grip.

Unlocked.

The suction of the opening door pulled a mini flurry of feathers out across the tops of Evan's boots. The door swung inward a few inches and then caught on a slashed throw pillow. Evan shoved through the wadded-up fabric and peered inside.

The lobby was trashed. Leather couch cushions punctured, framed pictures shattered, a sheepish fern rising naked from a mound of soil and pottery shards.

Behind Evan a strangled noise escaped Max's throat.

They eased through the reception area. Files strewn across the carpet, reference books torn from shelves, the chairs upended. The desk looked violated, drawers extracted from the slots like teeth pulled from a wooden mouth.

Evan said, "Impressive job."

Max wiped his forehead. "Can't quite find it in me to marvel at the professionalism."

Grant's office showed more of the same. The cylindrical locks had been popped neatly out of the big file cabinets, the contents rifled through. On the desk an even row of unplugged cords edged the blank rectangle where a computer would go. Evan felt like he was connecting the dots that the Terror had connected days before, walking in his footsteps. He placed his hand on the leather blotter, wondering if the computer had held the address of Grant's cabin in Big Bear.

The afternoon sun slanted through the blinds, chopping the bare desk into noirish bands of goldenrod. A dedicated monitor on the wall showed a livestream from the bullet camera in the hall. Were it not for the time stamp counting off minutes and seconds, it might have been a still life: *Stairwell Door at Rest.*

Awards had been raked from the dark walnut cabinets and flipped from the walls, rubbling the base of the old-timey wainscoting. KIWANIS CLUB COURAGEOUS CITIZEN AWARD. FRIEND OF LAPD. KEY TO THE COMMUNITY OF LA CRESCENTA. Plaques praising Grant's work heading up ethics oversight and peer review for the California Board of Accountancy had been snapped in two, the splintered edges rearing from the heap.

Look on my Works, ye Mighty, and despair!

Evan's eye caught on a photograph near the tip of his boot. It showed a family reunion, a raft of Merriweathers crowded together with smiling faces and matching T-shirts naming kin and year. Family reunions were yet another American custom that Evan viewed with an anthropologist's remove: *Decennially, relatives of the species* homo sapiens *gathered to wear coordinated garb, swap origin tales, and compare like-expressed genetic traits.*

Pillar-of-the-community Grant was front and center in the picture, surrounded by a subcluster of his immediate family. Evan searched for Max's face but didn't see it.

Max followed Evan's gaze, said, "Yeah, I didn't get invited to stuff like that. Especially after Violet."

"Your ex," Evan said.

Emotion bloomed behind Max's face, glassing his pupils, weighing on his cheeks. He nodded. Cleared his throat.

"When I saw that guy—the Terror—with the knife, I thought . . ." Max paused. "They say your life flashes before your eyes. But it doesn't. Just your biggest regret. Just one." He wet his lips. "I was never good enough for her. I just wanted to pretend I was."

Evan studied him. He was unsure why Max was telling him this, what would drive a man to share such a thing in the midst of this wreckage.

Max fixed him with a questioning gaze. "You've never met someone who makes you want to be . . . I don't know. More?"

"Than what?"

"Than what you are," Max said. "A different person, even?"

Evan thought of his last dinner at Mia's house. She'd cooked linguini with red sauce, a combination he'd never encountered. They'd sipped wheat-based Ukrainian vodka aged in wood for six months. Afterward they'd kissed in the doorway like a couple from a movie, from TV. Her mouth had been soft and promising. A domestic scene unlike anything he'd experienced before and would likely experience again.

He said, "No."

He moved on, picking through some of the mess on the floor.

Max watched him for a time. Then said, "Come on, man."

Evan looked at him.

"You're telling me you're never up at night reviewing everything you've ever done wrong?" Max said. "Overwhelmed by the whole . . . I don't know . . . fuck, fragility of the universe?" He looked exasperated, raw with exhaustion and stress. "Late at night I can tell you every last thing I've ever screwed up. Every time I hurt someone's feelings. Every faux pas. Every dumb thing. In junior high I was the second-smallest kid in my class. So I held Ryan Steck underwater in the pool during PE. He was the smallest kid. I thought it would make me feel better." He took a breath. "When I think about it, I still feel it. Like an ache in my chest."

Evan thought of a round man with a bullet hole in the back of his head, slumped forward, his face in his soup. All these years later, he could still hear the rattle of the hanging curtain beads, the static-tinged foreign words spilling from the old radio. He still felt the Makarov pistol, warm in his hand.

"Do you think he still remembers?" Max said. "That *he's* up somewhere late at night thinking about what a dick I was?"

Evan said, "If he's still alive and that's what tops his list of concerns, I'd say Ryan Steck has it pretty good."

Max looked unsatisfied with that, but Evan wasn't here to provide satisfaction. He stepped behind the desk once more, turned over the extricated drawers, checked the bottoms.

"They got through every lock in this office," Max said. "Whatever that key leads to is long gone."

"*If* the lock was in this office," Evan said. "This is the most logical place someone would look. Which means Grant probably wouldn't stash anything here."

"So why are *we* here?"

"To see what we can find that might point us to another location."

The First Commandment: *Assume nothing.*

Crouched above a shard of coffee mug, the echo of the Commandment in his head, Evan froze.

He said, "What if the key isn't a key?"

Max said, "If the key isn't a key, then what is it?"

Evan dug it out of his pocket again, stared at it on his palm. Shiny gold. Pristine. Slightly too big.

Like a prop.

He crossed to the rubble at the wainscoting, picked out a fallen shadow box, brushed away the shards. KEY TO THE COMMUNITY OF LA CRESCENTA. An indentation in the foam backing cast a familiar shape in negative relief.

Evan slipped the key off the chain connecting it to the Swiss Army knife and thumbed it into place.

A perfect fit.

"Wait—*what?*" Max said. "That doesn't make any sense. Why would he give me a fake key?"

Evan said, "He wasn't giving you a key. He was giving you a key *chain.*"

With the edge of his nail, he pried open the attachments from the red casing. The key chain was diminutive, the attachments few. Penknife, scissors, file.

Max crouched opposite him, their eyes level. Evan pressed the edge of the penknife into the pad of his index finger. It didn't cut.

A dummy blade.

He pinched it between thumb and forefinger. Sure enough, it slid off its casing, revealing the metal head of a USB plug concealed beneath.

A thumb drive.

Max blew out a breath. "Grant was clever. I'll give him that."

Etched into the metal stub of the USB connector, visible only if tilted to the light, was a logo formed of the union of two letters, the right slant of the M forming the first rise of the A. A nifty little piece of branding for Merriweather Accountancy.

Over Max's shoulder Evan registered movement on the wall monitor. A slender man emerging from the stairwell, turning his shoulders to slip through the barely cracked door. A black wool balaclava covered his face, save for two almond-shaped eyeholes. He looked too skinny to be the Terror, at least based on Max's description, but the exposed forearms were also ridged with carefully inflicted scar patterns.

His hands turned ghostly white by latex gloves.

One held a pistol, the barrel stretched wickedly long by a suppressor.

11

Much More Force, Very Specifically Directed

Evan hustled Max out of Grant's office and into the lobby, careful not to slip on the scattered files.

Already he was running scenarios. Grant's killers had hacked the new security feed to monitor the office. When the bullet camera had mysteriously swiveled, they'd sent a man to investigate.

A man with a suppressed pistol.

Evan and Max neared the front door, and Max balked, jerking back.

"Wait a sec," he said in a hoarse whisper. "Shouldn't we hide? Or run the other way?" His jaw was clenched, veins standing out in his neck. "Do you even have a gun?"

"We don't want him dead," Evan said.

"I don't want *anyone* dead," Max whispered. "Especially me."

Evan grabbed his collar and shoved him through the door, staying at his back.

Up the length of the hall, the masked man stood beneath the swiveled bullet camera, staring directly up. Under the hem of black wool, his Adam's apple floated between the flexed pillars of his neck muscles.

The almond-shaped eye cutouts snapped down at Evan and Max, standing in full view before the door.

The man's shoulder tensed, the pistol starting to rise.

Evan propelled Max up the intersecting corridor toward the elevator doors.

A muffled pop sounded behind them, and a puff of plaster dust lifted from the wall.

Evan shoved Max toward the elevator. "Push the DOWN button. *Go.*"

Max ran.

Evan swung open the wall-mount cabinet, freed the fire extinguisher, and unleashed a cloud of carbon dioxide behind him. Particulates filled the hall, visibility instantly reaching blizzard conditions. The man would be cautious turning the corner; now he'd be doubly so.

Evan backed up, swinging the nozzle, storm-making. He could hear Max jabbing at the DOWN button over and over. At last the elevator doors opened.

Dumping the extinguisher, Evan turned and swept Max into the waiting car, shoving him into the protected front corner. He spun into the opposite pocket, jamming his thumb into the OPEN DOORS button.

"What the holy fuck?" Max said, sliding to the floor. "Let's go!"

But Evan kept the button depressed. His body was clear of the line of fire. Only a sliver of his face was exposed as he peered through the swirling particulates, waiting for a human form to take shape.

Another two pops. A pair of rounds embedded in the back of the elevator.

Max's knees were tucked under his chin, his arms covering his head. He stared up at Evan. "What the hell are you *doing*?"

The next shot blew out the light casing above them.

At last Evan sensed a change in the textured air, a billow of white preceding the man's approach.

Evan released the OPEN DOORS button.

Flattened to the wall.

The bumpers started to shut.

The man's gun hand shot forward between the closing doors, the long barrel bucking once, twice.

Evan caught the arm at the wrist, jerking it forward, locking the elbow. The elevator doors bump-bump-bumped against the limb but did not retract.

Through the cage of his arms, Max's eyes looked huge.

Evan said, "You might want to look away."

Max complied.

Hyperextending the arm, Evan dealt a sharp heel-hand blow to the forearm on the thumb side near the crook of the elbow.

The radial head gave a wet pop as it dislocated.

The man screamed.

The pistol dropped to the floor, bounced once on the threshold, rattled through the gap, and vanished.

Evan let go, the limb slithering back into the thickening whiteness.

He tapped the button for the lobby.

It was unlikely that Max's pursuers would have sent more than one man to deal with a security-camera irregularity and more unlikely still that they'd want to have a shoot-out in a public lobby. But if they did, Evan was game.

The elevator doors eased shut, a gentle whir announcing their descent. The air was clear, but a chemical taint lingered, the smell of an aggressively treated Jacuzzi.

The speakers piped in a flute rendition of Christopher Cross, perennially stuck between the moon and New York City.

Evan's ARES remained holstered, invisible beneath his shirt.

The injury he'd inflicted was a precise one. And rare.

Nursemaid's elbow is generally seen in children because their bones are more cartilaginous than those of adults, which means that the radial head pops in and out more easily. It requires much more force, very specifically directed, to dislocate the bone in adults.

Evan had very specifically directed much more force.

Their would-be assassin would have trouble turning his wrist in either direction. His forearm would be locked in a midrange position. Grasping would be difficult.

It's hard to be an assassin if you can't grasp.

So he'd require medical attention.

Rare injuries are easier to track.

Which can prove useful when you're dealing with a professional killer wearing a balaclava and latex gloves.

Max gulped a few breaths. Then stood up. He shuddered off a chill and shifted his weight, pulling up the lank hair falling across his eyes. His gaze darted over to Evan, and then he shuddered again less violently and cracked a wry almost-smile.

"Okay," he said. "So *that* just happened."

12

A Thousand Brittle Pieces

Riding across town to his apartment, Max stuck his arm out the passenger window and let his hand skim across the passing air.

The Nowhere Man—who'd given only a first name of Evan—drove the Chevy Malibu at a steady pace, the needle pointed at the speed limit. He kept his gaze ahead, but his eyes stayed on constant rotation around the rear- and sideview mirrors. The guy seemed pensive, chewing on his thoughts.

Max's heartbeat had slowed at last, but he still sensed the after-wash of adrenaline in his veins. His skin felt dead; it felt like the color gray. He wondered if he'd ever sleep again.

Evan finally broke the silence. "What did you mean?" he said. "That Violet made you want to be more than you were?"

The cool wind buffeted Max's arm, whipped his hair around his eyes. He realized he was using it to jar himself out of numbness.

He thought for a beat, cleared his throat. "I was from the wrong side of the tracks," he said. "I mean, only by comparison, but still. Her parents basically disowned her. I was trying to support her on a construction worker's salary, going to night school to finish my degree. You know the kind of pressure that puts on you?"

Evan said, "No."

Max laughed. "Well, if you ever have a shot with someone who's worth it, try not to fuck it up." He looked at Evan ruefully. "Man, did I try not to fuck it up. Me, in night school." His chuckle, even to his own ears, held no amusement. "Pulling double shifts. And then when she got—" His breath snagged. "When she got pregnant." He shook his head. "But I wasn't. More. I was still just me."

They coasted along the blacktop, sliding between cars, the city flowing by indifferently.

Max said, "When I first saw her, I knew, right? I know that sounds lame, but right away, she just . . . She hit me in the spinal cord. She was gambling. Slots. And the seat next to her was empty."

The scene played in his head now, polished to jewel-like clarity by a million viewings. Sensation started to prickle his skin again, warmth spreading beneath the surface.

"I sat down and hit a jackpot with my first pull." Max smiled. "And you feel like a hero, right? Like you're in the movie and someone's writing your lines for you?" He paused. "You ever have that?"

Evan said, "No."

"Well, I guess you don't need it. I mean, with what you do, you're already there. But for me? In that moment? All of a sudden, it was like the whole world was open to me. If you could've seen how she looked just sitting there, doing nothing. And I remember thinking, If I can get this right, this one thing, all the other pieces will fall into place. And I got it. But they didn't." Max felt the loss now—a pressure at the backs of the eyes, his throat pressing upward. "Because I'm a fuckup. Who was I kidding that one thing could make everything fall into place?"

He stared at the passing cars, the work-casual folks on the sidewalk clustered around gourmet-food trucks. The oily taste of car exhaust left a bitterness at the back of his throat.

"Everything's a story," Evan said. "You want that to be the story of you, it can be."

Max shifted to look over at him. "What's the story of you?"

"That's not what this is," Evan said.

"What *what* is?"

"This isn't a therapy session."

"Well," Max said, "given what you do, it sure as hell seems like you're working *something* out."

The Nowhere Man didn't appear to like that answer. "So what happened?" he asked. "To you and Violet?"

Max closed his eyes, breathed the pollution. The wind poured through the window, cooling the sweat on his face. Evan had refused to answer any of his questions about personal shit. So he figured he was entitled to do the same. Especially about this. But he was already back in it now.

Awakened by screaming.

Violet in the bathroom.

Red drops on white tile. Thin rivulets down the insides of her thighs. She was crying in a way that he'd never seen, sobbing and hyperventilating at once, bent over, one bloodstained hand gripping the lip of the sink. She didn't seem to register him there at her side, but when he touched her, she crumpled into him, a dead leaf collapsing into a thousand brittle pieces.

The only thing harder than postpartum depression, they were informed by the well-intentioned ob-gyn, was postpartum depression after a failed pregnancy. And the only thing harder than that was simultaneously grappling with the knowledge that their hope for future children had been excised as surgically as her ruptured fallopian tube.

Violet was wrecked, relentlessly battered by a confusion of hormones. And he was barely functioning, hollowed out with grief. They started fighting daily. By being born, he'd lost a mother. By losing a child, he feared he'd lose his marriage. He buried himself in work and overtime and night school. Violet grew sluggish, her broken heart a millstone at her core. She said she wanted to die. That she didn't see the point of going on. How could she go back to work and spend her days surrounded by throngs of adorable kindergartners?

It was just talk, of course. The kinds of things you say when you're trying to give shape to god-awful emotions roiling inside you, when you're trying to process and vent and purge. He thought they'd figure it out. He thought they'd move on. He thought they would be fine right up until he came home from an evening class to find her in the bathtub, the cooling water the color of merlot, her floating arms etched from the razor.

Evan parked several blocks away and scouted Max's apartment to make sure no one was watching it. Then he went back and retrieved Max, the two of them making a quick approach through the parking lot, skirting the building manager's trusty Buick in the front spot. On the second floor, they ducked the manager's window and eased into Max's place, closing the door silently behind them.

Standing in the apartment, Evan noted how bare it was. It was a mess now, certainly, after the Terror had taken a tour through all of Max's belongings and the drywall, but there hadn't been much to begin with. Sawed-open couch, shattered TV on the floor, toppled coffee table. A few plates—now shattered—and some silverware dashed on the chipped linoleum in what passed for a kitchen nook. A bureau's worth of clothes hurled around the bedroom. A few empty packing boxes piled in the corner.

From what Max had told him, it had been about two and a half years since he'd rented this place after Violet, and yet it seemed he'd never really moved in.

Maybe he didn't want to.

Maybe moving in meant acknowledging that she was gone.

While Evan stood watch at the big front window, Max scurried around his bedroom grabbing personal items—clothes, toothbrush, and whatever else reasonable people considered to be necessities.

The second-floor corridor was empty, the street quiet. Evan cast another glance across the sparse apartment.

The habitat of a man who had figured out how to exist but not really live.

Evan wondered if his own place was merely a dressed-up version of the same. He had the thumb drive out, tapping it against his palm. He was eager to get to a secure location, plug it into his laptop, and see what the hell had started this ball rolling.

Max finally emerged from the bedroom, a bag slung over his shoulder. "Now what?"

"Now we tuck you away somewhere safe."

"Like where?"

Evan considered. From what he'd heard of the Terror and seen of the shooter at Grant's office, he figured these were street-level guys. Dangerous men, sure, but he doubted they had access to classified databases. Even so, he was reluctant to put Max on an airplane or check him in to a hotel.

Evan kept a number of safe houses scattered around Los Angeles, equipped with load-out gear and alternate vehicles. The locations were, like Evan's financial holdings, fully off the books, buried beneath an avalanche of shell corps and offshore holding companies. Because all transactions around the safe houses had to be double-blind, they took a hefty investment of resources to acquire and maintain.

The instant a client entered a safe house, it was blown forever. He'd use one if absolutely necessary but preferred not to.

"We have a few options," Evan said. "Number one: I give you a bundle of cash and a burner phone, you get in the Chevy Malibu and drive away. Then you keep on driving. You find a hotel five states away, pay cash for everything, and I contact you when it's over."

Max said, "No."

"Why no?"

"Because," Max said, "I gave my word." He looked like he needed to sleep for a month. "I'm not just gonna run away. I may not be much help, but I have to be around in case you need me. Until it's . . . you know, settled. And everyone else is safe."

Evan gestured at the tufts of stuffing stripped from the gutted couch. "You didn't give your word for this."

"I told Grant I'd take care of it for him. That I'd keep it away from his wife and kids. That I'd see it through for him. So I have to do that." Max swayed a bit on his feet and then said again, "I gave my word."

"You don't have to prove anything," Evan said. "Not anymore."

Max gave a hoarse laugh edged with self-loathing. His gaze was loose, unfocused.

"So what?" Evan said. "If you do this thing for Grant, it'll prove you're a good person?"

"No," Max said. "It'll prove I'm worth *something*." His eyes moistened, and he looked quickly away. "I thought, just one time, it might be nice not to let anyone down, that's all. It sounds so fucking juvenile, but . . ."

"What?" Evan said.

"I just . . . I could use a win, you know?"

His voice had grown husky, and for a moment Evan thought he might actually break down under the strain of it all. But then he seemed to shake off the thoughts and reset himself. "The other options," he said. "What are they?"

Evan gave a nod, glad to move on. "You have anywhere you can go? Anywhere safe?"

"Not really," Max said. "I mean, my dad's still around, but my family's not really . . . Like I said, we're not really close."

"Family's not an option," Evan said. "We can't put them at risk."

"Not that we have to worry about that," Max said. "Them sticking out their neck for me, I mean."

Evan said, "Okay."

Max pressed his palm to his forehead. "Shit," he said. "There is one— No, never mind. Shit. Okay. There might be one option but it's . . ."

"It's what?"

"Hard."

Evan stepped on a cushion on the floor, the knife slash gaping. "Harder than this?"

Max swallowed. The last bit of color had drained from his face.

"Yes," he said.

13

The Badness of My Heart

The cottage in the gently rolling hills of South Pasadena was tucked behind an ivy-covered brick wall. The streets were wide here, the sunshine plentiful even in the late afternoon, even in November. Polished fenders, moist green lawns, spit-shined windows—it all had a big-ticket gleam.

Evan had taken every precaution approaching the residence, but it was evident that there was nothing on this patch of neighborhood but an excess of money. Beside him Max shuffled from foot to foot.

The doorbell gave a resonant chime that belied an interior far deeper than what the cutesy stone-and-stucco façade implied. Evan felt the key chain—and the thumb drive it hid—pressing against his thigh through the tactical-discreet pocket of his cargo pants, right beneath one of his backup magazines.

Footsteps sounded.

Max said, "Maybe I should just wait in the—"

Violet opened the door.

She was as striking as Max had described. Glossy black hair lay pronounced against her pale skin, a single forties wave peekabooing one eye. Bloody red lipstick. Sharp, intelligent irises the color of espresso.

She wore leggings and a gauzy loose sweater over a fitted midnight-blue shirt. Instinctively she tugged at her cuffs, covering her wrists with her sleeves, but not before Evan saw the telltale marks. Thin raised scars, white as milk, like the branches of a dead tree.

Her eyes sharpened further, her brow twisting. For an instant her face wore a bare expression of unadulterated hurt, and then it hardened, locking down the softer emotion.

"Get him off my property," she said.

Evan said, "His life is at risk."

"Yeah? So was mine."

Max stared at the porch, at the tops of his shoes. Evan could feel the heat from her glare, and he was certain Max could, too.

"I can't believe you'd show your face here," Violet said.

Max nodded and faded back off the porch, never lifting his gaze. He waited in the grass, a salesman afraid to approach.

Violet looked at Evan, and he could see the strength in her. She was breathing hard, her neck flushed, her clavicles pronounced on the inhalations.

Evan said, "He did a favor for someone, and now a crew of hit men are after him."

Violet's focus moved past Evan's shoulder to Max. Her blink rate had picked up. She pressed her lips together. Unrolled them. "I'll give you this, Max. At least you don't make the same mistake twice. You find yourself a whole new one."

Her voice now was steady. Not a tremor. *This is what pain looks like when stoked to a bright light*, Evan thought. *It gets cold.*

"If I don't get him off the street and hide him," Evan said, "he will be killed. He said your parents are—" He almost said "slumlords," corrected course. "Real-estate kingpins. With thousands of holdings in questionable neighborhoods. He said you work for them now."

"Yes," she said, each word diamond-hard. "I do. Now. It was the best option, and I took it." She was going for a wounded kind of pride, but her misery at the admission was evident.

Evan asked, "Can you find a place that's between tenants in a"—*shitty part of town*—"lower-income area?"

"For what?"

"To hide him. To save his life."

"Why should I put myself at risk for him?"

"You're nearly three years divorced. And it wasn't amicable. It's incredibly doubtful anyone would think Max would come to you—"

"You can count me in that group," she cut in.

"—and be able to connect the dots from you to the business of your parents—who dislike him—and then to one of countless places they own around Los Angeles." Evan paused. "Let's just say it's beyond a long shot."

"You misunderstood my question," she said. "I didn't ask *if* I'd be at risk for him. I asked *why* I should put myself at risk for him."

A patch of roses breathed a lovely scent that seemed out of place amid all the bitterness.

Evan said, "I can't answer that."

She said, "Who are you?"

"Someone who's helping him?"

"Out of the goodness of your heart?"

Evan considered this. "Out of the badness of my heart, I suppose."

She seemed to appreciate his candor. "It's really life-or-death?"

"It is."

"Fine. I'll find somewhere. Somewhere *really* crappy. On one condition. Ask him what he did to me. You make him tell you. You should know who you're helping."

The breeze from the rose garden now smelled saccharine, a sickly indulgence.

Evan said, "I will."

"I'll give you three addresses," she said. "Unrented places. Pick whichever you like. Do *not* lose the keys. Return them when you're done. And then I never want to hear from you—or him—again. Also? I don't know anything about this."

Evan said, "Copy that."

"And tell him . . ."

"What?"

"Tell him I'm sorry about Grant." Her scowl returned. "Wait out here."

The door closed abruptly. The footsteps padded away, more sharply than before.

Evan exhaled through his teeth and eased back until he came level with Max on the front lawn.

Max said, "Look, after she . . . after she tried to commit suicide, I was lost. I remember going to the drugstore one day to buy shampoo and just standing there, paralyzed, because I couldn't decide what to get. Like for twenty minutes, just *frozen*." He wet his lips, swallowed. "We were gonna be parents. And then, all at once, we weren't."

"What did you do to her?" Evan asked.

"I felt so fucking helpless," Max said. "Just . . . at a total loss, you know? She didn't want to go on, and I didn't know when she'd do it again. She was sick with grief. She was sleeping all day and throwing up when she ate, and I couldn't help her. I couldn't do anything but hold her hair, and she looked . . . she looked like she had nothing inside her anymore. Like she'd already gone and left a husk behind. I would've done whatever I could to help her, but I didn't have the answers. I didn't have any of the answers. Everything I tried just made things worse. I would have done anything. You understand? Anything."

"You couldn't handle it anymore," Evan said.

Max took in a breath. "I guess not."

"So you left."

Max plucked a glossy rose petal from the bush, ground it between his thumb and forefinger. "Sure," he said. "I left."

A silence ensued, nothing but the cheery chirps of songbirds on the scented breeze. The closed door confronted them like a moral rebuke.

Evan felt Max's eyes on the side of his face.

"Lemme guess." Max's tone was sharp, but it was clear that just served to hide the shame. "That makes you not like me."

Evan said, "I don't have to like you to protect you."

14

Take Names

Violet had seen through her promise to find a supremely crappy place for Max.

The ramshackle house was bedded into the side of a hill, the crumbling rear wall patched with fiberglass siding. A trash bag duct-taped over a smashed window fluttered with sporadic violence, a bat trying to tear free of a trapped wing. The plumbing appeared to be intact, the pipes visible at intervals in the decaying drywall. The few overhead lights hummed with exertion. A cracked sliding glass door let onto a narrow bog of long-sitting water in the backyard, the rotted fence spitting distance from the threshold.

A Best Buy box under one arm, Evan paused in the main room and took in the place. It was unclear whether it was in the process of being torn down or rebuilt.

He supposed he could say the same for Max.

Lincoln Heights wasn't as bad as it used to be, fair-trade coffee-houses staking a tentative hold on corners that used to be gang-held. But it was still the Eastside.

Over where the kitchen used to be, a pair of work boots, a loaded tool belt, and a McKenna Properties baseball cap lay where they had fallen, as if the worker who'd owned them had ascended to heaven, leaving his earthly belongings behind.

As Max poked his head into the dorm-size bedroom, Evan tugged the Dell laptop out of the box, shedding the Styrofoam bookends. It had cost a little over two hundred dollars, money well spent for a clean device on which to test Grant's thumb drive. When Evan dropped the box, it stuck to the floor with a thud, impaled on an exposed length of tack strip where the carpet had been ripped up.

A new tile floor had been laid in anticipation of a kitchen so Evan sat there cross-legged, resting the laptop on the shelf of his knees.

As it booted up, he pulled the Swiss Army knife key chain from his pocket and flicked up the thumb drive. Max returned from the bedroom, leaned against the wall, and looked at Evan.

Evan plugged in the thumb drive.

A series of files populated the screen. He frowned at the confusion of numbers.

Max cleared his throat. "What is it?"

Evan said, "Spreadsheets."

"Of what?"

Evan didn't answer. He clicked. And he read.

For a long time, there was no sound save Max's breathing and the occasional tap of water dripping from a sweating pipe. The glow from the dim can lighting was as faint as the laptop screen, a chiaroscuro contrast of shadows and silhouettes.

Max said, again, "What is it?"

"Gimme a sec," Evan said.

"It's been forty minutes, man."

Evan checked the Victorinox fob watch clipped to his belt loop, the time surprising him. "Come over here," he said.

Max shoved off the wall and joined Evan in the weak orb of light thrown by the laptop. "It looks like a set of books."

"*Two* sets of books," Evan said.

"Why two?"

"One cooked. And one real. The real one shows the actual money flow."

"Laundering," Max said.

Evan scrolled through entry after entry of figures in the low thousands. Dozens a day. "See—they're smurfing it through these entities, breaking it up into amounts small enough not to raise any red flags."

The light reflected in Max's eyes. "That's gotta be three, four million dollars a month," he said. "What do you think it's from?"

"Could be anything," Evan said. "Drugs. Foreign money. Gun-running."

"No wonder Grant was digging into it. But who was he working for?"

"See this client code?" Evan pointed to where *"HWDPD"* recurred at the top of each page. "That's Hollywood Community Police Station."

"They hired him?"

"Yes. Seems like a big case for a community station—this sort of stuff usually gets kicked downtown."

"Even if the crimes are taking place in their jurisdiction?"

Evan nodded. "I'm thinking they were piecing it together, prepping it for the handoff to Vice." With a knuckle he tapped the screen. "This set of spreadsheets tracks the three steps of the process—injection, confusion, and acquisition. You inject the cash into the financial system. Then you camouflage its source through wires between various accounts. Look here. Then it loops through there, see?"

Max nodded, tracing a figure between documents on the screen. "And then back into this account."

"Right. And once it's been run through the system and cleaned up, the money's acquired 'legitimately' here. See these withdrawals? Grant was still figuring it out, helping Hollywood PD shore up the case."

"Against who?" Max said.

"Doesn't say. We have the dirty books but not the names attached to them. I'm guessing these codes here are initials. But there are plenty of blanks and question marks. The case was still being built. Grant was in the process of identifying the players. Which explains why the cops couldn't protect him. They weren't sure who to protect him from."

"So what next?"

Evan thought of the shooter from Grant's office, nursing that injured arm. Right now he'd be fighting off the inevitable. Trying to convince himself that it would get better, that he could deal with the pain, that he wouldn't have to go in and get that dislocated radial head popped back into place.

Evan said, "Next I take names."

He snapped the laptop shut and stood. Max found his feet as well. "Should we turn this over to the cops?"

"Sure," Evan said. "They'll continue the investigation. Send you on your way. And you'll wind up like your cousin or Lorraine Lennox."

Max's eyes got glassy. "Right. But how are you gonna figure out who's behind it?"

"Not being bound by the law enables me to be more . . . efficient."

Max nodded a few times rapidly. "Grant dealt with a lot of criminals. But something about these guys was scary enough for him to decide to put a break-glass-in-case-of-emergency option in place. And the guy at my apartment? He makes the dude who shot at us look like a minor-leaguer. These are bad men."

Evan handed Max a roll of hundred-dollar bills and a burner cell phone. "I've dealt with a lot worse than money launderers and street-level hit men." Evan started for the door. "Don't use any credit cards. Don't contact anyone. Don't leave this place except to buy food. Use the phone I left you only to reach me. I'll come back and update you on my progress tomorrow."

The air of the entryway was humid and thick, tinged with the soggy reek of mold.

Evan had his hand on the doorknob when Max said, "Wait."

He turned around.

"I didn't have a chance to thank you," Max said. "I don't know where I'd be if it wasn't for you. No—scratch that. I'd be dead already. I know that after the stuff with Violet . . . You may not be glad you're helping me. But I am."

Evan nodded. When he opened the front door, the chill night air blew across him, a refreshing break from the stillness of the house. He stepped out onto the porch.

"They say being brave doesn't mean you're not scared," Max said. "It means you're scared and do it anyway."

Evan halted. He didn't answer. But he turned around.

Max scratched at his neck, his fingernails raising red streaks. He was backlit, the shadows catching on his face, veiling his eyes. "Is that . . . is that true?"

Evan said, "I'm not scared yet."

15

Predacious Douchenozzle

Westwood Village hugged the south edge of UCLA, a jumble of restaurants, movie theaters, bars, and shops hawking college gear. As was the case in the rest of West L.A., the real-estate market had blown sky-high, but the students streaming through left the neighborhood pleasingly shabby in places. Frat-house lawns littered with beer bottles, pizza by the slice, sublet condos losing a war of attrition.

In the warren of streets east of Veteran Avenue, Evan approached a three-story apartment complex, assessing the security measures. The windows were single-pane, flimsy in their frames, easily breakable. The mounted light by the call box was broken, casting the entrance in shadow. The guard plate on the door had come loose enough to be pried free with a screwdriver. He raked the dead bolt in all of ten seconds with a half-diamond pick and took the stairs to the second floor.

Midway down the hall, he paused outside an apartment door backlit with a bluish electronic glow. In the thin gap by the frame, he could see that the three dead bolts had been left un-locked.

Lazy.

The doorknob lock looked to be as old as the building itself. Evan flicked open his Strider folding knife, slipped it into the doorjamb, and angled it to catch the ramped latch. Before he slid it back into its housing to free the door, he hesitated.

With his free hand, he took out his RoamZone and texted: YOU FAILED YOUR SECURITY ASSESSMENT. I'M COMING IN NOW. DON'T JUMP ME.

A moment later the reply hummed in: THEN DON'T GIVE ME A GOOD REASON 2 JUMP U.

He thumbed in: KAY.

With a tilt of the blade, he opened the door.

A workstation pod consumed the entire front room, towers and servers stacked atop a circular desk. Monitors were mounted three high on metal racks, hiding the chair from view. The sound of fu-rious clacking echoed off the walls and cottage-cheese ceiling, low-level violence being visited upon a keyboard.

As Evan closed the door behind him, a feminine voice said, "Hang on," and then a teenage girl emerged from the circular desk through a missing slice.

A too-big flannel hung unbuttoned from her lithe, muscular frame. The red T-shirt beneath boasted an image of Hello Kitty brandishing an AK-47. Lush brown-black hair tumbled past the girl's shoulders and mostly covered the shaved strip above her ear on the right side.

Joey Morales was the finest hacker Evan had ever encountered.

She was also a washout from the Orphan Program. She'd once had a target on her head, but Evan had saved her, and in a manner of speaking she'd saved him, too. She'd been the last of the Or-phans whom Jack had trained. His dying wish was that Evan look after her, a burden that had become a responsibility that had in turn morphed into something deeply meaningful to him in ways he could neither understand nor express.

Evan had cleared her out of the country, parking her in a Swiss boarding school until he could eliminate those who wanted to eradicate her and anyone else with Orphan training. Once the threats had been neutralized, he'd relocated her here. Or, more precisely, she'd relocated herself.

He'd come home one night to find his unpickable front door unlocked and his impenetrable alarm system incapacitated. He'd drawn his ARES 1911 and made an adrenalized tactical approach across the great room only to find Joey sitting barefoot on the couch eating Flamin' Hot Cheetos.

Napkinless.

Though she never admitted as much, she wanted to live close to him. And though he never admitted as much, the feeling was mutual. So after he didn't shoot her on his couch, he oversaw her move to the apartment a few miles away. He'd already set her up with some money stashed in a trust and with fake documents making her a legal adult, so she'd rented the place herself and furnished it with hardware befitting her genius hacker brain. As part of his ongoing attempt to mainstream her into normal civilian life, he insisted that she enroll in courses at UCLA in the coming semester, an arrangement she wasn't happy with and was already no doubt scheming to undermine.

He'd spent the past few months doing his best to keep track of her.

Keeping track of a sixteen-year-old girl, he'd learned, was more challenging than neutralizing a high-value target inside a guarded desert training camp.

She currently held a Big Gulp, which she waved in his direction. "What's with the 'kay'?"

She seemed indignant.

Evan said, "What?"

"'Kay' is angry in textspeak. Like, passive-aggressive pissed off, you know?"

"I don't know."

"And the worst? Is the *lowercase-k* 'kay.' 'Cuz you know the person put *effort* into taking off the caps lock. Lowercase *k* is a declaration of war." To punctuate the point, she raised the Big Gulp to her mouth and slurped a hit of soda through the wide red straw.

"There are words coming out of your face," Evan said. "But they don't make any sense in the actual world out here."

"Come on, X. Get with the times."

He pointed back at the door. "You have to throw the dead bolts. Every time. How you do anything is how you—"

She was mouthing the Second Commandment along with him, her eyes rolled to white. She stopped when he stopped, a thumbprint dimple marking her right cheek as she grinned. She had a radiant smile that got her out of trouble more often than it should have.

"Don't worry," she said. "Anyone breaks in here, you know I'll beat his ass silly."

Evan circled the massive workstation and checked the broken latch on the window. It was the second floor, but still. "They haven't fixed this yet?"

"Could you puh-*lease* get a hobby?" Joey said.

The windowsill was covered with all order of elaborate Rubik's Cubes—magic cubes and speed cubes and shape-shifters blown out in all dimensions. Some kids played video games to pass the time; Joey did cubes thirteen rows deep and high that would've knotted Evan's brain into a pretzel.

He almost knocked over a giant Megaminx twist puzzle as he fussed with the faulty window latch. "You need a dog," he said. "A guard dog."

"I don't need a dog. I need more money. Like, an allowance."

"An allowance? I gave you a trust fund that pays a monthly dividend of—"

"Do you *know* how expensive hardware is?" She disappeared back into the workstation and collapsed into a rolling gamer chair. Leaning over, she petted a rackmount Brutalis box. "This eight-GPU password-cracking monster was over twenty g's."

"I'd rather you spent your money on a safer apartment."

"If I paid for a safer apartment, I couldn't afford all this hardware. Which—I seem to recall—you make regular use of. So it's not really an allowance I'm asking for. It's more like a *raise*."

Evan came into the pod and leaned against the inside curve of the desk. The temperature here in the inner sanctum was at least ten degrees hotter, and the air carried a whiff of burning rubber.

He crossed his arms. "A raise."

"That's how I like to think of it, yeah." Another slurp of Dr Pepper. "Do you have any idea what my mad skills would go for if I turned black hat?"

Evan sank his face into his palm.

Joey grinned at his feigned bemusement. "Didn't anyone tell you how hard it is to raise assassin children in Los Angeles?"

"I'm not raising you," Evan said. "And you're not an assassin."

"Yeah, 'cuz you wouldn't *let* me."

"You're grounded."

She snickered. Then she spun around in her chair. Her hands played across one of a succession of keyboards, Beethoven pounding out a concerto.

In his pocket his RoamZone made a woeful noise. He sighed. Then he tugged it out and looked at it. Red bars had appeared across the screen. She'd locked him out.

In the event of an emergency, he'd given Joey partial access to the back end of his digital operations. Which in her hands had quickly turned into full access. That was the thing with kids. Give 'em an inch.

"Very funny, Joey."

"I think so." She really seemed to be enjoying herself now. "Oh, wait. I forgot the best part." She spun back to the keyboard. More frenzied typing.

A message materialized on his RoamZone: FOR USE OF THIS DEVICE, PLEASE WIRE $250,000 TO ACCOUNT NUMBER—

He lifted his eyes. "You can't blackmail me for use of my own phone."

"Pretty sure I just did." She was all but glowing. He had to admit, it was a pretty charming little routine. Charming and infuriating. "Could be worse," she said. "I could change your ringtone to something, like, *really embarrassing.*"

"Unlock my phone. Now."

She bounced a bit in the chair. "Sure you don't need a sweater?"

Wearily, Evan took the bait. "Why?"

"'Cuz of all this shade I'm throwing your way?"

"Josephine."

"Okay, okay." Back to the keyboard. The red bars and the joke ransom note vanished from the RoamZone. "Happy?"

"No," he said. "But I'm less unhappy."

"Now, what brings you here in the middle of the night?" she asked. "Girl trouble?" She finished her drink and tossed it into a trash can filled with three other empty Big Gulps, which went some way toward explaining her caffeinated patter at this hour. "What's going on with that DA lady? Mia?"

"Nothing."

"But you guys would be *so good* together. You get all flirty and nervous around her. It's cute. I mean, in an old-person way. Why aren't you guys at least dating?"

"Because if she finds out who I really am, she'd have to prosecute me."

Joey pulled her mouth to one side. A pensive pause. "That is complicating. But we can find you someone else. You should date some . . . I dunno, athleisure-wear model."

Evan forged onward. "I need you to check all emergency-room records in the area."

"For what?"

Evan explained. Joey listened intently, for once not running her mouth. He was a reasonably skilled hacker, but she was an Olympian. She'd have the hit man tracked down in a fraction of the time it would take him.

When he'd finally finished his account of what had happened at Grant's office, she was perfectly still with focus, her emerald eyes large. "So you fucked up his arm in a specific way just so you could track the injury?"

"Language. But yes."

She shook her head slowly. "That's pretty badass, X." She swiveled back around, fingers flying across her keyboard. "Bet you're glad I bought this Brutalis box now," she said over her shoulder. "Here's what I'm gonna do. Correction: Here's what I'm *doing*. I'm hacking into the two electronic medical-record systems used in these here parts—Epic and Cerner. For research purposes the records can be searched by patient, diagnosis, billing codes, everything else. So we hit the central research databases for both EMRs, check patient visits from the past twenty-four hours. . . ." Windows flashed open on multiple monitors, overlaid by others before Evan could even register them. "Diagnosis of nursemaid's elbow in the right arm. Search parameters: men between twenty and forty, ERs within a fifty-mile radius, and . . . Wa-la!"

Evan leaned forward, reading the case record. At 11:37 P.M. a twenty-eight-year-old man was discharged from the Palmdale Regional Medical Center's emergency room with a diagnosis of radial-head dislocation of his right arm. Right on schedule. The patient had provided no ID, given his name as "Frank Jones," and left against physician advice without paying.

Evan said, "Let's get into the security cameras in the waiting room and . . ."

Joey was pointing at the monitor beside his head.

He turned.

A freeze-frame image from the ER lobby at 10:34 had captured the man squared to the camera. Evan didn't recognize his face, of course, given that he'd worn a balaclava during their run-in, but the tapestry of patterned scars sleeving his bare arms was familiar. One of the markings, riding the outer ledge of his triceps, looked like a meringue cookie smashed flat. The Armenian eternity sign.

"Okay," Evan said. "Now you should grab facial recognition and—"

Joey pointed at another monitor behind him.

He turned further.

Panasonic FacePRO was already churning through the Internet, searching for matches of the captured image. It chimed twice, hitting on an Instagram profile.

BigggPapa69.

There Big Papa was, taking a selfie with two Budweiser girls at an Irish pub.

Next a posed shot in the gym as he dead-lifted eight plates.

Now behind the wheel of a Maserati, wearing reflective aviator sunglasses.

Predacious Douchenozzle

Evan said, "Can you slip into the profile to get us a real name?"

"Hang on." Her hands were a blur. "He's got double authentication, which is a pain. But wait—wait. Check this out."

She'd cyberstalked backward in his profile, finding a post from last year. Big Papa on an airplane with a friend, flashing a boarding pass and the hang-ten sign. The caption: HEADING TO MAUI TO SLAY SOME FRESH YOUNG HAWAII ASS!! His tongue was sticking out, his mouth framed with a pencil-thin goatee.

"Look at his dumb sexist face," Joey said. "I mean, what the actual fuck."

She clicked the mouse angrily, grabbing the image and whipping it across an arc of monitors until it rested on the screen in front of her. She zoomed in on the boarding pass name: *Michael Papazian.*

Before Evan could react, a rap sheet had magically come into being on the monitor at his elbow. Papazian's priors included violent rape, battery, possession of illegal firearms. Numerous plead-out charges and a few short prison stints. Current address unknown.

By the time Evan looked back, Joey had decrypted the barcode image from the ticket, revealing a six-digit number.

Evan said, "How . . . ?"

Joey shot up her wait-a-sec finger, and he clamped his mouth shut. Now she was using the six-digit passenger ID and Papazian's last name to log into the airline's website. All of a sudden, Evan was looking at Michael Papazian's frequent-flier number, travel preferences, credit-card information.

And address.

"You'll find him there." She flicked a hand at another monitor in the circle that showed Papazian's Netflix account. He was currently streaming an episode of *Luther.* "Distracted."

Evan shoved up from his lean on the desk. He rested a hand on her shoulder. "Good work."

"Yeah," she said. "It was." Her tone was morose, her face sullen.

Like Evan, she'd come up through a variety of foster homes. It had been harder for her because of assholes like Papazian. She didn't like to talk about it, and he never pushed her.

She glared at the Instagram picture. "Before you kill that predacious douchenozzle," she said, "tell him that the adjective is 'Hawaiian.'"

Evan looked at her blankly.

Her lip curled with disgust. "As in 'Heading to Maui to slay some fresh young *Hawaiian* ass.'"

Evan cleared his throat and said, gently, "I'll do that."

16

System Overload

Michael Papazian nodded off on his couch, his injured arm supported by a pillow. On the TV, Idris Elba stalked through gray London streets.

One room over, the screen door clanged softly in the desert breeze. There was nothing beyond his porch but a dirt driveway and a half mile of dunes leading to a trailer park and the horizontal bar of the 138 Freeway as it cut through Palmdale.

The screen clanged once more, louder than before, straightening Papazian on the couch and tightening his good hand around the Browning P-35 pistol resting on the cushion beside him.

He stared across the unlit stretch toward his front door.

First there was darkness.

Then a pair of hands, pale and floating.

A face.

Two strokes of the shoulders.

A form, advancing. Papazian found his feet, squinting at the man inside his house.

The man stopped in the doorway of the room, his lower half still lost to shadow. The faint glow from the TV played tricks, illuminating edges of his face, a collection of Picasso parts.

"I wanted to resume our interaction," the man said. "The one we started outside Grant Merriweather's office. I want to know who the Terror is. I want to know how many of you there are in the money-laundering ring. I want names and addresses."

Papazian lifted the pistol and aimed it with a shaking fist. He wasn't used to shooting with his left hand. "You have no idea who you're fucking with, chief."

"Also," the man said, "the adjective is 'Hawaiian.'"

Papazian cocked his head. "You cray-cray, bitch?"

"You're in a heightened state of alert," the man said calmly. "Your heart rate's up over a hundred beats a second. Which means your fine motor skills have already deteriorated and your gross motor is compromised."

Papazian jabbed the gun at the air. "Say *what*, motherfucker?"

Evan stepped forward into the room. They faced each other across the couch.

Riding Evan's back in a sling, angled like a samurai sword, was a matte black Benelli M1 combat shotgun. He made no move for it.

Instead he studied the pistol aimed at him, the barrel tip three feet from his forehead. The Browning P-35, known more widely as a Hi-Power, was one of the first successful double-stack mag nine mils. The thirteen-round capacity made it a favorite of many of the world's militaries since World War II, a sidearm of choice from Aussies to Venezuelans. Nonstop production in Belgium and licensed countries for nearly a century had put it so heavily into circulation that it could be considered nontraceable.

As with all self-loading semiautos, the Hi-Power cannot fire when the slide isn't locked fully forward in battery. A mechanical disconnector prevents the hammer from dropping.

A design element easily exploited when someone held the weapon within reach.

Evan shot his hand out, cupped the top of the slide, and pushed it back a quarter inch.

Papazian tugged the trigger, but nothing happened. His face

frozen with disbelief, he yanked it once more, the pistol bobbing in their shared grip.

Evan twisted the weapon to the side, hyperextending Papazian's elbow, and jammed the heel of his free hand into the forearm. There was a grinding of bone and tendon and the pop of the radial head unseating.

Nursemaid's elbow redux.

Now Papazian had a matching set.

Evan stripped the pistol from Papazian's hand and flung it behind him. It clattered across the floor, pinging off the wall in the darkness. Evan reached over his shoulder, unsheathed the shotgun from the sling, and whipped it down to rest on Papazian's shoulder.

The boom was bone-shuddering. Behind Papazian digital London transformed into a cloud of splinters.

Papazian staggered but kept his feet.

Evan said, "Now you're near two hundred beats per minute. Your cognitive processing is starting to go. Time dilation, visual narrowing, auditory exclusion."

He popped the shotgun up over Papazian's head, thunking it down on the other shoulder as if knighting him. He pulled the trigger again, the stock kicking back. Another boom, this one biblical.

Evan raised his voice so Papazian would hear over the concussive din in his head. "You're spiked over two fifty now. System overload. Perceptually shut down. Full-blown tunnel vision. Voiding instinct. That warmth you feel spreading down your leg? You might think you've already been shot, but it's just piss."

Papazian's eyes looked like dinner plates. His breaths came in hiccups.

Evan lowered the shotgun to aim at his knee. "Next time it won't be."

Mr. Omar answered his door wearing boxer shorts and a tattered blue bathrobe that was oddly feminine. He blinked up at the two men in the hallway. Cuffed sleeves, pressed slacks, polished shoes.

The taller of the two wore an LAPD baseball cap. "I'm Detective Nuñez, and this is Detective Brust." For good measure, he nudged the badge dangling around his neck on a lanyard. "I understand you're the landlord here?"

Omar scratched at his thigh. "Landlord no. Building manager yes." He smiled, revealed perfectly straight, large yellow teeth. "Instead of cashing the checks, I deal with much hassles. Not a fair trade-off if you ask me, my friend. But my rent is free, and—"

Brust tried on a smile as he cut in. "Have you seen Max Merriweather?"

"No. His apartment has been broken in, and he is missing. The other cops came and took the report. They told me not to fix yet. That it is evidence." Omar lifted a finger skyward. "And I have not."

"We saw that report, thank you," Nuñez said. "We're from the Hollywood Station, investigating a different aspect of the case. We need to know if Mr. Merriweather has been in touch with you in any way? If he's come by here?"

Omar shook his head. "I've been much worried about him. Always behind on the rent, but he is good man." His eyes were baggy, raccoon-ringed with darker skin. He tugged at his wattle. "But he vanished like this." A snap of his fingers.

Brust stepped forward and handed Omar a card. His partner was impeccable, but Brust had a coffee stain on the left side of his shirt, a brown dribble that wouldn't be coming out anytime soon. "If you hear anything—anything at all—please call us."

Omar pinched the card at the corners so it bowed inward. He stared at the number, brow twisted with worry. "Yes, I will. I will."

When he looked up, the detectives' faces were clouded with concern. "He's in grave danger," Nuñez said.

"What danger?" Omar asked. "How *much* danger?"

The detectives had started for the stairs, but Nuñez paused and looked back, his expression heavy. "More than he's even aware of."

17

Right Side Up and Upside Down

Evan—or more precisely the Benelli combat shotgun—had convinced Papazian to give up what information he had in exchange for a painless exit. Evan now had to stage the next phase of the mission, which meant getting to the databases and buckling down. By the time he returned to Castle Heights, an early-morning buzz had already filled the lobby. The tenants were clustered around the love seats, some dressed for work, others lounging in retiree leisure wear.

Evan lowered his head and vectored for the elevator.

"Ev. *Ev!* Come over here. My God, you won't *believe* what happened to Ida."

Lorilee's face looked Saran Wrap–tight beneath the bright lights of the lobby. He glanced down and halted at the sight of the crimson mist across the toes of his boots.

He had not been counting on prework social hour in the lobby.

He glanced at the group. "Maybe you could tell me later."

A storm of objections assailed him, the loudest from Hugh Walters, 20C. Hugh was the HOA president and never tired of reacquainting the residents with that fact. "I think you need to hear this," he said, his long face drawn longer with stageworthy distress. "It represents a security threat to this building's residents. And it can't wait for tomorrow's HOA meeting."

Evan's shoulders lowered another notch. He'd made a great effort to forget about the HOA meeting and the "nibbles" he was tasked with providing.

Stalling, he snuck another glance at the dappled red on his Original S.W.A.T. boots. There was no way he could join the others without their noticing. He raised one foot as if to scratch the opposing calf, wiping Papazian's blood onto the back leg of his cargo pants. He had to do the same with his left boot without looking obvious.

And without looking like he was performing a rain dance.

Everyone waited on him expectantly.

He had no choice but to shift his weight and fake-scratch at his other leg.

At that moment a burst of music exploded from his pocket: *AAAH LIKE BIG BUTTS AND I CANNOT LIE!*

He fumbled out the RoamZone, saw Joey on the caller ID.

YOU OTHABROTHAZ CAN'T—

He thumbed the green button to stop the atrocious ringtone.

Joey's voice came through. "Well, did you find him? What happened?"

Turning slightly from the stunned residents, Evan said in a low voice, "Impeccably bad timing. And the ringtone? Better go away."

"Oh," Joey said. "Oh, yeah. Sorry 'bout that."

He hung up, gave a quick check of the wiped-clean toes of his boots, and approached the love seats. As long as he faced the others, they wouldn't see the blood streaks on the backs of his pant legs.

He said flatly, "What happened to Ida?"

"Okay," Lorilee said, shouldering her way to the front. "Well, I was stuck at my place last night because the cleaning lady was coming. And then I had to rush out to Pilates and, let's see, grab an açai bowl for dinner—"

"Lorilee." Evan told his face to smile but managed only an impatient twitch of the lips. "What happened to Ida?"

"Right. Sorry. So I got back late and found her *bleeding* on the sidewalk right out front."

Evan felt his irritation harden into something sharper-edged. "What happened?"

Lorilee's face broke, an approximation of sobbing. She threw her arms wide. "Can you just hold me?"

Evan said, "No."

But it was too late. She collapsed into him, crying. Her breasts had about as much give as cannonballs.

Awkwardly he patted her back twice and extracted himself. "What happened?" he asked again.

"She got robbed," Johnny Middleton said. "That classy necklace she was showing off? A guy clocked her and ripped it off. Sounds like some fucked-up shit, man. If I was there, I woulda . . ." He made a few *choku-zuki* punches in the air, his fist position too low and then too high. It looked like semicoordinated flailing. "I mean, who the hell decks a eighty-something-year-old lady?"

"It's important that we all take proper precautions," Hugh said. "Until this maniac is caught."

"Is she at the hospital?" Evan asked.

"She's back home now," Hugh said with a paternal nod. "Resting."

Evan felt that sharp-edged anger shift inside him again and reminded himself that Ida Rosenbaum and her antique jewelry were not his concern. He wouldn't let anything derail him from the mission objectives.

"Thanks for letting me know," Evan said. "I'll keep an eye out." He backed away toward the elevators, not wanting to expose the bloodstains at his calves.

Everyone was still looking at him. He found himself offering another little wave, a ridiculous flare of the hand that had inexplicably become his trademark.

It wasn't until the elevator doors closed behind him that he realized he'd been holding his breath.

The instant he'd shut his penthouse door, Evan stripped naked. Using his boots as a tray, he carried his clothes across the great room and laid them before the freestanding fireplace. He fished two steel shanks from the ashes and a scorched watch fob, all that remained of his outfit's last iteration, and then fired up a trio of cedar logs. Once the flames were sufficiently robust, he fed them the clothing he'd worn to Papazian's house.

Then he padded down the rear hall to the master suite and scoured himself in the shower. After drying off and stepping into boxer briefs, he went to his dresser.

The top drawer held a stack of unworn 501s on the left and a stack of unworn cargo pants on the right. Each item was folded so crisply that it looked stamped from a mold. After putting on a fresh pair of cargo pants, he donned a V-necked dark gray T-shirt that he peeled from the leftmost of three identical columns housed in the second drawer.

He'd switched around which drawers held which articles of clothing at least a half dozen times over the past year. His brain told him that the compulsion came from seeking maximum efficiency, but his mind sent a different message, that he was enacting the ritual to soothe some part of himself that needed soothing.

He could handle chaos in the world as long as there was order at home.

The closet came next. He removed a new Victorinox watch fob from its packaging and clipped it to his belt loop, then grabbed the top shoe box from the tower in the corner and stepped into a fresh pair of Original S.W.A.T. boots. Ten Woolrich shirts hung from hangers in perfect parallel, as equidistant as the slats in a set of vertical blinds. Careful not to disturb the spacing of the others, he slid free a shirt and pulled it on, the magnetic buttons clapping together.

He exited the closet, stepped into the still-wet shower, and placed his hand on the hot-water lever. A brief delay as it scanned his palm print, and then an electronic hum announced the opening of the door hidden in the wall tiles. It swung inward, differentiating itself from the wall, the lever serving as a handle.

The Vault didn't look like much.

The four hundred square feet of walled-off storage space was accessible only through the secret door. The unfinished box of a room trapped the night cold. Toward the rear the ceiling crowded down in the shape of the public stairs above that led to the roof.

An armory and a workbench lined the back wall. A sheet-metal desk shaped like an L held a profusion of servers and computer towers. But there seemed to be no monitors.

At least until Evan clicked his keyboard and three of the four walls came to life. The OLED screens, made of meshed glass, were invisible when not animated, clear panes showing nothing but the rough concrete walls behind.

Now they displayed a menu of hacked security feeds from Castle Heights and an abundance of links to federal and state databases. The screens to his left held the status of several of his bank accounts, including the main one, hidden in Luxembourg under the name Z$Q9R#)3 and protected by a password consisting of a forty-word nonsensical sentence. As Orphan X, Evan had been issued enormous sums of money straight off the presses from Treasury. Jack had helped him stash it in numerous accounts in numerous nonreporting countries, buried beneath beaver dams of trusts and shell corporations.

When Evan had operated as Orphan X, it was essential that he be fully funded and fully self-sufficient. His job had been to enter territories the United States could not and commit acts that it would not. He knew the target he was to neutralize and nothing more. The ultimate cutout man, he had no useful information to relinquish if he were captured no matter how enhanced the interrogation got. The very government he served would deny any knowledge of him, leaving him to be tortured in a Third World dungeon or worn to a nub in a hard-labor camp.

By the time he'd bolted from the Program, he'd known where a lot of the bodies were buried; he'd buried most of them himself. If he'd been killed by now, plenty of people at the highest level in D.C. would be able to sleep more soundly.

He let his eyes scan across the digital offerings that wallpapered the Vault.

His e-mail, the.nowhere.man@gmail.com, showed no messages. He and Jack used to communicate inside the Drafts folders, but since Jack's passing, the e-mail had lain largely dormant.

Evan fired up his hardware and hit the databases, connecting through a four-step process of anonymous proxies and encrypted tunnels. The last step obfuscated any remnant of a digital address that might have remained, hiding Evan's imprint in a sea of noise, a droplet in the ocean of the Internet.

Michael Papazian had given him the names of those who constituted the money-laundering scheme that Grant Merriweather had been closing in on. Four men, led by David "The Terror" Terzian. Though they kept more hired muscle beneath them, they were the only ones with operational knowledge. The money itself wasn't generated from drugs or guns. But from gambling. The Terror had been running a hugely profitable underground fighting ring. Bets taken in cash were then mainstreamed through the operation.

Within seconds Evan filled the screens cloaking his walls with criminal histories, rap sheets, case files, investigative trails, court cases, social-media profiles, and related news stories.

Terzian was a burly man, thick with muscle. A close-shaven beard roamed high on his cheeks, crowding within an inch of his eyes. Early photos from his Facebook page showed him to be your basic street soldier—loose plaid shorts, white undershirt, gold-tinted sunglasses, a big cross around his neck. He had AP tattooed by one temple with three attendant teardrops for the enemies he'd dispatched. He liberally flashed gang signs—"OK" thumb circles held against his chest right side up and upside down like German quotation marks.

He and his inner cadre—the three other names Evan had extracted from Papazian—had been investigated for a variety of crimes. Drugs. Extortion. Kidnapping businessmen from the community and ransoming them back to their families in various stages of intactness. Set plays straight out of the Armenian Power playbook.

Right Side Up and Upside Down

The gang was a newer addition to L.A.'s underworld, forming in Hollywood, North Hollywood, Burbank, and Glendale during the eighties to offer immigrant students protection against the more established Latino gangs. Strength on the streets eventually meant numbers in the system, Armenian Power gaining a solid foothold within the state prisons.

As Evan scrolled through Terzian's digital history, he noticed a transformation taking place. Terzian and his cadre began to move into more sophisticated financial crimes. Medicare and mortgage fraud. Debit-card skimming. ID theft. Bank-account-draining scams run on elderly homeowners. Rather than tattoo their flesh, they started to carve it, overlaying lines of ink with scarification. Bringing a more menacing look to softer targets meant tilting the scales even further to their advantage. Wolves roaming among sheep.

A rare conviction had ensnared Terzian two years ago. He'd beaten his girlfriend severely and then forced her to cover her head with a pillowcase when he was home so he wouldn't have to look at her damaged face. Simple battery, a misdemeanor that carried with it a two-thousand-dollar fine and six months in L.A. County.

To Evan that seemed an exceedingly light punishment.

Since Terzian's release, records of his activity were sparse. That was presumably when he'd graduated to richer pastures, a new money-laundering scheme that kept him off the radar and returned millions of dollars a month.

Evan was not surprised to find Lorraine Lennox's name on the byline of several journalism pieces pecking at the edges of Terzian's domain. Though much of her work was unrelated—a dog-napping ring, a secret cabal of unidentified city leaders doing secret-cabal things, the rising risk of shark attacks in Malibu—she had deep-dived into the criminal networks gaining traction in Hollywood. She'd been sniffing around, getting familiar with the topography, which was undoubtedly why Grant had chosen her to receive the cache in the event of his demise.

As Evan closed out the open windows, he did his best not to note how much his processing speed lagged behind Joey's. Then he clicked to the Google Earth images on the address Papazian had coughed up.

The location was a local TV station abandoned several years ago in the wake of a merger. Buried behind high fences in a run-down part of Hollywood, it was an ideal criminal headquarters. Evan zoomed in on several buildings on the lot, everything looking dusty and disused. Papazian claimed that he was due to report back to the team there after dark tonight, which was when they generally met up.

Evan would get there early to observe. And then approach.

For now his work was done. Which gave him the rest of the morning to relax.

He logged off and exited the Vault, stepping through the shower stall and heading into his bedroom.

A safe distance from his floating bed, he removed his treasonous boots. Then he sat in the middle of the mattress in a slant of morning light, closed his eyes, and focused on his breathing.

The coolness of the air at his nostrils, in his windpipe, filling the crevices of his lungs. The weight of his bones tugging him down. A heightened awareness where the air met his skin, where his skin met the bed.

He'd not yet fully descended into his meditation when an image intruded.

A grown man punching Ida Rosenbaum in the face.

Tearing free a necklace from around her neck.

Her fragile bones striking the sidewalk.

He opened his eyes. Looked at the door.

"Goddamn it," he said.

18

The Terrible Intimacy
of the Mundane

With a single knuckle, Evan tapped gently on the door to 6G. In the event Ida Rosenbaum was sleeping, he didn't want to wake her.

He gave it a well-I-tried moment and then backed away.

Before he could get two steps, the door opened.

Mia leaned through the gap, the door and frame pinching her shoulders on either side. She wore a white blouse that looked a size too big and a brown pantsuit befitting a Baby Boomer congresswoman.

Her head cocked with puzzlement. "What are you doing here?"

"I heard what happened and wanted to check in on her."

Mia let the door hinge open. "She's pretty shaken up. I called a detective to handle it, a West Bureau guy I like. He just left. She wanted me with her while she gave her statement. It's important that everything gets handled properly."

He wasn't sure, but it seemed Mia's gaze was a bit loaded. She stayed in the doorway, not giving him enough room to enter.

"I'm handling this," she said. "Don't go near it."

"Why would I?"

She studied him a moment longer and then stepped back.

As he crossed the threshold, he realized he'd never been inside Ida Rosenbaum's condo. Or anyone else's at Castle Heights, save Mia's.

The place was dimly lit, heavy velveteen drapes drawn against the morning sun. Furniture crowded the living room, as if the Rosenbaums had kept too many pieces when they'd downsized from a house. Porcelain bric-a-brac covered most surfaces, impeccably arranged and free of dust. An array of Lladró figurines held unlikely poses of daintiness.

Spotlit on the mantel, a ballerina swooned over crossed arms, her swanlike neck bowed. Evan came up short before the figurine, wondering at the circumstances that compelled someone to put an item like that on beatific display. He supposed that if you had a mantel, you had to put something on it.

The complexities of everyday life never ceased to fascinate him.

Ida's voice powered up the hall, holding no small measure of irritation. "Well? Who's that, then?"

Evan caught Mia's eye. "I see the assault hasn't left her overcome with newfound humility in the face of life's vicissitudes?"

Mia's mouth curled up on one side. "I think that's safe to say."

He followed her back.

Mia's jacket still held creases from being folded or shipped. A transparent sticker down the back of the sleeve listed the suit's size.

He reached for it and peeled it off.

At the sound, Mia turned, and they faced each other in the narrow hall. Close enough that he could feel her breath on his neck. He had to remind himself not to look at her lips. Instead he held up the tag, and Mia said, "Shit. Thanks. Now that I'm downtown, I'm in court so much I had to rush-order some new outfits." She gave a half turn. "I think this color's wrong. Does it make my hips look wider?"

Evan said, "Yes."

Her mood, which he'd interpreted as mildly flirtatious, immediately shifted, lost behind a glower. But then a laugh seemed to catch her off guard. "You don't know anything about women, do you?"

Shaking her head, she turned away and continued down the hall, veering through a doorway at the end.

Evan stepped in after her.

Ida rested against a fan of pillows. Geriatric bruising mottled her right eye and cheek, the papery skin the color of eggplant. Orange pill bottles crowded her nightstand, penguins jockeying for position above shark-infested waters. A sterling hairbrush held a place of prominence on the old-fashioned vanity beside a peacock burst of framed photographs.

The largest, an eight-by-ten with a color palette that suggested the seventies, captured husband and wife side by side on the prow of a cruise ship. A short, stubby man with a dignified bearing, Herb wore a gray flannel suit and tortoiseshell eyeglasses. They'd been a matching set, he and Ida, in the way of couples of a certain era. Same height, same build, same aura of fortitude. Ida's hair, gray even then, was taken up in loose curls. Resting over the buttons of her shirtwaist dress was the purloined necklace, marcasite and amethyst gleaming in the pelagic sunlight. Tucked in the Tiffany picture frame was a cruise-ship ID card in Herb's name.

A sense of trespassing gripped Evan. The bedroom hadn't likely seen a visitor for a decade and change, and here he was amid the terrible intimacy of the mundane, disturbing the air, gawking at personal possessions. A faint whiff of dried sweat reached him from the pillow—the smell of aging, of death, of the inevitable future.

Ida raised a hand self-consciously to cover her bruised face. "What do *you* want?"

He said, "To see that you're okay."

"Do I look okay?"

"Actually, yes, ma'am."

She scowled. "I don't need any help."

"I'm sure you don't. You never have before."

At this her lips pressed together with satisfaction, maybe even delight.

"Since I'm here anyway," Mia cut in, "why don't I get another cold compress for you?"

Ida said, "Fine."

Mia padded out, leaving them in awkward silence.

Evan said, "What did he look like? The guy who attacked you?"

Ida said, "He wasn't a black, if that's what you're implying."

"That's not what I'm implying."

"He had one of those hooded sweatshirts that the kids all wear. The hood was pulled up. I couldn't see his face. Just this dark oval, and then . . ." Her lips trembled, and she turned away.

Evan took the opportunity to orient back toward the vanity. Holding his RoamZone low at his waist, he zoomed in on her necklace in the photograph and clicked a picture. He'd just pocketed the phone when Mia reentered with a soaked washcloth.

She moved to set it on Ida's face, but Ida took it from her roughly. She dabbed at her swollen temple. Then her free hand clutched at the sheets by her side and a dry, graceless sound escaped her.

It took Evan a moment to realize that it was a sob.

"Herb would be so embarrassed by me," Ida said. "Swanning around with that necklace like I was something special."

Mia was taken aback, literally on her heels.

Evan crouched and took Ida's arthritic hand. He said, "You are something special."

"No," Ida said, using the pretense of the washcloth to keep her eyes covered. "I'm an eighty-seven-year-old widow. That's about as unspecial as you can be. And that young man today . . . That young man proved it."

"I don't see it like that," Evan said.

She took a few wet breaths. "No?"

"You get through each day by your own strength. You live according to your principles. And you do it alone. The guy who assaulted you is nothing in the face of that."

Ida's diminutive chest rose and fell, rose and fell. "Nonsense," she said, but her tone was softer. And she didn't let go of his hand.

He could sense Mia's gaze on the side of his face. Intense, as if she were seeing him for the first time.

Ida dropped the washcloth and lowered her hand beneath her

neck, touching the place where the necklace would have been. "I just wanted to feel close to him again," she said, her voice cracking.

He stayed at her bedside. She clutched his hand a bit tighter.

He let her.

In the Vault, Evan plugged his RoamZone into one of his computer towers and uploaded the close-up he'd taken of Ida's necklace. Seconds later an enlarged version appeared on the OLED screens mounted on the wall in front of him.

He isolated the piece, removing the background, and then crisped up the pixelation with a digital enhancer.

He dragged the image into a visual search engine and set the parameters. If the item appeared online for sale, he would receive an alert.

He glanced over at the wall to his left, where the Google Earth view of the abandoned TV station waited. The headquarters of Terzian's quartet.

Evan had plenty of time to get over to Hollywood and scout the surrounding area. And the area around that. The Third Commandment: *Master your surroundings.*

At nightfall they'd be expecting Papazian.

They'd get the Nowhere Man instead.

19

Not That Fight

The useful thing about TV stations, if you're a money-laundering murderous thug requiring headquarters, is that they are generally enclosed. The cluster of drab concrete structures—offices, studios, a cafeteria—was protected by barbed-wired chain-link that, like the buildings themselves, had seen better days.

The neighborhood at the edge of Little Armenia was not a nice one. Evan had plenty of time to absorb it, spending six-plus hours in the seat of his Chevy Malibu. He'd observed the buildings from enough vantages that he could have rendered each in a cubist painting.

The disused property showed signs of having been recently overtaken. Chicken wire sutured up slashes in the rusting fence, and shiny new chains and padlocks secured the access points. A rolling gate protected the driveway and a rear entrance.

Terzian had arrived about an hour ago, tossing a laden Dickensian key ring to a neck-challenged bouncer type at the rear gate. Over the following ten minutes, Terzian's three compatriots had appeared, easily identifiable in their German sedans and aura of ill-gotten privilege. Evan had studied them in the Vault and knew well the ugliness that lay beneath the designer suits. The four principals had retired to the front office building, leaving a dozen hired men in charge of operations. The men seemed to be readying the cafeteria for a big event.

It looked like tonight was fight night.

Sure enough, the next hour saw a stream of gamblers pour through the choke points, all men exuding a cagey excitement. Anticipation electrified the air, the promise of blood spilled and money won.

Evan moved the car once again, sidling up to the curb several blocks distant, the grille angled for a quick getaway. Across the street a group of boys played basketball with a frayed soccer ball and a shopping cart hung on a dumpster as a hoop. A spray-painted tag on the dumpster's side read AxP, the Armenian Power tag.

These were the streets that Terzian had graduated from.

Evan got out. An old man with skin the color of mahogany sat in a weather-beaten recliner on his porch, smoking a pipe, a Chihuahua nestled in his lap blanket. As Evan passed through a sweet drift of tobacco, the man removed the pipe from his mouth and tilted it toward him in greeting. Evan nodded back.

Nearing the former station, he joined a band of young men crossing the street. Redolent of beer and liberally applied cologne, they chattered excitedly. "—best motherfucking fighters in L.A.—"

"—taking the over-under on Tiger going a full minute—"

They logjammed at the rear entrance, the bouncer types eyeing everyone and shooing them all quickly inside toward the cafeteria. The young men around Evan held up their cell phones with e-mailed invitations, but the bouncers barely checked them.

Evan brought up the photo of Ida's necklace and waved it past the nose of the nearest bouncer, timing it when the man's attention was split between two other gamblers.

He was ushered through.

As he passed, he brushed up against the bouncer, bump-frisking him. No gun, which confirmed Evan's suspicion that they were low-level rented muscle.

A few more bouncers were positioned along the walkway, herd-ing people toward the cafeteria. Evan could hear a buzz of voices inside, the crowd preparing for the fight.

He walked past the open doors, catching a glimpse of the space. Stacked bleachers framed what looked to be a sunken court in the center. The flooring had been torn up, an arena dug into the earth itself, a street-fighting competition that was literally underground. From the doorway Evan couldn't see the bottom of the pit. The bleachers were about a third filled. The rest of the attendants mobbed a betting station formed of folding tables.

Evan kept on past the open door, turning the corner sharply and backing to the wall when he heard someone approaching. One of the bouncers swept past, carrying a shrink-wrapped block of hundred-dollar bills. That helped fill in the picture of how Ter-zian generated the huge amounts of cash he'd been laundering.

Once the bouncer's footsteps faded, Evan stole to the front office building, where Terzian and his three lieutenants had holed up, conveniently segregated from the others.

There was no guard out front. The door was unlocked. Here in his domain, Terzian the Terror was confident.

As Evan eased inside, he heard voices in the back. He breezed through the lobby.

In a glass-walled conference room, the four men sat in a row behind a table. An expansive one-way mirror of a window over-looked a concrete path and the cafeteria beyond. Before each man was an old-fashioned phone and an open ledger. They were all on calls, receivers pressed to their faces, scribbling notes, their sleeves cuffed up to display the patterned scars beneath.

The big bets, coming in telephonically.

Before the men, steam misted from comically delicate espresso demitasses. The man on the right end, Raffi, sipped beer from a green bottle.

As Evan strode through the door, none of them looked up.

Terzian called out, "Are my fighters ready?"

Evan said, "I'm not sure."

In concert the four men lifted their heads. In another context the coordinated reaction might have been funny, a disruption at ye olde-fashioned switchboard. Terzian moved the phone slowly away from his face, the person on the other end squawking until he cradled the receiver.

The others followed suit.

Terzian crossed his arms, the cuffed sleeves bulging over his ribboned forearms. "I thought you were my boy Big Papa."

Evan said, "He couldn't make it."

The phones started up again, ringing at uneven intervals.

Raffi took a slug of Stella Artois. He was the largest of the men, barrel-chested and tall. "Ah. He's somewhere having his fun? Big Papa's a dirty dog. Out there humping legs."

To his left, Serj said, "Or women."

Yeznig chimed in, "Same difference."

They chuckled.

But Terzian did not smile. His mouth pouched, wrinkling his lips.

The phones kept on, an unnerving cacophony. In the background a faint rumble came on, the roar of the crowd warming up.

Terzian said, "You here for the fight?"

Evan said, "Not *that* fight."

Terzian's hand moved beneath the table. The Kydex holster felt cool pressing against Evan's appendix through his gray undershirt. His Woolrich button-up hung just loosely enough that no one would be able to tell if he was carrying.

Terzian's lips twitched. "Are you sure this is a fight you want to start?"

"I'm not starting a fight," Evan said. "I'm here to finish one."

The others chuckled again. Their hands remained by their ledgers in full view, signaling to Terzian, the alpha dog, that they were confident to leave this to him.

"What fight is that, friend?" Terzian said.

"The one you started with Max Merriweather."

Terzian tilted back in his chair. Withdrew his hand from beneath the table. Rested a Browning P-35 on top of his ledger, keeping his hand firm on the grip. The barrel pointed at Evan. It seemed the Hi-Power was the gun du jour for money-laundering assholes.

"Max is a friend, is he?" Terzian smiled, enjoying himself. "Good.

Then you tell him this. What I did to his cousin Grant? The electrical cables. The clamps. Those sensitive areas of the flesh. It will *pale* in comparison to what we will do when we catch up to him."

The others followed Terzian's lead, matching his grin at the pledge of violence. His gaze remained on Evan, unbroken.

"You're a fawn," Terzian said, "who just wandered into the lion's den."

"I understand you think that," Evan said. "And your track record has given you good reason to believe that you're scary. You've got the look down. The manicured tough-guy beard. The handiwork carved into your skin. But I want you to do something. Look at me. Look at me closely. And ask yourself: Do I look scared?"

The phones persisted, insistent and abrasive, a xylophone being Whac-A-Moled. Terzian glared at Evan. Then he shoved back his chair abruptly and rose.

Evan stood motionless.

Terzian stalked around the table, waving the Browning. "You walk in here tonight. A night when I have business." At this he jabbed the pistol at the one-way window and the cafeteria beyond. Through the walls Evan could make out the sound of countless feet stomping the bleachers in unison. "And you come here on behalf of someone who sought to *fuck with* my business?"

Wisely he kept a distance from Evan, regarding him over the top of the Browning. It was tilted sideways, gangsta style, the muzzle aimed just above Evan's left shoulder. "Clearly you don't know my name," Terzian said. "Clearly you didn't do your research." His hand tensed around the grip. "Because if you think you stand *any chance* of walking out of this room alive—"

All at once there was a hole in his forehead.

An awareness dawned in his eyes that a round had passed through his skull, that he was already dead. The ARES was steady in Evan's hand, the sights still lined on the trajectory of the Speer Gold Dot hollow-point round, his gun frame parallel with Terzian's still-raised Browning. Evan's parted shirt fluttered, and then the buttons found one another again with a metallic clink, hiding the empty holster.

Terzian gurgled blood, a powdering across the lips.

Evan reached out and grasped the canted Browning as he fell away.

Raffi was caught stunned, beer lifted mid-sip, but Serj and Yeznig were already drawing.

Evan spun the Browning around in his right hand, catching it upside down with his thumb jammed inside the trigger guard. He made a split-second adjustment to aim both pistols and fired simultaneously, shooting Serj through the mouth and catching Yeznig in the breast.

In a room filled with gunmen, a still target is a dead target. But Evan was already moving. A spin kick brought him within range as he let his foot fly above the table and hammer the raised bottle into Raffi's face. Raffi toppled back in his chair, an arc of shattered teeth and glass tracing his descent.

Too late Evan saw that Yeznig had twisted away from the round so it had caught his torso in glancing fashion, tearing free a hunk of flesh and fabric.

With a roar he flipped the table over at Evan, phones, ledgers, and espresso flying. Evan ducked down and in, letting it twirl overhead and getting off shots to Yeznig's shin, knee, and gut before it all crashed onto the floor behind him.

Yeznig groaned, clawing at the glimmering hole in his abdomen, his pistol out of reach.

Before Evan could pivot, Raffi charged him, his face awash in blood. He struck Evan in a football tackle, crushing the RoamZone against Evan's thigh. Despite its Gorilla Glass and hardened black rubber casing, the phone crunched as he fell.

Raffi swung blindly, a rage-fueled battering. The Browning flew from Evan's grasp. He tried to angle the ARES, but they were at too close quarters for him to risk firing. Raffi overpowered him, fighting his gun hand down and then swatting the ARES away.

They grappled on the floor, close enough to kiss, arms locked, teeth bared. Raffi's shattered face was inches above Evan's, dripping blood. From the corner of his eye, Evan sensed Yeznig dragging himself toward his gun.

Evan relaxed his arms, relenting. As Raffi's weight came down on him, Evan twisted away. Swinging around Raffi's torso like a wrestler and seizing him in an arm bar, Evan braced the elbow joint with his legs. But the limb was sheathed with muscle; it was like trying to snap a log.

Straining against the arm, Evan leaned back to shoot a glance behind him. Still short of his fallen pistol, Yeznig expired with a shuddering wheeze. One of the phones miraculously had managed to stay plugged in, and it rang, rang, rang, earsplittingly shrill.

Raffi was too strong, bucking and ripping his arm free before Evan could break the joint.

Evan rolled onto his back, already reaching for his belt. With a single jerk, he whipped it free of the loops. Popping onto his feet, he fed the leather end through the buckle. Raffi was on his stomach, gathering himself to rise when Evan slung the makeshift noose over his neck.

Placing one Original S.W.A.T. boot on the back of Raffi's head, he firmed his grip on the belt and jerked back.

A crackle as the vertebrae gave.

Raffi twitched. And then he didn't.

Evan scooped up his ARES and surveyed the mess of a conference room, his shoulders bowed, catching his breath. The noose of the belt dangled from one fist.

The phone continued to ring, but Evan saw now that the cords had all snapped free when Yeznig had hurled the table at him.

Something moved in his peripheral vision—Terzian's hand reaching for a gun?—and Evan swept the ARES over and fired through Terzian's heart. But the corpse absorbed the round without complaint.

Another ring and something moved again on Terzian's chest.

A cell phone inched further into view, worming up out of his breast pocket.

Evan recognized the rectangular slab of technology as a Turing Phone. Boasting end-to-end encryption on a security-geared operating system, it was engineered out of a rare alloy of zirconium, aluminum, silver, copper, and nickel, marketed under the comic-book name Liquidmorphium. It was physically unbreakable, unlike the RoamZone, whose broken pieces were jabbing Evan's thigh through his cargo pants.

Evan fished the Turing Phone out of Terzian's rumpled shirt.

It would do for now. At least until he got back to the Vault and replaced the shrapnel in his pocket with a new RoamZone.

Given Max's circumstances Evan had to be reachable at all times, so he thumbed off a text to Max: THIS IS ME. USE THIS NUMBER IN CASE OF EMERGENCY.

Then he pocketed the Turing. He was just about to rethread his belt through the loops when shouts rained in from the lobby door, the no-neck brigade arriving in force. Through the glass wall, Evan saw two of the bouncers breach the lobby, no doubt in response to the commotion.

Putting his back to them, he raised the ARES and shot out the one-way window. Ducking through the shower of glass and holstering his pistol, he jogged toward the cafeteria and the rear gate beyond.

As he neared, a pair of bouncers spilled around either side of the cafeteria, walkie-talkies to their faces, blocking Evan's way. They spotted Evan and froze.

He had blood on his shirt and a noose-shaped belt in one hand. Conspicuous.

They sprinted at him.

He shot a glance over his shoulder. The other bouncers emerged through the shattered maw of the window onto the walkway. They looked stunned from the violent aftermath they'd witnessed inside. And they looked angry.

He didn't want to kill them.

Holstering his ARES, he spun back around. The men pinched in at him from both directions.

Directly ahead, no more than twenty yards away, the side door of the cafeteria lay open. The gunfire had spurred a flurry of panicked movement inside. Most of the gamblers stood in the bleachers, confused, but a few were already running, strobing across the doorway.

He sprinted for it.

The bouncers closed in around him. He snapped the belt to the side, the buckle smacking a meaty chin and causing the others to veer and duck.

Without slowing his momentum, he flew through the doorway.

As soon as he cleared the threshold, he clipped the shoulder of a hulking guy in a biker jacket. Muscle and leather, undentable. Physics assigned them the roles of bumper and pinball.

Evan felt himself go weightless, the floor scanning by several feet below.

He hit the polished floorboard in a spin and slid a few feet. He'd just rotated around to see the gaping pit in the floor before he was weightless again, falling ten feet into the fighting arena. Impact jarred the breath out of him. Dirt in his eyes, under his nails. Grit against his chin, his cheek. The smell of musk, feces, and blood.

The bouncers appeared at the lip, leaning over Evan. They were laughing, which did not strike him as good news. Beyond them loomed the jeering gamblers in the bleachers.

The dirt was moist, warm, sticky. When Evan lifted his hand, his palm came up bright red with blood. Not his own.

The crowd roared. Feet stomped vociferously on bleachers.

And he heard growling coming from either side of him.

He swung his heavy head and blinked through the tangle of his bangs.

The scene down here took a moment to assemble.

Near the dirt wall by a knotted rope ladder stood a man with a bald crown, a horseshoe of stringy hair curtaining his shoulders. His gut bulged out between his dirt-stained T-shirt and tattered sweatpants. He held an empty syringe in each hand.

Not a fighter.

Evan blinked again, trying to clear his head.

There was a stainless-steel transport crate just in front of him.

And another behind him.

Each crate was ventilated with narrow slits through which he could see a creature snarling violently, cords of saliva dangling from scarred pink jowls, yellow eyes bulging with steroidal rage.

And each cage had a guillotine door on the end.

Tied to the top of each guillotine door was a rope that stretched up out of the arena and looped around a suspended pulley.

Not That Fight

That's when it dawned on Evan.

Terzian hadn't been running a street-fighting ring.

He'd been running a *dog*fighting ring.

The man who'd administered the steroid shots to the dogs finished hoisting himself up the knotted rope ladder and out of the pit.

He looked down at Evan from the rim. A carpenter's belt hung around his waist, filled with the tools of the trade. One of the bouncers grabbed the man's arm. Evan couldn't hear his words over the hyped-up crowd but he could read the bouncer's lips.

Do it.

The man dropped the syringes and grabbed the ends of the ropes.

There was a screech of metal against metal as the guillotine doors lifted in unison and the animals shot free.

20

Living Plaything

From both directions the dogs flew at Evan, barrels of muscle tapering to bared fangs. One looked to be a pit bull–mastiff mix, the other a bully kutta with leopard spots and cropped ears. Their heads and chests bore scars from battles past.

Each was easily 180 pounds.

Evan got his foot up just in time to ram it into the bully kutta's jaws. Caging his head with his forearms, he rolled sideways and the pit-mastiff blasted past him, claws skidding in the dirt.

Clamped onto the abrasion-resistant outsole of Evan's boot, the bully kutta shook his head violently, flinging Evan's leg back and forth.

Evan felt his boot rip free. The bully kutta reared up, jaws still locked around the boot as the pit-mastiff collided with him.

Overhead the audience thundered.

Evan had an instant to draw his ARES and shoot both dogs, but the Tenth Commandment—*Never let an innocent die*—applied here as surely as anywhere else. He couldn't hurt a victim even if that victim wasn't human.

The pit-mastiff regrouped, readying to sink his fangs into the bully kutta's flank.

Evan's belt, still looped into a noose, had landed in the dirt to his side. Rising to his knees, he snatched it up and slung it over the pit-mastiff's head from behind just as the massive dog lunged.

The dog's momentum yanked Evan off his knees, scraping his chin through the blood-softened earth. Even so, he held on to the belt, a fallen water-skier refusing to release the tow rope.

He pulled himself up onto the big animal's back and ratcheted the belt tight, forcing the jaws agape. He fought the prong through the tightest punch hole, gagging the dog and shoving him clear just as the bully kutta dropped Evan's boot from his mouth and attacked.

Evan got an arm under the muzzle as the dog landed on him, pounding him into the earth. Claws dug at Evan's chest, the snapping teeth inches from his face. The dog's steaming breath smelled of meat and the sour chemical tinge of the juice firing his system.

Evan had to turn his cheek to the dirt to avoid having his nose taken off. At the far side of the arena, the pit-mastiff was shaking his head furiously, gnawing at Evan's belt with his molars and making headway.

Evan groped on the dirt, his fingers finally closing around his chewed Original S.W.A.T. He rammed his hand through the throat of the boot and shoved it at the bully kutta's face. The dog took the bait, snatching the boot, twisting it off Evan's fist, and flinging it aside.

Evan rolled back over his shoulders onto his feet and dove for the transport crate. He landed on top with enough force to dent the stainless steel.

Charging in his wake, the bully kutta skidded into the crate, claws scrabbling for purchase on the metal floor. The crate rocked when he struck the far end.

As the dog regrouped below, Evan grabbed for his Strider, snapping the blade open as he whipped it from his pocket.

He swiped at the rope tied to the guillotine door, severing it. The stainless sheet screeched down an instant before the bully kutta collided with it, trying to escape. This time the impact rocked the crate up off the ground, sliding Evan neatly off the top and depositing him back in the dirt.

The pit-mastiff was on top of him instantly, gathering him between his legs and pressing his gagged-open mouth to Evan's shoulder. Miraculously, the belt held, but even so the distributed pressure of the oval of teeth pressed into Evan's skin.

He shoved the dog off him and heaved himself upright.

The bleachers were in a frenzy, gamblers standing and screaming, waving their tickets, cords standing out in their necks. The bouncers stared down uneasily.

Evan drew his ARES and fired straight up into the ceiling.

The gunshots broke the bloodlust spell, cheers turning to shouts, the gamblers stampeding for the exits. The bouncers backed away from the pit's edge, turning to run.

Another noise rose now above the din—police sirens, maybe a few blocks away.

The pit-mastiff collided with Evan's leg, mouthing his calf around the belt. Evan tore his leg free and kneed the dog aside. The dog spun up onto his paws again, lowering his head. The wide jaw of his square head pulsed, the belt snapping like a rubber band, freeing his fangs.

Evan ran across the arena, jumped onto the far crate, and leapt from there up onto the knotted rope ladder.

The dog followed on his heels, sailing in his wake, growling and snapping right up until he collided with the dirt wall just below Evan. Still snarling, he fell away.

Evan hoisted himself up, gasping, and flung himself over the side.

He knocked into something—a plastic gate—and landed on his belly.

He looked up to see that he'd taken down the wall of the warm-up pen.

Three revved-up dogs-in-waiting charged him.

He had no time to react, let alone cover himself from three sides.

This was how it would end, then. Torn to shreds in the cafeteria of a defunct local TV station.

At the last instant, the dogs jerked away from him, flying backward, yelping in pain.

Each had hit the end of its respective chain.

Now they turned and tried to attack one another, but the chains had been measured to keep them just out of reach. Another strategy to hold them at the red-hot edge of attack, fired up and ready to go.

They raged against their choke-chain collars, their snarls amplified off the high ceiling.

On all fours Evan backed away slowly, rose, and turned to go.

The cafeteria was largely empty by now, the last of the gamblers making for the exits. But the man who'd injected the dogs remained, bald pate shining, wisps of sweat-darkened hair rimming his shoulders.

He must have twisted an ankle during the stampede, because he bent one leg back now to hold his foot off the floor. His hands were raised defensively at Evan as he hobbled back another step toward the door.

"Look, man. I'm sorry. They told me to let them loose. I don't hurt people, man. I'm just the vet. I just wanna—" He stepped wrong and winced. "Please. I'm just in charge of the fighters."

The sirens were louder now, compounding the racket inside the cafeteria. In the arena below, the pit-mastiff was going insane, hurling himself against the wall beneath the rope ladder.

Evan glared at the vet, his teeth grinding. He felt the weight in his holster, the ARES calling to him.

But he turned to head for the far exit.

At the periphery of the chained fighters, just out of reach, another animal lay facing away, a hump of fur matted with blood. At first Evan wasn't sure what it was. A mammal yes. But it took a moment for him to register that it was a dog.

He took another step and saw the duct tape wrapped around the dog's muzzle, depriving him of the use of his mouth. The tape had been in place long enough to start digging through the flesh, the surrounding skin inflamed. Another ring of shiny silver tape bound his hind legs. His chest had been gashed, and a flap of skin hung loose from his cheek.

A strip of reversed fur down his spine identified him as a Rhodesian ridgeback, like the one Evan had grown up with in Jack's house. This guy looked to be a puppy around a year old, tall but not yet filled out with muscle. Oversize paws showed that he was going to be a big boy.

He'd been bound and tossed to the larger animals to rile them up further.

A bait dog.

He'd managed to squirm his way barely out of the orbit of the fighters, who snapped at him now from either side. Quivering, he lay on the tiny patch of safety between the snarling mouths.

His eyes rolled imploringly to Evan.

Evan's jaw set. He looked at the bait dog, debilitated and thrown to the others as a living plaything, an appetizer to whet their appetite for blood.

Evan turned around. Glared at the vet. Dangling from a loop on his tool belt was a roll of duct tape.

The vet stumbled away from Evan on his twisted ankle, circling the edge of the sunken arena. Below, the pit-mastiff roiled, raging against the walls. "Look," the vet said. "It's necessary to rile up the main contenders. It's just my job."

Evan said, "If you ever do anything like this again, I will find you. And I will do to you what you did to that dog."

"Okay," the vet said, holding up his hands, the stink of fear emanating from him. "Oka—"

The dog nearest him lunged, fully airborne before the chain snapped him back to earth.

The vet jerked away, stumbling on his injured ankle, and slipped over the edge. He screamed on the way down.

A clang as he hit the metal crate.

More screaming. And then the sounds of the pit-mastiff doing what the vet had primed him to do.

Evan rushed to the edge and peered down, but it was too late, the vet's screams terminating in a failing gurgle.

Evan staggered back to the bait dog. The prong collars forked into the flesh of the surrounding fight dogs as they strained to tear the puppy to shreds. Crouching, Evan grasped the ridgeback's bound rear legs and slid him gently through the narrow safe zone, fishing him free.

Hoisting him up into his arms, Evan ran for the rear door.

Outside, the gamblers flooded from the studio lot into the surrounding streets. Sirens chirped, cops on their loudspeakers issuing orders for everyone to freeze.

Cradling the injured dog to his chest, Evan sprinted up the street, losing himself in the fleeing crowd. The missing boot lopsided his gait, a grime-heavy sock flapping from one foot. As he jogged to the car, the dog looked up at him with bulging eyes. He didn't whimper or whine. He didn't make a noise.

At Evan's back, police units made progress up the packed road, veering through the gamblers. Cops spilled from vehicles, rounding everyone up, closing in.

Evan reached his car and fumbled at the lock, juggling the injured animal. The old man in the recliner watched him with dark eyes from the porch.

"*Beveria darte vergüenza,*" he said angrily, stroking his tiny dog. "*Nos deberias hacer a perros pelear.*"

He stood with a groan and set his dog down lovingly on the blanket behind him. Stepping forward, he raised a hand to alert the cops to Evan.

"*Le estoy rescatando,*" Evan said. "*Tengo que llevarlo al veterinario. ¿Me ayuda?*"

The old man studied him.

An officer broke through a cluster of handcuffed gamblers. Evan was right in his line of sight, but the cop was focused instead on the old man.

"Sir?" the cop shouted. "What is it, sir? Did you see someone getting away?"

The old man hesitated. Then pointed to the alley next to his house, away from Evan. The cop bolted up the alley.

Evan rested the puppy gingerly in the backseat and pulled out. Driving away, he nodded his thanks at the old man. The old man nodded back.

21

I Know What You Did

"I dunno, man," the young woman at the animal shelter said. "It looks pretty bad. The vet might be a while."

The exam room smelled of ammonia, the linoleum floor showing streaks from a recent cleaning. Evan sat on the floor with the bait dog in his lap, stroking his ears. The dog hadn't made a sound, his golden-brown eyes still fixed on Evan.

The duct tape remained dug into his muzzle. His hind legs, wrapped together, twitched.

"How long?" Evan said.

"At least a half hour."

"Can you at least cut the tape off his mouth?"

"I'm not messing with that," she said, tugging at her septum ring. A spiderweb tattoo clutched the back of her neck, and she wore a loosely stitched black sweater and an armful of metal bracelets that jangled when she moved. "Don't wanna hurt him worse, poor guy."

The service bell dinged up front, and she shot the dog an apologetic look and vanished, closing the door behind her.

Evan checked the Turing Phone, but there'd been no contact from Max. Evan had already assessed the phone to ensure that it was as secure as advertised, with no GPS features or spyware that would allow it to be tracked or monitored.

In his lap the dog lay heavily, seized up in a freeze response. His nose was sweating, his cheeks filling with the exertion of breathing through bound jaws.

Evan lifted the pup onto the exam table. Then he searched the cabinet, finding trauma shears in the second drawer down. He returned to the dog.

"This is gonna hurt, buddy," he said. "I'm sorry."

He reached for the swollen muzzle, but the dog pulled his head back, terrified. Evan leaned over him, putting his elbow behind the dog's neck to trap his head in place. Very carefully, he worked the blunted end of the trauma shears between the tape and the raw skin and sawed through.

When the tape finally released, the dog panted heavily, pink tongue lolling. The gash on his cheek looked bad, but the flesh was intact and could be sutured back into place.

Evan stroked his flank a few times. Then got to work on the hind legs.

He freed the limbs, leaving the tape stuck to the fur. Removing it entirely would be a substantial job better left to a professional but at least the boy was no longer bound.

The door opened, and the vet entered, a curly-haired woman with huge dark eyes and caramel skin. She noted the trauma shears in Evan's hand. "You're not supposed to do that," she said.

"I'm sorry. He was having trouble breathing."

"Jaycee said you found him in an alley?"

"Yeah. Dogfighting ring, obviously. They used him up and threw him out."

She shook her head. "We've seen more of it lately," she said. "Especially around Little Armenia." She pinched her lip with her teeth. "It's such a disgrace. There are so many hardworking folks, and then a few *bozi tghas* give us all a bad name."

"'Sons of bitches'?"

"'Sons of whores,'" she said. "If you wanna get technical."

She moved closer to the dog, held her palm out for him to sniff, and started examining him gently.

Evan said, "Is he gonna be okay?"

"We'll get him patched up," she said. "I just hope we can place him afterward."

"And if not?"

"He'll have to be put down. We're overcrowded. As in *really* overcrowded."

Evan said, "Oh."

"I can let you know," she said. "Though we're not supposed to give dogs to people with . . . um, housing challenges."

Her eyes dropped to Evan's exposed sock. Suddenly aware of his bloody, mud-streaked shirt and clawed pants, he realized that she thought he was homeless.

It had been a long two days.

He grimaced, eager to wrap up the mission and get home to a freezing vodka and a hot shower.

"I could let you know first, though," she said. "Unofficially. If you had somewhere I could reach you by phone . . . ?"

"That won't be necessary," Evan said.

He started for the door. With his hand on the doorknob, he hesitated. Turned back. He walked over and rested a palm on the dog's shoulder above the gash. The dog strained to lick his knuckles, the tape flapping atop his snout.

Evan thought, *Goddamn it.*

He jotted down an ordinary phone number that forwarded to his RoamZone and left it with the vet.

Stepping outside, he fished the Turing Phone from his pocket and dialed.

Max's words came at him in a rush. "What happened?"

"The Terror is no longer a threat to you. Neither are any of his men."

"*Seriously?*" Max said. "Wow. Just . . . wow. So it's over?"

"Looks like it."

Evan cut through a back lot onto the neighboring block, where he'd left the Chevy Malibu behind a life-insurance shop that advertised in three languages. The asphalt of the parking lot felt cool through his ragged sock. He walked to where he'd parked next to a dumpster in the darkness at the far edge. Broken glass crunched under his boot, prompting him to mind where he set down his other foot.

Max said, "I can go to the cops now, right? Hollywood Station? I can deliver the thumb drive into the right hands like I promised?"

Evan felt an urge rising in his chest—to wrap this up, put the Nowhere Man to bed, and move on with his life the way he hoped Max would move on with his. But the First Commandment reared into his awareness, casting a shadow over his optimism.

"It looks like the problem's been handled," Evan said. "But I don't want to assume anything just yet. Give me a day or two to make sure this thing is tied up neatly before you go in and let the cops take over."

"Okay," Max said. "Okay. What do I do then? When this is done?"

"You can start over," Evan said.

It struck him that he was speaking for himself as much as for Max. This was the first time his own freedom had been aligned with a client's. When this mission ended, they'd each be able to turn a new page. He had to be certain that his keenness to do so didn't make him careless.

The insurance shop's exterior lights were mostly burned out, so Evan had to slow to study the ground for glinting shards.

"I've been so focused on surviving I haven't given much thought to what I'm going back to," Max said. "Or what I'm *not* going back to."

Evan remembered his first time on a shooting range. Jack's callused grip encasing his twelve-year-old hands, shaping them around the pistol stock, showing him how to aim. What would Evan aim at once he left the Nowhere Man behind?

He kept on across the parking lot, stepping around the shattered brown hull of a forty-ounce. "Maybe it's time to start."

Max said, "I still can't believe it's really over."

Neither can I.

Evan signed off and put the phone away. He aimed the key fob at the Chevy Malibu, and the car responded with the double chirp of a mating call. As he reached for the door, the shrill ring of an old-fashioned telephone broke the silence. The sound was so out of place here in the dark parking lot that Evan had to register the vibration in his cargo pocket to realize it was coming from the phone he'd just hung up.

He took the Turing Phone out again. Caller ID showed: UN-IDENTIFIED CALLER.

Evan clicked to answer and held the slab of rare metal to his cheek.

"The Merriweather job isn't done." The accent was hard to place. Maybe Armenian, maybe Georgian, the consonants slow and the vowels deep, forced through gravel.

Evan paused with his hand hooked under the cold metal of the door handle. He felt his flesh sitting heavy on his bones, the weight of exhaustion. He'd been awake for two days, shot at and chased, tackled and punched, bitten and clawed. He'd wanted the mission to be over, and that wanting had obscured his clarity.

Unidentified Caller was an unknown threat. A moving target. Another mask sliding forward to front a faceless enterprise.

"No," Evan agreed. "I thought it was. But I guess not yet."

He could hear the man breathing across the line. "I know what you did, boy. You interceded on his behalf. You put down Terzian and his men." He sounded older, into his fifties at least. The words held the dead calm of a man accustomed to dealing with challenging circumstances.

Evan did not like the sensation spreading like acid in his stomach. That he'd underestimated the situation. That he was up against something more complex and dangerous than he'd anticipated. That things were about to get a whole lot worse.

"Who are you?" the man asked.

"Don't worry," Evan said. "You'll find out soon enough."

"Sooner than you think," the man said.

Evan pulled the door open slightly, but something in the man's voice made him hesitate. Picking his way across the glass-strewn lot with his eyes on the ground, Evan had neglected the Third Commandment. He shot a glance over his shoulder, but the dull yellow glow of the shop windows illuminated only a flurry of moths beating themselves against the glass.

"I don't know," Evan said, tugging the car door handle. "I might be harder to track down than you think."

"Oh," the man said, "I don't need to track *you*. I just need to track the dog you rescued."

A snap of breaking glass announced itself from the darkness by the dumpster. Evan just had time to look up over the top of the open car door when a form melted from the pitch-black, arm raised, aiming at Evan's stomach.

So, he thought. *This is it, then.*

Muzzle flash strobed, a trio of gut shots slamming into Evan, and he sensed himself suddenly weightless. The asphalt reared up, smacking the back of his head and filling him with blackness.

22

Not Yet

He was dead.

Of that much he was sure.

What he was less sure of was why he still felt a throbbing between the temples, his head pulsing as if preparing to explode.

His eyes were open, but he wasn't seeing right. The stars were wobbly streaks, and the outline of his car, visible over the tips of his boot and his sock, was fuzzy and indistinct. His shirt had tugged up, night air cool against his ribs. One arm was flung overhead as if he were plummeting into the underworld, but his other hand had landed on his belly, which felt smooth and seemingly intact.

Not dead, then.

When he tried to lift his head, a wave of nausea swept through him so intense that it washed the pain away. He lowered his head, blinked through the haze. The stars streaked even more, slashes of blinding light. A tuning-fork ringing warbled in his ears.

Concussion.

From his head slamming into the ground.

He reassembled the previous minute. Walking to his car, his attention on the ground. Unidentified Caller. Shooter by the dumpster.

Stupid, he thought.

The door of his Chevy Malibu stood open before him, the plastic interior shattered by the force of the shots. He'd hung Kevlar armor inside the panels, as he did on all his vehicles, and it had absorbed the shots, slamming the door into him.

Again he tried to get up, and again nausea enveloped him.

The door pulled itself closed, seemingly of its own volition. But then he realized that the shooter had approached from behind it and kicked it shut. Now the man stood in its place, revealed. His arm was still raised, the gun pointed down at Evan, and this time there was no convenient armored door between them.

The head cocked. "Damn, you're tough," the man said.

Evan's hand slid off his stomach.

And caught on the edge of his Kydex holster.

His pistol wasn't visible in the darkness, but there was no way he'd be able to draw it unnoticed. When he tried to say something, his voice squeezed out of his throat as an unintelligible croak.

The man said, "Say what?"

Evan let his hand slip around the grip of the ARES. He could barely move, but he did his best to flatten his thigh and his knee, clearing the way. The highly molded Kydex would retard the full cycling of the slide, so he'd get off only a single round with the pistol in the holster.

One shot.

He'd better make it count.

He croaked once more, and the man took a step forward. "I said, 'Say what,' motherfucker?"

Evan closed his eyes, prayed that the flesh and bone of his leg were out of the line of fire, pigeon-toed his foot to clear it, and pulled the trigger. The first shot blew out the bottom of the holster and the man's shin. As the man screamed, Evan ripped the ARES free. Barely able to lift his head, he smacked the magazine's base plate against his thigh, hooked the rear sight on the outer edge of the holster, and ran the slide. The case ejected, spitting to the side, a fresh cartridge chambering, the whole tap, rack, and ready drill done before the man's howl reached its apex.

Evan cinched his finger around the trigger and kept tugging, the rounds going in the same place but catching different parts of the shooter—knee, hip, gut, chest—as he collapsed.

Evan couldn't see the man beyond his feet, but he listened carefully and knew him to be dead.

No onlookers, no police sirens, no one drawn by the shots. Any second that would change.

"Get up," he told himself. His voice came out slurred.

He rolled onto all fours and stayed that way for a few deep breaths before heaving himself to his feet. Moving through a fog, he staggered to the car. The grouping of shots in the door panel had been tight enough to result in a single crater that resembled a collision more than bullet holes.

He collapsed into the driver's seat, risked a peek in the rearview, and saw what he'd feared—his right pupil, blown wide. Big and dark, it seemed to consume the entire eye.

Hunched over the wheel, focusing carefully on the blurry road, he drove away.

He got four blocks before he screeched over, flung open the door, and vomited into the gutter. He leaned half in the car and half out, the pain behind his eyes so intense that he heard himself laughing dryly.

He'd had plenty of concussions.

None this bad.

A blow this severe actually changed the chemical levels in the brain. Usually it took a week for him to stabilize. He didn't have a week. He needed rest. He wouldn't get that either. Not with Unidentified Caller out there.

The fog would thicken at every exertion and stress. He'd have to protect his head at all costs. Second-impact syndrome—getting another concussion before the first had healed—could be fatal.

Maybe the rest of this mission wouldn't have any exertion or stress or blows to the head.

There it was again, that dry laugh, barely audible over the sustained ringing.

The guy who'd done this to him wasn't better than anyone else Evan had faced.

He hadn't been damaged by a top-tier operator. He'd been damaged by statistics. Being one of the best assaulters in the world meant a 99-percent success rate. Evan had done over a hundred missions. His number had come up. If he kept this up, someday, maybe even someday soon, he'd draw an even worse number.

Wouldn't that fit the cliché, taken down as he coasted toward the finish line?

Wiping his mouth, he gathered himself, breathing until his vision regained some semblance of normality, until the glare of the streetlight overhead no longer felt like a needle through the eye.

Then he tugged the car back into gear and headed to Max.

Evan parked up the block from the Lincoln Heights house and changed his clothes. He kept an extra set in a black duffel bag stored in the trunk but had neglected to pack backup boots.

The stripped-off rags reeked of blood and wet dog. No wonder the vet had mistaken him for a homeless person. He shoved them through a drain curb and moved along a sidewalk that tree roots had rubbled to post-earthquake effect. He was still having trouble with his balance, and the uneven concrete didn't help.

Duffel slung over his shoulder, he tapped twice on the front door. Max opened it. "I thought you weren't coming for another day."

"Let's go inside," Evan said.

Max's eyes widened, beads of sweat suddenly visible at his hairline. They drifted inside. The lack of lighting in here was a godsend, backing Evan's headache off the red line.

The air hung heavy in the main room, the trash bag taped over the broken window sagging lifelessly. The standing water in the backyard stank. Evan could see up the hall through an open doorway into the bedroom where Max's possessions were neatly stacked against one wall. It reminded him of a prison cell.

His face drawn and blanched, Max looked Evan over. "You're missing a boot," he observed.

Evan said, "Really."

"What's wrong?"

"Someone else emerged. One of his men shot up my car."

Max's lips quavered, the strain of the past three days breaking through. "Who?"

Evan could still taste bile in the back of his throat. "I'll find out," he said.

"I thought it was just this one problem and we were done."

"Now there's a second problem."

"Okay." Max nodded a few times too many. Trying to settle himself. "Thank you. I appreciate it. I appreciate your sticking with me."

"I'm here until it's finished. That's the deal."

Max crossed to the kitchen counter, where a few take-out containers rested. He'd closed them back up and lined them against the wall. Taking a bit of pride in looking after his space, even here.

Evan watched him in the dim light. Max picked at the edge of one of the containers, his head bent. Moonlight glowed through the fiberglass patchwork on the rear wall, turning his skin amber. A few days' stubble darkened his face, with some gray flecked in, adding a touch of rakish charm to his hangdog features.

"Think about what Grant did," Max said quietly. "I mean, he had colleagues and brothers and kids. But he gave the thumb drive to me."

A few blocks away, a car horn bleated. The house felt small and safe and glum, a carved-out hiding space in a city of four million.

"You're saying he trusted you?" Evan asked.

"I'm saying I'm the only person he knew who didn't matter. Who no one would miss."

Evan thought back two-thirds of a lifetime to an East Baltimore boys' home. Pent-up energy and quashed dreams, the smell of a dozen boys in close quarters. Bunk beds lined the room like racks on a submarine. As the smallest, Evan slept on a mattress on the floor between the bunks. Most mornings started with one of the kids sliding out of bed, accidentally stepping on him.

The Orphan Program had sent a recruiter sniffing around the Pride House Group Home to check out its wares for a variety of reasons. But the most important was that the kids who lived there were expendable.

He felt an urge now to gloss over Max's grief, to point out the nearly two dozen electrical shocks that Grant had endured before giving up his name. The crime-scene report had been stomach-churning. Grant hadn't *wanted* to put Max's life at risk.

But he'd been willing to.

And Evan wanted Max to shove the thought away because of how painfully that same reality lived inside him—how little he was wanted, how little his life had been valued. Max's recognizing it meant that Evan had to recognize it, too, the anguish resonating in his bones like a deep-struck note. But Max was owed more than another voice giving him false assurances, so Evan kept his mouth shut and sat in it with him.

Max dug his thumbnail into a Styrofoam lid. "'No one would ever think of you.' That's what Grant told me. That's the thing. I don't really matter. I'm not really family."

Evan breathed in the dark space. "Maybe they're still mad at you for moving on from Violet."

"Moving on?" Max raised his head, the amber light catching half of his face, the other lost in eclipse. "When you love someone like that? You never move on. They get into your cells. They live inside you even when they're not living with you." He lowered his gaze again. "This whole mess with Grant, it took me right out of life. But that gives me a better view of it, you know? My life. Like I'm outside looking down at it. And I guess my fear is . . ." His lips bunched. "My fear is that maybe Grant was right."

"If you don't like what you see," Evan said, "change it."

Max's laugh died quickly in the small room. "I wish it was that easy."

"It is. It's everything else that's complicated."

Max didn't seem to like the sound of that.

"Maybe this will give you a chance to do something different." Evan noticed that his enunciation was loose, slightly slurred from the concussion, and that once again he was talking to himself as much as to Max.

Max went back to picking at the take-out container. He did not look convinced.

Evan fought to speak more clearly: "You know the two best words in the English language?"

Max shook his head.

"'Next time.'"

Max blew out a breath. He leaned on the counter, his elbow trembling.

Evan picked up Max's disposable phone from the counter, dropped it down the disposal, and let it run until the pieces rattled vigorously. Then he took a fresh phone from the duffel bag, peeled it out of the packaging, and tossed it to Max.

"Just to be safe," Evan said. "Use this now. Same rules. I'll have 1-855-2-NOWHERE up and running again as soon as I get home. I'll be in touch."

"When?"

"When I take care of the second thing."

Max chewed at the edge of a thumb, his shoulders curled inward. Wrecked with worry. "What should I do in the meantime?"

"In the meantime?" Evan considered for a moment. "Figure out what you want to do with your life when we get it back for you."

Detectives Nuñez and Brust sat on the overstuffed couches in the front room of the Beverly Hills house, sipping black coffee out of bone-china teacups. Grant Merriweather's widow sat opposite them, a frail woman with an expensive haircut and toned rich-wife muscles.

"So Max Merriweather stopped by here on Monday," Nuñez said. "What did he want?"

"I don't know." Jill shook her head, her layered chestnut locks swaying. "He'd heard that Grant was killed. He said he wanted to offer his condolences, but it seemed like he was nosing around."

"For what?"

She raised her head with a kind of affected dignity, the lines of her neck pronounced. "To see if Grant had left him anything."

The detectives looked at each other.

"Like what?" Brust asked.

"In the will, I assumed. Money. Something. Max was always . . ." She reached over to adjust a willow branch rising from a massive vase. It scratched against the crystal. "He was always the family disappointment."

Brust frowned. "Have you noticed any unusual people hanging around who might be dangerous? Was anyone with Max when you saw him?"

"We've covered all this already," Jill said. "And besides, why all the interest now? Why not when Grant was scared for his life?"

"I'm sorry your husband wasn't protected from this, Mrs. Merriweather," Nuñez said. "He was a courageous man who was working on some high-stakes cases, cases other people might not have had the balls—if you'll excuse my language—to take on. We're worried he struck a hornet's nest. And we're doing our best to make sure no one else gets hurt."

"Like who?" She snorted. "Like Max?"

"Yes."

"You think the people who killed Grant would want to kill Max?" Jill said. "Why? Grant was important. Prominent people make enemies. No. *No.* The only overlap between Max and Grant would be if Max implicated my husband in some dirty business. In which case—"

She caught herself. Resumed adjusting the willow branch.

"You're saying you think we need to look at Max Merriweather as a suspect in this investigation?" Brust finally asked.

Jill's face contorted with grief briefly before it hardened back into an angry mask. She glowered at the detectives.

"I'm not going to tell you how to do your job," she said.

23

The Snack Docent

By the time the elevator opened on the twenty-first floor, Evan was dead on his feet. More precisely—he was dead on one sock and one boot.

He trudged down the hall, squinting against the painful light of the wall sconces, eager for the silent embrace of his penthouse.

He looked up to see Mia, Peter, and Lorilee standing at his front door, waiting expectantly. Peter jabbed the doorbell, and Mia hooked him back against her legs and said, "That's enough."

Evan walked up behind them. Cleared his throat.

They swung to face him. "Oh, thank God," Lorilee said. "Just in time."

"In time for . . . ?" And then, with horror, he remembered.

The fucking HOA meeting.

"We started fifteen minutes ago," Lorilee said. "Hugh was worried you forgot."

"No." Evan scratched his forehead, hiding the dilated pupil. "I got hung up with a work thing. I just have to run inside to grab the . . ." He cringed slightly. "Nibbles."

Mia stared at him. It seemed she couldn't believe the word had come out of his mouth any more than he could.

He smelled of dog and sweat and vomit, so he bladed through them as swiftly as he could and fumbled the key into the lock. The internal security bars gave a clink as the lugs withdrew from the steel frame.

Peter said, "You're missing your boot again."

Evan looked down. "I guess that's right."

"This time it's the *other* boot, though."

"You've never lost a sock in the laundry?"

"Huh?"

"I'm kidding. It's a new workout. Calf conditioning." Evan was inside now, peering out, closing the door as he spoke. "I just need a . . . Be down in a . . ."

He closed the door. Put his back to it. Shot a breath at the high ceiling.

Then he ran to the bedroom. He kicked off his boot and grabbed another oversize shoe box from the closet. Pulling on the new pair, he stumbled into the Vault, grabbed a replacement RoamZone, and dumped his ARES into a medical waste bucket. On his way out, passing the bathroom mirror, he froze at the sight of the dark orb of his right eye. In the second drawer, he kept a few sets of specialized contact lenses for precisely this contingency. He popped one in, masking the damage, and immediately noticed two dark lines seeping through his shirt across the stomach.

He ripped off his shirt, exposing the claw marks from the pit-mastiff. Superficial gouges, reopened in his mad dash around the penthouse. He tore open a pack of styptic swabs that he snatched from the medicine cabinet. Grabbing two, he painted over the cuts, the sting setting his nerves on fire.

An annoying level of pain, too high to ignore, too low to take seriously.

"Ow, ow, ow." Hopping back into the bedroom with one boot raised so he could tie the laces. Pulling on a new gray T-shirt, he sprinted to the front door. He'd just reached it when he remembered: nibbles.

Back to the refrigerator.

It held five saline bags, a jar of pearl onions, several ampoules of epinephrine, and a half-eaten doorstop of Huntsman cheese. The vegetable drawer was filled with vials of Epo, an anemia med that hastened the creation of red blood cells, kept on hand in the event of a bad injury.

Not helpful.

A sleeve of water crackers, a box of jasmine rice, and two types of lentil pasta peered back at him from the roll-out pantry. He shot a desperate glance at the living wall. Nothing there he could readily alchemize into a crudités platter.

To the fridge yet again. At the back of the top shelf stood his collection of cocktail olives. Grand Barounis, Spanish Queens, pitted Castelvetranos. He juggled the jars to the concrete island and then started slamming through the cupboards looking for any sort of serveware, as if he'd unknowingly purchased some in the event he suddenly had occasion to distribute canapés.

No appetizer bowls had magically materialized on the shelves. Water glasses would have to do.

He upended the jars over the sink, using his hand as a sieve, and jammed the olives into the glasses. All the movement made him dizzy, and he paused for a moment, leaning on the counter to catch his breath.

The freezer drawer held a murderers' row of the world's finest vodkas. He grabbed the Syvä because it came packaged in a manageable bottle, short and plump. Encircling the glasses with his hands, the vodka swaying beneath one fist, he hurried out the door, kneed it shut, and rode down to the ninth floor.

As he elbowed into the social room, the conversational hum halted abruptly. Evan turned to take in an array of the usual suspects rimming the oval expanse of the fine-grained conference table. More tenants stood against the walls, Ida's mugging clearly having escalated the meeting to standing room only.

Hugh Walters was of course installed at the table's head, a despot's perch from which he could hold forth at length on topics ranging from parking regulations to chlorination levels in the pool.

"Delighted you could make it, Mr. Smoak," he said. "Generally a resident makes arrangements to be here early when he is responsible for refreshments."

Evan blinked away the rising tide of his headache. "Sorry. I got stuck with a work situation—"

"We're *all* busy." As Hugh leaned back and folded his hands, Evan sensed he was warming to a platitude. "We all have jobs and responsibilities. Everything in life boils down to priorities. It's not like you're a firefighter or a doctor where you can't responsibly control your schedule."

Evan's grip was slipping, so he held the collection of glasses against his stomach, refusing to wince as his shirt pressed into the scrapes.

Lorilee wiggled in her swivel chair, her eyes lighting up to match her surgically fixed expression of perpetual surprise. For a moment he thought his vision was blurring again, but then he realized that was just her face. "You brought . . . olives?" she observed.

Evan set down his offerings with a clink. Forty or so sets of hungry eyes lasered to the woeful glasses. It was surprising how inadequate they looked there on the massive wooden table.

He armed sweat from his brow. His fake contact was starting to itch. "Not just any olives."

Seated on the far side, Mia took mercy on him. "Are these different kinds, Evan?"

"Yes." He cleared his throat. "The Spanish Queens are a classic, though you'll want to rinse them before you put them in a glass so you don't brine the vodka."

"Vodka?" Johnny Middleton said.

"Oh, right." Evan picked up the bottle, realizing too late that he was displaying it like a servile waiter. "This is a rye-based small-batch. You'll taste a bit of smoke in it, a toasty charge on the tongue. It's made in a distillery in northeast Minnesota on a farm built by Swedish immigrants a century ago, so it retains that plainspoken Finnish pedigree. The grain oil hits mid-palate, and if you pay attention, you can grab a hint of orange peel and laven-der. . . ."

Everyone was staring at him in a manner that suggested they were captivated less by what he was saying than by the fact that he was saying it at all.

His voice lost steam. "The Castelvetranos are best with a flavor-less vodka, something delicate. . . ."

Lorilee, evidently the only person worse at reading the room than he was, brightened above even her elevated baseline. "I like olives stuffed with red pepper."

He suppressed a shudder. "It's a martini. Not a tapenade."

For reasons unclear to him, this remark caused a stir. Mia tipped her mouth into her hand in an attempt to hide a smile. Peter flopped onto the table, kicking his legs to propel himself toward the center. He dug his dirty fingers into the nearest glass, retriev-ing a fistful of Grand Barounis.

"Peter, *please*," Mia said. "You look like you're rooting for truf-fles." She grabbed the rear of his belt and slid him back across the table, even as he shoved several olives into his mouth.

Hugh banged his empty coffee mug on the table, a judicial re-buke. "Please don't make me regret lifting the child-attendance embargo, Ms. Hall." His patronizing gaze found Evan. "And if you consult Reg 13.8, you'll see that alcohol is disallowed at these meet-ings."

Evan wondered how anyone got through an HOA meeting *with-out* alcohol but decided against raising that objection.

Hugh pointed to the sole empty chair at the table. "That spot is held for the snack docent."

A familiar feeling of unease resurfaced, that Evan was a traveler in a foreign land, observing native customs and rituals without understanding their purpose. Being concussed didn't exactly clar-ify matters.

"That's okay," Evan said. "Maybe someone else would like to—"

"Please sit down," Hugh said.

Evan sat.

He looked across the table at Mia, who bit down a grin and rolled her eyes. She surreptitiously pointed at the lonely olive-filled glasses, untouched since Peter's plundering, and mouthed, *Nice nibbles.*

"Before you swept in," Hugh said, "we were about to vote on the new carpet initiative." Wielding a clicker with lightsaber proficiency, he brought up a PowerPoint presentation comparing pile densities and anti-stain treatments.

As Hugh droned on about estimated HOA assessments, the air conditioner breathed a current of dry air onto Evan's neck. The room smelled like the cabin of an airplane. There were a jaw-dropping number of incredibly specific questions. Evan found himself wishing that the ringing in his ears was even louder so it could drown out the deliberations.

He stared longingly at the bottle of Syvä, verboten by Regulation 13.8.

It took a moment for him to register that his right thigh was vibrating.

The Turing Phone.

He removed it from his cargo pocket and set it on his knee beneath the table.

A text from the Unidentified Caller he'd spoken to an hour before: I WILL FIND OUT WHO YOU ARE.

The letters blurred and then snapped back into focus. He could practically hear that voice, unrushed and hoarse with age, delivering promises of violence. The cool air at the back of his neck felt suddenly unnerving.

"Wait, wait, wait." Johnny Middleton held up a hand, stubby fingers splayed. The overhead light illuminated his hair plugs, symmetrically planted like rows of corn. "Does the Emerald Forest Green come Scotchgarded?"

Lorilee cut in, waving a pad on which she was—for some reason known only to herself and God—taking notes. "What's the tuft-twist rating on the Juniper Bloom?"

Peter tossed an olive into the air and tried to catch it in his mouth, but it bounced off his forehead and skittered across the table.

The Turing Phone vibrated again: I SHOULD WARN YOU, BOY. THIS ISN'T SOME DOGFIGHTING RING YOU CAN WALK INTO LIKE A THIRD-RATE

GUNSLINGER. NOW YOU'VE GRADUATED. YOU HAVE MY COMPLETE AT-
TENTION. I HAVE NOTHING ELSE ON MY AGENDA EXCEPT YOU.

"—need to turn our attention to the most important matter at
hand," Hugh was saying. "I know we're all enormously concerned
about the incident that took place last night when Ida Rosenbaum
was brutally assaulted."

Now Evan's other pocket vibrated. He tugged out his Roam-
Zone, rested it on his left knee.

It was an alert from the image search he'd run on Ida's necklace.
MATCH FOUND. He thumbed the link, opening up a Los Angeles
Craigslist posting. "*MINT* beatifull silver + purpel necklace. $500.
Dont waste my time w/ fake offers. Local only, cash handoff, text now.
Jerry Z."

Evan tapped Jerry Z's phone number into his RoamZone.
Through his VOIP provider, Evan was able to set his caller ID to
any name or number in the world. It was currently programmed
to identify him as Jean Pate with a San Bernardino area code. The
French approximation of John Doe was a source of secret amusement for him.

LOVE THIS NECKLACE!! Evan typed from behind the fake ID,
cringing slightly at the double exclamation point required to stay
in eager-buyer character. WANT IT FOR MY LADY. WILL PAY IN FULL.
WHEN CAN YOU MEET?

"Mr. Smoak!" Hugh's voice held an insistence that indicated
that this wasn't the first time he'd called Evan's name. "I implore
you to pay attention. This is as severe a security challenge as we've
faced at Castle Heights in my seventeen years as HOA president."

As Evan nodded, the Turing Phone went again. He flicked his
eyes down to scan the text: I'M GOING TO HAVE MY MEN SKULL-FUCK
MAX MERRIWEATHER TO DEATH AND MAKE YOU WATCH.

Eyes back up to Hugh. "I understand the gravity of the situation," Evan said.

On Evan's left knee, Jerry Z's reply arrived on the RoamZone:
MCDONALD'S @ CRESSENT HEIGHTS + SUNSET TOMOROW @ 10PM DONT
B LATE BRING ALL THE CASH

"We are simply not safe until this madman is in custody." Hugh
removed his black-framed glasses with soap-opera aplomb and

wagged them at the captive audience. "Now, as many of you know, Mia Hall is helping with this issue. It's not often we get a big-case DA overseeing a robbery. She has graciously offered to update us on the investigation."

Under the table Evan tapped a reply to Jerry Z. NO PROBLEMO. SEE YOU TOMORROW.

Another hum on his right knee, another threat from the Unidentified Caller on the Turing Phone: AND THEN MY MEN WILL DO WORSE TO YOU.

Mia rose slowly to address the group. Noting Evan's distraction, she frowned at him with concern and mouthed, *You okay?*

He flashed a low thumbs-up.

Left knee: I'M AFRAID WE'LL HAVE TO PUT THE DOG TO SLEEP TOMORROW.

Evan had a moment of confusion until he saw the 323 area code. This was the animal shelter now, not Jerry Z, purveyor of stolen jewelry.

Left knee: WE'RE WAY PAST CAPACITY, AND NO ONE WANTS A FIGHT DOG.

Right knee: YOUR TIME IS COMING, BOY. I AM CONSULTING THE KAMA SUTRA FOR NEW IDEAS ABOUT HOW TO VIOLATE YOU.

Left knee: EVEN BAIT DOGS. SAD BUT TRUE.

It was like Dada poetry but even more awful.

"Can we have pets?" Evan blurted out.

A painful silence ensued. Mia's hands were clasped, her shoulders squared. Clearly he'd interrupted her closing-argument-level focus. Her head was cocked more in disbelief than irritation.

"Absolutely not," Hugh said, punching the words to make clear his irritation at the non sequitur. "This is a strictly allergy-free building. No pets, no smoking. Even the plant life in here requires a board approval process."

Right knee: IT WILL BE LONG.

Left knee: I'M SORRY.

Right knee: AND MORE PAINFUL THAN YOU CAN POSSIBLY IMAGINE.

Left knee: THERE'S NOTHING WE CAN DO.

Across the table another tossed olive struck Peter's chin and flew into Lorilee's cleavage.

Peter reddened. "Oh, boy."

Evan used the distraction to ease back from the table and slip away.

Though his balance was still in and out, Evan managed a shower, bracing himself against the wall. Toweling off brought forth a swell of nausea, and he rushed to sit down on the bed. He wanted to go to the bureau to get a pair of boxers, but his head hurt too much, and the city lights, diffuse through the window, started to streak.

The RoamZone indented his sheets where he'd tossed it, and he picked it up, thumbing down the brightness as a concession to his light sensitivity.

A deep, long sleep could be incautious; a patient was supposed to be awakened every hour and checked for focal neurological abnormalities that would suggest damage worse than a simple concussion.

To be safe, Evan set the RoamZone alarm and turned the volume all the way up before collapsing onto his side. A clammy sweat enveloped him. Closing his eyes seemed to intensify the pain where his head met the pillow.

He told himself to doze lightly so the alarm could pull him out for a self-exam.

Before he went under, a parting thought glanced off his consciousness: It would've been nice to have someone here to look after him.

24

Amphetamized

Bouncing footsteps sounded inside the apartment after Evan rang the doorbell. Then a voice: "Are you a rapist?"

"Not funny, Joey."

"So that's a no, then?"

"Open the door."

She did. Her lopsided grin faded when she saw the bag of kibble tucked under his arm. Her gaze tracked down to his hand and then along the leash he gripped to the Rhodesian ridgeback puppy panting at his side.

"Uh, *no*," she said. "No way."

Evan said, "They're gonna put him down."

"Why is that my concern?"

"You need a guard dog anyway."

"I do *not* need a guard dog. Plus, it's all banged up."

"He was a bait dog."

"A bait dog?"

"A dog they throw to bigger dogs to tear up so they're blood-hungry before a fight."

"Fuckers."

"Language. But yes."

After his oft-broken night's sleep, Evan was feeling somewhat better. He could still feel the aftereffects of the concussion, but the symptoms had receded significantly, the ringing in his ears faint enough to ignore. The dog had been nicely patched up, the vet suturing his wounds and treating his raw skin. At Evan's request she'd removed the dog's tracking device and stitched up that incision as well.

"What's with the stripe down its back?" Joey asked. "Did it have spine surgery or something?"

"No. He's a ridgeback. They're lion hunters from Africa."

At this, Joey's eyebrows lifted a millimeter, a poker tell that she was ever so slightly impressed. She stepped back with a sigh, her shoulders sagging operatically. "Fine. You can park it here—just until it heals up. I'm *not* keeping it."

"He's a him," Evan said. "With the requisite parts and everything. At least most of them."

The dog padded in at his side, nosing Joey's hand as she walked off. She flung her arm away. "It got schlop on me. So gross."

In a fall of pale early-morning light, a half-eaten breakfast burrito rested on the kitchen counter next to the ubiquitous Big Gulp. Music pulsed from the pod of the workstation—some remixed dance number heavy on percussion.

"Do you *ever* sleep?" he asked.

"Not with you coming over at all hours bearing dogs."

Evan set a prescription bottle on the edge of her desk. "You'll have to give him these antibiotics twice a day. Just mash the pill into a piece of cheese or something."

"Great. A *sick* dog."

"He's not sick. It's to prevent an infection from his injuries."

She flicked a hand at the dog. "Go over there."

The dog looked at her.

"It's really well trained," she said.

"He's better trained than you."

"That's hysterical. And inaccurate."

"You should name him."

"No."

"Why?"

"If I name it, it could get attached to me."

"Joey."

"Fine. Didn't you have a dog way back when? With Jack? What was its name?"

"Strider."

"Like the knife company?"

"Yes. But that was before there was—"

"You're such a *guy*." She crossed her arms, displeased. "Fine. I'll name it 'Dog.'"

"Careful you don't spoil him with too much affection."

Dog sat, wagging his tail, staring up at her. She tugged off her sweatshirt and coiled it in the corner beneath a pull-up bar bolted to the wall. A makeshift bed. "Here. Come over here, Dog. Dog, come!"

The dog furrowed his brow, regarding her intently.

She glared at Evan. "Why's it tilting its head at me?"

"Dogs are incredibly attuned to their owners. They want to know your mood at all times."

"I'm not its owner."

"They watch their owners' mouths—their teeth—to see if they're bared. Or smiling. His muzzle blocks his view of the lower half of your face so he's cocking his head to clear his field of vision."

For the first time, she didn't have a ready answer. "It cares that much how I'm feeling?"

"He does."

She crouched and patted the sweatshirt. The dog padded over, circled the puddled fabric a few times, and lay down, licking at the raw skin where the duct tape had stripped off his fur.

Joey rose, cracked her knuckles. "Okay. Did you need something, or were you just dropping by to complicate my life?"

"Without complications life is sterile."

"Who said that?"

"Confucius."

"Really?"

"No."

"Who then?"

"Me."

She rolled her eyes, transforming from a striking young woman to a stubborn kid. A sixteen-year-old could be either, Evan had learned. Or both at the same time.

"I need you to track an unidentified caller who dialed this phone." He produced Terzian's cell phone. "Which will be challenging, given the encryption."

"Look at you, getting all tech-porny over a Turing." She snatched it off his palm and disappeared into the circular desk, only the top of her head visible behind the monitors. "It's built like a tank, sure, and waterproof—cool, I know—but there's no micro USB, which is their fancypants ultra-secure move—lame, right?—and no headphone jack, like if you're doing super-encrypted shit, you don't wanna jam to—what do people like you listen to? Josh Groban? Michael Bolton?"

"I don't know who they are, but I sense that's below the belt."

From behind the row of monitors, she leaned into sight, shot him a winning smile, then swooped back offstage. More amphetamized typing.

"It sucks for mobile gaming, too—not that you've ever played a game in your whole life—I know, I know, 'Chess is a game'—and it barely achieved a twenty-five hundred rating on Geekbench 3, if you can call that 'achieved.'" She snorted. "I get that it's for security, not performance, so whatevs, but still, can't these people walk and chew gum at the same time?"

Evan circled to the opening in the desk. "Look, I doubt you'll be able to uncloak—"

"'Uncloak'? What is this, Middle Earth? Easy, Gandalf, I just need to grab the IMEI—that's international mobile equipment identifier for you mouth-breathers in the room." At this, she directed a pointed look at Evan and then at the dog, snoozing in the corner. "It's the fifteen-digit number burned into each phone they use to authenticate you to the network, charge you for minutes, all that. Then I'll just jump into the maintenance channel of the telco switch and use their SS7 hacks to look up which number texted this IMEI at . . ." Scrolling through the Turing's text messages, she cocked her head, not unlike the dog. "Wow. Kama Sutra, huh? Here we go—9:37 last night—and *wham*. Call detail record, bitches!"

He stared blankly at the wall of numbers on the screen. "So how do I . . . ?"

"Subscriber data's in another part of the database, dummy." She tucked back in, fingers blurring. "Lookee here. Your caller's account is registered to . . . Three Monkeys Café in Glendale."

She spun around in her chair, pulling in her knees, a full 360 ending with her bare feet stomped down and jazz hands.

"I'd express admiration for what you just did," Evan said. "But your ego doesn't need any shoring up."

"Who is this guy anyways?"

"Looks like I'll have to head to Glendale to find out."

"No, I mean, who is he, like, contextually?"

"Seems like he's the boss who unleashed Terzian," Evan said, plucking the phone from the desk and backpedaling out of the cockpit-like enclosure. "Which means the money-laundering operation's bigger than I thought."

"Why don't you bring me the thumb drive, let me take a spin through the spreadsheets?"

"I already analyzed them."

She stripped a Red Vine from a plastic tub and flopped one end into her mouth. "I'd think by now you'd have learned to extrapolate what my insulting reply to *that* might be."

He held up his hands. "Okay. Uncle. I'll bring you the thumb drive when I can."

As he started out, she called after him, "Take the dog with you."

"Can't hear you over the music."

The ridgeback lifted his head from his paws, his forehead wrinkled in a show of intense interest. Or concern.

"Take the dog with you!"

"Sorry, still can't hear you."

Evan winked at the dog and closed the door behind him.

25

An Unusually Painful Slip

At the third hour, things got interesting.

Evan had parked himself across Brand Boulevard, Glendale's commercial thoroughfare, on the second-floor terrace of a career college. Flopped open before him were several dog-eared study guides he'd bought used downstairs. To blend in with the denizens, he'd picked up an abomination of an iced-coffee drink with whipped cream and caramel streaking the insides of the clear plastic. It reminded him of the cheapo peanut-butter-and-jelly combo jars they used to get at the foster home around Thanksgiving when the churches donated baskets. The drink was the size of a fire hydrant and contained enough caffeine to make a racehorse's heart explode. Or to fuel Joey for fifteen minutes.

Up the street the Alex Theatre's gaudy Greco-Egyptian façade funneled into a hundred-foot art deco column, lit with neon and topped with a spiked ball befitting a medieval flail. The theater was hosting a Buster Keaton marathon, the signage bringing Evan back to late nights in the study with Jack watching Buster scurry around a locomotive like an ant surveying a leaf. Jack rarely laughed, but he'd prop his cheek on his fist, the wrinkles at his temple conveying something like pleased contentment. It was rare to see Jack at peace with his place in the world, even if only for the two-hour running time. Every other waking second was spent striving for the ever-receding horizon of perfection. Evan drank up those precious moments of leisure with Jack. He imagined for most people that was what life generally felt like. He sensed that once this mission was completed, that would be the sensation he'd search for.

But today Evan wasn't here for the movie theater. Or the steroidal coffee.

He was here because of the view, as clean a vantage as he could have hoped for across four lanes of traffic onto the entrance of the Three Monkeys Café.

Half of Glendale's population was composed of folks with Armenian roots. The café, with its overpriced khash and khorovats, seemed to cater to the upper slice of the community. The whole area had an upscale gleam not unlike that of Violet's South Pasadena neighborhood. Sun-kissed buildings, breeze-ruffled foliage, pop-up shops selling artisanal ice cream or hemp purses or accent tables made out of driftwood.

It brought to mind how far Los Angeles proper had slid. From downtown sidewalks cloaked in a forever haze of freeway exhaust to Eastside shanties ready to topple from a strong wind or a stray bullet. These surrounding towns and incorporated neighborhoods with their own taxes and budgets fared better than the great wheezing city, a beast of burden bearing the load of four million souls.

A convoy of Town Cars interrupted Evan's musings. Three heavy-duty Lincolns, black as pitch, rolled up to the valet. Six doors opened in concert. Twelve loafers set down on the asphalt. Even at this distance, the clunk of the closing doors was audible, armored metal reseating in reinforced frames.

The large men formed a rugby scrum that moved without obvious purpose but still encapsulated the passenger in the middle car as he emerged. Evan caught only a fleeting glimpse of a man with silver hair and a dark beard before his men cocooned him and conveyed him into the café. Everyone else knew the drill as well, swinging into motion as if mechanized, the valets nodding deferentially, a hostess materializing to hold the door, the maître d' standing at attention inside, armed with a leather-bound wine list.

The scrum swept inside without a hitch. One of the men had peeled out of formation to stand at the curb, overseeing the parked Town Cars.

Evan left the used workbooks on the table. As he jogged down the stairs, he felt no residual dizziness from the concussion. As long as he took it easy, he seemed to be functional.

He crossed the street. The valets didn't nod at him deferentially. No hostess appeared to hold the door for him. The maître d' didn't bother to look up from his reservation ledger, which he pondered Talmudically.

All that pointed inattention gave Evan a moment to scan the bustling café. Tables spread artfully across a Moroccan tile floor. A few sleek wooden fans circled leisurely overhead. French doors let onto a small courtyard with a single table where the convoy's sole passenger sat with two other men, sipping espresso. The bodyguards stood around the courtyard and at the French doors, on alert.

The diners didn't seem to take notice. A mother ate with one hand on a baby stroller, rolling it gently back and forth. Her husband lolled in his chair and jabbed at a molar with a toothpick, his stomach a testament to suburban sprawl. Near the door to a unisex bathroom, a family of six rimmed a round table, their heads bowed as if in prayer, each lost to a different screen.

No one seemed bothered in the least by the bodyguards.

Which meant Unidentified Caller was well known in the community, his presence here a dash of local flavor: the neighborhood connected guy who ate where the good food was.

The patrons were unaware that they were providing him protection, allowing him to hide here in plain sight. Cops and rivals would be less willing to make a move with such a high likelihood of collateral damage. And in the event that they did? Having civilians around to distract, confuse, and catch the occasional stray bullet would provide useful protection.

An Unusually Painful Slip

At last the maître d' pried himself from the ledger, looking up through his wire frames. "Yes, sir?"

"May I sit in the courtyard?" Evan asked.

"I'm afraid that table is taken."

"Today?"

"Always."

"Oh. Is that the owner?" Evan flicked his head toward the silver-haired gentleman. The cut of his suit was impeccable, the fabric breaking in all the right places, as if the folds had been penciled by a sketch artist.

Evan had looked into the café's business records but found only a snarled fishing line of parent companies, subsidiaries, and loan-outs.

The maître d' said, "I'd be happy to seat you inside, sir."

Putting a name to Unidentified Caller would take a bit more hoop-jumping, then.

"That would be fine. I'd prefer something away from the door. Maybe there?" Evan pointed to an open table with a partial view of the courtyard.

The maître d's grin looked as if he'd read about how to smile in a textbook and was trying it on under duress. But he seated Evan where he'd asked.

Evan ordered an Armenian coffee and settled in to observe.

The bodyguards were on point, focused on movements, windows, doorways. The courtyard looked to be sheltered from the view of the surrounding buildings. The armored Town Cars out front were under constant watch.

Unidentified Caller hadn't lied. This wasn't some dogfighting ring Evan could walk into like a third-rate gunslinger.

For this he'd have to bring at least his second-rate game.

These men seemed to be stitched into the fabric of the community. Kids in private schools, gated houses with circular driveways, three-year leases on luxury SUVs for the missuses. Nicer suits, finer espresso, a courtyard of one's own.

When acoustics allowed, Evan could make out the occasional snatch of conversation from the table, though only the voices of the other men.

Removing the Turing Phone, he texted Unidentified Caller: ANY HEADWAY WITH THE KAMA SUTRA?

He stared across the dining room, past the bodyguard, through the French doors.

Waiting for confirmation.

It took a few seconds for the text to skitter its way through the encryption. But at last the silver-haired man reached inside his lapel. He removed a matching rectangular slab of Liquidmorphium. Eyed the screen.

His lips pursed with amusement.

He held up a finger, and the men around him ceased talking.

He typed.

A moment later his text appeared: IF YOU STILL HAVE YOUR SENSE OF HUMOR, YOU DON'T COMPREHEND THE FATE YOU'RE FACING.

Evan: THE TERROR TRIED TO TELL ME THE SAME THING. RIGHT BEFORE I PUT A HOLLOW POINT THROUGH HIS FOREHEAD.

The man stared at the screen, the amusement fading from his face. As if he'd taken a joke too far with a child and was no longer willing to countenance any acting out.

He returned the phone to his lapel pocket, nodded at the men, and the conversation resumed.

Evan had to identify him. He needed a name. If not Unidentified Caller's, then at least that of one of his associates or bodyguards. He could backtrack from there.

Were Evan not sitting in clear view of two of the bodyguards, he might have risked raising his phone to take a picture.

But the facial-recognition route would not be an option.

There were three men at the table, and a lot of espresso sipping was going on.

Which meant it was only a matter of time.

Surprisingly, it wasn't one of the associates who moved first. It was the bodyguard from outside, the one watching the vehicles. He entered and nodded at the man by the French doors, who nodded at one of the redundant guards in the courtyard, who slipped outside to cover as the first guy headed into the bathroom. A seamless rotation.

Evan waited a moment. Then he rose and entered after him.

An Unusually Painful Slip

It featured only stalls, as befitted a unisex bathroom.

From behind the closed stall door came the sound of a torrent of urine.

Evan quietly threw the dead bolt behind him. He cupped his hands under the sink, sprinkled some water on the concrete, and then entered one of the vacant stalls. As he waited, he noted that his body temperature felt higher than usual, and then all of a sudden he was sweating as if someone had ramped up the heat. A familiar fogginess rolled over him, altering his perception, fuzzing the edges of the stall, the latch lock, his own hand held before his face. He didn't know what an ideal time was to have a flurry of concussion symptoms, but this was not it.

The guy finished, zipped up, and cleared the stall, moving to the trough sink.

Evan closed his eyes, focused on his breathing, willed his body temperature to lower. He had to be swift and precise in order to avoid any kind of physical altercation. He couldn't risk another knock to the head.

Once he felt steadier, he emerged, giving a neighborly nod when the guard looked up to eye him in the mirror.

As the man reached for the paper-towel dispenser, his weight shifted forward, moving him up onto his toes on the water-slick concrete. Evan grabbed the nape of his neck, swept his ankles back, and slammed his forehead into the lip of the sink.

The man's knees buckled forward, and he sat froggy style, his torso flopped back over his legs. His eyes were open a sliver, showing a seam of white, and his breath came evenly and jaggedly. He would come to in a few seconds. The overwhelming likelihood was that he would remember nothing and dismiss it as an unusually painful slip in the bathroom.

Evan lifted the unconscious man's weighty arm, adjusting his grip around the right index finger, and rolled the finger pad onto the back of his own right thumbnail.

A nice hard surface that would hold the print.

He released the arm, and it slapped to the floor.

Evan adjusted his hair in the mirror and exited.

He hooked left through the lobby and was out on the street in seconds. Too late he realized that in his slightly dazed state he'd inadvertently dined and ditched, which would make him memorable, especially to the snotty maître d'. Now he'd be unable to return to surveil the area if the mission called for it, the first concrete cost of the concussion he'd sustained. He vowed it would also be the last.

Next door a concrete office building the color of sandstone rose five stories to a steep slope roof. The building probably didn't offer a useful view of the courtyard, but it was the best and only option.

Evan gauged it from outside and then rode to the top level. The lights of the elevator seemed unnaturally bright, aggravating the aching in his brain, making him squint.

A dermatologist and an internist shared the floor. A bathroom conveniently took up the center of the southwest side.

Evan entered the bathroom, slid open the window, and stuck his head out.

He could see down onto the top of the courtyard but not quite to the table.

Another five feet or so would get him there.

But he didn't have five feet. There was only open air. The ground gave a vertiginous swirl, and he took in a lungful of fresh air and moved his gaze upward.

A faint commotion stirred on the sidewalk outside the Three Monkeys Café, the valets rushing to assist one of the bodyguards as he helped his fallen comrade out the door and into the front Town Car. He was squeezing his forehead and staggering. Evan could relate.

The bathroom door squeaked open behind him, a few workers entering. He pulled back from the window, offering a bland smile to their inquisitive stares. It was a busy bathroom on a busy floor.

Evan went back downstairs, walked two blocks, and got into his truck.

Driving home, he was careful to keep his right hand fanned off the steering wheel so as not to brush the fingerprint invisibly preserved on his thumbnail.

26

Small Talk

Back home in the Vault, Evan harvested the fingerprint from his thumbnail using lycopodium powder and lifting tape, converted it to digital, and ran it through the FBI's Integrated Automated Fingerprint Identification System. Unsurprisingly, the bodyguard he'd knocked unconscious in the bathroom had a criminal record, which provided a convenient ID. Evan leapfrogged from there, running through known associates in the databases until he arrived at a photograph of the silver-haired Unidentified Caller he'd watched sip espresso at the Three Monkeys Café.

Alexan Petro. Evan figured the surname for an Ellis Island special or a crime-lord affectation.

Either way Petro was a busy man, with a history that ranged from money laundering to racketeering. Armed with a strike team of attorneys and advantaged by a pattern of convenient key-witness disappearances, he'd proved slippery. As he'd telegraphed through his texts to Evan, he was the head of the snake to Terzian's operation, the upper echelon of corruption.

The six bodyguards who formed Petro's inner cadre were a gruesome lot, rapists and child abusers who'd been implicated in multiple murders but—thanks to the selfsame superb legal representation—had skipped free each time. Reviewing some of the evidence later deemed inadmissible, Evan found himself wishing he'd slammed the bodyguard's forehead into the sink with a bit more emphasis.

A quick glance at Google Maps showed that Petro's mansion, perched atop a hill in a gated Oak Park community, had been turned into a guarded compound. Security stations, spiked fences, armed patrols—the setup was worthy of a cartel leader or a high-value terrorist. Getting in wasn't merely a serious-risk venture; it would require weeks of planning. Evan pondered detonating Petro in his armored Town Car, but the possibility of collateral damage was unacceptable.

Especially when there was a better option.

To get it done, he'd need the help of a friend who could bring— quite literally—a unique perspective to the challenge.

The South Central apartment building was run-down, the carpet worn, the paint peeling around the doorframes, the numbers rusting.

But one door had recently been sanded and painted. The buffed brass numeral was precisely centered beneath the peephole. A literal welcome mat—a mat reading WELCOME—covered the frayed carpet edges.

All this precision made Evan feel at home.

He was holding a pizza. More precisely, a pizza with pineapple and yellow bell peppers and pepperoni.

He rang, and a voice called out, "Who is it?"

"Pizza delivery."

The peephole darkened. "No, it's not. It's you with a pizza."

"Right," Evan said. "It's a joke."

Trevon Gaines opened the door. "I did what you said and found somebody else and gave him your phone number."

"Yes, you did." Evan looked up the hall. "Can I come in?"

"Oh, shoot. Kiara told me good hosts are supposed to ask. Hang on."

Trevon closed the door. Evan stood there, the pizza box warming his palm. An instant later the door opened again.

"Hi, um, um, would you like to come in?"

"I would. Thank you, Trevon."

He entered. Trevon's cat, a slender tabby who hated Evan with motiveless malignancy, arched her back like a Halloween cutout.

Evan hesitated. "Is that thing gonna . . . ?"

"Don't worry," Trevon said. "She's just saying hi."

The cat hissed at Evan with the terrifying savagery of her jungle superiors and darted down the hall toward Trevon's room. Exhaling, Evan set the pizza on the round kitchen table and flipped up the lid with theatrical aplomb. "Here you go. Only yellow and orange food groups per your vehement preference."

"Um, um. Pepperoni's a darkish red."

"I put it more in a rich orange category."

"I don't."

"Okay," Evan said. "If I pick it off, will you eat the pizza?"

"No," Trevon said. "I can't. I'm sorry. And thank you. I . . ." He pressed his flat palm to the side of his head. "Would you mind getting it off my table?"

Evan closed the box, carried it to the kitchen, and shoved it into the trash can. Then he faced Trevon across the counter, stocked with bananas, mac-and-cheese boxes, Cap'n Crunch's Orange Creampop Crunch, Cheerios, and a bowl of clementines.

Trevon had been Evan's previous client. Just like Max, he'd run into the wrong kind of men. They had destroyed his family and done their best to destroy him, too, but Evan had intervened. He normally made a point of staying away from prior clients, but Trevon was special in more ways than one, and Evan checked in on him from time to time.

"How are you doing?" he asked.

"I'm good. I miss Mama, but I see Kiara twice a week 'cuz she's family and family takes care of you. I'm, um, um, I'm dating a girl." An embarrassed smile sprang up, and he covered it with his hand, dipped his head. "She's five-two and a hundred forty-seven pounds but it's not nice to say so because that's not a good social cue 'cuz a lady never says her weight but it's obvious and I don't see what the big deal is anyways but ladies are confusing."

Trevon was like that. A human tape measure and digital scale. He saw the world as if through a set of binoculars with stadiametric rangefinding.

"She's high-functioning like me but she doesn't like sand or wind or 3-D movies so it makes it tricky to go out on dates."

"Then you'd better raise your game. A yellow-and-orange picnic."

Trevon checked his watch. "Are you gonna be here long? 'Cuz small talk gives me a headache and I'm supposed to shower."

"I need a favor."

Trevon checked his watch again, cleared his throat uncomfortably. "What favor?"

Evan pulled out a hundred-dollar bill and rested it on the counter. "I need you to take yourself to lunch."

Trevon stared at the bill. "Um. Why?"

"I can't show my face at this particular café again. So I need you to go in my stead."

"And do what?"

"Eat," Evan said. "And look around."

"Why do you need me to look around?"

"Because you see things I can't."

"Like what?"

Evan told him precisely like what.

27

The Edge of Visibility

Despite the Las Vegas midday sun, a November chill prickled the skin at the back of Evan's neck. The low-slung building ahead rose from a stretch of dirt road and desert sand like a woebegone settler's cabin in a Western. A rusting auto-repair sign threw shade across the sturdy metal door, but the neon was unlit as always, the business unlisted in any directory. Husks of cars and the occasional engine block rested in the scrubby brush, arrayed like props, which was precisely what they were.

Carrying the weighty medical-waste bucket under one arm, Evan lowered his face from the sign where the front security camera was housed and rapped on the door. A popping sound from within answered him.

Gunshots.

Or, as he thought of it, the soundtrack of Tommy Stojack.

Evan pounded more loudly with the heel of his hand.

The gunfire ceased.

Silence.

And then the door yawned open, a burly figure standing in the dismal lair, pistol in either hand. He was backlit by a feeble shaft through a barred skylight and the glow of a gooseneck lamp clipped to one of a half dozen workbenches. A range of machinery completed the torture-dungeon motif of the shop. It smelled of gun grease and spent powder, coffee and cigarettes.

A Camel Wide lifted to the man's face, the cherry illuminating the stub where the forefinger had been blown off at the knuckle. An inhale crackled the paper, the orange glow at last bringing the face to the edge of visibility. Biker's mustache. Lip bulged out with a tobacco plug. Deeply expressive, melancholy eyes bedded down above crescent bags of puffy skin. A tumble of gray hair falling over a lined forehead twisted with wry amusement.

Tommy's machine shop, which Evan thought of as a lair, provided a variety of services for a variety of government-sanctioned black-ops groups. Preproduction. Proof of concept and R&D. Prototyping and fabrication. Weapons procurement. Evan didn't know specifics about Tommy any more than Tommy knew specifics about him.

He knew only that he trusted Tommy absolutely and that he was a world-class armorer.

Tommy spit a comet of tobacco juice skillfully past Evan's shoulder, took another hit off the cigarette, and scratched at a nicotine patch adhered to his neck that had peeled away from the skin in either protest or despair.

"I'm glad it's just you," Tommy said.

Evan stepped inside, crouched to reach for a hidden outlet, and unplugged the security camera, as was their policy. "Who were you expecting?"

"Got a new broad hooched up with me. Figured maybe she was feeling lonely, talked herself into making an unannounced drive-by. That woulda gone down like a Japanese Zero. But forget that shit. How's things?"

"Good. You?"

"Any better, I'd expect to get indicted." Tommy jogged the pistols in his hands, showing each one off against a callused palm.

"Working on some modifications for a couple of the ninja ballerinas."

"Ninja ballerinas?"

"SWAT. This puppy's an FNX tactical."

"A .45?"

"Nobody makes a .46, do they?" Tommy let one palm drop, lifting his other one, Lady Justice with a gun fetish. "And this thing of beauty is an S&W .359 NG. Fixed combat sights, beveled cylinders, Crimson Trace grips. It's got built-in laser, puts a dot on the forehead—insert offensive Indian joke here."

"You got my next batch of ARES pistols?"

Tommy swiped the gun back and ambled toward the nearest workbench. An oft-injured warhorse, he had the broken-down gait of a retired bronc rider.

As Evan followed him into increasing dimness, Tommy stepped across a roll of what looked like green conveyer belt. At least fifty feet long, it stretched along the oil-spotted concrete floor, a python lying in wait.

Evan squinted down. Puttyish substance, thirty-six inches thick, like a parcel of linoleum ready to be unrolled. "Is that— Wait, Tommy. Is that C-4?"

Tommy paused, tugged at his mustache, and looked down. "Not just any C-4," he said. "Detasheet from a stash that predates the mandatory addition of taggants. Totally untraceable—no coded microparticles in this slab o' goodness. I took the lot off the books in '82." He smiled, showcasing the slender gap between his front teeth. "'Expended in training.' Had it in my inventory ever since, but I finally got around to slicing and dicing it for the Balls-Deep State."

He detoured around a heavy-barrel Browning M2, giving it a loving nudge with his boot. "Been restoring this .50-cal meat chopper. It ain't the aircraft version, but you'd better eat your Wheaties if you wanna lug this hog around. And over here . . ."

Years of experience had taught Evan to pry Tommy off show-and-tell as quickly as possible, so he set down the medical-waste bucket on the workbench, the ARES pistols inside clanking like hammers. "I need you to puddle these, turn them to slag."

Evan always dispensed with his pistols after using them. The ARES were impossible to trace, sure, but each round still bore the signature from the individual barrel it had been fired from, as well as scratches introduced during the loading-and-feeding process. This meant that if he used the same gun in two shootings, a connection could be established between the incidents. Even if the projo was mangled, a fired case left on the scene carried distinctive tool marks from the firing pin, extractor, ejector, or the breech face. He always collected shell cases when he could and wore latex gloves while loading magazines, but if there was one thing Jack had drilled into his bone marrow, it was that you could never be too sure.

"You're spoiling another set of perfectly good pistols," Tommy said. "You do realize that this little security measure of yours is an affront to my fine handiwork?"

The Second Commandment, Evan thought. *How you do anything is how you do everything.*

He gave Tommy a been-there look.

"Okay, okay." Tommy showed him his palms, relenting as he collapsed into a rolling chair behind the workbench. He spun a Pelican case to face Evan and popped the lid. Nestled in foam were a dozen fresh ARES 1911s. "I got your new EDCs here. Did an action job on 'em. Smoother than a frog's asshole."

"They're notoriously smooth, are they? Frog assholes?"

"I ain't field-tested it. But so says the literature." Tommy slid the case across to Evan. "If they don't understand English, make sure they understand lead."

Evan picked one up to feel the familiar heft, like an extension of his arm. Yet another reason he'd chosen the aluminum pistols as his everyday carry.

He lined the sights on the coffeepot gurgling behind Tommy like a witch's cauldron. Then he ran a quick target-acquisition drill, swinging the muzzle to a cutting torch, a set of welder's goggles, an ashtray made from a ship's battered porthole. He was pleased to note that his vision stayed crisp—no double images, no blurring, no light streaks. Getting the concussion behind him was a necessity, given what lay ahead.

"That'll steer you into the fray," Tommy said, chinning at the pistol. "Then you hit 'em with the 'iles.' Agile, mobile, and hostile."

Evan started to turn away, but Tommy snapped the intact fingers of his right hand. "Take it for a spin, please."

At the back of the space, Tommy had a few paper targets strapped to bales of hay and more bales stacked up against the wall. Evan put on eyes-and-ears protection, firmed his stance, and went for the one-hole drill—all the rounds through the same hole.

The first eight shots went according to plan, but then a rush of light-headedness fuzzed his vision, his brain reminding him that it was still displeased about being slammed into parking-lot asphalt. His ninth shot edged south, turning the solitary hole in the target into a figure eight.

Intense focus or quick movements seemed to dial up the symptoms. Not helpful given that everything to come would be dependent on intense focus and quick movements. He lowered the pistol, blinking himself back to normal and hoping Tommy didn't notice the sheen of sweat that had sprung up on his forehead.

Tommy cluck-clucked. "You got 'How'd I do?' syndrome. Peeked up and dropped the last shot. Didn't no one teach you shit?"

When it came to shooting, Evan knew better than to compete with Tommy even when his head was clear. He returned the ARES to the foam lining and clicked the Pelican case lid shut. "I also need a sniper rifle."

"For what?"

"To snipe."

"I'm getting some FN Ballistas in next week that'll make your socks roll up and down."

"I don't have till next week."

"What range we talking?"

Evan told him.

Tommy waved him off with a four-fingered hand. "You don't need a highly specialized sniper gun for that. You can just zero a deer gun."

Evan said, "You're thinking a 700 Remington?"

"Most common hunting rifle in North America. Millions of them. Hits your checkmarks for traceability and availability. Hell,

I got a heap in the back. We pimp it out with an old-school Swarovski scope, you are GTG."

Tommy kicked back in his Aeron chair, rolling across the slick concrete and disappearing into the shadowy fringe of the lair. A racket ensued—rusty hinges lifting, curse words, something clattering to the floor. The whir of the wheels presaged Tommy's return. Sure enough, he sailed back into view, Remington rifle across his lap. He lifted it in triumph.

Evan said, "You got it in tan?"

28

Eleventh-Hour Surprise

In the corner of Joey's apartment, Dog the dog lapped water from a Red Vines tub. Evan sat on the floor and looked him over. The laceration on Dog's cheek was healing nicely, though the restitched flap of skin on his chest was red and inflamed. Evan smeared some Neosporin over the stitches and then checked the strips of exposed flesh at the muzzle and hind legs where the duct tape had been removed. Healthy white skin, the fur starting to grow back. Dog shoved his wet nose into the hollow of Evan's neck, and Evan steered the big head away, scratching behind the ears.

Joey's typing, a white-noise constant since Evan had given her Max's thumb drive a half hour ago, contributed a pleasing background hum.

"Dog's doing well," Evan said.

"You like it so much, you should find a permanent home for it," Joey said. "Sooner rather than later. We don't want it getting comfortable."

"He's still healing," Evan said.

"I know. It kept me up whimpering all night."

"It's hard work taking care of someone else," Evan said.

Joey snapped around in her chair to glower at him from her workstation. "What does *that* mean?"

"Precisely what it sounds like it means."

"I take care of someone else already." She was wearing the Hello Kitty–with-an-AK T-shirt again, the sleeves hiked up, showing off her well-defined arms. "You. I have to, like, spoon-feed tutor you when it comes to hacking."

"I assume you're unfamiliar with the Dunning-Kruger effect," Evan said.

"Dunkirk-who?"

"Never mind." Evan rose and walked to the circular desk, Dog following closely, pressing into the side of his leg. "What did you find?"

"Your boy Petro's got all the angles." Dog the dog was whimpering, and Joey paused, annoyed. "Can you get it to be quiet?"

"When's the last time you took him out?"

"I don't know."

"You want him to pee on your floor?"

"Yeah. I'd totally love that."

"Let's go."

She grimaced and then dug beneath her desk and came up with a leash and a black fabric collar with a cutesy skull-and-crossbones motif.

Evan said, "You bought him a collar?"

"Just so it's easier to take him out. Everything doesn't have to mean some big thing."

Evan noted her first use of the masculine pronoun but kept his mouth shut.

When Joey crouched to pull on the collar, Dog licked her cheek. She didn't smile. But she didn't protest either.

They rode the elevator down and stood outside, Joey holding the leash while Dog the dog sniffed the grass, moved a few feet, sniffed it again. Lifting his leg, he unleashed a fire-hose stream onto an elm sapling.

"Are you feeding him Big Gulps?" Evan said.

"He's a big animal—a lion hunter, like you said. That's just how they pee."

"It's okay. You don't have to defend him."

"I'm not *defending* him. But while I'm stuck babysitting him, I've learned how he rolls. That's all."

Despite wanting to needle Joey more, Evan changed course. "So what'd you get on Petro? From Grant's files?"

"Well, you're right—he's definitely upper management. Oversaw the washing process with the cash that Terzian and his crew brought in. The books are light on proper nouns, but I pieced together some of the EINs. They were laundering money through—wait for it—kebab vans and plumbing companies. I know, right? These guys didn't take the sensitivity workshop on ethnic stereotyping. But it's a lotta money. Like, a lotta lotta money. After a while kebab vans and plumbing trucks just wouldn't do. So Petro got himself a bank."

Dog the dog was still going. The elm sapling looked woeful. At last he lowered his leg and shook his head, his ears giving off leathery snaps against the sides of his skull.

"A bank," Evan repeated.

"Yeah," Joey said. "I broke the code on the routing numbers in, like, ten seconds. It was simple-stupid—middle-aged men playing at a girl's game. Oh, yeah!" She did some sort of dance move with her hands shoving the air upward. Evan and Dog the dog stared at her. "So I followed the trail. Know what 'bank capture' is?"

"It's where you buy a controlling interest in a bank in some nonreporting jurisdiction or a tax haven with shitty records. Then you channel your money through it, and no one's the wiser."

"Impressive. How'd you know that?"

"Because I've done it," Evan said.

"What? *What?* When did you own a bank?"

"It was a onetime thing," Evan said. "Long story."

"O-*kay.* Anyways. You said Hollywood PD's trying to build a case. But I don't get why the feds aren't involved, since we're dealing with banks in Singapore and whatnot."

"Because," Evan said, "they don't know it's that big yet. They don't have the thumb drive. We do."

Dog the dog stretched languidly and yawned, curling his tongue and emitting a tired whine that bordered on adorable. A crew of guys made their way up the sidewalk toward Evan and Joey, roughhousing and joking. With their gym muscles and notched-in side parts, they looked sparkly clean and uniform, rolled off an assembly belt. But Joey wasn't looking at them with annoyance. Not in the least.

She snapped out of her daze, noticed Evan watching her. Blushing, she tugged on the dog's leash to move him back toward the lobby. "Can we please get inside already? Us being seen together is social suicide, okay?"

Evan said, "For me or for you?"

"With all that training you got, it woulda been helpful if they'd included a crash course in, like, actual humor."

In the lobby a few workers had appeared, measuring the flimsy single-panes and jotting notes on clipboards.

"New owners," Joey said. "They're fixing the place up, taking care of all those oh-so-scary security holes you're so fussy about. Happy?"

Evan looked back at the loose guard plate on the front door. "Partly."

"Are you *ever* happy?"

He thumbed the elevator button. "When I'm ballroom dancing."

Joey's emerald eyes widened. "Really?"

"No."

Back upstairs, Evan crowded into the cockpit with her and studied the screens.

He pointed. "I'm assuming these initials are code names?"

"Yeah. Lower-end workers, payoffs, bribes, whatever. I guess I could run them down, tracking the precise amounts of the payments and then digging through bank records, but it'd be a slog."

"Do it anyway. It would be helpful to match the code names with real identities."

"For what? These are peripheral players."

"Once I take care of Petro and his goons and Max is in the clear, I'll send him into a police station with that thumb drive. If they know the names of the bottom feeders, it'll help them put a ribbon around the case later, tie up the loose ends. Plus, I want to make sure I know the extent of it."

"What do you mean?"

"This mission already telescoped on me once. Last time I thought it ended with Terzian. Then I found out about Petro. I could do without another eleventh-hour surprise."

Joey reached down, unplugged a zip drive from a port, and tossed it to Evan. "Here's a copy. I'll keep chipping away at the original."

Evan squatted to scratch the dog's ears. "Okay. Take care of Dog."

"Where are you going?"

Heading out, he glanced at the Victorinox fob watch clipped to his belt loop. In less than an hour, he was due to meet with the jackass who had mugged Ida Rosenbaum—Jerry Z of the frequent typos and the rationalized orthography. As if Evan didn't have his hands full already with money launderers and organized-crime outfits.

Evan said, "McDonald's."

Both Joey and Dog the dog cocked their heads at him in concert.

Evan said, "You know that thing about how owners start looking like their dogs?"

He ducked the Big Gulp flying at his head and closed the door behind him.

29

A Man Moves Through the Night

Due to its West Hollywood location, the McDonald's at the corner of Crescent Heights and Sunset aspired to be high-end. That meant clean booths, ample napkins, and additional seating upstairs.

As Evan neared the entrance, two moms with gym-attenuated limbs passed by, pushing strollers and sipping kombucha. They cast a wary eye at the fast-food joint, as if it were a den of iniquity. No line-caught salmon or free-range chicken in there.

Evan entered, hit with a stream of ketchup-scented air-conditioning, and looked around. A few high-schoolers comparing iPhone pics. A homeless guy bundled into a booth, hands encircling a cup of water. A musclehead in a gym tank top plowing through a Big Mac with lawn-mower efficiency.

None seemed likely suspects.

As Evan mounted the stairs, his RoamZone rang.

He paused, checked caller ID, then answered. "Now's not the best—"

"It's sixty-four yards off the ground," Trevon said. "The first measurement you asked for. And the second distance is six hundred seven yards. They say 'as the crow flies' but that doesn't make any sense 'cuz crows fly all sorts of ways—"

"Can I maybe call you in a—"

"—like if they're hungry or see a worm or maybe they're coming to land on a telephone wire. So you don't really know how they fly, do you, which makes it an imprecise standard of measurement."

"Trevon, thank you. But I have to call you back."

Evan hung up the phone, slipped it into his pocket, and continued up the stairs.

The tables were sparsely populated—a few couples, a group of kids with Fairfax High sweatshirts, a pair of elderly women.

And a heavyset white guy clad in an Adidas sweat suit with thick gold chains, pierced ears, and orange-tinted Oakley Razors worn backward so the lenses rode the fat rolls on the nape of his neck.

Evan circled the table, bringing Jerry Z into view. Steps notched into the sides of his light blond hair. A wispy beard clutching his chin. Pebble eyes set in a wide, boyish face. At the moment those eyes were fixed on the elderly women, no doubt considering the pearl necklaces resting against the folds of their blouses.

Evan sat before him.

"You Jean Pate?" Jerry Z pronounced the first name hard, like "Gene."

"Yes. Do you have the necklace?"

"You a cop?"

"No, I'm not a—"

"You hafta say, you know. Or it's like entrapment or some shit."

"No. I'm not a cop. May I see the necklace?"

Jerry Z hunched forward, his massy chest pressing into his picked-over tray and bringing forth a waft of body odor that smelled vaguely like barbecue potato chips. He shot a glance over his shoulder, taking in a couple holding hands at the booth over by the stairs. They looked like models. Or fitness trainers. Or television doctors.

"I always forget how many faggots there are all over WeHo," Jerry Z said. "Always checking out my shit."

Evan noted his gel-sticky hair, the unwashed scent, the 1989-vintage shaved lines in his hair. "I'm sure they find you irresistible."

Jerry Z reached into his sweat-suit jacket, retrieved a black velvet bag, and spilled its contents onto the table next to his tray. A jumble of rings, several necklaces, solid-gold bracelets hinged open like horseshoes.

A diamond earring with dried blood on the post.

Evan imagined Jerry Z sidling up behind a woman and tearing her earrings straight through the lobes. He pictured Ida Rosenbaum in her bed, one hand raised self-consciously to block the bruising that had turned the right side of her face into a mottled mess. *I'm an eighty-seven-year-old widow. That's about as unspecial as you can be. And that young man today proved it.* Compared to Ida, Jerry seemed like a different species. A man of his size hitting a woman of hers. Closed-handed. In the face.

Evan set his jaw, reached for the First Commandment: *Assume nothing.*

"Whoa," he said, in his best Jean Pate–from–San Bernardino impersonation. "You're not a fence, are you?"

"What? No." Jerry Z's stubby fingers picked through the jewelry and plucked out Ida's necklace. "I get all my shit legally. Trust me. I procured this particular item myself."

"Where'd you get it?"

Jerry's smile conveyed more menace than joy. "My granny."

Evan reached across the table and lifted the necklace from Jerry's hands.

"Your grandmother was into Victorian marcasite, was she?"

"Yeah, you fucking racist. Or classist. Or whatever the fuck."

Evan turned the glinting amethyst pendant around. An inscription on the back, worn from a thousand touches. TO IDA, I'LL ALWAYS BE HERE BY YOUR HEART.–H.

"And she was named Ida?" Evan said. "Your grandmother?"

Jerry flattened his hands on the table. His face tensed, a fan of crow's-feet bunching his left eye. Trying to figure out how to play it. He swung his Oakley shades from the back of his head to the bridge of his nose. Crossed his arms. Leaned back.

"Fine. Tell me what you wanna hear. My cousin runs a pawn-shop?"

The group of students headed out, two of them arguing vehemently, a girlfriend on tilt. "Well, maybe if you stopped dating your *phone . . .*" The others weighed in, offering support, stoking the fire. The attractive couple by the stairs were tucked into their Quarter Pounders, occupied with chewing. In the reflection of the Oakleys, Evan could see the elderly women behind him lost in conversation.

He pooled Ida's necklace in the palm of his hand. Pocketed it.

"The money," Jerry Z said.

Evan held up a wait-a-sec finger. Then he plucked the straw out of Jerry's orange soda.

"The fuck you think you're doing, bitch?"

Evan folded the straw twice, gripped it so the triangle of bent plastic protruded a quarter inch from between his index and middle fingers.

A makeshift push dagger.

He couldn't risk a fight, not after the concussion. He didn't want to raise his heart rate. He didn't even want to break a sweat. Any action he took would have to be efficient and immediately debilitating.

"Okay," Jerry Z said, leaning in and conveniently bringing his forehead into range. "I been cool about all this. But you're about to find out who I *really* am."

Evan dealt a single quick strike, the edged straw slamming into Jerry Z's forehead.

At first the big man didn't move. He stared at Evan, shock enlarging those pebble eyes. His forehead was split neatly in a five-inch line above the brow, a cracked egg that had yet to seep.

Then the blood came.

A controlled rush into both eyes.

Jerry blinked once, twice, sagging forward. Evan palmed the top of his head and slammed his face into his tray. The plastic muffled the noise, but it was enough to put him out.

Evan rose and set his chair back in place. Heading down the stairs, he removed his phone, changed the settings, added a voice filter, and dialed 911.

"You'll find a man bleeding and unconscious on the second floor of the McDonald's at Sunset and Crescent. He has thousands of dollars of stolen goods in his possession."

As he reached the main floor, commotion erupted upstairs. A manager shouldered past Evan, lunging for the stairs.

Unseen and unnoticed, he stepped out into the cool night breeze.

Walking away, he dug the necklace from his pocket. The pendant spun gently beneath his fist, the cursive words coming clear at intervals: *I'll always be here by your heart.*

What had Max said? That when you love someone, you never move on. They get into your cells, live inside you even when they're gone.

Evan had been trained to remain aggressively alone. To never show vulnerability. To ignore pain. To protect the mission at all costs.

Intimacy, it seemed, required the precise opposite. It required baring yourself to the best and worst that the world could generate. It required living alone in a bedroom filled with old photos and memories long after the warmth and light of a relationship had faded to ash. It required giving someone a marcasite necklace to wear after you're dead.

He thought about Max, broken down by life and the loss of a baby, helpless in the face of his then-wife's suffering. *Everything I tried just made things worse. I would have done anything. You understand? Anything.*

Max had reached a breaking point where he couldn't take any more pain. And Evan had judged him harshly for that. He'd judged him for trying and failing at something that Evan lacked the courage to even attempt.

Closing his hand around the antique necklace, he wondered at the myriad elements that constituted bravery and counted those he was lacking.

The door to 6G floated a half inch above the threshold. Sometime before midnight Evan crouched above the welcome mat and slipped a crisp envelope beneath. The bump within caught a bit of friction, but the package slid through.

He had written nothing on the envelope, and there was no message inside. It was empty save for a piece of jewelry with a lifetime of sentiment attached to it.

He'd cleaned the necklace upstairs with dishwashing liquid and water, removing any oil and sweat residue. The envelope, fresh from the box, contained no fibers or trace DNA. His fingertips were coated with a thin layer of superglue, and he wore latex gloves on top of that. He'd glitched the hallway security camera to ensure that his late-night visit would not be memorialized.

He would have indulged these habits even if he didn't share a building with a perspicacious district attorney who had her eye on him in mostly unflattering fashion. But knowing that Mia was here six floors up made him pay even more meticulous attention to every last ritual.

He had to be perfect.

Especially in light of the impossible task he was going to undertake tomorrow.

Perfect meant invisible, autonomous, without emotion.

He rose and stood a moment in the empty hall.

He was never here. He wasn't even here now. He had no fingerprints, no footprints, no image captured by the eye of the lens overhead.

It was a koan worthy of Jack: If a man moves through the night and no one sees him, does he really exist?

Sometimes even he wondered.

30

Trapped Sweat and Spilled Blood

If you looked at the side of the building, you'd see nothing at all. If you squinted hard, perhaps you'd discern the faintest bulge at the fifth floor, the sandstone façade curving outward.

What you wouldn't detect was the semi-stable folding platform, two feet wide and five feet long, cantilevered out from the ledge of the open bathroom window. You wouldn't see the mechanical bracketry rigged to the mouth of the sill and braced against the wall outside because it was all—the platform, the bracketry—painted the precise color of the sandstone.

Nor would you see the man atop the shooting platform, literally suspended in midair in a supported prone position sixty-four yards above the sidewalk.

He wore a Crye sand-tan pullover combat shirt, matching cargo pants, and a matching pair of Kevlar-and-leather aviator gloves. Cammy paint on his face and wrists, also the shade of a desert dune, further blended him into the backdrop.

For the short time before engagement, Evan Smoak was nothing more than a slight disruption of the visual field, a tiger standing in tall savanna grass.

Spray paint had worked fine on the Remington 700. There was no need for any intricate design, just enough shading to break up the outline of the rifle. To further ensure his invisibility, he used a killFLASH honeycomb, a metallic anti-reflection device clamped over the scope to dampen any glint or glare.

He'd required a vantage into the courtyard of the Three Monkeys Café that didn't exist, a shooting position floating in space. A seemingly unsolvable problem that he had, with a little help from his friends, solved.

His toes hooked over the sill behind him, protruding into the room above the row of urinals. The bathroom door was locked, a cleaning cart positioned in the hall outside, accessorized with a mop tilting from a yellow bucket and a RESTROOM BEING SERVICED A-frame sign. The cart featured a canvas basket nicely sized for carrying industrial laundry loads or a portable sniper hide.

A 607-yard shot from a sixty-four-foot elevation wasn't a hard shot. It wasn't an easy one either. Especially not with a head sporadically swimmy from a concussion.

The built-up Remington had been modified to accommodate a detachable mag that took ten rounds, which were all Evan would require. The rifle was set up on a bipod, the Manners stock resting against his left shoulder. He was so still that he might have been statuary carved into the building itself, a gargoyle with a sniper habit.

Getting the measurements from Trevon in advance was enormously helpful. Evan had already checked the range card taped to the stock, so he knew how much holdover he needed for the distance and how much cosign compensation the downhill angle required. The combination baseline for scope and rifle was zeroed at four hundred yards, and he'd already ascertained his hold for the round he was using, a 168-grain Federal Gold Medal Match. Knowing ahead of time where to hold on the optic meant that there was no need to mess with the scope.

There Alexan Petro was, tucked into his café table in the restaurant courtyard, sipping espresso and talking on his Turing Phone. He sat alone, which seemed only to enhance his status: Important Man Conducting Virtual Business. Five of his bodyguards were spread around the courtyard and restaurant. Nineteen minutes ago Evan had watched them enter, counting them off like cattle headed to the abattoir. Only two of the men inside were visible at the moment.

That would change quickly.

The sixth member of Petro's core team waited outside by the armored Town Cars, leaning against a fender and thumbing at his phone.

But Evan wasn't focused on the bodyguards now. He was focused on Petro.

A handsome man by any standards. That rich mane of silver hair. A certain grace of movement. The overcompensatory noblesse oblige of the newly affluent.

Evan's world narrowed to a circle marked by stadia reticle increments. He felt his vision get loose, verging on blurry, but he squeezed his eyes shut, and when he opened them again, everything he saw obeyed the normal rules of physics. He was a left-eye-dominant shooter, a stroke of luck since the dilated right pupil was harder to coerce into cooperating at the moment.

His earpiece activated on voice command, sparing him the slightest movement. "Dial."

The RoamZone in his cargo pocket complied.

Through the scope he saw Petro pull the Turing Phone away from his cheek to check caller ID. His features set in a show of amusement. He clicked over, and a moment later his voice spoke in Evan's ear. "Hello, boy."

"Petro."

The man's face, magnified in the scope, tightened. "So you found a name. Am I supposed to be scared?"

"Not by that." Evan kept gentle, steady pressure against the comb of the stock and gauged the come-up, adding the superelevation below the horizontal line.

Petro smirked. "Then by what?"

"By the fact that you had Grant Merriweather killed. And a doctor and two nurses. And Lorraine Lennox. And that you tried to take out Max Merriweather."

"You think those names mean something to me?"

"No," Evan said. "I think they mean nothing to you. Or to your men."

A low ticking laugh came across the line and then the purr of that ten-grit voice. "The world, my world, is a much bigger place than you think. Expand your perspective, boy. At least for the few remaining days you have on this earth. My men have done things for me you can't even imagine. I've watched them take people apart piece by piece while keeping the heart beating until the very end. Do you have any idea how much skill that requires?"

"Anything you'd like to say?"

"Before?"

"I mean, any last words?"

Petro's eyes darted around. Then he relaxed back in his seat, smoothed the lapel of his suit, and grinned. "If you expect to scare me, you don't know me at all."

"How about your men? You want to ask them if they're scared?" Evan made a microscopic adjustment, dropping the crosshairs to the spot where Petro's arm met his trunk. The Timney trigger split the pad of Evan's index finger. "At least the five within earshot right now?"

It took a quarter second for the words to clear the Turing Phone's encryption. Another quarter second for Petro to register their meaning. His neck corded, a sheet of muscle as his flesh tightened with panic.

Evan applied 3.5 pounds of trigger pressure, and a crimson rose bloomed on Petro's shoulder. He toppled back in his chair, landing splayed in clear view on the stone of the courtyard.

The platform gave the faintest wobble from the recoil but held firm.

Through the earpiece Evan heard the clatter of the Turing as it struck ground. He cycled the bolt, the expended case spinning in a lazy arc past his temple, and buried the next round in the meat above Petro's left thigh. Petro gave a pained animal howl, bellowing for help.

The next two bullets knocked out the visible bodyguards.

Evan swept the Remington across the restaurant rooftop until he saw the bodyguard standing rigidly before the Town Car, one finger pressed to his earpiece. He found the man's sweaty forehead, badly bruised from its encounter with the bathroom sink. The instant before he squeezed off another round, his vision streaked and then doubled, the glare of the windshield turning into a comet of light.

The shot sailed past the bodyguard's ear, shattering the polished windshield.

The bodyguard turned to stare at the Town Car in disbelief. By the time he tensed to run, Evan had partially regained his focus. He squinted to bring the two images of the bodyguard into one and found the forehead once again. The next round splattered the hood.

Gritting his teeth, Evan rotated to the courtyard again. An ache started up at the back of his head where he'd cracked it on the asphalt.

Pandemonium had erupted in the restaurant, the patrons pouring out. He'd counted on the crowd response, bystanders going one way, bodyguards the other.

Each party ran the pattern as predicted, but to Evan's view they looked like smudges of color. Sweat trickled down his forehead; he armed it away before it could reach his eyes.

Slowing his breaths and trying to fight off his nausea, Evan locked the sights on a single point of entry for the courtyard. From here there were no tricky adjustments; if he could manage to hold position, he'd be able to get it done. As he'd anticipated, Petro's cries drew his remaining men in neat succession, Evan headshotting them in order. The men piled across the courtyard, heaped on top of one another, the last falling across Petro and pinning him to the ground.

Petro's face had turned to a blurry oval. Then it floated apart like a cell dividing. A ghost image of Petro hovered above the man himself, a spirit debating whether to depart. Sweat stung Evan's eyes. He laid the crosshairs on the nose of what he took to be the real Petro, blew out a breath, squeezed off his final round.

And missed.

A spray of chips flew up from the flagstones, shredding Petro's ear. He twisted around and dug at the ground with his finger-nails, trying to worm his way out from beneath the bodies.

Aggravated, Evan reached back to the rope bag on his right thigh and freed a lengthy two-inch-thick hawser rope. It unfurled to the side of the platform, feeding out until the bottom whip-snapped up and then settled to sway a foot above the sidewalk.

Nice to see that even Trevon could make a twelve-inch miscal-culation.

Evan had already set the anchor in the platform, so he simply rolled off the side, leaving the rifle behind as he fell. Cinching the rope between his gloves and the insteps of his boots, he fast-roped down. The sandstone whirred by as he kissed thirty miles per hour, a firehouse-pole slide. The pavement flew up and caught him, a healthy jolt to the ankles and knees, and he flung the gloves from his hands with a single violent shake. They lay on the side-walk, steaming with friction heat.

Roughly a half second had elapsed since he'd un-assed from the platform.

He took an instant for the pavement to stop spinning from the sudden exertion. The headache expanded, a pressure at the temples.

Finish it, he thought. *Then you can rest all you want.*

Despite the steel shanks, warmth rose through the soles of his Original S.W.A.T.s. His hands gleamed white from the latex gloves he'd worn beneath the aviators.

As part of his prep, he'd sliced and restitched his sand-tan com-bat shirt and cargo pants to make them tearaway, and he ripped them off now, a quick snap of his fists that left the fabric pooled on the ground. Beneath he wore a gray V-neck and jeans.

No passersby. No rubberneckers in the cars drifting past. The few people across the street remained distracted by the commo-tion over at the Three Monkeys Café.

Evan dug a Baggie out of the front pocket of his jeans. A wad of moist baby wipes waited inside. He freed a few and swiped at his face, brisk scrubs that cleared the cammy paint.

As he stepped off the curb, crossing the street to the restaurant, he looked like an ordinary pedestrian. His gait was unsteady, so he took great care to even it out.

He entered the side door to the kitchen. After the gunfire it had been abandoned hastily. Plates of lavash basked on the counters beneath heating lamps. Pans remained on the burners, hissing garlic steam. A pot boiled over, sizzling on orange coils. He felt the glare of the overheads in his spinal cord.

As Evan passed through, he turned the oven knobs off.

He emerged onto the main floor. Chairs knocked over, tables shoved clear, a high heel on its side.

Through the French doors, he could see the heap of bodies he'd left. The remains of Petro's men.

Evan unholstered his ARES and stepped into the courtyard. The air felt humid, trapped sweat and spilled blood heated by the midday sun. The nausea swelled. His stomach thought about lurching, but he did not allow it.

Petro faced away, still clawing at the flagstones, trying to pull himself out from beneath the last of his fallen bodyguards. Given the destruction of his right arm, he was making little headway. One of his buffed fingernails had snapped off and lay shimmering on the ground, an ivory curl.

He was moaning repetitively. A fine mist of blood speckled the side of that glorious silver hair.

In Terzian the Terror, Max had thought he was facing one problem. It had led to a second problem in Petro.

Soon there would be no problems.

Evan was close enough now to offset the effects of the concussion. He raised the 1911, thumbed off the safety.

At the click Petro froze.

Then he rolled onto his side, regarding Evan over his shoulder. None of that well-cultivated confidence was on display, not anymore. Above Petro's biceps tattered cashmere fluttered at the edges of the wound. A pair of reading glasses had spilled from his breast pocket and lay shattered on the ground beside him. The bent wire frames lent a small touch of humanity to the gruesome tableau.

At the end Petro was just a man, like so many Evan had walked past on the street or ridden next to on the subway or put in the earth.

The wail of sirens reached him now, still miles out. They both knew that help would not arrive in time.

Petro's face trembled. "Who is Max Merriweather to you?" His voice held something more than fear. Something like outrage.

Evan said, "Someone who needed my help."

Petro stared at him, his forehead twisted in disbelief. Spilled espresso snaked between the flagstones, joining a rivulet of crimson. The dead air smelled of dark roast and iron.

"Who are you to him?" Petro asked.

Evan said, "Nobody."

Petro's dark beard bristled around a wavering mouth. No words emerged.

Evan said, "But now it's over for him."

Petro coughed, and blood speckled his lips. He smiled a wobbly smile that put a twist in Evan's gut.

The sirens notched up, ever louder, ever closer.

Evan sighted on his forehead.

A final round ended the mission.

31

The Whole Story

Evan found Max in the swampy backyard of the Lincoln Heights house, staring at his reflection in a brown puddle. His shoes were muddy, as were his arms up to the elbows. He held a wrench cloaked with slime.

When Evan stepped through the cracked sliding-glass door, Max started and grabbed his chest. "Jesus. Why didn't you knock?"

"I did."

"Oh. I guess I zoned out . . . I don't know, contemplating the human condition."

"In a mud puddle?"

He shrugged. "Where better?"

Evan frowned, conceding the point. His eyes snagged on the wrench. Max followed his gaze to the dripping tool in his hands.

"I figured there was a broken connection down there. Usually the T-joint stubbing up to a sprinkler head."

"But there are no sprinkler heads."

"There used to be," Max said. "See how the ground's mounded

up there?" He pointed with the wrench, but Evan saw only mud and more mud. "So I went in and fixed it."

"For who?"

Max shrugged again. "I figured for once it might be nice to leave a place better than it was when I got there." He looked at his hands, the dirt now cracking across the knuckles. "I don't have a lot of ways to say thanks anymore."

"To Violet?"

"To anyone." When his gaze lifted, Evan was surprised by the dread it held. "What happened?"

"I took care of the other thing," Evan said.

"How?"

Evan pictured Petro lying pinned beneath his bodyguard in the courtyard. That speckling of blood in his silver hair. He hadn't raised an arm against the bullet like so many did.

Instead he'd smiled.

Evan hadn't liked that smile. Had it held something knowing? Or was it merely a final show of pride, a refusal to give in to fear? Maybe it was that simple—he hadn't wanted to give Evan the satisfaction.

Evan said, "They're all gone."

Max took a step back, his shoe plunking in the puddle. It pulled free with a sucking noise. Around them mosquitoes whined and swirled. "Am I safe now?"

Evan hesitated, caught a flash of Petro's dying moment in his mind's eye. He'd asked about Max. What had Evan said? *Now it's over for him.* And then Petro had smiled.

Why the hell had he smiled?

Evan had eliminated Terzian and his crew. Unmasked the laundering ring. Run up the chain of command to the man at the top and left him lifeless on the flagstones of a courtyard beneath a mound of bodyguards.

It was done. Any peripheral players who remained no longer had an operation to plug into. Their leadership was dead, the files blown. They likely had no idea who Max Merriweather was, and even if they did, no incentive remained for them to harm him.

Joey would continue to do her best to match code names from

Grant's books to the bottom feeders in the scheme, but it was time to get the case back into the hands of the authorities, where it belonged.

What was Evan supposed to do? Keep Max holed up in a teardown house indefinitely? Because of a smile?

"Am I safe now?" Max asked again.

Evan's head throbbed and then throbbed some more. "Yes," he said.

"So where . . . where should I go?"

Evan tossed Max the zip drive onto which Joey had copied all of Grant's files. "Hollywood Station. Let them finish what your cousin started."

Max wiped his hands on his jeans and pocketed the zip drive.

Evan said, "You never called me. You never met me. You never saw me. You went to Grant's office alone, and a guy tried to shoot you. You got scared, went underground. That's your story. The *whole* story. Understand?"

Max nodded.

The first thing Evan would do was remove the dried-out contact lens and climb into bed. He'd rest until his head stopped throbbing, the nausea receded, and his vision stopped playing hallucinogenic games with the world. He thought about the row of bottles in his freezer drawer, the world's best vodkas chilled and waiting. Once the symptoms were gone, he'd go with something smooth and nuanced, like CLIX. Shake it so hard that crystals would mist the surface off the pour. A sprig of basil from the living wall. Maybe a stainless-steel martini glass to retain the cold. He wanted the first sip to make his teeth ache.

A nice reward after a long three days' work.

But Petro flashed into Evan's mind once more, interrupting his vodka reverie.

For a dying grin, it had looked awfully smug. As though Petro knew something Evan didn't.

As if he had a secret.

Evan replayed the conversation they'd had, how readily Petro had deployed his braggadocio: *The world, my world, is a much bigger place than you think.*

The Whole Story

Max said, "Would you mind driving me to my truck?"

Evan resisted a temptation to clench his jaw. He wanted to squeeze the bridge of his nose, dig his thumb and forefinger into his eyelids to stave off that incipient headache. He wanted to put a check next to the mission, deliver Max back to his life, and then—for the first time—start his own. A life of his own making.

But yet. That smile.

"I don't want you to go back to your truck just yet," Evan said. "I'll take you to a random street corner and call you a cab."

"I thought you said it was safe."

"It is," Evan said. *But I don't like how a guy smiled right before I shot him. And my paranoia has no limits when it comes to interrupting a long rest and a good drink.*

Was it paranoia? Or was he reluctant to let go? Because once he admitted it was over, then the Nowhere Man was over, too. And without the Nowhere Man, who the hell was Evan Smoak?

Max was squinting at him impatiently.

"We'll destroy your disposable phone, and I'll give you a fresh one," Evan said. "Don't turn it on unless you're in trouble or until you're done talking to the cops. Then call me again. I'll go with you to your truck. And then to your apartment."

"Why? Is this over or not?"

"It's over," Evan said. "But no one ever got killed by being too careful."

32

Awful Shit

Alone in the backseat of the cab halfway to the police station, Max had a change of mind. "Hang on," he told the driver. "Make a U-turn. I need to take a quick detour."

"Your wish is my command," the driver said, spinning the steering wheel with the heel of his hand like he was turning around a big rig.

Twenty minutes later they were coasting up a broad street, palm trees nodding overhead. The block was lined with parked cars.

"Looks like someone's having a party," the driver said.

"Could you slow down, please?"

As they passed the house, Max spotted the catering vans in the driveway and felt a familiar hollowness at his core. "Pull up here on the right," he said. "Up a little farther. A little farther."

The cab crept beside a tall hedge at the neighbor's house. "If I didn't know better," the driver said, "I'd think we were trying to hide."

Awful Shit

Max opened the door, set one foot on the curb. "Would you mind waiting for me?"

"Your dollar, your desire."

Leaving the idling taxi behind, Max eased out from behind the hedge, the Spanish-style mansion edging into view. On either side of the porch, immense concrete pots held artfully spiraled lilies, a tornado of white buds.

The post-funeral reception.

The front edge of dusk muted the sky, making the house lights pop. The drawn front curtains allowed a panoramic view of the expansive front room and the crush of well-wishers it accommodated—cops and cousins and colleagues. Scattered throughout, men and women with coiffed hair and impressive bearings seemed to have their own gravitational fields, drawing whirlpools of beholders. Community leaders, no doubt, like Grant.

Wearing an elegant widow-black dress, Jill was in the thick of it, directing traffic in between fusillades of cheek kisses. Despite her concerns she was managing the event with the family's usual aggressive competence.

The swinging door to the kitchen emitted a steady stream of servers bearing silver trays laden with canapés. Failed actors in white shirts and black vests scurried from the catering vans, hauling Saran Wrapped serving platters, royal chafers, crates of glassware.

Standing among the impeccably trimmed juniper cones, Max suddenly felt quite small. Whatever he'd planned on saying, it wouldn't get said. Not here, not now.

And yet he found himself unwilling to take his eyes off the scene inside. As he scanned the crowded room, he realized he was searching for Violet.

One of the servers hauling food from the van paused en route to the house and caught Max lurking there among the shrubbery. A flash of white teeth. "Hi. Are you with the party?"

Max's T-shirt was rumpled, his jeans worn, and he was three days unshaven. He'd cleaned off his shoes before getting into Evan's car, but smudges of mud remained at the outsoles.

"Yeah," Max said. "But now I'm feeling a little overdressed."

The guy laughed. His tray was spotted with what looked to be endives filled with candied walnuts.

Max said, "I was his cousin."

"I'm sorry. That sucks. What happened to him."

Max nodded.

"Well, come on in. There's certainly plenty to eat." The server hoisted his tray and vanished inside.

To avoid further attention, Max took a few strides to the side of the house. Two years and seven months later, and here he was blending into the vegetation, risking humiliation. Just to catch a glimpse of her.

The sounds carrying over the adobe wall signaled that the reception had already filled the backyard, too. The wall wasn't much taller than Max's head, but he wasn't going to risk peeking over.

As he turned to leave, the hardwood arched gate clicked open and his father walked through, head lowered, extracting a cigarette from his shirt pocket. They almost collided, the Marlboro falling to the gunmetal-gray wood chips carpeting the flower beds.

"Oh, excuse m—" Terry looked up, recognized his son, and froze. "Max. I was just . . ." His hands circled as if to conjure up a better excuse. "Sneaking a smoke." He patted the air. "I know, I know. I'm too old, they'll kill me, lung cancer and blood clots. I just have the occasional stick. When I'm . . . upset."

His expression slackened for an instant, and Max saw the grief he'd been holding in. His father had always loved being Uncle Terry to Grant. It was as though the image of himself he saw reflected back in Grant's eyes was better than what he'd been expecting.

Until Violet, Max had never gotten it. How you could like yourself better just because someone else did. With her, for a brief time, he'd seen his own promise and potential. Even his own deep-buried flaws and vulnerabilities had been teased to the surface and warmed by the light of her gaze until he understood that maybe they weren't so unique, so shameful. They were just other pieces of himself that he had a shot at accepting because, after all, she had.

He hoped he'd done all that for her, too.

Before.

Max crouched to pick up the fallen cigarette, and as he handed it back, he saw that his father's eyes were rimmed red. They stayed that way after he cried, all the next day. Max remembered from his childhood—mornings after his mom's birthday, their wedding anniversary. He wondered what Grant's death had loosed in Terry. Another life cut short, another truncated family member. It had to have set the tectonic plates shifting inside him, rupturing along old fault lines. It struck Max that he'd been too goddamned scared these past days to notice that it had done the same to him.

"Thanks, son." Terry gave him an awkward pat on his shoulder, and Max smelled beer on his breath. "Why—" He halted.

Max finished the thought for him: "Why am I here?"

"Goddamn it, can't I say anything without . . ." Terry tucked the cigarette back into his pocket. "Do we really have to do this again? Here?"

"I'm not doing anything, Dad. Except standing here."

A sudden flare of anger. "I did my best, okay? I did what your mother would've wanted me to. And maybe if you had a kid of your own, you'd understand how hard it is, that you can't be perfect no matter how much you try."

The words echoed between them. *Maybe if you had a kid of your own.*

Terry shoved the heel of his hand to his forehead, eyes wrinkled shut with dismay. "Oh, God. I didn't mean it like that. I swear I didn't. Christ, I'm sorry. I can't say anything without feeling like an asshole. Look, I didn't mean you shouldn't be here. I just meant you're not dressed for it. That's all."

"I didn't know the reception was today. I was coming to . . ." Max paused. He'd sensed why he was coming but hadn't considered it head-on. It sounded so foolish now.

Through the open gate, he could see clutches of people around the infinity pool. Tealights floated in the aqua water on origami rafts, and paper lanterns had been strung along the pergola. Elegantly dressed women sipped chardonnay from voluminous wineglasses probably suited to the varietal. A string quartet fronted a bank of roses by the greenhouse, trickling notes across the yard with muted reverence.

It was all so ridiculous. Not the reception, but Max's being here beholding it.

And then he spotted Michelle. She was sitting on the back end of the diving board, her dress shoes off, rubbing her feet. They got sore when you were pregnant—he remembered that from Violet. It took a toll, making a human.

Seeing his niece sitting quietly amid all the movement, Max felt a stab of pride in knowing that he had kept her safe. He had kept them all safe, and there was a private kind of honor in that.

He looked back at his father, the answer suddenly clear. "I came to tell them."

Terry's eyebrows hoisted. They were fuller than Max remembered, a few rebellious strands twisting out. His father's rugged, handsome face was just starting to transform into that of an old man. Max felt the awareness like a fresh cut. The years were pouring through his fingers, and he couldn't do anything but watch.

"Tell who?" Terry said.

"I don't know. Jill, the cousins, Nona." *You.*

"Tell them what?"

"That what happened to Grant wasn't my fault," Max said. "That *he* pulled *me* into the mess, not vice versa, and I kept it away from the family to protect you. All of you. And I did. I protected them."

"How?"

Max looked through the gate again, saw his grandmother sitting on a cushioned deck chair in a dour funeral dress, various grandkids playing at her elbow. The purse in her lap looked like a bowling bag. Life in ordinary motion.

Max shook his head. "Never mind."

"Grant's business?" Terry said. "The stuff he uncovered that got him killed? You cleaned it up?"

"With a lotta help. But yeah."

Terry looked into the backyard. "And you were gonna tell the family. But?"

"I don't want to now."

"Why?"

"I don't know." Max started to walk back to the taxi, his dirty shoes crunching on the designer wood chips.

"Son?"

Max turned.

Terry tugged at his mouth. "I'm proud of you."

Max swallowed and then swallowed again, something simmering inside him, rising to the brink, threatening to spill. "I don't need you to be proud of me *now*."

Quickening his pace, he weaved through the juniper cones, stepping onto the front walk.

And coming face-to-face with Violet.

She wore a black dress with long sleeves—always long sleeves—and she looked a bit wobbly in wedge heels. Her mouth was ajar, her eyes flared with surprise, and Max thought if she came at him hard after his run-in with his dad that he might just come apart altogether.

"Max." She stepped back, away. "I . . . I guess you have more of a right to be here than I do."

"I suppose that's one perspective."

"Oh. You weren't . . ." She couldn't quite get out the word "invited."

"You know how it is, Vi."

"Are you out of danger? Or whatever?"

He nodded.

"So you're good?"

She'd always been able to read him at a glance, and right now especially he felt like he had no control over what his face might show. He didn't know where to look. Had her eyes always held that much yellow? A tendril of hair twisted down her cheek, touching the edge of her mouth. Her perfume—orange blossom and vanilla—brought him right back to that casino floor, sitting next to her for the first time.

Can I sit here?

I'm having an unlucky run. If you're smart, you'll get as far away from me as possible.

Don't worry. I'm not that smart.

He forced his gaze downward. "I'm good," he said. "You doing okay?"

She laughed. "I live in South Pasadena. I'm working for my parents. *My* parents. Overseeing housing units. And I'm doing my best making sure the tenants have what they need, you know? Making sure we're good landlords to them, at least better than my dad would be, but it's still . . . I'm in this job I hate in a life I hate and I swore I'd never be here again and it's all my fault and all my own choices and here I am wondering how the hell it happened." She wiped at her eyes. "So no. If we're being honest, I'm not very good."

"I'm sorry." The same two stupid words, but he said them with everything he had, and she must have sensed it in his voice, because for the first time it seemed she actually heard them.

For a few moments, they stood in the breeze, not knowing what to do. It was no longer dusk; night had happened all at once, the gathering inside vivid behind plate-glass windows and the two of them out here, invisible.

"It got so awful," she said. "Between us. And we said awful shit. But I would've gone through it with you. I would've been awful *with* you. Until we weren't."

She was crying freely now, and there was no anger, only pain laid bare, and whether that was from the rawness of Grant's death or the moment, he didn't know.

"I understand," she said. "Believe me, I understand. Maybe that's why I'm so angry."

"Understand?" Max said. "Understand what?"

"That I was . . ."—she had to fight out the word—"*damaged*." Her voice was constricted, squeezed tight with grief. "You didn't want to be with me because I couldn't have kids anymore."

The words cut through him like a scythe.

"What?" He fought to catch his breath. "No. No, no, never. Violet—*never*."

"Why, then?" she said. "Why?"

He opened his mouth. It clutched, but nothing came out.

He couldn't tell her.

He could *never* tell her.

Awful Shit

She studied him an instant through glassy eyes and then turned and hurried away, arms crossed around her stomach to hold herself together.

He stayed rooted to the walkway, the faint melody of conversation and string instruments reaching him on the wind.

At some point he told his legs to carry him back to the taxi, and they obeyed. And then somehow he was in the backseat, bathed in the scent of the pine Little Tree freshener spinning from the rearview.

The cabdriver tilted the mirror and for once didn't offer a smirky crack. "Where would you like to go?" he asked.

Max considered the question in a larger context and realized he had no fucking idea. He had to clear his throat twice before he could speak.

"Hollywood police station, please."

33

Reduced

By the time Evan went to his safe house, traded out the Chevy Malibu for his Ford F-150, fought through clotted traffic on the 405, and reached Castle Heights, he was fit only for sleep and vodka.

He turned in to the porte cochere more briskly than usual and waved off the valet, who feigned annoyance as usual. It occurred to Evan that this was the closest thing to a domestic ritual he had.

The run-flat self-sealing tires screeched on the ramp as he veered down, powerful headlights raking the subterranean parking lot before landing on Mia Hall standing directly between the concrete pillars that defined his spot. Her glare was unrelenting, her arms crossed.

He was bent into the wheel from hitting the brakes abruptly, the grille steaming five feet from her, but she hadn't budged an inch. She hadn't even flinched. Leaving the truck running, he climbed out. Walked around. Stood in front of her. The dank space smelled acrid from the brake pads. Her mouth was set, her full lips compressed into a thin line of displeasure.

"Something on your mind?" he asked.

"His *head* was split open," Mia said.

"Who?"

"Don't fuck with me, Evan." She jutted her jaw forward, stared over his shoulder at nothing, took a deep breath. "The guy who robbed Ida. He was terrified, confessed to everything. His forehead, split like a melon. He had bruises all down one cheek."

"As I recall, so did Ida."

"Eye for an eye? The law doesn't work that way."

"No," Evan said. "The law shouldn't. It can't."

She was radiating more than anger, something like thundering moral authority, and he understood how defendants must feel in the face of her righteousness—undressed, despite their courthouse suits. "I told you I was handling this," she said. "I told you to stay away from it. And you *lied* to me."

Her expression loosened for only a split second, but he saw what was beneath, how badly he'd hurt her. The betrayal she felt.

He wanted to tell her that he hadn't lied, not precisely, but he couldn't assemble the words. He didn't have the faintest notion how to navigate a situation like this, but he did know that a semantic argument right now would be a colossal misfire.

And besides, he'd missed his opening.

"What is it you do, exactly?" What Mia's voice lost in volume, it gained in sharpness.

"I help people," Evan said. *Or at least I used to.*

"What does that mean?"

"I protect them."

"Without limitation?" She grew frustrated at his silence. "You'll go anywhere? Do anything?"

The garage whirled a little, and he rocked to regain his balance but recovered before she noticed. "Yes."

"When you split Jerry Zabala's head open, how were you *protecting* Ida Rosenbaum?"

"Allegedly."

In the headlights her eyes had turned impenetrable, wishing-fountain dimes throwing back a midday glare. "Excuse me?"

"When I *allegedly* split Jerry Zabala's head open."

"Answer the fucking question, Evan."

He took note of his core temperature, a faint rise in heat through his torso. A steady exhale brought it down to normal. He observed her as if she were someone he was seeing for the first time. Nostrils flaring with each inhalation. Faint flush through her cheeks. Leaning forward onto the balls of her feet. An aggressive bearing all around.

To de-escalate, Evan answered in a dead-calm voice, hoping Mia would subconsciously match it. "For five hundred dollars, Jerry Zabala put Ida Rosenbaum in the hospital. But the damage was worse than that. She was *reduced*. Treated as if she were invisible. No feelings of her own. No power over her own body. No dignity. That's how she feels right now." He pictured Ida's frail frame, bones beneath the bedsheets, bolstered by pillows. That age-curled hand rising to cover her bruises, hiding her eyes behind a washcloth. *I'm an eighty-seven-year-old widow. That's about as unspecial as you can be.* Evan met Mia's glare. "She deserves to be shown that she matters."

"A lot of people deserve a lot of things," Mia said. "That doesn't mean you're allowed to just go out there and get it for them."

"Maybe if you were in her situation, you'd feel differently."

"Right. Because when my husband died of pancreatic cancer and I had to pick up the pieces for myself and my three-year-old, I felt empowered as hell."

"We're not talking about cancer," Evan said. "We're talking about willful, considered choices that people make to tear others down. And what should be done about it."

"You mean what *you* should do about it?"

He shrugged. "Not anymore."

"What's that mean?"

He said, "I don't know."

They considered each other in the headlight's glare, the engine growling behind them like something feral.

"How could you? Hold those views? Do those things?"

"You're a district attorney," Evan said. "You don't know what it feels like. To have no recourse. No power. Nothing."

"And you do?"

Reduced

He pictured himself at twelve years old, the scrawniest of the boys at Pride House Group Home. How he'd slept crammed on the floor between bunk beds, every day starting with kids sliding out of the sheets, pounding him into the floor. Charles Van Sciver, two years older and one head taller, used to flick mac and cheese across the table onto Evan's shirt, his face, daring him to respond. Even now in the garage, Evan could feel the heat of the asphalt against his palms and knees that day behind the handball courts. Drooling blood onto the cracked black tar, his head still ringing from a backhand. Squeezing his eyes against the bright-lit pain, blinking himself into a reality that was hardly any better.

He locked down his face, his body. Total control, no nonverbal cues, the perfect stillness of an Orphan. The truck grumbled at his back. He gave Mia no answer.

"You interfered with a criminal case," she said. "*My* case. And you committed criminal actions of your own." She stepped forward, tilted her head, studied him. The flush on her cheeks remained, her anger on a low boil. "I've never seen you before," she said. "I've never seen who you really are."

He said, "I hope you never have to."

He'd spoken softly, his words sincere. He had already saved her and Peter once before, but she had no idea how far he would go if he had to. She took his words entirely the wrong way. As a threat.

He saw something in her eyes that horrified him.

Fear.

She drew back her head. The high beams bleached the fringe of her lush, wavy hair. She squinted, collected herself. "You're a thug," she said. "If you mess with one of my cases again, I will take you down."

After her footsteps faded away, he stood for a time there between the pillars. The headlights spilled over his shoulders, silhouetting his shadow on the concrete wall. He stared at it.

It stared back.

34

Nightmare Scenario

As the taxi pulled away, Max lumbered toward the police station at the corner of De Longpre and Wilcox. The low-slung building, concrete and brick, suffered from a paucity of windows. Like so much else within the cash-strapped L.A. city borders, it was losing a war of attrition, too many weeks grinding by with not enough funds. Chewing gum spackled the Hollywood stars embedded in the pavement. Sun-baked plants crumbled in the dirt beds lining the entrance. The bricks, faded and chipped.

A bail-bonds shop across the street perkily advertised 2 percent down, the glitzy yellow sign a lighthouse beacon shining through the night, drawing the fallen like moths. This was real Hollywood, the tattered velvet underbelly, a spiderweb stretched wide and hungry to catch overreaching souls in free fall.

Max's hand, shoved into his pocket, made a fist around the zip drive loaded with Grant's files. His palm was sweaty.

Taking a deep breath, he walked up the ramp, yanked open the weighty glass door, and stepped into a trickle of air from a failing fan. Unhappy folks filled the molded plastic seats. The desk officer didn't look up from her iPhone. She was frowning down at it, tapping away with one finger. "Your complaint?" Her voice emerged tinny from a speak-through grille punched through the bullet-resistant glass screen.

"My cousin, Grant Merriweather, was a forensic accountant working on a case for someone at your station. I have information about the investigation." Max's mouth felt dry, the words rough and raspy on the way out. "He was murdered last week."

At this she looked up.

She dropped her phone on the blotter and pushed back in her rolling chair, coasting to the left side of the horseshoe desk. Plucking up a landline, she poked at buttons with the end of a pencil and had a brief conversation. Then she called over to him. "Max Merriweather?"

"That's right," he said, surprised. "That's me."

She finished the conversation and rolled back over. "Please have a seat, Mr. Merriweather. The detectives working the case are on their way."

Max settled in between a dozing homeless man and a young woman with a ragged cable sweater and a black eye. A water stain marred the ceiling. Beyond the security glass, officers shuttled victims, witnesses, and suspects between desks and rooms. The whole place felt drenched in exhaustion and despair, the everyday aftermath of lives that had collided with other lives, or with vehicles, or with bullets. And yet Max felt a swell of gratitude that he was here, another anonymous citizen with a problem that could—at last—be handled by the proper authorities. The Nowhere Man had succeeded in delivering him out of a nightmare scenario.

What had he told Max? *Figure out what you want to do with your life when we get it back for you.* Max was finally seeing through his promise to Grant, delivering the cooked accounting books that would dismantle the remnants of the money-laundering operation that had cost his cousin his life. He could make this the first step on the long road back.

On the wall above the desk officer's head, LAPD's logo was stenciled in dark print: TO PROTECT AND SERVE.

Max leaned back in the chair and closed his eyes, the snore of the man beside him as regular as a metronome.

For the first time in five days, he felt his muscles unclench.

CLIX vodka's name, derived from Roman numerals, represents the 159 times it has been distilled. The initial batch consisted of only two thousand bottles, each a numbered crystal decanter with a stopper.

Evan had liberated his from the handmade burlwood case so it could take its place in his freezer drawer. He stared down longingly at it now, about to reach for it.

He hesitated, a chill mist gusting up at him.

Again he pictured Petro's dying moment in the courtyard of the café. Pinned beneath a fallen body, his lips curled faintly with amusement.

What did he know that Evan didn't?

Sipping a single glass of vodka would barely dull his senses. But still. Once Max was done with the cops, Evan had promised to accompany him to his truck and his apartment to ensure that all was quiet on the Western Front. If he was a half percent loose from alcohol, it was a half percent too much.

The Second Commandment was also the most onerous.

Giving his concussion an alcohol overlay, as tempting as it was, seemed not the wisest choice. Booze would exacerbate the symptoms. So would pretty much everything else. The only thing that had ever helped crisp his focus for a few minutes was an injection of epinephrine, but the synthetic adrenaline would prevent him from resting, so he didn't want to go that way either.

He sighed, shooting the CLIX decanter a parting look. "It's not you," he said. "It's me."

Grabbing an ice cube, he padded across the great room, giving the heavy bag a spin kick for good measure. Down the hall, into the bathroom, through the shower wall to the Vault. An aloe vera plant resided atop a bed of cobalt glass pebbles in a bowl by his mouse pad. The size and shape of a pinecone, it—she—was his sole companion. Vera II. He nested the ice cube in her glass bowl and gave her a pat on the spikes.

Back into the bathroom. He peeled off his shirt, stripped off his pants and boxer briefs, and regarded himself in the harsh LED lighting. The claw marks on his chest had reddened, the first flush of an infection. He had a healthy bruise on his left thigh—also from the pit bull–mastiff?—and a splotchy contusion over his right kidney that he couldn't match to a specific blow. Broken capillaries mottled his collarbone, probably from grappling with Raffi on the floor of the deserted TV station. The back of his head was tender and swollen, and his brain still felt like it had been pressed into a belt sander.

He slid the specialized contact lens out of his right eye and was dismayed to see that the pupil hadn't constricted in the least. It stared back at him vacantly, a well-placed bullet hole. He flicked the contact into the trash and irrigated with hydrating drops.

From beneath the sink, he retrieved an olive-drab pack designed to SEAL team medic specs and dug through the packages—ACE bandages, field dressing, morphine vials—until he found the alcohol pads. He swabbed at the puffy skin around the claw marks, ignoring the sting. Then he nudged the glass shower door aside once more on its barn-door track and loosed the nozzle until steam filled the stall.

He exhaled deeply and evenly, felt his shoulders sink, his head tug forward with exhaustion.

He was just stepping in when his RoamZone rang.

He hesitated, annoyed.

Then backed out, wormed the phone from his pant pocket, and checked caller ID. He clicked to answer, but before he could speak, Joey's voice flew at him in an excited rush.

"Guess what?"

Evan said, "You've amended your position on the capitalization of 'kay' in text messages?"

"No. Lowercase 'kay' is still an atrocity. But this is *almost* as important. Are you ready?"

He stood naked in the bathroom, the blue-purple splotches on his skin drawing his eye in the mirror. "Bated breath."

"So Grant's files? I've been whaling away at them since, like, forever o'clock, right? And then I noticed something super uncopacetic."

205

The shower was still running, the steam beckoning. Evan couldn't wait to get his battered body to the tiled bench inside and sprawl out as if he were in a Muscovite *banya*. "Which was?"

"Well, it occurred to me—'cuz I'm a friggin' genius—to check the memory. It shows four gigs on the thumb drive, but all of Grant's files only add up to a little more than three gigs."

This time he failed to keep impatience from his voice. "Which means?"

"Dude! Hidden file! C'mon, X. So I right-clicked and ran as administrator to look for the removable file. Then I typed in 'attrib-s-h-r /s /d' and wa-la—the hidden files all came visible."

Dread flickered to life, augmenting the throbbing at his temples. He sensed that the thread of this discovery would somehow lead back to that mysterious smile Petro had summoned when Evan had told him it was over now for Max.

In killing Petro he thought he'd cut the head off the snake.

Yet what if he wasn't fighting a snake at all?

But a hydra.

Sever one head and two more grow.

His voice sounded tight even to his own ears. "What'd you find, Joey?"

"More wire transfers, more bank accounts. And a key to the code names for more low-level scumbuckets Petro had in place. The dirty management at his bank and the workers at the front companies—even the bagmen who courier the cash back and forth from the dogfights."

"Okay," he said cautiously, still trying to slow the thrum of his heartbeat. "Good work. We can get all that stuff to the cops."

"Yeah," she said. "About *that* . . ."

He reached into the stall and turned off the shower, a growing void hollowing out his insides. The sudden silence was unsettling. "*What*, Joey?"

"Two of the names who took payoffs? Ignacio Nuñez and Paul Brust? Are dirty cops. Looks like Petro flipped them nine weeks ago, just before Grant's investigation started. And guess where they work?"

Already Evan was yanking on his pants, flinging his shirt over his head, his feet slipping on the shower mat, sending the bandage rolls spinning. He fought the phone back to his face in time to hear her say, "Hollywood Station."

Max drifted through the Morongo Casino, his head delightfully swimmy from a few beers. An orchestral version of "Bad to the Bone" piped through the speakers, accompanied by the clang and din of slot machines. Carnival chaos reigned all around—spinning cherries, flashing coins dumping into payout trays, balls pinging around roulette wheels.

Max cradled a brimming bucket of quarters to his chest, each step jarring a few free.

Up ahead Violet occupied her same mythical stool, but this time she faced away, a strand of silken black hair wound around her finger. Her sandals lay on the floor where she'd kicked free of them, one slender bare foot resting on the base of the stool beside her, the stool that was his to occupy.

He drifted up behind her and said, "Can I sit here?"

She didn't turn even now, facing rigidly away, and he felt an up-tick in his chest, tendrils of fear winding themselves through his ribs.

"If you're smart," she said, "you'll get as far away from me as possible."

Slowly she turned, bloodred lips pronounced against alabaster skin, her eyes dark and impenetrable. She wore a white blouse, gauzy and loose, and as he looked on in horror, crimson began to seep through the fabric above her wrists, spreading up her arms.

"I'm sorry I disappointed you," she said.

Max came awake with a jolt at the hand shaking his shoulder. Coiled in the plastic molded chair, he took a moment to get his bearings.

Hollywood Community Police Station. Lobby. Two faces leaning in over him, one white, one brown—officers wearing slacks and white button-ups with suspenders, badges dangling around their necks.

Max pressed himself upright and ground at his eye with the heel of his hand. "Sorry," he said. "Must've drifted off."

The homeless man and the young woman with the black eye were gone, replaced by a few other ragged folks spread among the chairs, looking at him.

The taller of the two men straightened up, firming his LAPD baseball cap on his head. "Max Merriweather? I'm Detective Nuñez, and this is Detective Brust. You said you had some evidence in your cousin's case?"

"Yeah, I do." Max dug the zip drive from his pocket and wagged it proudly between thumb and forefinger.

Their smiles flashed in concert, as if someone had flipped a switch. Brust turned and nodded at the desk officer, who hit the button to buzz open the security door.

"Excellent, Mr. Merriweather," Detective Nuñez said. "Why don't you follow us back right this way?"

35

Into the Lion's Mouth

Evan rocketed up Sunset Boulevard in his reinforced Ford F-150, bulling sports cars out of his way. His latex-gloved hands alternated between gripping the steering wheel and wiring an electric cap and detonator into the Nokia in his lap. Because they published their circuits in their manuals, Nokias made for quick and easy receiver phones.

Miraculously, he managed to prep the bang while not T-boning any Porsches—and he got across the city in nineteen minutes flat.

Despite all that, he feared he was already too late.

Having crushed Max's last burner phone and ordered him to preserve the new one until after his meeting with the cops, he had no way to warn Max that he'd delivered him into the lion's mouth.

Which meant he had to intercept him.

He was going to raid a police station.

He'd have none of the benefits that generally gave him an operational advantage—no advance scouting of the target location, no analysis of the building's blueprints, no disabling of security equipment.

He'd like his odds a lot better if he wasn't largely making up the plan as he went along.

He'd been caught flat-footed when the second problem, Petro, had led to a third problem.

It was becoming a pattern.

Evan whipped into a parking space a block away and jogged for the police station, winding an ACE bandage around his head. Feigning injury was the only way he could thwart surveillance and mask himself without drawing suspicion—or drawing fire.

Once his face was sufficiently mummified, he tucked the wrap in the back and affected a fragile, stumbling walk. He peered out through the slit in the bandages, noting the security cameras positioned at intervals around the building. Then he hovered his hands over his cheeks as if he were in great pain. Given his perennial headache, it wasn't a terrible stretch.

He hesitated at the side of the station.

He'd carried out his share of improbable missions. But even for the Nowhere Man, this was a bit much.

He ran through the few contingencies he'd anticipated, the few supplies he'd brought. He didn't have a gun because he'd be unable to smuggle it past the metal detectors. He'd have to get it done with the hastily rigged flashbang in his pocket, a wad of medical gauze pads in a Baggie, and more luck than he liked to count on. A wing and a prayer and not much more.

Last chance to back out.

His own words from the garage echoed in his head like a bad memory: *I protect them.*

Without limitation? Mia had asked. *You'll go anywhere? Do anything?*

Yes, he'd replied, like a virtue-drunk imbecile.

He'd made his pledge—to Max, to Mia, to himself. Now he had to back it up.

If he still had time.

Staggering forward, he leaned against a dumpster and doubled over in ostensible agony. He used the pretense of gripping the side to drop the flashbang in. The duct-taped package—Nokia and grenade—struck the inside of the metal box with a hollow clang, signaling that the dumpster was empty. When the time came, that would help the amplification.

Nearing the entrance, he took a series of rapid breaths, his best impromptu simulation of hyperventilating. He wanted his breathing to sound fast and panicked when he entered. It sent his lightheadedness into overdrive, and he pulled back a bit, careful not to overdo it and trigger his other symptoms.

He moved through the door, shuffled to the desk officer. "Officer, I'm . . . I'm—" He cut off, bending at the waist, floating his palms trembling again above his bandage-wrapped face.

The desk officer found her feet, leaning toward the bullet-resistant screen. "What? What happened?"

"My girlfriend threw burning water on my face. She lost her . . . *fuck* . . . lost her *fucking mind*—"

"Have you sought medical attention?"

"Not yet. Her daughter's still in the house with her—and *fuck*, ow, ow . . ."

"Sir. *Sir!* I need you to calm down."

He shuddered and straightened up, leaning against the screen. The bandages shielded his eyes, which let him peer around her without seeming too obvious. He was hoping for an open record log or a whiteboard showing which cops were occupying which interrogation rooms. But there was nothing in plain sight. The information probably resided on her computer, and there'd be no getting in there.

Evan said, "I'm scared for her daughter, and before I go to the ER, I have to—"

"I understand. I'll have someone speak to you immediately."

"Thank you." He let his shoulders tremble as if he were fighting off sobs. "Thank God."

The desk officer called across into the bullpen, and a weary-looking detective rose, his rumpled shirt spotted with a coffee stain. He slapped down a file on his desk and blew out a breath that lifted his scraggly bangs. "Okay," he said. "I'll take it."

A grating buzz sounded, and the security door clicked open.

Evan placed his RoamZone in a red plastic basket and stepped through the metal detector.

It did not alert.

Gathering his phone, he entered the inner sanctum.

Max sat down at the table and folded his hands on the surface. Brust and Nuñez kept their feet. Nuñez crossed his arms and shouldered against the rear wall while Brust set his knuckles on the table and leaned in. The thumb drive rested between him and Max like an avant-garde centerpiece.

"We're so glad you came in," Brust said.

Nuñez chimed in from the back. "Really happy to see you."

"You're a solid citizen—"

"—who was put in a terrible position. We understand that."

Max cleared his throat. "You were working with my cousin?"

"Yes," Nuñez said. "Very smart guy. Very capable." He scratched his cheek. His fingernail was polished, his cheeks shiny from a close shave. He grinned, but the skin around his eyes did not wrinkle in the least.

Max shifted in the chair. Cleared his throat. "Yeah, he was. Grant was good."

Brust placed his forefinger on the thumb drive as if it were a poker chip he was considering adding to the pot. "Do you know what this is? I mean, have you looked at what's on here?"

"Yeah." Max's unease grew, but he heard himself still talking. "They look like spreadsheets. Real and fake." He suddenly felt detached from the situation, as if he were floating above the table looking down at himself answering the questions like a good little boy. "Some kind of money-laundering operation, from what I could tell."

"Ah," Brust said, the single note holding disappointment.

"That's too bad," Nuñez agreed.

"Has anyone else seen this?" Brust asked. "I mean, did you share your cousin's work with anyone?"

"No," Max said, shaking his head. "Just me. I went to Grant's office, and some guy shot at me, so I got scared and I went into hiding." Sweat trickled down his neck, burrowed beneath his collar. Something was wrong, but he couldn't put his finger on it. And yet the conversation kept proceeding, and he felt bizarrely incapable of stopping it. "Look, is there . . . ? I mean, is something wrong?"

Those automated smiles once more. "No," Brust said. "Everything's finally right. You did great. You did great bringing this here to us."

He slid the thumb drive off the table and tossed it to his partner.

"Where did you say you went?" Nuñez asked, coming off the wall to pocket the drive. "When you were hiding?"

Max looked over at the bullet security camera wired into the corner of the ceiling. In the curved black lens, he caught a distorted fish-eye reflection of the room—Nuñez's broad shoulders stretched to Olympian proportions; Brust looming over the desk, his torso swirled; and Max in the center, shrunken and diminutive.

His gaze caught on the sticker adhered to the camera's side: IronKlad Kam. The same equipment had been installed in the hall outside Grant's office, an unsettling coincidence. And something was different. When he noticed what, he felt the awareness as a chill tightening his flesh, making his scalp crawl.

No glowing red dot to show it was recording.

Which meant that Brust and Nuñez had turned it off.

What reason would they have to be in here with him and not want to be recorded?

"Is there . . . ?" Max's voice went hoarse, and he had to start over. "Is there someone else I could talk to? Another cop?"

"Oh, no," Brust said. "I think it's best we keep this discussion between these four walls."

Nuñez's eyes were shaded by the brim of his baseball cap. "All nice and soundproof."

Brust keyed to Max's gaze, traced it to the security camera. "Ah," he said. "All these budget shortfalls have us operating on a shoestring."

Nuñez again. "Sometimes we have to turn off the cameras. You know, to save electricity."

The words were pleasantly delivered, without a trace of menace. Max was having trouble processing them. Was he reading into some dark intent? Was this all in his head?

Nuñez fished a digital recorder from his pen-laden shirt pocket. He half turned, shielding Max's view with a muscular shoulder, and spoke into the microphone softly.

"Wait," Max said. "What are you saying?" He looked at Brust. "What is he saying?"

Nuñez's voice carried to him then. "—can be used against you in a court of law."

"Guys," Max said. "What's—"

"*Shit!*" Nuñez shouted so abruptly that Max jerked back in his chair. "Oh, shit—grab him, he's—" He fumbled the recorder in his hands purposefully and then clicked it off. Immediately he was as calm as before. He tucked the recorder back into his shirt pocket.

Nuñez and Brust looked at Max silently. Expressionless.

Max had broken out in a full sweat. He stared at the two faces, but they gave nothing away.

And then Brust set his foot on the chair across from Max and hiked up his pant leg. Strapped to his ankle was a banged-up, nickel-plated .22. He plucked the pistol from the holster and set it on the table between them.

"What . . . what's that?" Max asked.

"Oh, that?" Once again Brust gave with the grin. And once again Nuñez mirrored it. "That one's yours."

The bullpen was bustling, abuzz with overlapping conversations, most of them unpleasant. Perched on a hard wooden chair to the side of the detective's desk, Evan made sure that each breath sounded labored, pushed through increasing pain.

The detective—O'Malley by his nameplate—looked exhausted, dark bags beneath his eyes. He wore sweat-matted brown curls in no discernible style and was slender to the point of frail. Lower body weight would prove useful.

His security key card was in full view, clipped to his belt, but his holster was empty. Evan guessed O'Malley had either locked his weapon in the drawer or secured it in the gun safe before he'd entered the chaos of the bullpen.

His desk was one of four currently occupied in the immediate area, the other cops conducting similar interviews, keying in similar reports. A drug-animated prostitute waved his arms around, using a high-pitched voice and noodle arms to illustrate his story. "—thought you were my brother-in-law when I approached the vehicle, uh-huh, that's right. It was all a big mix-up, sweetie pie."

The other cops burrowed further into their desks, trying to focus. That was helpful.

A corridor across the bullpen, guarded by a key-card-protected security door, led back to what Evan guessed were the interrogation rooms. That's where Nuñez and Brust would have taken Max. They'd need privacy to talk to him. And to do whatever else they needed to do.

O'Malley slurped at his coffee and reviewed the monitor onto which he'd begun to input the complaint. "Okay, so surname 'Case,' first name 'Justin.' Is that right, sir?"

"Yes."

A few desks over, the prostitute grew increasingly agitated. "Bitch, puh-*lease*! I'm a upstanding member of this mothafucking community!"

Evan set his RoamZone on his knee. Then he dug the Baggie from his pocket, rested it on his thigh just out of O'Malley's line of sight. He took a deep breath, held it, and cracked the zippered seal. Given the state of his brain, the last thing he needed was a whiff of this stuff.

The cop at the adjacent desk was no more than five feet away, but his face stayed down as he chicken-pecked at the keyboard with two fingers, his brow furrowed from the effort. The faintest turn of his head and he'd have Evan dead to rights.

O'Malley squinted at the monitor. Taped to the top was a frayed photo of a dachshund wearing a Spider-Man knit sweater. No wedding ring. He rubbed at his eyes once more. "Wait a sec," he said. "'Justin Case'? 'Just in case'?"

His face snapped over to Evan. Already Evan had the sodden gauze pads in his palm. With his other hand, he hit REDIAL on the RoamZone.

There was a half-second delay as the call routed through to the Nokia in the dumpster outside. The flashbang's effect, compounded within the metal walls, literally vibrated the building, the boom loud enough to send a passing officer airborne. Coffee rose from his cup in a brown fountain. The detective to Evan's side hit the floor, hands laced over the back of his head.

Evan was up beside O'Malley in an instant, cupping his hand over the detective's mouth and nose, steadying him and pretending to lean over the desk in an improvised duck-and-cover.

Desflurane was Evan's preferred halogenated ether. Its TV-trendy cousin, chloroform, was nearly useless, taking a solid five minutes to be effective and requiring ongoing inhalation to keep the target unconscious. In Evan's experience the onset of action for Desflurane hovered around two minutes, but a lightweight individual like the unfortunate Detective O'Malley would be functionally incapacitated at the thirty-second mark.

The drug was also much safer than chloroform, a key consideration if you were planning to knock out an innocent cop.

Over the furor in the lobby, the desk officer shouted, "Everyone please evacuate in a calm and orderly fashion!"

As the bullpen cleared, Evan caged O'Malley's head with his arm, tilting him forward at the big monitor to hide his face and the soaked gauze from view. O'Malley whipped his head back to crack into Evan's, and Evan pulled away just in time so it thudded ineffectively into his chest. A heartbeat slower and Evan would've been laid out on the floor with second-impact syndrome, a second concussion ballooning the first, leaving him unconscious or dead.

Exhaling with relief, he held his grip firm. O'Malley's knees rattled against the underside of his desk, but already they were losing steam. His eyes rolled up to Evan, showing white, and Evan whispered, "Don't worry. It's harmless. I'm not going to hurt you."

At last the detective slumped, but Evan maintained the seal over his nose and mouth.

By now the detectives and cops had grabbed their weapons and were streaming toward the front, herding the citizens with them. Evan held Detective O'Malley in place in his chair and spoke to his unconscious face loudly, "Okay, okay. I'm coming. It just hurts if I move too fast."

The exodus from the bullpen was nearly complete, the last of the cops filing through the door to the lobby.

Evan lowered O'Malley gently to the desk, resting his forehead on the mouse pad. Then he unclipped the key card from the detective's belt and crossed the bullpen.

He had no weapon. But he had no time either.

With a tap of the key card against the pad, the security door clicked open. The corridor beyond had three doors on either side. Except for one, all stood open, likely left ajar in the explosion's aftermath.

If Nuñez and Brust had taken Max to a back room as Evan anticipated, they'd have good reason to remain behind during an evacuation. They'd require the privacy.

Evan gritted his teeth. He had to enter the fray unarmed and face whatever came at him. But he could not afford to take another blow to his head. It would put him out, maybe for good.

The closed door was locked, so Evan stepped back and kicked it in.

It smashed the wall, the doorknob sticking through the drywall.

"Hurry up and—" Nuñez cut off his words to his partner, his eyes lighting with alarm at Evan's bandage-wrapped face, his hand already reaching for his sidearm.

At the center of the room, Brust stood facing Max over the table, one arm extended, his Glock aimed at Max's head. An executioner's pose.

Before Evan could move, Brust fired.

36

Deadweight

Evan filled the open doorway of the interrogation room, the echo of the gunshot ringing within the reinforced walls.

Max was gone, knocked clear out of his chair by the head shot, lost somewhere beneath the table, bleeding out.

Adrenaline surged at the reins, threatening to break free and bolt through Evan's bloodstream, but he tightened his hold. If Max was dead, he'd still be dead three seconds from now.

Evan couldn't waste a split second. He was in close quarters with two homicidal cops. They had Glock 22 Gen4s, each with fifteen .40s stacked in the magazine.

Evan had an ACE bandage wrapped around his head and a lingering concussion.

But he'd been trained to slow down time in a firefight, to assess the freeze-frame progression of movement and angles.

Brust remained in side profile, having just fired across the table at Max. A slow-motion ripple spread through the cheap cotton of his shirt behind the right shoulder, stirred into existence by the recoil. He was pivoting toward Evan, his head leading the turn.

At five feet away, Nuñez was the closer threat. Forty pounds heavier, he was the larger one, too.

But Brust would have Evan in his sights first. Evan couldn't reach him in time.

As he played through the extrapolation of the next three seconds, a pair of thoughts struck him. One: Given his concussion, he hadn't run the simulated scenarios as quickly as he usually did. And two: That split-second delay meant that he could not cover both men.

There was no version that didn't end with him getting shot.

That's when the table scooted of its own accord, skittering forward two feet and slamming into Brust's thigh. Brust staggered, buying Evan another instant to focus on Nuñez.

The big detective's hand had already reached the hip holster, the Glock rising, not yet clearing leather.

Evan drove into Nuñez.

As the Glock rose, swinging to target Evan's critical mass, Evan swept it to the side with a cupped hand, accelerating the momentum from the draw. Curling his fingers over the top of the slide, Evan steered Nuñez's arm along the trajectory it was already traveling, the weapon carried in a straight-armed swivel.

It whipped through another fifteen degrees, and then Evan jerked the weapon to a halt, the jolt causing Nuñez's hand to clench.

His finger constricted around the trigger.

Evan had halted the pistol with the front sights aligned on Brust's head.

Droplets painted the rear wall.

Brust crumpled.

Nuñez gasped, a screeching intake of air.

To his credit he did not release the Glock. He had a better grip on the weapon and was much stronger to begin with, so Evan released the barrel. His other hand was already grabbing for the pens in Nuñez's shirt pocket.

As Nuñez took a clunky step to the side to regain his balance, Evan tore a pen free. He spun into Nuñez, throwing his weight backward, slamming his shoulders into Nuñez's chest, tilting his head forward to protect it from colliding with Nuñez's chin.

As Nuñez barked out a grunt, Evan tightened his fist around the pen and slammed it down past his own hip into the inside of Nuñez's thigh.

Now the big man dropped the Glock.

He lurched back stiffly, struck the wall, and slid down to a sitting position, his legs kicked out before him. With disbelief he looked down at the pen protruding from his thigh, the dark stain spreading through the fabric of his slacks. Then he curled his hand around the pen, holding it in place.

Evan looked past Brust's fallen body and the knocked-askew table to where Max sprawled on the floor, tilted back on his ass. His foot was still raised from when he'd kicked the table into Brust.

Behind him there was a black hole where Brust's round had buried itself in the wall; it must have missed his head by inches when Max hit the floor.

Evan unwound the Ace bandage from his head, enjoying his first clear breath of air since he'd entered the station. "Thanks."

Max's nod looked like a tremor.

Evan moved over to Brust and started tugging off the detective's shoes. The big man's legs hung from Evan's grip, deadweight.

In the corner Nuñez choked out a grunt of pain.

Evan finished with the loafers and got to work on Brust's belt. "You're gonna want to keep pressure on," he said, not bothering to look over at Nuñez. "The pen is buried in your femoral artery. If you let go, you'll bleed out in seconds."

Nuñez grunted, eyeing his fallen service weapon a few feet past the tips of his shoes. So tempting.

Evan stripped off his own jeans and stepped into Brust's pants. A bit loose, but they fit well enough. The button-up took a bit more doing. The collar was stained, but not terribly. Next Evan worked the badge lanyard carefully over the mess of Brust's head and ducked into it.

He made for a passable detective.

Deadweight

Nuñez watched the fashion show, his upper lip wrinkled back from his teeth like a dog's.

As Evan adjusted Brust's belt around his own waist, Nuñez let go of the pen and lunged for the Glock.

Blood spurted onto the tile, powerful blasts timed to his heartbeat.

Evan shook his head. "Mistake."

Nuñez toppled over. His hand pawed the floor a few times and then stopped. He stared glassily at nothing.

Evan smoothed down the shirt, adjusted the badge at his stomach, and freed the handcuffs from the hard leather belt pouch. Then he walked over and tugged the baseball cap from Nuñez's head. It fit perfectly.

Max still hadn't moved. He remained on the floor, breathing hard.

"Look at me," Evan said. "Look at me. You're okay. Get up."

Max obeyed.

"Turn around."

Max did.

Evan slapped the cuffs on him and started to march him out.

"Wait," Max said at the door, his voice hoarse with shock. He chinned back at Nuñez. "The thumb drive. He has the thumb drive in his pocket."

Evan went to Nuñez's slumped body and dug through his pant pockets. As he extracted the thumb drive, a slab of smooth metal slid out and clattered on the tile. Not just any metal.

Liquidmorphium.

Evan glared at the Turing Phone. Then he scooped it up, wrapped it and the thumb drive in his jeans, and tucked the bundle under his arm.

They exited into the corridor.

The bullpen was still empty save for O'Malley, who was just now stirring at his desk. As they passed, Evan paused behind the slender detective. "Apologies." He picked up the soaked gauze from where he'd dropped it on the desk, pressed it over O'Malley's nose and mouth once more, and left the detective sleeping on his keyboard.

Gripping Max's cuffs in the back, Evan steered him roughly out onto the sidewalk.

The uniforms were setting a perimeter, holding off onlookers. By now most of the detectives had clustered around the dumpster, comparing notes and shaking their heads. A few looked up at Evan and gave him a nod.

He nodded back.

Evan manhandled Max across the street, into an alley, and out the other side.

The Ford pickup chirped twice and unlocked when Evan hit the key fob. He released Max's cuffs and let them fall into the gutter as Max climbed into the passenger seat.

Evan shed Brust's badge, left it with the handcuffs in a trickle of dirty water by the curb drain, and drove off.

37

Whac-a-Mole

Returning to the Lincoln Heights house felt like defeat.

And yet here Evan and Max were, standing on the splintered floor of the living room, a grim silence filling the darkness between them. They'd barely spoken on the drive here, staring through the windshield, lost in separate thoughts.

"I thought it was over," Evan said. "I was wrong."

Max's posture was clamped down, his arms half crossed, one straight, the other gripping the opposite biceps. His knuckles were bloodless, his hand shaking down by his thigh. It looked like if he let go, he'd fly to pieces.

"Max. *Max.*"

A focus came back into his eyes.

"You're safe now," Evan said. "Right now, in this moment, you're safe."

He took out Nuñez's Turing Phone and thumbed through recent calls. The directory had been completely wiped.

Except for one outgoing call.

He felt a tickle at the back of his skull, the next threat worming its way to the surface. Three problems had arisen. And he'd dispatched all three.

But if this mission had taught him anything, it was that the next problem was waiting just around the corner, blade in hand. And if his concussion had taught him anything, it was that he was playing Russian roulette. There were only so many dry clicks he'd get before the hammer dropped on a live round. It seemed cruelly fitting that his final outing as the Nowhere Man refused to end, as if the universe itself would not allow him to let go.

The time stamp on the Turing showed that the number had been dialed shortly after Max entered the Hollywood Station and turned himself in. The call had lasted twenty-seven seconds.

As the lead officers on the case, Nuñez and Brust had been alerted to Max's presence by the desk cop. And then Nuñez had immediately contacted whoever was at the other end of that phone number.

Not Petro, since Petro was dead.

But another shot caller, even further up the food chain.

Nuñez and Brust had gotten their marching orders. And then headed to the Hollywood Station to murder Max.

The Turing Phones were links in a chain stretching up. How high that chain went remained to be seen.

Evan slid the shiny slab of Liquidmorphium back into his pocket.

"What's that?" Max asked.

"Something else I have to handle."

"Something or someone?"

Evan said, "Both."

"How are you gonna handle it?" Max asked.

The headache had resumed, a vise clamping Evan's brain. "I don't know yet."

Max rasped a hand across his stubble, peppered with gray. "I thought they were gonna kill me," he said. "Two detectives. In a police station. And then . . . and then you busted in there with your head all wrapped like some kind of deranged King Tut. . . ." At this, the first sign of amusement teased his lips. But just as quickly it was gone. "Did you see Brust's head? I've never . . . never seen anything like that."

He blinked hard a few times as if clearing his mind and then walked over to the mud-caked wrench on the counter. He picked it up and turned it over in his hands. Only a few hours had passed since he'd used it to repair the pipe outside, but to Evan it felt like weeks. He figured that for Max it felt even longer.

"Why did they want to kill me?" Max said. "I mean . . . they're *cops*."

"They worked for Petro. He managed to flip them before Grant was hired."

"But those guys are the detectives running the investigation *against* Petro. Why would they have opened the case to begin with? Why hire Grant to start digging?"

The sound of a car engine rose on the street outside, and Evan and Max tensed. But it kept on, motoring into the dead of night.

"I'm guessing Petro knew that an investigation was coming," Evan said. "The dogfighting arena and a number of the smaller businesses used to launder his cash are in Hollywood. So he paid off two detectives in the local station to take point on the case, contain it at a smaller level, and bury it before it got kicked to Vice downtown."

Max said, "So Brust and Nuñez were making sure the investigation went nowhere."

"That's right. They needed to hire a forensic accountant to cover their bases, figuring he wouldn't get very far. They could check the right boxes, steer the case from the inside, then drop it for insufficient evidence. But it looks like Grant uncovered more than they were bargaining for."

"Grant was too good." It seemed the words were weighed down, hard for Max to say. He let the wrench slip from his hand onto the counter. "I thought I'd hit bottom. Now I'm implicated in the murder of two cops. What the hell's next?"

Before he'd died, Petro had faced down Evan, smiling into the bullet that would end him. Evan sensed in his bones now that whatever Petro had been smiling about was more dangerous than a pair of dirty cops.

The First Commandment: *Assume nothing.*

Or in the case of this mission: *Assume it can always get worse.*

"One of my associates uncovered new files," Evan said. "We're going to go through them entry by entry and make sure there are no more surprises."

Max said, "You have associates?"

It was, to be fair, an inflated term for a sixteen-year-old and an injured rescue dog in a Westwood one-room apartment. But Evan would take Joey over an NSA cyberwarfare group any day of the week.

Evan moved on. "When this is over, you'll say that an assassin in Petro's operation carried out the assault on the police station, that he killed Nuñez and Brust as part of the cover-up. He took you to force you to give up the thumb drive's hiding place. But you managed to escape."

"No one'll believe that."

"When we hand over files tracing all the payments to Nuñez and Brust, they will."

"I don't know," Max said. "Every time you put down a threat, another pops up. And this thing, it keeps getting bigger and bigger." His face, sallow in the ambient light, held a worn-through dread. "Imagine if Grant had never given me that thumb drive. Hour after hour I replay that scene in my head, and I think what if I'd just stood up for myself? What if I'd just said no? Was I that desperate for his approval? That desperate to show everyone that I wasn't . . . I don't know, *useless*? 'Come on, Mighty Max. For once in your life, maybe step up, shoulder some responsibility.'" A bitter laugh escaped him. "And now I dragged Violet into it— Christ, just seeing me she has to relive it all, and I swore I'd never put that woman through anything ever again." His voice quavered, his eyes brimming. "Now everywhere I look, someone's trying to kill me, and I can't do anything but hide in this *fucking house.*"

His voice rang off the walls. He lowered his head, eyes on the floor, his face coloring. Water dripped somewhere, an unnerving *plink-plink-plink*. The lights were off, the walls receding into darkness, so it seemed the space stretched out forever, a dank underworld.

"I'm sorry," Max said. "You don't need this."

"Pick your head up," Evan said sharply.

Max wiped at his eyes roughly.

And then he lifted his gaze.

"You had my back in that interrogation room," Evan said. "Show yourself the same respect."

"What's that mean?" Max asked.

"'Act like the person you want to be.'" It was one of Jack's favorite quotations; just thinking of him put a rasp in Evan's voice. "If we want to get through whatever's coming, we're gonna have to face it head-on."

The protracted silence was broken only by more drops against the subfloor. When Max spoke again, his words were little more than a whisper. "I can't see a way out anymore."

Evan said, "Then I'll find it for us."

38

Worse to Come

Dog the dog backed into Evan, shoving his rear end into his thigh, demanding to be petted. It was crowded enough inside Joey's workstation without a Rhodesian ridgeback wedged in along with them.

Evan scratched just below the ridge, and the dog curled his back with pleasure, his mouth wrinkling into a smile. His wounds looked to be healing nicely, the stitches almost ready to come out. A tube of Neosporin and a scattering of Q-tips lay on the floor in the corner; despite her objections Joey was taking good care of him.

Joey kept on at the keyboard resting in her lap, her shoulders rippling beneath a wife-beater tank top. "God, you two," she said. "Get a room."

Evan returned his attention to the monitors rising three high around the circular pod. Joey had hacked into reverse directories to source the 213 phone number Detective Nuñez had dialed. It belonged to a preloaded SIM card that had been bundled with a batch bulk-sold to an LAX shop three months prior. Now she was backtracking to see which cell towers had been pinged during the call, hoping to approximate a location for the recipient.

Petting the dog, Evan did his best to quell his impatience. The mission had turned into a game of Follow the Turing Phones. Terzian's had led to Petro's had led to Nuñez's, each electronic slab a nerve-racking blank slate that held the promise of worse to come. Bathed in the unstirred heat of the apartment and the steady clacking of Joey's progress, Evan felt a familiar unease. Like they were reeling up a lure from the shadowy depths, unsure of what was tugging on the line.

The slats of the vertical blinds were angled skinny. Wee-hours blackness blanketed the panes, pinpricked by a few streetlamps. The room had the sticky-sweet smell of convenience-store food—candy bars, Red Vines, Dr Pepper—with an overlay of canine funk. Evan was debating how to extract himself from Dog to open a window when Joey said, "I can't believe you busted into a police station." She shook her head and grinned, that hair-thin gap in her front teeth making her look once again like a goofy kid instead of the young woman she was slowly, relentlessly becoming. "Damn, you a maniac, X."

"That's the job," he said.

"To boldly go where no man has gone." Joey looked at him over a shoulder sculpted with muscle, still typing away. He wondered how she ate the way she did and maintained her rock-solid form, and then he remembered she was sixteen. The *rat-a-tat-tat* of the keys took on an aggressive edge. "To do anything for your clients. To go anywhere."

The caustic note caught Evan off guard. "Sure," he said.

Her left cheek tightened, a lopsided scowl. "And if you die?"

Joey armored over her vulnerability with anger. He knew this. And yet the quickness of it surprised him every time.

"If I die," he said, "take care of Dog."

Joey turned away from him. "That's not funny."

"It's a little funny."

But this earned no response. She was lost again to the myriad screens, leaning forward, chewing her lip. And then she stiffened.

"God*damn* it." She flopped the keyboard onto the stretch of curved desk before her. At the clatter, Dog the dog tucked his tail and scurried out of the pod. She glared after him. "Some lion hunter you turned out to be."

Evan gestured at the inscrutable wall of code on the monitor. "What's wrong?"

"First of all, you're pointing at the wrong monitor." She grabbed his wrist and swung his finger to the adjacent screen, which contained an equally inscrutable wall of code.

Feigning forbearance, he waited for her to explain.

She didn't disappoint. "The shitty SIM outfit leases their cell towers from real companies. Which means they can't keep location logs—no access. So I can't pin down where the caller is." She rocked back in her gamer chair so far that he thought she might topple over. "Incompetence can be an infuriatingly effective defense."

Sometimes she was almost as quotable as Jack.

He could sense her magnificent brain powering away, could practically feel the heat rising from her head. He knew to keep his mouth shut and let the engines churn.

Scrunching her eyes tight, she flipped her mane of brown-black hair to one side, revealing the shaved strip above her right ear. Ten seconds passed, and then ten more. He was about to clear his throat pointedly when she said, *"Unless."*

"Unless what?"

She bounced forward, her hands locking back onto the keyboard as if magnetized. "We do it in real time."

"Track the call."

"Yeah," she said. "If you make a live call, I can capture the IMEI with my Stingray."

"And triangulate the cell towers."

"More like advanced forward link trilateration," she said. "But we can't expect the mouth breathers to grasp the difference." She held up her fist.

He bumped it. "Indeed not."

"If it's an urban area with denser cell towers, I can pin him within fifty meters. Rural could be a miles-wide zone, which is tougher. But also easier 'cuz, like, fewer buildings."

"I know, Joey. Even the mouth breathers can grasp—"

She plucked the Turing off the desktop, a cord swaying beneath like the tail of a kite. She shoved it at Evan. "Go. Talk."

"Do I have to keep him on the line for a certain amount of time?"

"Yeah," she said, "especially if you teleport into a movie from 1987." She spun around on the chair, and Evan had to lean back to avoid getting kneecapped by the armrest. Tucking into another section of her circular desk, she cluttered the screens with windows that, he gleaned, showed the inner workings of several telephone networks. "Just do your whole Nowhere Man thing. You know"—now a self-important frownie face with a husky voice—"'Do you need my help?' 'How did you get this number?' 'Hold on, I have to crack some walnuts between my buttocks.'"

Her impression of him was accompanied with more head wagging than seemed fair. But then again: artistic license.

"That's totally off the mark," Evan said. "I usually crack the walnuts in my chin cleft."

But she was dialed in to the monitors now, the scroll reflecting like rainfall in her deep green eyes.

The heat thrown off by all the hardware was starting to get to him. Gripping the phone, he pushed up from his lean against the inner desk and a surge of unsteadiness hit him. He staggered to right his balance and put his hand down hard on Joey's keyboard.

Her head snapped over. "What's going on?"

"Nothing. I'm fine."

"Bullshit. Why are you dizzy?" She was on her feet. "Wait a minute. Your right pupil looks like a fucking shark eye."

The contact had been drying his eye, so he'd left it out to take a break, a choice he now regretted. "Language."

"Do you have a *concussion*? How long have you had this?"

"I don't know. A couple days."

"A couple *days*?" She appeared to be livid, though he had no idea why. "Do you have *any idea* what Jack would say? 'Take care of your equipment.' Now, I know your brain's your least valuable piece of gear, but still. I mean, look at that thing." She grabbed both of his cheeks and angled his head down, but he pulled away. "You know the cure for a concussion? Rest. Do the last coupla days look like rest to you?"

"I've been fine. I've been feeling steadily better. Plus; I haven't hit my head again—"

"Well, bravo, X. That gets you a bronze in the Dipshit Olympics. You know what you're supposed to do. And what you're supposed to *not* do. You and I both had the same lectures from Jack. No stress, no exertion. Avoid shit that's physically and emotionally demanding. Like, you know, *every single thing* you've been doing."

He lifted the Turing Phone. "Are you going to help me do this or not?"

She glared at him, her jaw sawing back and forth. She looked like she wanted to give him a secondary concussion herself.

"Fine." She plopped down in her chair. "But when you *do* get your head bonked, don't except me to be a pallbearer at the funeral."

"I'm not planning on having a—"

"It's a figure of speech!"

She stayed facing away, focused on the monitor, hands on the keyboard. Ignoring him.

He thumbed the Turing to that sole outgoing call. Stared at the 213 number. Somewhere—nestled in a pocket, resting on a nightstand, plugged into a dashboard—a phone waited.

And a shot caller sufficiently powerful to order two LAPD detectives to execute an innocent man inside a police station.

Evan pictured Max, his head lowered in that hangdog manner of his, wiping at his cheeks. *I can't see a way out anymore.*

He tapped the number.

It was the dead of night, but the man answered after the first ring. "Nuñez?" He sounded wide awake.

Evan said, "Nuñez can't come to the phone right now."

The puff of an exhalation fuzzed the line. And then another. In the background Evan heard a metallic clang.

"And why is that?"

"Because I killed him."

"Ah," the man said. "May I ask who you are?"

The voice carried the hint of an accent like the others'. But the man—the shot caller—projected utter placidity. There was none of Terzian's rage, none of Petro's slickness or theatrical arrogance. He seemed not merely composed but unflappable, a man burnished by tough negotiations and tougher choices. A man too self-assured to raise his voice or resort to rudeness.

Each rung of the operation Evan scaled seemed to bring with it an upgrade in professionalism. Under different circumstances, he might even have admired a man like this.

Another clang came audible, one heavy object striking another, perhaps, or machinery flexing its muscle. Was the man in a factory? A plant? A junkyard?

Evan said, "The Nowhere Man."

"I see," the man said. "It had occurred to me when I heard the manner in which my efforts were being interfered with. Can I inquire after Detective Brust?"

"I killed him, too. And I'll kill anyone else you send after Max Merriweather."

"Hmm." The syllable conveyed a moment of genuine reflection. And then, "You can keep killing them. But I can keep sending them."

"I've dealt with mob bosses before."

"A mob boss? No, nothing so glamorous. I'm just a businessman."

"For a businessman you have an appetite for assassinations."

"I suppose," he said, sounding rueful. "Or maybe I'm just honest. I've distilled business down to its essential elements. Profit. And loss. I have responsibilities. I protect my bottom line."

"Then it looks like you and I will have to have a face-to-face," Evan said. "Like I did with Nuñez. And with Brust."

"Good luck with that," the man said.

"Don't worry," Evan said. "I'm sure I can arrange it."

"No, Mr. Nowhere Man. Even you can't arrange this."

The line went dead.

Evan's mouth had gone sour, sweat cooling across the back of his neck. He'd nearly forgotten he was in the room with Joey.

She was facing away, but he could see her hand pulsing around the elaborate mouse, rolling the sensor ball and clicking. "Good news," she said. "We're downtown. Close cell towers, so I should be able to peg him pretty closely, and—"

She froze, as still as death in her chair, her hands floating above the keys. The abrupt cessation of noise was unsettling. Across the room in his nest of dirty laundry, Dog raised his head, sniffing the shift in the air.

Joey laughed a hard, ugly laugh. "Oh, boy," she said.

"What?" Evan said. "Where is he?"

At last she turned to look at him, and her face was more serious than he'd ever seen it. "Twin Towers Jail."

Evan rubbed his eyes.

He said, "Fuck."

39

No Margin for Error

Evan blew through the lobby of Castle Heights, Joey hustling to keep up, Dog the dog prancing along beside her, his collar jangling against the leash. The empty expanse had an early-morning sheen, pink light spilling across the dated marble, the smell of coffee emanating from a stately silver urn on a side table. The mission loomed large in his mind, impassable and impossible, a towering wall of stone. He had only the roughest shape of a plan, just a few handholds he hoped might get him up the cliff face.

Evan was talking hard, his voice low. "I need *everything*, understand? Procedures, schedules, security measures, equipment, guard shifts. I need names, heights, weights, and profiles for prisoners. I need to know gang affiliations—what they're in for, who's in which cell block, when they're being released. I need security-camera positions, surveillance gaps, what you can alter, delete, control. I need to know—"

"Jesus, X." A sheen of perspiration sparkled at Joey's hairline. "You can't do this. Not with your head the way it is."

He pivoted to face her, walking backward without breaking stride. "Joey. I have to."

She shriveled a bit beneath his glare, and he realized that the intensity of his tone had scared her.

"Chillax, okay?" Her voice sounded small, intimidated, and he hated himself for it. "I got you."

"There is no margin for error."

"I understand, okay?" She held up her palms, a rare show of submission. "What's the plan?"

"I don't know yet," he said. "I've never done anything like this."

As they reached the elevator doors, Joaquin called out from behind the security desk. "Hey, Mr. Smoak. And Ms. . . . Janie, right?"

"Joey. She'll be staying with me for a few days. Please give her access."

"Uh, the no-pets policy?"

"He's a service dog," Joey said. "I have a severe psychiatric disorder."

Joaquin looked at her, gauging whether or not she was serious. Joey stared back, unblinking.

Joaquin pursed his lips. "Why don't we just make sure we keep it inconspicuous so we don't have to show Mr. Walters any paperwork to that effect."

"Mr. Walters?" Joey said.

"The HOA president," Joaquin said. "He takes his HOA'ing pretty seriously."

"I appreciate that," Evan said.

He and Joey faced the closed elevator doors, breathing the crisp lobby air. Evan noticed he was clenching fists at his sides and did his best to still his hands. The floor indicators showed the car making glacial progress. Dog the dog sat, bent his head, and licked himself with abandon.

"You hear the latest on Mrs. Rosenbaum?" Joaquin called out.

Evan shook his head. Did not turn around. He felt the heat of Joey's gaze on the side of his face.

"I guess they caught the guy," Joaquin said. "And someone returned her necklace for her. The old-fashioned one from her dead husband? Slid it right under the door."

Evan said, "Is that so."

"Yeah. I pulled the security footage to see who, but the system was down."

Joey turned her head to look at Joaquin, her hair flicking like a horse tail. Then back to Evan. "How odd," she said flatly.

"Yeah," Joaquin said. "Guess we'll never know who the Good Samaritan is."

"Maybe it wasn't a Good Samaritan," Joey said. "Maybe it was a bad guy who had a change of heart." She shot Evan a glare. "Or a bad guy who doesn't listen to anyone but himself."

Evan felt his face tighten, but before he or Joaquin could respond, the elevator chimed. Saved by the bell.

Or not.

He heard her voice before the doors parted. "—this case goes sideways on me one more time, so help me God, I'm gonna go full-on Sherman's March to the Sea."

The elevator rattled open.

Mia stood inside, phone pinched between ear and shoulder, bulging satchel briefcase in one hand, Batman lunch box in the other. Somehow her lunch-box hand managed a travel coffee mug as well, and she was caught mid-slurp, steam rising past her puffy eyes into the wild tangle of her curls. At the sight of Evan, her eyes flared, the cup frozen against her lips.

With a pang of sadness, he realized how readily he could read her, how familiar he was with the cogs and gears by which her life ran. Darkness beneath her eyes, second cup of coffee to go, and the file-heavy briefcase meant she was working a big case. Up late last night, up early this morning to drop Peter at math tutoring, court-ready suit in case she had to file a motion.

She let the phone slip from her cheek and fall into her gaping briefcase. Beside her, Peter tilted back in a partial limbo, his over-stuffed backpack sagging past his rear end. He was firing bullets from a paper-towel roll he'd embellished with a Magic Marker, turning it into a futuristic gun.

Right now he was shooting out the overhead lights. *"Pew pew pew!"* He turned and saw them. "Evan Smoak! And niece-person Joey! And a awesome dog!" He swung around and fired the paper-towel roll at Evan. *"Pew pew pew."*

Mia looked how Evan felt: mortified.

"Pew pew pew."

The doors started to close, and Mia stuck out a foot, knocking the bumpers back. "C'mon, Peter. Let's go."

"No," he said. "He has to shoot back." For good measure he swept the cardboard barrel to cover Joey, too. *"Pew pew pew."*

Mia hustled Peter out of the car, but he bucked away.

"C'mon! You haveta shoot back. That's how you play."

Heat crept up Evan's throat, spread beneath his face. Reluctantly he made a finger gun and aimed it at Peter. "Bang," he said.

Peter flung himself against the wall, crunching his backpack against the marble. He clutched his chest, gasped theatrically, and slid to the floor, legs splayed before him in a manner not unlike Detective Nuñez's final pose.

Mia's face was flushed, her tone sharp. "Get up *right now*, Peter. We're gonna be late."

As Peter reanimated, Evan and Joey stepped past him into the elevator, tugging Dog the dog with them.

"Wait, I didn't get to pet the dog," Peter said as Mia dragged him away. "Mom, can we get a dog? Just a little one?"

The car sealed off Peter's continued entreaties. As the elevator rose, Evan blew out a breath through clenched teeth.

"What was up with *that*?" Joey said. *"Awk*ward."

Evan said, "It's complicated."

"Okay, Facebook."

"What?"

"Nothing."

They rode the rest of the way in silence.

40

Your Average Lowlife

For what was coming, Evan couldn't have any tactical gear on him.

No cargo pants with discreet pockets for hiding spare magazines. No Woolrich shirts with magnetic buttons. No Original S.W.A.T. boots. No ARES 1911 or Strider folding knife.

He had to look like your average lowlife.

He grabbed a pair of dark 501s from the bureau drawer and stepped into them.

The door to the bathroom was open, the shower door slid back, the hidden door ajar. And Joey was inside the Vault at the commands, a pilot driving a spaceship, shouting her findings out to him. "Unshockingly, Twin Towers Jail hasn't updated their security systems in ages! Budget shortfalls, blah-blah-blah. I mean, a noob with a Compaq and a USRobotics dial-up modem writing their hack in Visual Basic could get in here in, like, thirty seconds." She gave a self-satisfied snort.

Evan went toward the walk-in closet, buttoning his jeans. "I don't know what any of that means."

Joey's voice boomed out at him. "Jail surveillance bad. Joey good."

At the foot of the bed, a scattering of dog hairs rested on the concrete floor, pronounced beneath the overhead lights. He blinked his eyes hard, opened them, but they remained. He'd have to deep-clean the penthouse when this was over with.

He tore himself from the sight and entered the closet. Past the neatly stacked cartons of boots was a bin holding several pairs of sneakers he'd dragged behind his truck, scuffing them up for undercover work.

This would certainly qualify as undercover work.

"So get this!" Joey shouted. "Like, half of the surveillance cameras are still using the factory default passwords." She laughed heartily.

It never ceased to amaze him what the girl found amusing.

He stomped into his sneakers and swept the hanging shirts aside to reach a cubbyhole cut into the drywall. A dozen metal cases, each the size of a deck of playing cards, were stacked inside. He slid the top one free and cracked it open. Slotted neatly into the black foam lining were twenty glass microscope slides. An oval of silicone composite film half as wide as a strand of dental floss resided inside each, suspended in a ghostly float.

Fingerprint adhesives.

As he slid the case into his pocket, Joey rattled on. "They have everything hooked up to the Internet. Typical. Like, let's get everything online and vulnerable and then not update it, 'cuz we're stupid city bureaucrats. So I banged in there with Shodan."

"Shodan?"

"Dude, c'mon, X. The search engine for Internet-connected devices? Every device that sends data out has a string that IDs what it is. Shodan searches all those strings, feeds you the geolocations based on the IP addresses. I bust into the cameras, and I'm looking at a bunch of ugly-ass felons sitting in jail. Oh—and a deputy in the control room picking his nose. *Aaaand* he's eating it."

Pulling on a T-shirt, Evan ducked into the bathroom and fingertipped in another specialized contact lens to cover his dilated right eye. Then he yanked open the other drawers, searching their contents.

"I'm gonna drop in a zero-day exploit now," Joey said. "Make that two, so I have one for insurance. Hang on, and . . ."

Evan heard the pounding on his keyboard and wondered if she'd actually break it. It struck him how odd it was to hear another voice within the walls of his penthouse. He was used to drifting through the rooms accompanied only by the sound of his own breathing.

"The more secret digital doors into the system software we have, the better," Joey was saying. "Then, to cover your ass, I can always slew a lens to face a wall or spoof a frame to show an empty room or just burn down the whole house with a distributed denial of service attack and be all, 'How ya like me now, bizatches!'"

Beneath the sink he found the bottle he was looking for. Charcoal pills. He pocketed eight of them and stepped through the shower into the Vault.

Joey had shoved Vera II to the side and yanked the keyboard into her lap so she could type while cocked back in his chair at a breaking-point angle. Her dirty bare feet were up on the sheet-metal desk. A glass of orange juice rested on his foam mouse pad.

As he entered, the projection light hit him in the face, streaming glare and shadow across his eyes. He lifted the sweating glass off his mouse pad, swiping at the condensation ring with his wrist. "Don't they teach the use of coasters in evil-hacker school?"

"Shockingly not on the curriculum," Joey said.

Dog the dog lifted his leg and urinated in the corner. Joey swiveled her head from the dog to Evan, trying unsuccessfully to bite down a smile.

He watched the trickle leaking out from the wall. "This isn't funny."

"Actually, it's really funny."

"You're gonna clean that. Paper towel in the kitchen and Clorox spray beneath the—"

"Whatevs. Once you see what I just did, you're gonna drop the whole OCD routine."

Evan came around the L-shaped desk, nearly tripping on her

kicked-off shoes, and stood behind her to take in the OLED screens horseshoeing the walls.

One photograph was front and center.

A bland-looking man in his late forties. Side part, affable features, totally ordinary.

"Who's that?"

"That's your shot caller." Joey flicked a hand over the mouse, bringing up a rap sheet for Benjamin Bedrosov. "Weird last name. I mean, I thought this was an Armenian operation."

"Quite a few Russian Armenians had their surnames changed to end in '-ov' somewhere along the way," Evan said. "Like Garry Kasparov."

"He that actor in all those westerns? *High Noon* and shit?"

Evan knew that a withering look would be wasted on her, so instead he studied the rap sheet more closely. A host of dismissed charges. Two failed convictions. A deep bench of defense attorneys with Century City and Beverly Hills addresses—a clear upgrade from Alexan Petro's array of legal firepower. Under Aliases a single nickname was listed: *Bedrock*.

"He's a full-on businessman," Joey said. "Bernie Madoff motherf—" She caught herself. "Homey's got a I-banking firm downtown, slick crib up Beachwood Canyon, on the board of a half dozen companies. Check out the fancy website. If you didn't pull his rap sheet, you'd think he was legit."

Evan couldn't help marvel at the photo again. Bedrosov wore a suit jacket and a button-up shirt loose at the collar. He wasn't smiling exactly, but his face was set in a pleasingly mild expression. It was the kind of portrait you'd see on bus benches and billboards, a Coldwell Banker Realtor conveying can-do competence.

Evan leaned over Joey and thumbed up Bedrock's booking photo. The suit jacket was gone, but the same inoffensive expression remained, a businessman you could rely on to be steady at the helm through rocky waters.

It called to mind that well-trodden line about the banality of evil.

Dog the dog tapped his way over, circled a few times at Joey's feet, and lay down with an old-man groan.

"How'd you find this guy?" Evan asked.

"The payments to the dirty cops didn't come from Petro," she said. "They came from this *other* account. Which is funded with incoming wires directly from a shell corp that happens to also have *the* controlling interest in—you guessed it—Petro's Singapore bank. The shell corp lists Benjamin Bedrosov as the principal. I'm guessing this guy has a few Petros under him scattered around the city, all of whom feed his bank for a small piece of the owner-ship."

"And he's currently in Twin Towers."

"Awaiting trial for wire fraud," Joey said. "Looks like he'll be tried under Penal Code 186.10 as a felony. Been there about a month and a half."

Evan checked the date. "Right around when payments began to Brust and Nuñez."

"Like you said, he put the detectives in place to cover his ass and squelch the investigation. I'm not big on reading legal mumbo jumbo, but from the prosecutor's internal memos here"—she swiveled to an investigative document projected onto the south wall—"it looks like they know they don't have a solid case. The bureau director himself called it 'thin' twice in the case-review memo." Click, highlight. "Like, youch, right? Bedrosov'll probably walk, same as he did every time before. The guy does an exceptional job insulating himself from Petro and everyone else beneath him."

"Which makes Grant's files that much more damning," Evan said. "Wires, accounts, transactions, code names—all linking back to Bedrosov. And the cash thresholds are probably high enough to take the case federal. Then you're not talking a few years in prison for a conviction. You're talking twenty per. That doesn't just put him away. It sinks him for good."

He thought back to Grant Merriweather's final moments, confused and depleted. He'd given his life uncovering the evidence to take down Bedrosov's operation. He'd been hired by dirty cops with a hidden agenda. By doing his job well, he'd turned it into a death sentence. For himself and for Max.

If Evan didn't shut Bedrosov down, he'd send the next wave of hit men after Max. And another wave after that.

Evan stared at Grant's thumb drive, currently slotted into a USB port. The attached Swiss Army knife key chain protruded, a mundane hiding place for a data dump that had cost twenty lives and counting. Bedrosov had presided over the whole bloody mess with calm upper-management demeanor, a pleasing façade, and a psychopath's willingness to dispatch anyone in his way.

Evan had faced evil before in various guises—dark and dirty, passionate and zealous, powerful and cruel. But he'd never gone up against someone so . . . ordinary. This mission moved against the grain of all those that had come before. Rather than winding into increasing perversion and turpitude, it seemed to arc upward toward a kind of warped legitimacy. He kept looking for a clear enemy, but the faces he continued to encounter were seemingly interchangeable. Terzian and Petro and Brust and Nuñez and Bedrosov were variations on the same theme, a progression of men seeking profit at any cost.

As if reading his thoughts, Joey said, "I thought we'd finally get to some master villain, you know? Someone who looks the part. But he's not a villain any more than those dirty cops were. It's like they're all *pieces* of a villain that have to be put together for us to see. And that makes them worse, almost. 'Cuz they can pretend none of them are to blame." Her dark eyes were shiny, her hair twisted down to cover one eye. She'd withdrawn into herself, but Evan could hear in her voice how keenly she felt the outrage. "The guy does whatever he wants to whoever he wants and gets away with it."

"Not anymore," Evan said.

Joey's eyes were glassy, drinking in the evidence writ large on the walls.

Evan thought about the epiphany that had hit him after he'd taken out Petro: That he wasn't fighting a snake but a hydra. That the fanged mouths would keep multiplying until he reached the commanding head and severed it. He hoped that was Bedrock. But this time he had to make sure of it.

"While I'm doing this," he said, "you dig into Bedrock's connections, bank records, comms, e-mails, *everything*. I've been caught on the back foot three times now. I need to know that if I walk out of this alive, I'm done."

Joey's eyes flared at the "if," but he gestured her aside, not wanting to get bogged down. After she vacated the chair, he rattled around in Google, coming up with a slew of articles from April about Armenian pride rallies. A San Diego feature contained several photographs depicting some of the marchers and naming them in the captions.

Evan started highlighting names and running them through the databases.

"What are you doing?" Joey said.

He waved her off. From her dish of cobalt pebbles, Vera II looked on in support.

The fourth name, Paytsar Hovsepian, threw back a useful report from NCIC. A stoned outing in his senior year of high school had ended with a conviction for vandalism. He'd made threatening remarks to the arresting officer, earning him a position on the Violent Person file.

Even more helpful was his profile information. Mid-thirties. Lean build. Average height. Just an ordinary guy, not too handsome.

Evan went back to the online article depicting Paytsar holding a sign that read NO PLACE FOR DENIAL. With his other hand, he flashed the peace sign.

Evan double-clicked on the high-res photo. Great focus, strong lighting.

Precisely what he needed.

He zoomed in on the two fingers held aloft. Tighter, tighter.

"X," Joey said, "why are you dicking around with this right now?"

From his other side, Vera II cheered him on silently. Another reason to prefer the company of plants.

The photo resolution held. He captured the image, sent it to his RoamZone.

"Wait," Joey said. "Is that . . . ? Are you . . . ?" She shook her head. "No way. No fucking way."

"Language," he said.

He grabbed his phone from the charger, scratched Dog the dog on the head, headed out of the Vault.

Paused halfway across the threshold, one foot in the shower.

"You coming or not?"

Joey scrambled off her chair.

41

Your Usual Four-Alarm Emergency

"Are you fucking crazy?" Melinda Truong asked.

The accurate answer, Evan figured, was yes.

Joey had ridden shotgun on the drive to Northridge, laptop across her thighs, running through procedures and regulations and pop-quizzing him on the players inside. It wasn't nearly enough, but it was what he had.

Melinda set her tiny, capable fists on her hips, and Evan realized that she wasn't going to allow him to dismiss the question as rhetorical. He looked to Joey for air support, but her mouth only clutched a few times ineffectually.

Melinda was the first person Evan had seen render Joey speechless.

And fair enough. She was a force of nature. Stunning and lithe, a rope of jet-black hair hanging past the curve of her lower back. Yoga pants and a Lululemon sports bra hugged her compact form. Her skin was without blemish, perfectly smooth. Not a stray hair out of place. A pair of bright yellow Pumas capped off the precision athlete look.

Inside her warehouse-size operation in an industrial park, she presided over her restoration service with an emperor's iron fist. The operation placed vast resources and highly specialized equipment at her disposal. The dozens of workers—every one of them male, every one of them simultaneously terrified of and in love with her—spent their days and nights bent over giant square worktables with atomizers and palette knives, coaxing vintage film posters back to health. Some of the one-sheets sold for hundreds of thousands of dollars.

But that wasn't where Melinda made her real money.

She made her real money here, in this dark-walled photography room with blacked-out windows, as a world-class forger.

A 000 paintbrush, the most slender of them all, was tucked behind her ear like a pen. Pink tape wrapped its handle, a stamp of ownership ensuring that none of her workers would dare borrow it. Cradled in a hip holster like a six-shooter, her Olympos double-action airbrush was also padded with pink tape.

She looked like a lead character from one of the exploitation posters she so lovingly resuscitated.

From the main floor, sweatshop noises echoed down the hall at them—machinery and conversation and motorized equipment being revved. A horrendous crash sounded, punctuated by a cartoon aftereffect like a hubcap spinning out on asphalt.

Melinda snatched up a phone on a desk scattered with counterfeit passport stamps and hit the intercom button. Then she barked in her native tongue, *"You'd better unbreak whatever just broke, or I'll take it out of your hide."*

She slammed down the phone and turned crisply on her heel to face Evan again. "Well? Are you fucking crazy?"

He said, "Clinically or legally?"

She strode over to him, grabbed both sides of his face, and kissed him full on the mouth. At a hair over five feet, she had to rise to her tiptoes. Her mouth was soft, dewy from lipstick, and she smelled delightfully of lavender skin cream.

She finished and shoved him away. "You know what that is? That's your long kiss good-bye, Evan."

"It was worth it," he said.

Joey was still standing dumbly at his side, her jaw partially unhinged.

"Now we're never going to get married and have beautiful mixed-race children," Melinda said.

"You never know," he said. "I might survive."

She scowled, a focused effort that at last produced wrinkles. Just as quickly they were gone. All business, she snapped her fingers. "Let me see them."

He produced the silver case with the fingerprint adhesives. "They're silicon composite films," he said. "Fifty microns thin. Developed in a DARPA lab, but I managed to acquire a few sets. You've probably never seen anything like them, but—"

"You got ripped off." She screwed a loupe into her eye, examining one of the slides with a jeweler's focus. "These are at least seventy-five microns. The ones I deal in are a true fifty, which makes for better adhesion." She dumped them in a trash can and cast a look at Joey. *"Men."*

Joey said, "Right?"

Evan tried to steer the conversation back on track. "Look, I'm not sure if you have the printing technology to transfer someone else's fingerprints onto the adhesives—"

"My preferred method," Melinda said, "is to generate engraved plates from my 3-D printer. Since the silicon films are impressionable, etched casting surfaces are ideal."

She leaned over the computer on her desk, linked to an AmScope binocular microscope and a MakerBot Replicator+. A red glow lit the printer's black box, an intense spill of color that made the contraption evocative of a futuristic forge, which Evan supposed it was. She brought up the photo detail Evan had forwarded her, Paytsar Hovsepian's fingers raised in a peace salute.

She let out a hiss of delight through her teeth. "Nice detail. I can get a couple dozen ridge characteristics easy."

Evan could still taste her lipstick, sugary like frosting. "I pulled the rest of his fingerprints off NCIC. They were ink-rolled at a local station nineteen years ago, middling clarity, but I figure as long as we have two at high-res, you can improvise the rest."

"Improvising," Melinda said, "is my life." She straightened up, flicking her hair expertly over a shoulder.

Joey had to lean back to avoid getting whipped.

"What else do you need?" Melinda said.

"Fake driver's license," Evan said.

"Finally a reasonable request."

"With ink that fades after twenty-four hours," he added.

"That's not possible."

"Even for you?"

"I'm incredible," she said, "but not magical." A lash-heavy eyelid dipped in a wink. "Except in bed."

"First of all . . . um, *gross*," Joey said. "Second, how 'bout a chemical reaction? Layered under the laminate? Something that kicks in after a certain exposure time to oxygen or whatever."

"She speaks," Melinda said. "And reveals brains beneath that god-awful haircut." She went to Joey and smoothed her hair down, covering the shaved strip on the right side. Then she tucked Joey's locks behind her ears and caressed her cheeks. "Don't be afraid of how beautiful you are."

For once Joey didn't back away. She looked too shocked to react.

"Um, thanks?" she said.

"Or how smart you are. You can be both, you know, even if that makes the less-fair sex feel insecure." Melinda gave another crisp officerial pivot to Evan. "Now. I can play with some metal-compound inks, like cerium oxalate. One of my men, Giang, is an expert in acids. But this level of specialty work will cost you plenty." She picked up the phone again, hesitated. "I assume this is your usual four-alarm emergency. I'm almost afraid to ask when you'll need it by?"

"We'll wait here," Evan said.

Melinda licked her thumb. Then reached across the desk and wiped a smudge of lipstick off Evan's mouth. "Very well, sweetie," she said, already dialing. "But you'd best stay out of my way."

42

A Nice Visible Presence

Joey looked uncharacteristically small behind the wheel of the massive Ford pickup. Or maybe it was just the view from the passenger seat, which Evan was occupying for the first time. It felt dislocating. As they prowled downtown streets cloaked with dusk, he emptied his pockets into the center console. No money clip, no RoamZone, no keys. Last out were the eight charcoal pills. He started palming them into his mouth two at a time, swallowing them dry.

Joey said, "Once you leave this truck, you'll have nothing."

Evan felt an urge to comfort her with false assurances but knew better than to lie.

She shot a glance down at his hands, the transparent films invisible across the pads of his digits. "Not even your fingerprints. "No backup, no weapon, nothing." She clenched the wheel. "I know, I know." She reverted to head-waggy Nowhere Man voice. "'I am the weapon.'" He had to smile at that, but she just glowered at him. "This is stupid dangerous, X. Think about it. I won't be able to do anything to help you. *No one* can do anything to help you. You'll be totally at their mercy. If one thing goes wrong, you're done. Forever. And if you smack your stubborn concussed head in there? You could *die*. And it's not like fights aren't known to happen. Christ, X. This is dumb in more ways than I can count, and I'm really good at math."

The RoamZone rang, rattling in the console. Evan tensed, anticipating that it was Max with a last-minute complication. But then he saw the Las Vegas area code and picked up.

The voice, pure gravel and exuberance, poured through the receiver. "I got yer sniper rifle."

"I didn't order a sniper rifle."

"Sure you did," Tommy said. "When I outfitted you with that low-rent Remington, I told you I was getting Ballistas in."

Evan tossed the last two charcoal pills into his mouth. "I don't need a sniper rifle anymore."

"Any man worth his salt needs a precision pea-shooter. I'm in L.A. on Monday. I'll drop her by for you."

As Joey weaved through sparse traffic, they passed under the shadow of Men's Central, a blocky construction of intersecting concrete slabs rising behind a perimeter of chain-link. Beyond it rose the dueling chunks of Twin Towers, one seven stories of misery, the other eight, each a study in beige efficiency. Evan forced the pills down his gullet. "I'm a little busy at the moment, Tommy."

He'd barely thumbed off the phone when Joey was on him again. "You don't have to do this," she said. "We have enough on Bedrosov to turn over to the cops now. Let them run with the football from here. They'll put him away for good."

"The case will take months to prosecute," Evan said. He scooped a few coins and some beat-up singles from the ashtray, seeding his pockets. "And in the meantime? Bedrosov is a shot caller in jail. With access to a phone. And hit men on the outside."

He remembered Benjamin Bedrosov's voice over the line, his tone the epitome of reasonableness: *You can keep killing them. But I can keep sending them.* He might as well have been updating shareholders on an earnings call.

"X—"

"Even if he's found guilty and goes to prison," Evan said, "do you really think he won't see it through and end Max?"

Headlights swept the windshield, highlighting her hair, her full cheeks. Her eyes were brimming, and he was confused yet again by the turmoil of her moods.

"If it goes bad . . ." Joey paused, struggling, seemingly forcing each word out. "What happens to me?"

"There's enough in your account to—"

"I'm not talking about *money*," she said. "Goddamn it. You're such an idiot." She screeched the truck over to the curb. "Just get out. Here's as good as anywhere. Just go, okay?"

He sat in the passenger seat, watching her. She was turned partially away, but he could see her front teeth pinching her bottom lip to keep it from trembling. Biting down hard. Nostrils flaring with each breath. She blinked several times, fighting her way back to control.

"Joey."

She ignored him.

"Joey."

Still nothing.

Gently he said, "Josephine."

She pulled her face to profile. It was the most he was going to get.

"Take a breath," he said.

"Why?"

"Because you can't take a breath from the past. And you can't take a breath from the future."

He watched the words land on her. She took in their meaning. Then she said, "This is lame."

"Do it."

She closed her eyes. Inhaled deep. Let it go.

"Feel better?" he asked.

"No," she said. And then, "Maybe a little."

He reached to brush her hair out of her eyes, an avuncular gesture, and she let him. He sensed a hint of softness in her face now.

She said, "Why do you care so much about Max Merriweather? I mean, aside from the fact that he lucked into your phone number?"

Evan didn't reply right away. He owed her a considered answer. "He lost a baby, lost his wife, lost his bearings. He's been knocked down for years, trying to get up, and these guys came along and put a foot on his back. You know what that feels like."

Evan did, too.

He understood what it was to be born under a bad sign.

The few papers he'd been able to excavate after leaving the foster-home system indicated that his birth mother had traveled from out of state to relinquish him in Maryland for a domestic adoption. The post-placement visit to his new home revealed that the adoptive mother had suffered a series of strokes that she'd never disclosed, and her rapidly deteriorating condition left her and her husband unable to provide care to a newborn. The placement fell apart. A second placement became delayed when the agency tried to locate Evan's birth mother, as she had retained the right to select the adoptive family. But she'd traveled out of state to hand over her baby for a reason; she didn't want her identity known. And so Evan was frozen in a bureaucratic middle ground past one fate and shy of another.

The Nowhere Boy.

By the time the state had him officially declared "abandoned," he was no longer a palatable commodity, but a four-year-old who'd bounced through multiple foster homes.

No mother, no father, no early-childhood memories.

When his remembrances started to fade in, they were not of being treated kindly.

After Jack had rescued him at the age of twelve from one dangerous life and put him into another, Evan had asked, *Why'd you pick me?*

You know what it's like to be powerless, Jack had told him. *I need someone who knows that. In his bones. Don't ever forget that feeling.*

All at once everything felt heightened, the air crisp, the nighttime sharp all around them.

"I made it out," Evan said. "But I owed something still."

"To who?" Joey asked.

"To anyone who got left behind." Evan took a breath. "Jack never wanted . . ." His throat felt uncharacteristically thick. He cleared it. Joey was looking directly into him. He felt vulnerable, exposed, and had to look away for the moment. "It was never just about becoming a killer. It was about staying human. And it's not easy. If I started picking and choosing . . . If I looked at someone like Max and decided he wasn't worth it, then I'd be back to where I started. Where no one's worth it. And then I'd just be what they made me to be." His lips felt dry, cracked, and he wet them. "A murderer."

Joey's eyes were wide, brilliant emerald, glimmering with moisture or a trick of the light. They'd never talked about it, and the starkness of who he was, of who she was, too, lay there for an instant, as shimmering and vivid as koi in a stilled fountain. The words hung between them for a brief, searing moment, and then he cleared his throat and opened his door, disturbing the waters once more.

"You ever gonna really prove that to yourself?" she asked. "What you're *not*?"

"I don't know." He scratched the back of his neck, looked away. "But it's easier than figuring out what I am."

Or maybe it's the first step to getting there.

"How much more do you have to prove?" she asked. "When's it end?"

The ultimate question laid bare, slicing him to the bone. He stared over at the rise of the jail, shadowed and foreboding.

"After this," he said. "After this it ends."

She stared at him. Her lips quivered ever so slightly, and she pressed them together, clamping down. She reached across his knees to pop the glove box, grabbed a pint of Cuervo Gold, and smacked it against his chest. "Don't forget your tequila."

He took the bottle, climbed out, and looked back at her across the high seats.

"Don't worry," she said. "I'll do my job. Just make sure you do yours."

She peeled out, spraying his shins with grit, leaving him with a mouthful of exhaust.

She'd left him behind the El Monte Busway by a Denny's parking lot. He could see through Union Station's Gateway Plaza to where the threads of the railroad tracks gathered. A cop car was parked past the bus entrance. An officer leaned against his unit, a nice visible presence for all the commuters streaming by, catching their trains home.

Evan uncapped the cheap tequila and flipped the top to the side, heard it ping off across the sidewalk. Then he settled himself with a deep breath, banishing thoughts of the vodkas slumbering untouched in his freezer drawer, each as pure as the driven snow.

This was far from the worse part. But it would still be awful.

He scrunched his eyes shut and drank a third of the pint in a series of long pulls, spilling a bit on his shirt for good measure. It burned down his throat, coated his stomach. He listed like a hobo there on the grimy sidewalk, praying his concussion symptoms wouldn't come roaring back to life. Then he stumbled for the police officer.

As he crossed North Vignes Street, he took another healthy swig, let tequila dribble through his lips and down his chin. Headlights bored into him, an oncoming rush from a just-changed traffic signal. A Subaru veered to miss him, the driver laying on the horn, a sharp blare in the thickening night.

That drew the cop's attention.

Evan passed right before him, swinging the open container at his side, letting the tequila slosh over and douse his fist.

"Christ on a stick," the cop muttered. And then, "Sir? *Sir.*"

Evan wheeled around drunkenly, one shoulder lowered, the bottle dangling. The front edge of the booze was hitting, making the colors jump, cramping his vision at the sides. His throat felt raw, the air pleasingly cool on the inhale. The booze roiled in his gut, a molten slosh. The symptoms were just starting to return, light-headedness and nausea urged back to life by the booze. If they held here, he could manage them. The streetlamps started to bleed into streaks of yellow, the glare assailing his eyes.

"Come here please, sir."

Evan staggered up to him. The cop was handsome, fresh-faced, spots of color dotting his smooth cheeks. Uniform pressed and starched, duty boots buffed to a reflective shine. He stayed tilted back against the driver's door, one thumb hooked through his belt. It was affected and vaguely endearing, as if he'd studied what pose a cop should strike in this situation and was doing his best to measure up.

"You have an open container."

Evan looked at the bottle of Cuervo, feigned surprise at seeing it there on the end of his arm. "Guess so."

"Listen, it's a Saturday night." The cop barely bothered with eye contact, speaking at Evan while looking around, as if reserving his focus for more important matters. "You look like you've had a tough day. Maybe things aren't going so well for you right now. What do you say you just toss the bottle there in the trash and we call it even?"

Just his luck. A kindhearted officer.

Evan pretended to register the offer on a tape delay. Then he rocked forward onto the balls of his feet. "Don' tell me wha' ta do."

Finally the cop broke from the cool act, coming up off the car. "Look, man, I'm really trying to help you out here."

Evan had to figure some way to break the guy out of his hearts-and-minds campaign. As the cop came forward, Evan set his feet clumsily and swung at his face. The officer leaned back, and Evan missed by two feet. He pretended to lose his balance on the follow-through, letting the bottle slip from his booze-greased palm and shatter on the sidewalk. He wound up doubled over, breathing hard, fists on his knees, doing his best to signal that he was too compromised for the cop to bother restraining. The last thing he needed was for Officer Friendly to choke-hold his concussion back into high gear.

"Hey," Evan said. "You made me spill my drink."

The officer's voice washed down at him. "Whoa, pal. Settle. Let's pretend you didn't do that. That's a whole other kind of trouble, and you look like you don't need any more."

Evan blinked hard at the pavement and grimaced. Wondered what the hell he had to do to get arrested.

The cop was still talking to the top of his head. "I'm gonna give you a final warning. You do *one more thing*, I'm gonna have to take you in."

He'd arrived at the point of no return. This was it. The last hurdle and the highest. If he wanted to save Max. If he wanted to put down the RoamZone for once and for all and ride off into the sunset.

Bent low to keep his face out of view, Evan jammed his finger down his throat and vomited onto the cop's shiny boots.

43

Arrangements of a Muscular Nature

A conference room.

Bad things never happened in conference rooms. They smelled of dark roast and Pledge wood cleaner. The happenings within were illuminated by fluorescent overheads and the clear light of reason.

The Steel Woman was nothing if not aboveboard.

The office building in which she presided, an unassuming ten-story rise wedged into the skyscape at the north edge of downtown, housed midlevel hedge-fund firms, mortgage lenders, and limited-liability partnerships like the one she ran.

Well, perhaps not *just* like it.

Stella Hardwick was a businesswoman by trade. She'd aged into being something more than that, and she wore the signs of her experience proudly. Her face heavily lined, features accented with ellipses and underscores. She wore the gunmetal-gray hair from which her nickname derived in a bun that was so tightly wound it resembled a stone.

The boys had arrived a few moments prior, shuffling in with their dark suits and briefcases like escapees from the 1950s.

But if this were the fifties, she wouldn't have been running the show. She'd have been taking dictation.

They sat in the aforementioned conference room on the seventh floor, the picture windows offering a mediocre glimpse of the city. She could afford richer views, but she'd learned that ostentation carried risks, and if the Steel Woman believed in anything beyond profit, it was risk reduction.

She occupied her seat at the table's head and observed them. A group of men with similar proclivities. She'd painstakingly assembled them through a byzantine process heavy on allusions and reliant on introductions made by like-minded souls. The departments and agencies in which they operated were by and large clean. In each one she required only a single well-placed worker with flexible standards. They were the clockwork to her grand design, able to operate the levers of power without leaving any fingerprints. Investigations were steered, cases misfiled, dockets shuffled.

Their role was simply to stay out of her way and reap the benefits.

But tonight she required something more. That was the reason for the late-night confabulation.

She cleared her throat.

The boys fell silent.

She rested her elbows on the walnut slab of the conference table, the chill rising through the Armani featherweight virgin wool of her thin sleeves. The air conditioner, pegged at a steady sixty-five, kept the room pleasingly refrigerated. She found that the cold generally clarified her thinking.

"Whoever this man is," she said, "it's clear by now that he's a friend to Grant Merriweather's cousin. Which makes him an enemy to us."

"Grant didn't have everything," one of the men said.

"No," Stella said. "But what he did have could *lead* to everything."

Another chimed in, "From what we know, it seems highly unlikely anything can be traced to us."

Arrangements of a Muscular Nature

"I'm rarely content with what I know," she said. "I prefer to know what I *don't* know."

She let them grapple with that for a moment.

"We've insulated ourselves rather magnificently," she said. Even though she'd been the one to arrange all the insulating, she flattered them with the first-person plural because: men. "But our buffer is growing thinner."

The first speaker waved her off. "Hiccups," he said. "Nothing more than a few hiccups."

"The good thing about working with low-level scumbags," another weighed in, "is how replaceable they are."

Several chuckles picked up steam, confidence growing.

Stella spread a smile across her face. "And the two LAPD detectives?" she said. "Are they readily replaceable as well?"

This was greeted by silence and throat clearing as they waited for the heavyset gentleman on the left side of the table to chime in.

"Well, yes," Fitz said carefully. "But it'll take some time."

"And in that time, as we function without the benefit of their assistance, would you consider us stronger or weaker?" she asked.

She preferred not to dominate the committee members but to wear them out. They were strong. But they were men. They didn't have a woman's endurance. They'd rehash their arguments again and again and finally fold.

Fitz mumbled the appropriate response.

"But we have Bedrosov," another said. "As long as we have Bedrosov, everything stays intact. And there's no way in hell anyone's getting to him."

"One thing you've all been masterful at," she told the circle of men, "has been arranging for the unexpected."

A soothing current circled the table, the faces changing from sheepish to proud.

Until now she'd resisted making any arrangements of a muscular nature from inside the conference room of the climate-controlled seventh floor. However, circumstances had changed, and it was time to take a more active role in the steering.

Desperate times and whatnot.

"As long as we have inconvenient material floating around out there . . ." She waved a manicured hand to the glass wall, the city beyond. "We need to continue to arrange for the unexpected. Since the unexpected seems to keep coming for us, we require contingency plans—"

"Those are in place," Fitz said.

She pressed her crimson lips together in something like a grin. "And contingency plans to our contingency plans."

The man beside her folded his hands on the table and frowned ponderously. "What—" His voice went dry, and he coughed into a fist and started again. "What did you have in mind?"

She told them.

The silence afterward hummed with discomfort. The men had blanched. Their gazes remained on the table, on their hangnails, on the seam where the wall met ceiling. Eye contact was too threatening. Too human.

"But, Stella." Fitz fiddled with his wedding ring. "That's a whole other thing."

The Steel Woman smiled. "So are we, dear."

44

Mantrap

The Inmate Reception Center smelled overwhelmingly of industrial disinfectant and body odor. The ducts were working overtime, doing their best to diffuse a lingering trace of spent pepper spray. Beneath a splotch of blood where someone had tried to put a fist through the cold concrete, Evan sat on a bright orange chair seemingly molded for maximum discomfort. The aftermath of the booze, soaking into his addled brain, made his head feel as though it had been molded for maximum discomfort, too. He'd been waiting for nearly forty-five minutes while sheriff's deputies shuffled other arrestees through the system.

Happy hour was crowded at Twin Towers Booking.

In fact, every hour was crowded at Twin Towers, the world's largest jail.

There were forty-five hundred inmates jammed into a space running at 150-percent capacity.

Evan closed his eyes, breathed the stale scent of riled men, felt the heat from countless trapped bodies. Someone was sobbing and someone was screaming and someone was singing. Singing badly.

He'd already been processed by the baggy-eyed civilian employee with caked-on foundation. He'd stood at the counter hiccupping while she reviewed the probable-cause statement. It had been sent through the bulletproof glass in a transaction drawer along with a time-delay, self-destroying license with his face and Paytsar Hovsepian's information, ingeniously engineered by Melinda Truong. "Open container, drunk in public." She glanced up at the young cop by Evan's side, chewed the inside of her cheek. "Barfed on your boots?"

The cop said, "Yes, ma'am."

"Sounds like a charmer."

Evan had given her a loose-handed salute, and she'd smiled wryly in response.

His training had taught him to find quiet where he could, even in the most stressful of circumstances. He kept his eyes closed and breathed. His task right now, in this moment, was to do nothing but occupy his body. The charcoal pills had done their job, ameliorating the effects of the tequila, but the acrid taste of eighty-proof bile remained in his mouth. The light-headedness held on, wobbly shapes floating behind his eyelids.

A beefy deputy rapped him gently on the shoulder, and he opened his eyes. "Patser Hovsepian?"

Evan corrected him with a crisp accent. *"Paytsar."*

"Great," the deputy said, "okay. We'll be sure to get it perfect before you take the stage at the Dorothy Chandler Pavilion." He flicked two fingers the size of breakfast sausages. "Come with me."

Evan followed him into the booking room. Stations were set up three deep, sullen men being shuttled through like cattle. A jocker inked with the Aryan Brotherhood clover and trip sixes caught Evan's eye and flicked his tongue at him lewdly. Ignoring him, Evan looked around, assessing any loose items he might be able to palm and sneak in. A stapler on a desk in the corner. Pen tucked into a clipboard. A computer mouse.

His plan only covered getting in and—ideally—getting back out. He couldn't know in advance what the precise conditions in the jail would be. When it came to protecting himself and eliminating Benjamin Bedrosov, he had to improvise.

Predictably, any obvious tools or weapons were well out of reach.

The deputy gave Evan a prod, reminding him that he no longer controlled where his body went and what it was allowed to do. He complied readily, not willing to escalate to a situation that increased the odds of a blow to the head.

"Stand over here. Back up. Smile for the birdie."

Above the stalk of a skinny tripod, a tiny digital camera peered at him like the head of an exotic insect. Evan flashed A-OK signs against his chest, one circle up and one upside down. Armenian Power.

"Hey, dipshit. You sure you want *that* to be the look the judge sees at arraignment?"

Evan winked at him. There would be no judge, no arraignment. And Joey would have the digital photo wiped from the system within minutes of Evan's departure. Or—if things went badly— he'd be dead and none of this would matter.

The deputy sighed. "Your funeral."

The flash hit Evan, burning his eyes. He cringed away drunkenly. The alcohol leaching through the charcoal and the light sensitivity from his concussion made it easy to play the role.

"Hey," the deputy said. "You okay?"

Evan nodded. The deputy moved him to a bench bolted to the concrete floor. Before him was an electronic fingerprint scanner. The deputy collapsed into a computer station on the far side with an arthritic groan and said, "All ten on the glass."

Evan pressed his hands onto the wide plate, felt the heat rising through the fingertip adhesives as the light-emitting diodes rolled underneath. The deputy's monitor was tilted, granting Evan a slanted view of the CLETS database, waiting to spit out Paytsar Hovsepian's criminal history once the scan results registered.

Evan waited for the impressions laid into the fingerprint films to work.

But the onscreen timer kept spinning. The deputy knocked the side of the monitor in frustration. The false prints wouldn't register.

A sense of genuine dread descended on Evan, tightening his jaw. All it would take was a momentary computer glitch. The deputy would wipe down his fingerprints, discover the adhesives. And Orphan X, the country's most wanted former government asset, would no longer have to be hunted and taken down. He'd already have put himself behind bars, delivered himself with a bow. Right on the eve of his retirement.

The deputy tugged a few tissues from a box and swiveled his chair toward Evan.

The computer dinged, accepting the scan.

The deputy turned away and stuffed the tissues back into the box.

Evan eased out a breath through his locked teeth.

The CLETS interface brought up Hovsepian's prior conviction from high school. The decades-old booking photo showed a dull-eyed kid washed pale from adrenaline, a tangle of hair falling over his stoned eyes.

Evan's appearance was close enough, especially given that it had been nineteen years since the picture was taken.

The deputy didn't even bother looking. "You can take your hands off the scanner already."

Evan had been so tense he'd frozen in place. As he withdrew his fingers, he felt the film on his left pinkie tug.

The adhesive peeled free and clung to the glass plate.

Transparent yet in full sight, it remained curled up from the scanner like a contact lens.

Evan forced himself not to look at it. He set his hands on the table casually. The deputy turned and rested his elbows on either side of the scanner. His breath fluttered the pinkie adhesive.

"All your possessions on the table," he said.

Evan took out his driver's license, a few crumpled singles, and some coins. He dropped the change about six inches above the table, trying to make it look unintentional. A nickel rolled off the edge, and the deputy leaned to catch it.

As he dipped to the side, Evan swept his hand across the fingerprint scanner, the gummy adhesive clinging to his knuckle and peeling free. Annoyed, the deputy set the nickel back down atop the sad pile of cash. "Okay. So. Two dollars and seventeen cents. Gearing up for a big night on the town, were you?"

Pretending to cough, Evan brought his fist to his mouth. Slipped the film inside. Swallowed.

Only a momentary relief. If he wanted to leave no trace behind, he'd lost the use of his pinkie finger for the duration.

He wasn't sure what the optimal conditions were to enter jail but he imagined that they didn't involve a concussion and a non-operational finger.

The deputy swiveled back to the computer, logging the few items into the property-management system. He shoved a clipboard at Evan. "Review that this is all your stuff and sign."

Evan unclipped the two-page form and took his time reading it, scrutinizing each line of text, rubbing his eyes as if hungover. He flipped back to the first page again. Then back. The whole time he was careful to hold out his pinkie like a Jane Austen heroine.

"It ain't signing away your firstborn, high roller," the deputy finally said. "It's less than three bucks."

Evan slotted the pages back into the clipboard and signed Paytsar's name. Lowering his hand to his side, he returned the clipboard.

The deputy snapped his fingers. "Nice try."

"Oh," Evan said, "sorry."

He gave back the pen.

But kept the staple that he'd managed to pry free from the form. He straightened it with his thumbnail and squeezed it lengthwise between his ring and index fingers.

Another deputy had appeared behind him, tapping him on the side of the neck with the butt of a hefty Maglite. "The jail sergeant signed off for you to come with me, sweet cheeks. You've got a history of drug use. Which means it's time for your cavity search."

Evan grimaced.

"I leave that to Horace," the beefy deputy said. "He's got a stronger stomach than me."

Horace led Evan to a box of a room with a concrete bench. He held the flashlight like a baton, fist curled around the thick metal base. Evan's neck still throbbed from the love tap.

"Strip," Horace said.

Evan undressed, keeping his back turned as if in shyness. When he removed his sock, he shoved the staple through the tough, callused skin of his heel just beneath the surface.

"Turn around," Horace said.

As Evan rose, a blue fishnet bag hit him in the chest.

"Put your shit in here."

Evan obliged.

Horace clicked on the Maglite and adjusted his grip, clenching it up near the lens. At the slightest provocation, he could snap his hand forward and bring the metal shaft to bear. "Open your mouth. Tongue up. To the side. Other side."

Evan obeyed.

"Now turn around. Bend over. Spread."

After a moment Evan heard the light click off behind him.

"If you're lucky," Horace said, "you won't have to do that again. Now get dressed."

A perfect square of folded jailhouse clothes rested on the concrete bench. White boxers made from a papery fabric. An undershirt flimsy enough that the color of his skin showed through. Gray cotton socks. Vans-style slip-ons with thin soles, clearly manufactured by the lowest bidder. Dark blue uppers and lowers, loose-fitting because jail took all shapes and sizes. The shirt had a pocket at the left breast.

Evan followed Horace out of the concrete box to the next station, where Horace handed him off to yet another deputy. "This here's Willy. Please let him know anything he can do to make your stay more pleasant. Hypoallergenic bedding, mint on the pillow at turn-down service, maybe a yoga mat in case you need to do some light strength work."

As Horace grinned and faded away, Willy shot out an exhale, bristling a broomlike mustache fringed brown with coffee stains. He didn't wear a weapon, but a holstered Taser was one snap away. "I gotta classify you. Figure out who gets housed in which pod. We keep certain criminal elements together. So. State your affiliation."

Evan said, "I ain't no gang member."

"Fine. I'll just put you in with the Norteños. That should work out swell. Consider your cavity search a warm-up stretch."

Evan fiddled with his hands. "Armenian Power," he said.

"Shocking. Hov*sepian*." Willy checked the monitor. "You got no priors with them, but I see your booking photo here. Nice look. I'm sure the judge'll dig it at your arraignment."

"Yeah," Evan said. "I heard that one already."

Willy gave him a droopy glare. "Arraignment ain't till Monday. Sucks, that. Two nights in the can. You heard that one, too?"

Evan looked away.

"Gimme your left wrist," Willy said. Evan complied, and the deputy fastened a bar-coded wristband on him, clasping it with plastic rivets. "You'll be in 121 B-Pod with the other Armos. That's here in Twin Towers, so consider yourself lucky. Old-school MCJ is bursting at the seams with prisoners trucked in from the over-crowded prisons—six, eight to a cell. We can thank the state budget, which seems to spring new leaks every quarter."

Twin Towers had less brutal arrangements for the prisoners than Men's Central, but its precast cells, bolted steel furniture, and pod structure were also expressly designed to eliminate any access to tools, implements, or loose items. Every last object in Twin Towers was locked down and kept track of.

"It ain't exactly roomy here, but— *Hey*." Willy snapped his fingers to get Evan's attention. "I'm trying to help you out, punk-ass. I don't care how many signs you throw, your drunk-in-public's not gonna strike fear into the hearts of the motherfuckers on the other side of that wall." He palmed his mouth, tugging his mustache down. "Ah, fuck it. Why do I bother? Get up."

He steered Evan down the hall. Tile floors, endless windows. They passed the inmate property room, a vision from a dystopian future, part deep-freeze coat check and part grapevine. Thousands of blue fishnet bags hung from racks, filling the bay from floor to ceiling. All those worldly possessions suspended in time and space. Each blue sack matched a beating heart warehoused behind metal and concrete.

Evan's bag dangled somewhere among them, a drop in the ocean.

At the end of the wall waited a cart loaded with supplies. Before Willy had to prompt him, Evan grabbed one item from each stack. Sheet, towel, soap, rubber toothbrush. With his thumbnail he tested the end of the toothbrush, but the rubber yielded under the pressure. Too soft to whittle into a shiv.

"We had a stabbing last week, which means no disposable razor," Willy said. "If you stay longer, we will allow you to shave under supervision."

Evan's mouth had gone dry. He nodded, rasped a hand over his two-day growth. He'd purposefully gone without shaving today.

"We'd give you a TB test, but results take three days and you'll be out by then. So: Try not to cough on anyone."

Evan nodded. Willy shoved another clipboard at him. "Sign this."

"What is it?"

"It says if you contract Hep C or AIDs, the county's not liable."

Evan forced down a swallow.

"*Kidding*. It says you haven't requested that any prescription meds be supplied."

Careful to keep his pinkie lifted, Evan signed. Gave back the clipboard.

"Nice try," Willy said, and snapped his fingers.

Reluctantly, Evan handed over the pen.

Willy signaled to a guard in the control room. The electronic doors gave a bone-jarring clank and hissed open. Willy marched Evan into a mantrap, the door behind them sealing before the one ahead could release. They drew parallel to the guard window, Evan's wristband bar code was scanned, and the door before him rumbled open.

"You're in Cell 24," Willy said. "Try'n play nice with the others."

He prodded Evan forward, and the door slammed shut behind him, sealing him off from the world.

45

Deploying a Mop-Based Weapon

As Evan eased forward into 121 B-Pod, he was enveloped by a dull roar of background noise, a wave about to break. The unit smelled like death, the decay of organic matter deteriorating, uncleaned and unnourished.

The wall at his side held painted instructions with green arrows: COURT, VISITORS CENTER, RELEASE.

He couldn't help but note that they all pointed opposite the direction he was walking.

Two levels of rooms overlooked a central bay with bolted-down picnic tables sprouting up at intervals like brushed-metal mushrooms. The circular tables sat only four at a time to keep commiserating to a minimum, and they were occupied now. Punks and jockers, hustlers and cell lieutenants with muscle-swollen joint bodies—Evan could read the dominance hierarchy from their postures and positions. A few inmates dotted the stairs and catwalk, watching Evan's entrance with casual menace. The deputies stayed safely behind the glass, the prisoners left to police themselves. If the deputies did come in, they'd come with full riot gear, pepper spray, and stun grenades.

The walls were stained with water damage from the sprinklers, white paint bubbled out from the concrete. Dousing the two hundred or so prisoners jammed into the fifty cells was a common anti-fire, anti-riot, and anti-agitation technique.

From Joey, Evan knew all the camera positions and sight lines in here, when to lower his head and when to turn his face. She could glitch the cameras now or wipe the footage later, but he didn't want to make more work for her than necessary.

He kept on across the bay toward the stairs. An ACLU flyer fluttered by his head: *Do you not have a bed? Floor sleeping is a violation of your rights!* He noted the thickness of the paper, the dab of tape connecting it to the concrete. Passing a table of men playing poker, he next considered the playing cards, how they might be repurposed as something useful. He came up blank. Two prisoner-workers distinguished by yellow jumpsuits slid a bucket around, slapping mops across the floor. Evan did a quick mental breakdown: wooden mop handles, metal band wrapping the head, brackets holding the wheels, shatterable yellow plastic.

Promising.

A wide doorway led to the showers, another to the dayroom, where a television blared a talky news show. The screen was mounted behind armored glass, elevated above a few dozen chairs. Evan noted an assemblage of prisoners whose profiles he'd memorized with Joey's help, the Armenian Power heavies he'd assumed would be closest to Benjamin Bedrosov. They sat in a cluster around a chair centered beneath the television—the best seat in the house. Evan couldn't see the face of the man occupying the privileged position—just part of his shoulder and an arm—but he sensed immediately that it was the man himself radiating a nimbus of influence.

One of the men with teardrops inked at the corner of his eye—Argon Sargsyan, aka Teardrop—noted Evan's gaze across the bay and stood abruptly. A few of his compatriots rose as well, forming a human shield that blocked Bedrosov completely from view.

Deploying a Mop-Based Weapon

Evan averted eye contact quickly and mounted the stairs. An old inmate sat on the landing, scratching his neck and reading a newspaper. A zoo-house musk hung over the second floor. Evan moved up the catwalk, counting down the rooms.

He arrived at Cell 24.

He entered.

Two bunk beds at either side, a metal commode with a concave sink dimpling the top of the toilet tank, a window the size of a shoe-box lid with a browning miniature fern on the shaded end of the sill. The reek was stronger in here, a fight-or-flight hormonal dump shoved through pores and sweated into dank bedding. Contributing to the stench, a bulky bearded man around six-four crouched over the commode. His pants and underwear were dropped and pulled free of one shoe so they wouldn't tangle his ankles if someone tried to jump him. His wristband was coded *H* for highly dangerous. Evan couldn't retrieve his name, but he recalled his alias, Casper, earned for his ability to vanish from crime scenes. His magic powers had run out recently.

On the top bunk, skinny legs dangling like a puppet's, sat a nervous tweaker whose profile Evan hadn't reviewed. He pegged the guy as a lowest-level offender, probably possession or trespassing. A patchy beard sprouted along the man's jawline, and his eyes jerked sporadically. He twisted his hands in the rag he wore that used to be a shirt.

"Welcome . . . um, hi, hi, hello, welcome." The tweaker tilted his head, reading the name on Evan's wristband. "Paytsar was my uncle's name. You got any ramen?"

"No," Evan said.

"We got a extra bed still, which is a treat, a real treat, since Gonzo is laid up in the medical bay. He got shivved with a pencil, so they put us on lockdown and took all our shit. Hot plates, lighters, matches—everything. And now I can't make my ramen no more."

Casper wiped himself once and rose. "Shut the fuck up 'bout your ramen, Monkey Mouth."

"It's like cash in here, man," Monkey Mouth whined. "Better'n cigarettes." He broke off a dry strip of noodles from the cake in his lap and sucked the end. "It's my last one, don't have no more. Got two cigs, but can't light 'em, can't smoke 'em. No money on my card. Most of the phones is broke, so you're gonna wanna spring for cell minutes from one a the big shots."

The top bunk on the right was unoccupied, a mattress folded in half. Evan entered the tight space and flipped it open. He pulled the sheet neatly over the filthy mattress, hiding his soap and tooth-brush beneath and then smoothing out the wrinkles as best he could. Three folds of the threadbare towel took it to pillow thick-ness. He set it down atop the sheet, perfectly centered.

Casper sidled up to his side, breathed down on him. He dragged a dirty hand across Evan's sheet, bringing up folds in the fabric.

Evan stared at the mussed sheet but remained impassive, ready-ing to protect his head if a blow came.

"You're gonna sleep on the floor," Casper said.

Evan thought back to all those years as a kid sleeping on the floor between bunk beds at Pride House Group Home. He wasn't going to do it again.

He ignored Casper, straightening the sheet once more. Then he ran his fingers along the metal rails of the top bunk, checking the soldering for a loose bead of metal he might be able to strip off. No luck. He checked the posts as well.

Monkey Mouth rattled on, "Look, Paytsar, fighting's against the rules. If you have to, though, stick to body blows. Don't lump up anyone's head too bad. Plus, there're sharper bones in the face, right? They'll get you abrasions on your knuckles, which the screws see and then, fuck. And if they ask you anything, you'd better hold your mud, 'cuz it ain't good in here for snitches. It ain't good at all."

Evan said, "Noted."

He moved to the window, Casper shadowing him. A single piece of tempered glass cemented in place with no handle or rail. Evan felt for any vulnerable metal around the sill, but it was just a concrete lip holding paint flakes and dust and nothing else. The precast cell was a seamless block cemented in place. No bars, no bolts, nothing usable. He eyed the plant, but it rose from a Styrofoam cup that was useless for repurposing.

He kept part of his focus on Casper, idling in his blind spot, but Casper didn't make a move.

From the control room, deputies couldn't see into the cells. There were no cameras in here, but even so, if Evan sent the guy out on a gurney in his first minute, it could compromise his mission objectives.

Survive, kill Bedrosov, escape.

When he turned, Casper blocked his way. "Give me your shoes."

Evan said, "They won't fit you."

"I didn't ask if they'd fit me."

"Let's get this clear right now," Evan said. "I'm not sleeping on the floor. I'm not giving you my shoes. I understand you're bigger than I am and that *H* stamped on your wristband probably serves as a pretty big badge of honor for you in here. But I want you to look at me. Look at me closely. And ask yourself: Do I look scared?"

He stared up into Casper's bearded face. Unblinking.

Ten seconds passed. And then ten more.

Casper exhaled into Evan's face, settled his shoulders. He raised a meaty arm, pointed at one of the bottom bunks. "That's my Cadillac. You fuck with it, you so much as *breathe* on it, you'll be dancing on the blacktop. Got it?"

"Got it," Evan said. "Same goes for my stuff."

He started out.

"I know your type," Casper called after him. "You're a cell warrior. All tough talk in here. We'll see how you do out on the floor, fish."

Evan headed back downstairs, giving wide berth to the guy on the landing buried in his newspaper.

As he reached the main floor, the workers wearing yellow jumpsuits were just getting buzzed through a security door. A tempered-glass wall gave the deputies maximum observation of the pod with minimum exposure to the inmates. The deputies took the mops and the bucket, examining them thoroughly for missing parts, and then patted down the workers themselves.

So deploying a mop-based weapon was out. Evan needed another plan.

Actually, he needed several plans. As of yet he'd succeeded only in the easiest aspect of the mission: getting arrested.

He worked his way to the center of the bay to get a clear view into the dayroom.

The center chair was now empty, a throne awaiting the king's return.

Evan looked up along the catwalk, spotted two Armenian Power lieutenants standing watch outside the door to Cell 37. Clearly, Bedrosov moved with impunity throughout the jail. And now he'd withdrawn to his guarded palace.

Evan shifted his gaze to the overhead lights. The bulbs were well out of reach even from the catwalks, recessed behind bolted panes. No getting his hands on the glass, then.

Turning away, he drifted into the dayroom. A few men slumped in chairs, spaced out, arms crossed, resting dick faces on. No one was smoking, not after the deputies had confiscated lighters and matches in the wake of the shiv stabbing, but the room still reeked as if the tobacco had climbed into the walls. On the too-loud TV, the news cycled a story on President Victoria Donahue-Carr, the same panelists masticating the same tidbits about her assumption of the office and her predecessor's untimely departure.

Standing here breathing stale cigarette smoke surrounded by gangbangers, rapists, and murderers, he found himself considering again just how much he looked forward to ending this mission and beginning a different life.

He sensed someone approaching fast and turned, hands rising in an open-hand guard, one foot sliding back to set his base.

It was Teardrop.

He lunged at Evan, swinging for his face.

Evan flinched away hard, arms rising to cage his fragile head, his brain already aching in anticipation of impact.

But Teardrop stopped the punch mid-swing, brayed a staccato roll of laughter at Evan's overreaction. "Jumpy, ain't you, *bozi tgha*?"

Teardrop was Evan's size and build, the start of a scruffy beard pushing through sallow skin. Evan felt an impulse to deliver a *bil jee* finger jab to his trachea, but if they fought out here in full view of the cameras, he'd be hauled off to solitary and miss his shot at Bedrosov. Teardrop was in for a parole violation, coming to the end of a ten-day flash. If history were a guide, he'd be out a few weeks and then back in, out and in, living between worlds until a bigger bust hooked him for good.

He squinted, the pair of teardrops at the corner of his eye squirming like slugs. An ugly cut on his chin had scabbed over, sutures poking out through his stubble like the bristles of a caterpillar. "You taking an interest in Bedrock?"

"Who?"

"I saw you looking," Teardrop said.

Half hidden by the shirt collar, a tattoo rode the hollow of Teardrop's neck, the pinwheel of the Armenian eternity sign, the center of the swirl beckoning like a bull's-eye.

"Did you," Evan said.

"I did." Teardrop jammed a finger into Evan's chest at the junction of his arm. "Watch. Your. Step. *Bozi tgha.*"

He spit on the floor and knocked Evan's shoulder as he walked off.

Evan gave him some distance and then started back to his cell.

Over by the main door, a sheriff's deputy was feeding newspapers through the hatch to the men in the yellow jumpsuits, whom Evan took to be the pod leaders. A lineup of prisoners waited as the papers were distributed according to some predetermined pecking order. One paper was run up to Bedrosov's cell.

They were quickly gone.

Evan looked through the glass at the yellow bucket and mops. Out of reach, every rivet and screw accounted for. His thoughts rumbled, searching out a new angle.

He started for the stairs. The old inmate on the landing had moved on to today's *L.A. Times*, the earlier one folded beneath his ass. Evan stood over him until he looked up.

"I'd like a section of the newspaper."

"Three sausages for sports and entertainment. Two for the front page."

"What's the cheapest?" Evan asked.

"Dunno. Shit, lifestyle, prolly. One sausage."

"I don't have a sausage."

"No shit, fish. You just walked in. Tomorrow morning you'll get breakfast sausage."

"I need the paper now."

The man studied him with jaundiced eyes. Then he withdrew the folded section from beneath him and handed it off.

Evan said, "Pay you tomorrow."

"You'd motherfuckin' better, fish, or I'll take it out your ass."

Evan carried the lifestyle section to his cell. Casper was gone, but Monkey Mouth lay sprawled on his top bunk, talking at the ceiling. "—never called never called couldn't give a damn about me rotting in here—" He paused only to suck on his last bit of ramen.

All in all, not an enviable existence.

The cell was dark, a bit of streetlamp yellow leaking through the tiny fixed window. Evan took advantage of the relative privacy. He worked his thumb into a slight tear in the wall-facing side of his mattress, enlarging it. No springs, only stuffing. He snapped his soap into thirds, extracted the staple from his heel, and sank it into one of the pieces of soap. Then he stored that hunk and one other inside the tear and firmed the mattress once again to the concrete wall.

Focusing on the newspaper, he removed the centerfold and tore it down the crease. After stashing the excess pages beneath the mattress, he brought the single sheet over to the sink atop the toilet and doused it. Then he sat cross-legged on his upper bunk, hunching so the ceiling brushed the top of his head. Starting at one corner, he rolled the page as tightly as possible, pressing all the space out of each turn. His fingertips cramped with the effort of mashing every millimeter of the damp newspaper as tightly as possible. It took a solid fifteen minutes to roll the single sheet into a long cone. Then he climbed off the top bunk, sprinkled some more water over the flimsy cone, and smoothed it again and again and again until it was a single solid stick of newsprint rather than a bunch of compressed layers.

All the while Monkey Mouth rattled on and on, snatches of

phrases bumping across the contours of a terrifying inner landscape.

Casper came back in before curfew and Evan lay down on his upper bunk, placing the slender cone of newspaper between his arm and the wall so it could dry in the open air.

Casper clanked around, making plenty of noise. Then he took an endless leak, watered his dying plant—a losing battle—and kissed it good night. At last he settled into the bunk beneath Monkey Mouth, who was still motoring. "—and he made me, and I was so little, and he tasted like dirt—"

Casper kicked the bottom of Monkey Mouth's bunk hard, causing him to bounce up so high he nearly struck the ceiling. "Shut the fuck up!"

Monkey Mouth whimpered and settled down onto his mattress facing Evan. His eyes were wide, terrified, and his lips moved as rapidly as ever. But he made no sound. He was looking at Evan but not looking at him at all.

"G'night, fish," Casper said.

His big frame shifted around on the mattress a bit more, and then there was quiet.

In the pin-drop silence, Evan stared at the smooth ceiling above his face. Tried not to think about the men he was locked in here with. The forged steel and concrete surrounding them. The chain-link and razor wire beyond that.

He'd smuggled inside nothing but himself. He was his own Trojan horse.

He thought about Max across the city in Lincoln Heights, maybe sleeping, maybe not, but just as alone as Evan was here. That was his tether to the outside world, his purpose that would have to carry him through this hell and out to the other side.

He placed one palm on his chest, the other on his stomach. Closed his eyes. Tried to find a tranquil place inside himself, a place that looked a lot like an oak forest outside a two-story Virginia town house. Ceaselessly clear sky. Air crisp enough to sting the throat. Waving leaves and solitude and the calls of hidden birds.

He was at the brink of sleep when he sensed a stir in the air. He came fully awake just in time to spot Casper standing over his bunk, his massive fist looming.

It hammered Evan in the temple, his head flying across his makeshift pillow and smacking into the concrete wall.

46

Some Martha Stewart Shit

When Evan returned from the split second of perfect blackness, the pain was so excruciating it made no human sense. It had colors—orange and green—and it made noises—a hi-hat cymbal trilling under an insistent drumstick.

Before Evan could find his other senses, Casper's arm slammed down onto him, the blocky hand seizing his loose-fitting shirt. The right fist was already drawn back again, set for the follow-up blow.

The next punch would kill him. With luck he might survive second-impact syndrome. But there wasn't a name for third-impact syndrome because no one made it that far.

The age-old choice fired his lizard brain: move or die.

His thoughts weren't functional, so he relied on muscle memory. Through the black-and-white speckles clouding his visual field, he made a series of split-second calibrations. Top bunk. Casper standing. Leaning in. Firm grip. Punch imminent.

He seized Casper's wrist and, rather than fending the hand off, pulled it in tighter, throwing Casper off balance. Casper's right arm flailed to prevent him from toppling, so he couldn't land the strike.

Evan flicked a hand at the bridge of the big man's nose, shattering it. Holding the left wrist firm to keep Casper's arm locked across the lip of the bunk, Evan spun up and around, flying off the bunk sideways so his knees struck the top of Casper's braced elbow.

The impact carried the force of Evan's momentum and his full falling weight.

Elbows prefer to bend the other way.

The snap was loud enough to awaken Monkey Mouth in the next bunk.

Both men hit the floor, Casper on his back with blood spurting from his nose and his arm flopping loosely, Evan on his feet.

Evan's knees buckled, and he had to grab Monkey Mouth's bunk to hold himself upright. His brain seemed to jog in his skull, streaks of light and nausea crowding in on him.

He looked down at Casper, watching him writhe. He tried to talk, but his words came out a slur. He cleared his throat, shut his eyes against the pain, and tried again. "If you get to the medical bay quickly and tell them about how you slipped and fell, they can set that and avoid permanent damage."

It took everything Evan had to reach down, grasp Casper's good hand, and haul him to his feet. Mewling, Casper cradled his shattered arm and stumbled out.

The instant he cleared the cell, Evan collapsed. One hand on the concrete floor. Static bugs poured across the room, a sheet of movement. He crawled to the toilet and vomited, then vomited again.

He sat with his back against the wall, palms pressed to his skull, trying to fight down the throbbing. He imagined his brain inside, swelling, creaking the junction points of the plates.

"You should go," Monkey Mouth said. "To the infirmary with Casper. It's no good getting hit in the head like that."

But the last thing Evan could afford was for anyone to take a closer look at him and see that he wasn't Paytsar Hovsepian.

Which meant he had to muscle through the pain. Or die here on the cell floor.

Right now it felt like it could go either way.

A half hour later, an electronic bleat announced breakfast, sounding like an air horn going off between Evan's temples. It took him a solid thirty seconds to stand. By the time he did, Monkey Mouth was gone.

Evan took Casper's beloved plant from the Styrofoam cup, shook the clod of damp soil into the toilet, and flushed it. Then he tilted the miniature fern back into the cup, slid it to the other edge of the sill to absorb the direct morning sunlight, and staggered out.

Downstairs he joined the herd of inmates assembly-belting toward the metal picnic tables. His balance was terrible, tilting him into an inmate beside him and earning him a violent shove in return. But he kept his feet.

He scanned the mob of faces all around, searching for Bedrosov, but his blurry vision made it near impossible. The pod leaders circulated carts among the tables, serving the prisoners a few sad items each.

Evan took a seat at a table with other seeming outsiders, including the gray-haired inmate who'd sold him the newspaper section, and hunkered down over his tray. Powdered eggs, biscuit, three breakfast sausages. To repay his debt, he gave one sausage to the older inmate, who received it with an appreciative grunt. Then Evan arranged the food neatly, aligning the sausages so they were parallel. Set the rubber spork on the left edge of his plate. Unfolded his napkin and rested it in his lap.

The old guy across from him watched his preparations with wry amusement. "Nice picnic, fish. That's some Martha Stewart shit."

Evan heard the words as if underwater. When he looked down at his tray, his vision doubled, a spork doppelgänger springing into existence. He tried to stare it back into one utensil but failed, so he reached somewhere between the two images and came up with the actual object. He pressed the flimsy spork against his tray, but it had too much give to be useful as a weapon, so he set it back down.

With great effort he picked up his head and scanned the bay for Bedrosov. He didn't see him, but he did pick out Teardrop at a table on the far side of the staircase. Evan figured Bedrosov was sitting on the other side of the same table, just out of sight.

"What you looking for?" the guy across from him asked.

"I want a tattoo," Evan said, concentrating hard to get the words out cleanly. "Commemorate my time in here."

At this the other inmates chuckled.

"Anyone in here do that?"

"Shit, Cedric over there's a ink slinger," the gray-haired man said, chinning at an obese inmate two tables along. "But not no more since the screws took his kit in the shakedown. He got no more needles, no more spoon to mix the ink with toothpaste, no more lace to soak that shit up. So for the meanwhile you're stuck with your baby-smooth Martha Stewart skin."

Cedric sat with his legs spread to accommodate the dip of his belly. He'd already wolfed down his breakfast and looked to be jonesing for a smoke, rolling his fingertips against one another, sucking on the end of his spork.

Evan ate his eggs first and then the remaining sausages.

He folded the biscuit in his napkin and pocketed it.

When the alarm blared for them to return their trays to the carts, Evan stood up, lost his balance, and plopped back down onto his seat. No one paid any mind. His next attempt was more successful. Firming his equilibrium, he stared over at Teardrop's table once more. The ring of Armenian Power lieutenants parted, and Evan caught his first glimpse of Bedrosov.

He'd gained weight on the inside, his cheeks shiny, a curtain of fat hanging from his jawline. He looked like a bloated politician, sure-footed and entitled, as if he already knew the deck was stacked and just had to wait for the game to play out.

In the jostle to the cells, he and Evan locked eyes across the bay.

Some Martha Stewart Shit

Bedrosov's core of protectors carried him off, and Evan watched him vanish into the swirl of dark blue prison wear.

Back in his cell, Evan lay flat on his bunk until he was sure he wasn't going to vomit. Once the pain had receded a notch below all-encompassing, he removed the cone of newspaper from where he'd hidden it beneath his sheet. Though it had hardened as it dried, it was brittle enough to break if he tapped it against the wall.

While Monkey Mouth spoke to the ceiling in one endless unbroken sentence, Evan retrieved another sheet of newspaper from beneath his mattress and repeated the process, first wetting it, and then wrapping it around the fragile initial cone as tightly and meticulously as possible. He was careful to keep his exposed pinkie away from the paper to avoid leaving a print.

If all went well, his little craft project would wind up as evidence.

When he finished, he rested it in the gap between the side of his mattress and the wall. Then he rested, worn out from the level of concentration. Every half hour he would repeat the process until he'd built the cone up painstakingly, one sheet at a time.

He interrupted Monkey Mouth's monologue. "Can I trade a biscuit for your cigarettes?"

Monkey Mouth rolled his head to take in Evan with large, childlike eyes. He was scratching his arm repetitively, drawing blood. "Do you have any ramen?"

"I'm sorry, pal," Evan said. "I don't have any ramen."

The man's disappointment held the weight of the world. "Okay, then." He reached into his sock and pulled out two bent, sweat-stained butts.

From top bunk to top bunk, they exchanged items.

Evan split the cigarettes between his thumbs, exposing the tobacco. Then he pulled down his blue lowers and tore a shred of papery fabric from the leg hem of the jail-issue boxer shorts. Ripping the shred into two rough squares, he divided the tobacco between them, twisted the fabric at the tops to form tea-bag pouches, and tied off each with a thread plucked from the sleeve of his oversize top. He had to squint the entire time to keep everything from blurring.

He headed out, moving unevenly along the catwalk. The floating clock above the bay showed 11:59 A.M.

At the bottom of the stairs, Evan paused and stared directly at the top surveillance camera. He blinked four times. Each blink was a signal to Joey. She couldn't watch the feed around the clock, but when she reviewed footage, she'd note his blinks and count four hours forward from noon. At 4:00 P.M. they'd meet back here virtually and he'd give her the next set of coded instructions in real time.

He spotted Cedric the inker in the dayroom and wandered over to take the chair next to him. Cedric tilted back in a chair bowing beneath his weight. His fingers were still jumping around, searching for a cigarette, and he was sucking on his bottom lip. He stayed focused on the TV even as he addressed Evan. "What you want?"

"I know you're an ink slinger," Evan said.

"Can't make no tattoos no more," Cedric said. "Don't have shit for needles. No spoon, nuthin'."

"Do you have ink?"

"Maybe I managed to hide me some. But what good's ink for by itself?"

Evan took the two bound pouches of tobacco from his pocket and held them in his palm.

"What's that sorry-looking shit?"

"Pouch tobacco. You can stuff it in your lip like a Skoal Bandit."

Cedric leaned over, the chair creaking, and poked at the pouches. He made a face and shifted away, hugging his chest and pretending to watch the TV. He couldn't help but work his lower lip between his teeth, an oral fixation hamstering out of control.

Finally he sighed theatrically and withdrew a crappy Bic pen refill from his breast pocket. He slapped it into Evan's hand and snatched up the pouches. "I don't know what you're gonna do with that," he said. "Then again, I don't know what I'm gonna do with it neither."

Some Martha Stewart Shit

By the time Evan reached the door, Cedric had already tucked one of the pouches into his lower lip.

Wobbly on his feet, Evan walked back across the bay, glancing up to see Teardrop blocking the bottom of the stairs. As Evan approached, Teardrop shifted back on his heels, arms crossed high on his chest.

"The man wants to see you," he said.

"The man can come see me himself," Evan said.

Teardrop grinned a wolfish grin. "You don't wanna do Bedrock like that," he said. "Listen to me, bro, I may be getting kicked soon, but don't think I won't do one last job up in here."

"Then you *won't* get out of here anytime soon."

"Oh, I'm sure Bedrock'd make it worth my while."

Evan considered. Gave a faint nod.

He followed Teardrop to Cell 37, concentrating so as to not slip on the steps. The Armenian Power lieutenants, inked up as members of the Glendale chapter, parted to let them through.

Bedrosov sat on a makeshift king-size mattress built of two stacks of twins shoved together. Except for a single unoccupied bunk bed against one wall, the rest of the cell was empty, a testament to his influence. The bottom bunk was bricked in with packages of instant ramen, hundreds of them, the vision Monkey Mouth would see if he ever dreamed pleasant dreams.

Bedrosov's soft, plump hands were folded loosely between his knees. He looked at ease, a man without a care in the world. His voice was soft, that familiar pragmatic purr. "Paytsar Hovsepian?"

Evan said, "You know my name."

"You broke Casper's arm," Bedrosov said.

"Why do you care?"

"There's an order. When that order is disrupted, business is disrupted."

And to you, Evan thought, *there's nothing worse than business getting disrupted.*

Bedrosov's face smeared into a mocha streak atop a shirt. Evan blinked several times hard, and it reassembled itself.

"I didn't mean to mess with your gang," Evan said.

"Oh, I'm not one of these animals," Bedrosov said.

If Teardrop or the lieutenants were insulted, they gave no sign of it.

"I don't belong here," Bedrosov continued. "I'm only a part of this temporarily. But while I'm here, I like to ensure that things go as smoothly as possible for me."

"If Casper hadn't attacked me," Evan said, "things would still be going smoothly for him."

Bedrosov tilted his head back and examined Evan. He was an extremely still man, so every move seemed freighted with significance. "If that's the case, if Casper attacked you, I will let it slide. Be sure not to initiate any violence on your own during your stay."

Evan nodded, but Bedrosov remained motionless, the picture of control. His eyes were unblinking, reptilian. Evan had read once that there were more psychopaths in business than in any other field. The man before him seemed a perfect case study.

Evan started to back out.

"You seem vaguely familiar," Bedrosov said. "Have I seen you somewhere?"

A tingle of heat moved through Evan, dampening his undershirt with sweat, the electronic wristband sticking to his skin. "Not unless you service your car at the AutoZone at Washington and Hoover."

Bedrosov said nothing. He just stared.

Evan lowered his gaze as if intimidated and backed the rest of the way out.

47

Kill You Tonight

The next hour was like the one before and every one before and every one to come, stretched out in front of Evan like the horizon. He'd been in a few holding cells and interrogation rooms, even done a short stint in a Moroccan prison. He understood jail time. Institutional life was not unlike his early childhood. Warehoused like wine in a barrel, overheated and overripened, drying out or filling with acid.

He stayed in his cell, adding layer after layer to his brittle newspaper cone and trying not to think about just how thin the needle was that he had to thread to pull this all off.

Lunch was bologna with a green tinge, greasy french fries, and an orange sugar drink he couldn't make himself finish. He sat at the same table with the same outsiders, trying to stop his vision from rolling like an old-fashioned TV. His head felt full of soup.

As they streamed back to their cells afterward, he noticed several inmates stuffing crumpled newspapers down their collars.

Evan said to the gray-haired inmate at his side, "What are they doing?"

"Padding they undershirts against stickings," the man said. "Shit's going down. Soon."

"What shit?"

The man cocked his head, looked at Evan sideways. "Son, don't you know?"

Before Evan could respond, the man peeled off toward his cell.

Screened rec areas formed the backside of the top floors. As the inmates were let out from the stairwell into the semi-open zones, Evan realized that he'd forgotten what real air tasted like. He sucked in a few lungfuls, hoping it would help clear his head. The men spread out among the basketball courts and the weight-lifting turf. Industrial screen rimmed the building's edge. There was no good sniper vantage from any of the surrounding buildings.

He'd checked.

Bedrosov sat on a weight bench until a runner brought him a cell phone. Then he made call after call, and the deputies either didn't notice or didn't care.

Evan walked carefully around the screened perimeter, eyes on the ground, searching for anything useful. Balled up by the trash can was a foil pea of a chewing-gum wrapper. He crouched to pick it up, and the change in elevation brought the pain between his temples to a high hum. He squatted there a moment, catching his breath.

A skeletal crackhead leaned against the trash can, hugging his knees, pant cuffs tugged up to show what looked like a staph infection in the open wound on his shin.

Evan said, "You need to get to the medical bay."

The man stared at him with sunken eyes, his gaze dizzyingly vacant.

That's what time on the inside could do to you.

The possibility of failure curled around Evan's brain stem, and he shook it off. Defeat was too awful to even contemplate.

He rose and glanced over at Bedrosov on the bench making

phone calls, running his empire with impunity. Evan wondered if he was putting out another contract on Max Merriweather. If so, the only way to void the contract was to make sure there'd be no one around to pay it.

The whistle blew to signal the end of rec time, and Evan turned to go, nearly bumping into a huge inmate he didn't recognize. A ruinous mountain in jailhouse blues, acne scars so severe they looked like burn marks. "You the boy who hurt Casper." The man smiled, revealing a gleaming gold incisor. "We gonna kill you tonight."

A wave of light-headedness swept through Evan, and he had to step to the side to right his balance.

"Okay," he said.

At four o'clock sharp, Evan returned to his meet spot with Joey at the base of the stairs. He was en route to the shower, his towel and chunk of soap in hand. He paused a moment beneath the camera and ran his hand across the back of his neck, a subtle gesture that would go unnoticed by any current or future observer. He rubbed his neck five times, calling for her to glitch the surveillance system in five hours.

The newspaper cone, drying upstairs under his sheet, had been growing steadily throughout the day. He hoped it would be ready by nine.

He hoped everything else would be ready, too. Including his concussed brain.

Walking away, he stumbled a bit. He hoped Joey wouldn't notice. Continuing on into the showers, he stripped with a few other inmates and stepped under the lukewarm drizzle. His scruff had grown longer, approximating a beard, and he longed for a shave. He didn't duck his head beneath the stream, staying alert. Even the moderate heat of the water brought his temperature up, the symptoms simmering back to life. The room tilted one way and then the other, a slow-motion seesaw. He sagged into the wall, willing the static to clear from his brain.

That's when he noticed the other inmates trickling out.

No, no, no, he thought. *Not now.*

He stepped out of the stream, his body still slick with soapy water, staggered over to the benches, and hurriedly dressed. He'd managed to get into his boxers and pants when the lights went out.

Three elongated shadows fell through the wide doorway, stretching across the tile. When the men stepped into view, they were perfectly backlit, black outlines that looked like holes cut into the air itself. Casper's friends coming to settle the debt.

They advanced on Evan.

Evan didn't wait.

He charged.

Drawing first blood was the only chance he had.

The three men were counting on the intimidation factor and the element of surprise. All the set decoration—killed lights and long shadows in the proverbial shower—didn't buy them what they'd hoped.

The darkness meant he wouldn't see them coming.

But it also meant they couldn't see him coming.

The floor was slick with water, which would help.

In a three-man assault, the guy in the middle was usually the alpha, so Evan singled him out first, jabbing two fingers into the jugular notch at the base of his throat. The soft flesh in the U-shaped dent beneath the Adam's apple had plenty of give. The man fell away, hands wrapped around his thick neck, gagging and screeching for air.

The ringing in Evan's ears rose to a high-pitched whine, but he ignored it, ignored the nausea and the pain and the way the men's outlines were indistinct, like ghosts bleeding into the air. If he held it together, he could get it mostly right, and mostly right might just be good enough.

The other two came at Evan simultaneously, unsteady on the wet tile, but they were clearly spooked at having lost the drop. Slipping between them, Evan chambered his leg and pistoned his heel into the outside back of the smaller man's thigh, aiming four inches above the knee to target the spot where the peroneal nerve branches off from the sciatic. The pressure-point pain was profound and immobilizing and set off a sympathetic reflex in the other leg. The man tumbled to the floor, doubled over in an improvised fetal position so he could clutch his throbbing limb. His lips gaped, and even in the dim light Evan could make out the glisten of drool.

Evan faced the last man. He still couldn't see him clearly, but the guy was enormous, his shoulders rising and falling. Panicked breathing. His mouth was spread, a gold incisor glinting in the dim light.

The man from the rec area, then.

Not one of Bedrosov's lieutenants. That made the situation less complicated but still plenty dangerous.

Evan's two strikes had cost him. His muscles were spent, his head screaming. The tile rolled like a boat beneath his feet, threatening to dump him over.

Evan and the big man circled each other.

The others flopped on the tile, fighting for air, making animal noises.

Evan's view got swimmy and wouldn't come back. He could barely discern his opponent; he looked like a collection of ripples that made up a man.

There was no way Evan could fight him. Not right now.

He had to bluff his way out.

It took everything he had to produce the words without slurring. "If I'd kicked him four inches lower, I would've struck the knee joint. That would have produced permanent damage—cartilage tearing, tendons stripped from the bone, maybe a shattered patella. That's what I'll do to you. Unless."

They kept circling, sizing each other up. Evan's bare feet made slapping noises against the tile.

"Unless what?" the big man finally said.

"I don't want to hurt anyone too badly," Evan said. "And I don't think any of you want to get hurt too badly."

"Like you hurt Casper?"

"Yeah," Evan said. "Like that."

They shuffled around and around, the men's gasps and moans echoing in the darkness. Evan stopped, and the man matched him. The room, however, kept moving.

Evan summoned his toughest voice. "We good?" It sounded husky rather than weak, a stroke of luck.

The man hesitated. Then gave a nod. "We're good."

"Why don't you help your friends out," Evan said.

The man shouldered his cohorts and stumbled away. Evan stood in the darkness until the sounds of their labored retreat faded.

Then he sat on the bench, gripped it at either side, and did his best to figure out how to breathe again.

48

I Saw What You Did

After prepping the cell, Evan rested on his bunk, visualizing his brain as healthy and unimpaired. He thought about all his symptoms—the nausea and light-headedness, the headaches and blurred vision, the light streaks and dizziness, the ringing in his ears and trouble with his balance—and he willed each one slowly away.

If he guarded his head at all costs, he just might make it through intact.

When the time was near, Evan hopped down and eased onto the catwalk to check the clock—8:57 P.M.

Three minutes to go time.

He went back into his cell.

"Monkey Mouth," he said. "You should go to the dayroom."

Monkey Mouth paused his oblivious yammering. "Why?"

"It'll be safer there."

Monkey Mouth scurried off the bunk and hustled out.

Evan closed his eyes. In two minutes Joey would black out the cameras. That would give him a limited window in which to get it all done.

He took a few deep breaths.

Either it would work.

Or any recognizable version of his life would be over.

One minute.

Keeping his eyes shut, he felt the firmness of the concrete underfoot, the pressure of the soles in his shoes, the weight of the air. A coolness at his nostrils with each inhalation. The rise of his chest, his stomach moving as well, every breath expanding ribs and belly, reminding him that right now he was alive and safe, standing on a planet with seven and a half billion souls, many of whom had bigger challenges even than what he was about to face.

He keyed to the snow-globe swirl of his thoughts and emotions and waited for the sediment to settle.

Once the water cleared, he opened his eyes.

He felt neither stress nor trepidation. Neither weakness nor concussion symptoms. He'd consigned all emotion to the future. Right now he was a pulse and a weapon heated to 98.6 degrees. He was muscle and bone that if deployed properly would produce predictable results.

And he was moving.

A broken third of his soap bar rested atop his sheet. The staple he'd smuggled in was embedded in the chunk, curved out like a horseshoe and padded with the foil gum wrapper.

Plucking it up, he crouched by the electrical outlet. Careful to grip only the soap, he jammed the small piece of curved metal into the outlet. An arc ran through the center of the horseshoe.

He'd placed the dead plant, dried further by the day's relentless sunlight, on the floor beside his knee. He plucked up a stick of it now and touched it to the arc.

It caught, a makeshift match.

Scattered around him lay tufts of stuffing from his mattress.

Kindling.

He lit a tuft on fire. And then another. And then another. And then one more.

When the flames reached a sufficient pitch, he dropped one tuft atop each of the four mattresses in the cell, mini bonfires with fresh fuel.

Fire burned down into the heart of each mattress.

He picked one up by the edge, ran to the cell door to get up his momentum, and flung it over the edge of the catwalk. The inmates below scattered a moment before it struck a table, spraying sparks.

He hurled another mattress to a different part of the bay, spreading out the diversions so they'd be harder to source. Confusion reigned, inmates hollering, running to their cells, toward the sealed exit. He spotted Teardrop below, bolting from the dayroom, grabbing fleeing inmates and shouting questions at them. Across at Cell 37, Bedrosov's lieutenants leaned over the catwalk, staring down, also trying to assemble the picture.

Evan dragged a third mattress around into the neighboring cell. Four sets of eyes stared at him in alarm. He stood, wielding a raft of flame.

"Excuse me," he said, and they bolted.

He slung the sheet of fire into the center of that cell and pulled the other mattresses down around it.

As he reemerged onto the catwalk, mayhem spread below, brawls breaking out. Evan ran back into his cell, the heat as thick as paste. Safe from the flames, tilted in the corner near the door, was the result of his toil.

The papier-mâché newspaper, ten pages meticulously rolled, dried, and hardened into a single solid object.

A spear.

Not only was it too brittle to be used as a bat, it wouldn't survive a stabbing intact. It was designed for onetime use. He had to protect it until he got to Bedrosov. And he had to hit the mark on the first try.

Evan grabbed it, careful to keep his unsheathed pinkie lifted from the surface, and turned to go.

One of Bedrosov's lieutenants filled the doorway. "I saw what you did, you stupid—"

A single thought loomed, lit in neon on the inside of Evan's mind: *Protect your head.*

Curling the spear defensively to his chest, Evan whipped around in a spin kick, striking the guy with the edge of his foot, hitting him on the rise just beneath the sternum. The man flew up across the catwalk, landing on the rail with a backbreaking crunch. He slid forward onto his knees, puddling onto the mesh metal as Evan passed.

The other lieutenant remained in guard position in front of 37, fists raised, eyes darting from the floor to the various cells. He spotted Evan when Evan was twenty yards out, sprinting up the catwalk at him.

The man squared to fight, his left foot sliding back, which meant either a jab would come from the right or a cross from the left. His eyes bulged, veins squiggling in his neck. An overadrenalized fighter tended to lead with a power cross, and sure enough, as Evan closed in, the guy wound up for a haymaker.

Hurtling forward, Evan hugged the spear and ducked the powerful swing, his speed carrying him inside the man's span. The punch whistled past Evan's ear, missing by inches. A half squat set Evan's base, and then he erupted up into the man, crushing his ribs with his shoulder and lifting him up, up, and over the rail.

Given all the commotion, Evan didn't hear him hit the floor below.

His shoulder had done all the heavy lifting, his head keeping clear of the impact, his hair not so much as ruffled.

He turned.

Bedrosov had backed to the rear of his cell. Even from there he would have clearly seen Evan put his man over the railing. He was on his feet, the characteristic calmness washed from his face along with all color. His gaze dropped to the spear in Evan's hand.

"You're the one who phoned me," he said. "About Grant Merriweather's cousin. The Nowhere Man." He looked at Evan and did not seem to like what he saw. One hand lifted, patting the air, a we're-all-adults-here gesture betrayed by a tremor. "Let's be reasonable."

Evan crossed the cell in three strides, rotating the spear around his hand in an iaido-sword spin to draw Bedrosov's eye. Sure enough, the man staggered back, hands flailing. His head oriented to the spinning cone, leaving his neck exposed.

Evan sank the tip of the spear into the side of Bedrosov's throat and snapped off the end.

The tip protruded about an inch, a golf-ball tee sticking out of his neck.

Beyond that, nothing happened.

Evan dropped the newspaper stick. The two men stared at each other. Bedrosov blinked a few times.

Shocked, almost absentmindedly, he reached up and pulled the tip free. Blood spurted from his carotid, painting the wall to his side.

He sagged forward, knees bending but not giving way.

Another spurt and he struck the floor.

His cheek smashed into the concrete. A shimmering halo spread out beneath his head. One foot twitched and twitched again and then went still.

Evan scooped up a few packs of ramen and jogged back to his cell. Behind the tempered glass below, deputies were appareling themselves in riot gear, readying a charge. There was not much time left. As Evan vectored up the catwalk, he saw Teardrop down in the bay circling frantically around the fallen lieutenant's body, still trying to get a bead on what had gone down.

Evan whistled through his teeth. Loudly.

Teardrop's head snapped up.

He backtraced Evan's trajectory from Cell 37, and his face seemed to constrict around the angry points of his eyes. He sprinted for the stairs.

Evan hustled to his cell. Inside, a few tufts extinguished themselves on the floor, bits of lit stuffing rising like flares. Ash textured the air, instant twilight. The heat started to fire his symptoms, the first flush of light-headedness threatening.

Evan went to Monkey Mouth's bunk and rested the ramen packs on the slab of metal where his mattress used to be. At the end of his own bunk, only two objects remained—the Bic pen refill and that last third of the soap bar.

He squared to the door. Sparks swirled around his shoulders. It was like standing in a furnace. Footsteps hammered the catwalk, and then Teardrop wheeled around the corner, breathing hard, neck sheeting with muscle. Exertion and rage had turned his face a pronounced red that glowed beneath the patches of his scruffy beard.

"Glad you could make it," Evan said.

Teardrop flew at him. Evan sidestepped his first punch, hooking him around the stomach and hurling him back. Teardrop lunged to grab Evan's oversize shirt. Rather than step away as expected, Evan darted forward. Catching Teardrop's chest with both forearms, he drove him backward with all his force. Just before Teardrop struck the wall, Evan twisted his torso and thrust his own chest up into Teardrop's. The men were the same height and build, their bodies aligning maximally for a triple-tap slam into the concrete. Chest hit chest, Teardrop's shoulders slammed the wall, and then the back of his head cracked against the concrete.

A classic wall stun, perfectly executed.

Zero contact with Evan's head.

Evan hooked his hands behind Teardrop's neck, clamped his elbows around his ears, and slammed his face down into his own rising knee.

A crackle of gristle as bone and cartilage yielded.

Teardrop slapped the floor, unconscious, his face destroyed. Shattered nose, cheeks, and eyes already starting to swell.

Soon enough he'd be unrecognizable.

Clangs and hisses carried up from the bay, as well as warning shouts about the deputies' intrusion. "Fire on the line! Hats and bats coming!"

In rapid succession came three booms, the thundering percussion of flashbangs.

They'd be upstairs within minutes.

Evan grabbed his lump of soap and doused it in the sink. He used it to grease his wrist, and then, clamping his fingers into the shape of a tulip to narrow his hand, he tried to slide his electronic wristband off. The hard plastic edge cut into the meat of his thumb pad, but he ignored the pain, ripping it free.

He repeated the procedure on Teardrop and then switched the loose wristbands, fighting them into place.

Downstairs came screams, cries of pain, the hiss of teargas deploying. A deputy yelled, "Move it out *now*, or it's gonna feel like you went bobbing for french fries!" Batons banged against shields, the sounds of the conflict moving closer.

Evan wiped the soapy residue from his wrist and his hands and then bit the top of the Bic pen reservoir to crack it open. Using the metal side of the commode as a mirror, he squeezed out a dot of ink onto the pad of his bare pinkie and dabbed it three times at the corner of his eye, simulating Teardrop's tattoos. He couldn't tell if the reflection was blurry or if his eyesight had slipped further. He blinked hard, refocused.

The tattoos looked imperfect but passable.

Especially given Evan's growing beard and what he was about to do to his face.

He ran his palm across the floor, besmirching it with a layer of ash. Then he smeared it across his cheeks and forehead, even into the creases of his eyelids. For good measure he dirtied up his shirt as well. He streaked Teardrop's face heavily also until—between the soot and the swelling—he could pass for Evan's alter identity, Paytsar Hovsepian. The sutures in the cut on Teardrop's chin had strained but held, remaining obscured by his beard.

After finishing, Evan rose and staggered out onto the catwalk, doubled over, hacking as loudly as he could manage. With all the heat he'd breathed into his lungs and the fire blazing in the neighboring cell, it wasn't hard. He didn't have to fake being unsteady on his feet. A smoky yellow haze of tear gas billowed up from below, creeping through the metal mesh of the catwalk. The first sip sent him over the top.

Deputies ghosted through the haze below, turned insectoid in gas masks, herding inmates out of the pod. Many of the prisoners had removed their shirts and tied them over their mouths bandito style.

A few deputies pounded up the stairs, leading with their shields. Evan collapsed on the catwalk, curled up, coughing until he gagged. He balled a fist and rubbed his eyes hard, working the ash, grit, and tear gas deep enough to prompt swelling and redden them up even more.

They reached him and dragged him out. "Looks like smoke inhalation."

"Christ, let's get him to the med bay."

Evan found his feet, fought off an urge to throw up, and waved the deputies off. "I'm okay, I'm okay." His voice came out strangled, unrecognizable.

They steered him downstairs, out the security door, and through the mantrap he'd first entered twenty-seven hours ago.

The stream of prisoners passed the central control room, and then the men were packed into an adjoining dayroom insufficient to accommodate the pod's overcrowded population.

The room simmered, a press of bodies. Shoving matches broke out, threatening to erupt. Evan shoved his way to one side of the room and stood with his back to the wall to aid his balance. He needed the building to hold him up.

The temperature was on the rise, rivulets of sweat working down Evan's forehead. He mopped his brow and then finger-pasted more soot in its place, needing to keep the cover intact. He hoped the inked teardrops weren't running. He was seeing spots; he desperately wanted to lie down.

Tension escalated, skirmishes flaring, resolving, flaring again. Deputies patrolled, pulling out prisoners for the medical bay and taking others in groups to store in various locations. The room thinned out a little at a time. Around eleven o'clock a deputy swung open the door and rapped it with his fist. "Anyone due for release tomorrow, come with me."

Evan joined a half dozen other inmates, following the man out. More deputies materialized to flank them all the way to the inmate-reception center. Evan had to look down at his feet to make sure he was walking straight.

He found himself seated at a familiar table before a deputy he didn't recognize.

"Your lucky day, homey," the deputy said. "We don't let you go day of release, you can sue our asses. And since we gotta unfuck that mess in 121 B-Pod today, we're kicking you at midnight."

"Okay."

"Social and date of birth."

Evan had memorized Teardrop's personal information in advance, having chosen him for his size, build, and release date. But for an awful moment, he drew a complete blank. The ringing in his ears drowned out all recollection. The only thing he could picture was the awakening he'd received with Casper's fist on one end and the concrete wall on the other.

The deputy leaned over, muscular forearms bulging. "Well?"

And then, like a dream, the numbers were there again, rippling up to the surface of Evan's shattered thoughts. He recited the data quickly before it vanished once more into the deep.

The deputy grabbed Evan's arm and twisted it to bring the wristband into view. He scanned it and then rubbed his fingertips together, eyeing the filmy residue.

Soap.

"What's this?"

Evan fought not to alter his breathing. "I was washing up in my cell when the fires started," he said. "I didn't have time to—" He feigned another coughing fit, leaning over the table toward the deputy, who drew away.

"Okay, okay. Jesus." The deputy tossed him a blue fishnet bag. "Here's your shit. Get dressed."

When Evan stood, it took his full attention not to topple over. He carried the bag to the concrete room where he'd changed before. After stripping off his uppers and lowers, he pulled Teardrop's clothes from the bag. Wallet holding a debit card, driver's license, eighty-some dollars, and a tattered photo of a woman in a bikini. Pack of cigarettes. Pack of chewing gum. Filthy jeans and a blood-crusted flannel shirt that had no doubt been soiled during whatever altercation had split Teardrop's chin and landed him in here.

The two dollars and seventeen cents Evan had walked in with would remain behind, along with the fake license that would have faded to invisibility by the time anyone thought to pull it from deep storage.

Evan had to sit to yank on Teardrop's dirty jeans, and then he buttoned the soiled shirt. His fingers felt numb, and he had a tough time shoving the buttons through the holes. Caked blood blackened the collar in the front. Swallowing hard, Evan ground it against his chin, bits catching in his emergent beard. If anyone thought to look for a cut on his jawline, the mess would provide ample cover.

He stepped out of the room, cleared his throat, and said, "I'm ready."

As the deputy led him downstairs, he could hear his pulse whooshing in his ears. The air-conditioning blew down sharply on him, drying the back of his throat. His legs had turned to rubber, his knees threatening to buckle with every step. When he saw who was standing at the metal detectors in the front, he had to resist a powerful urge to draw up short.

It was Willy—the deputy who had classified him on the way in. His mustache, fringed with brown coffee stains, bristled as he bunched his lips.

He stared Evan straight in the face.

Evan lowered his gaze, prayed that the beard and soot and teardrop tattoos were sufficient cover. How many prisoners did Willy process through in a given day? Dozens? Hundreds? Moving past Willy, Evan sensed the man's glare on him.

He willed himself to walk. He could feel every bone in his foot struggling to hold balance as his weight rolled across it. One step. Another. Another.

He cleared the detectors.

The front door was ahead, and it was oscillating only slightly.

"Hey," Willy said, and Evan's skin went to ice. *"Hey!"*

He turned.

A drop of sweat trickled from his hairline, nearing the ink of the fake tattoos. He didn't dare reach to wipe it away. His head hummed, spots dancing everywhere, pixelating the deputy.

Willy squinted at him.

Each second held the weight of an hour.

The drop of sweat reached Evan's eyebrow, a few millimeters from smearing the teardrops.

Willy lifted a pair of scissors into view. For an instant Evan had a bizarre vision that the deputy might attack him here and now.

"Want me to cut it off?"

Evan cleared his throat. Cleared it again. "'Scuse me?"

Willy jerked his chin at Evan's arm. "The wristband."

"Oh," Evan said. "Yeah. Thanks."

He held out his arm.

A snip.

The wristband fell away.

Evan turned as the drop of sweat tickled down through the Bic ink at the side of his eye.

He walked out through the glass doors into the embrace of midnight.

The front gate, topped with concertina wire, rolled open. He nodded at the deputies and stepped through.

He had eighty of Teardrop's dollars in his pocket. He'd have to walk to the garment district, see if there were any street vendors who could sell him a fresh shirt. He'd find a gas-station bathroom to wash the ash, ink, and dried blood from his face. And cab home.

Then he'd finally get this mission in the rearview mirror once and for all. And set about figuring out who he wanted to be for the back half of his life.

The night sky brought not relief but a dull kind of terror, as if he were standing on the brink of an abyss. The time inside had reacquainted him with his inconsequentiality. *You know what it's like to be powerless.*

Yes.

He'd been within an eyelash of living it for the remaining seconds and minutes and years of his life.

If the spear hadn't worked—

If he hadn't been able to lure Teardrop into his cell—

If he hadn't been able to slide off the wristband—

If—

He was shaking. Even here beneath the open expanse of the sky, he couldn't draw a full breath. He staggered a block and then another block, and then he sat down on the curb. His beard rasped against the crusted collar. He couldn't stop his hands from trembling.

A voice washed down at him. "Hey, pal. Need some money?"

"No, thank you," Evan said. "I'm fine."

"I'm fine," he repeated.

"I'm fine."

49

An Orphan's Best Friend

The tonnage of Advil in Evan's system kept the pain in his head to a low roar as he disabled the various front-door locks and pushed into his penthouse. The first thing he saw: dirty plates on the kitchen island. The first thing he smelled: dog. The first thing he heard: pounding footsteps and claws scrabbling across the concrete floor.

He held up a hand as Joey and Dog the dog flew up the hall from the master suite. "Wait, my head's really—"

But Joey slammed into him with a hug, her cheek pressed to his chest. Despite the thunderous throbbing in his skull, he held her. The dog nudged his wet snout between them until Evan lowered his palm to be nuzzled. Joey's hair smelled of fresh shampoo, the shaved right side bristling against his chin. Her hands were clamped around the small of his back, ratcheting him tight enough that his bruised ribs ached.

But he didn't let go.

Not until she shoved him away, wiped her nose, and averted her gleaming green eyes.

"I'm glad to see you, too," Evan said.

"I'm not glad to see you," Joey said. "I'm just relieved you didn't get yourself killed. There's a difference."

"I understand."

She wiped at her nose again. Her face was still flushed. "I tore Bedrosov's life apart and didn't find anything else. I think you did it. I think he's the end of the line."

The finality seemed to weigh at them both. Was this really the end of the mission? The end of the Nowhere Man?

Evan broke the silence. "Nice work."

She nodded. "Remember that when you get all anal-retentive about the fact that me and Dog slept in your stupid floating bed."

"You let the *dog*—"

Joey held up a finger in warning. "Not a word. Except thank you."

Evan clenched his jaw. "Thank you."

"You look like shit. How's your concussion?"

"Okay."

"Good. It's over. Which means you do nothing now but rest. Got it?"

"Got it."

Joey snapped her fingers, and Dog trotted over to her side. "So me and this stupid dog you stuck me with better get out of here before anyone notices. Every time I took him out to go potty, we had to Scooby-Doo our way around that tight-ass HOA guy with the *Where's Waldo?* glasses."

"I have no idea what any of that means."

Already she was out the door, her voice wafting back. "You need a shower. And shave already. You look like a hobo. A *concussed* hobo."

The door closed.

He stood a moment in the quiet, trying not to let the crusted plates on the counter and the dog hair on the floor aggravate him. What a different way to come home. Footsteps, a hug, a warm muzzle in the palm.

Maybe his new life could include these things.

He took Joey's advice, showering, shaving, and then dressing in his own clothes. The bedsheets were swirled atop the mattress and flecked with dog hair. The floor was a mess. A half-drunk glass of OJ had left a ring on the nightstand.

All the imperfections felt overwhelming, scratching at his focus, and he felt a compulsion to clean and order, to curate the environment until it was pleasing to his eye. He entered the Vault and checked the corner where Dog had relieved himself. Joey had cleaned that up at least, though various plates were scattered across the L-shaped table. And crumbs. Was it that hard to position one's mouth over a plate while eating?

He supposed he shouldn't complain. He was finished now, with nothing ahead on the calendar but getting Max back to his life and doing some light cleaning.

He glanced up at the OLED screen and froze, his compulsion vanishing.

His e-mail, the.nowhere.man@gmail.com, showed a new message.

A rarity.

He glanced over at Vera II in her dish of cobalt pebbles. She, too, seemed surprised by the e-mail.

He moused over and clicked.

No sender. No subject line.

It contained nothing but a single phone number. A code word. And an extension.

(202) 456-1414. Dark Road. 32.

The main switchboard for the West Wing and the means to get directly through to the Oval Office.

Evan was not a friend to the Oval Office, nor was it a friend to him.

Especially recently.

He looked at Vera II. "What do you think?"

She exuded oxygen and an air of skepticism.

He said, "Me, too."

He wondered why the hell President Donahue-Carr would want to talk to him and concluded it was not for anything good. He just hoped that whatever complications arose wouldn't get between him and his retirement. One thing was certain: He needed to find out as soon as possible.

He dug a Pelican case from the corner of the Vault and headed to the parking level beneath the building.

Joey had returned his Ford F-150 pickup to his spot beneath Castle Heights. When he opened the driver's door, In-N-Out wrappers dribbled out onto his boot, a booby trap too perfectly aggravating not to have been devised.

He ensconced himself behind the wheel and dug for the Roam-Zone in the center console. The screen showed he'd missed a call.

An international number starting with 54, the country code of Argentina.

No message.

Puzzled, Evan stared at the screen. Twice before he'd received wrong-number calls, consumers looking to purchase refill vacuum bags. But perhaps the Oval Office had managed to run down this number and used it to attempt a second outreach. Had this been an attempted contact routed through a U.S. embassy? That didn't seem to make sense.

He hit REDIAL.

The call dumped straight into voice mail. A feminine voice, slightly throaty, one he didn't recognize. A mature woman, late fifties, maybe sixty. She spoke unaccented English: *You've reached my voice mail. Leave a message, or call back later, or do whatever else you'd like to do.*

She sounded more like a seeker of vacuum bags than a trained operative. Wrong number, then.

He hung up. Examined the RoamZone.

It was loaded with a preposterous amount of encryption, but if he was going to reach out to 1600 Penn, he'd have to take measures beyond the merely paranoid.

He slid the SIM card out, snapped it in two, and slotted in a virgin one. Pairing his laptop with his phone for a secure Internet connection, he hopped online and moved the phone service where he parked the number from a company in Reykjavík to one in Maracay.

Then he drove up the ramp, through the porte cochere, and got on the 60 Freeway heading east.

For two hours and forty-three minutes, he beelined it into the platter of the Mojave. At one point the throbbing in his head intensified to the point where he thought he might have to pull over, but then it subsided. He forged on, finally veering off at a random spot just shy of the Joshua Tree National Park. His window was down, the cool air slicing through his shirt. The headlight beams swept across stunted trees and jutting slabs of stone, a postapocalyptic landscape. He cut the engine, grabbed the Pelican case, and climbed out.

The moon was shining in force, caught in a haze of stars. A cicada buzz filled the air.

Evan took a knee over the Pelican case, ignoring the brief spell of dizziness. From the top he slid up a yagi directional antenna and aimed it at a distant cell tower. Then he accordioned out a small tripod and attached it to the case top, using an SMA connector and a small omni stubby antenna. He waited, crouched over the tight assemblage of equipment as if it were a campfire. The tiny makeshift GSM base station dodged all authentication between itself and the nearest cell tower, but it was now participating fully in the network.

His own personal rogue cell site.

Completely untraceable.

Only now did he thumb on his RoamZone's Wi-Fi hot spot, joining the LTE network.

He dialed.

When the switchboard operator picked up, he said, "Dark Road."

Then he punched in the extension.

He waited, the old-fashioned ring loud in his ear.

A moment later the president of the United States picked up.

Silence crackled over the line. A tarantula lumbered by, brushing the toe of Evan's boot.

At last she said, "X?"

Victoria Donahue-Carr had ascended to the throne after Evan had removed her predecessor in creative fashion. He'd always thought that she seemed principled, or at least as principled as a politician might be.

He waited. The RoamZone's sound filters would drown out the cicadas along with any background noise. He fed her the silence some more.

She said, "I'm interested in a face-to-face."

He said, "No."

"At a minimum I require a live video feed. Audio can be replicated, synthesized. How am I supposed to know you're you?"

He said, "You're not."

"We'd need to discuss terms, of course, but I'm confident we can reach an arrangement."

"I don't respond to euphemisms."

"An informal pardon," she said quickly. "I assume you don't want to spend the rest of your life looking over your shoulder."

Her words caught him completely by surprise. Here he was on the verge of walking away from the demands of being the Nowhere Man, and the offer had materialized out of the thin desert air, his deepest wish made manifest. How surreal that hours ago he'd been locked inside 121 B-Pod of the Twin Towers Correctional Facility, and now here he was conversing with the leader of the free world about his future. He took a moment to gather himself. He had to get to Max and close out the mission. Then he'd be ready to walk away.

"I'm not looking over my shoulder," he said. "Are you?"

The silence lasted a bit longer this time.

"Think about it," she said. "You know how to reach me."

He cut the connection. Broke down the gear and nestled it back into the black foam of the Pelican case. Removed the chip from his RoamZone, crushed it under his heel, and slid in a new one.

Sitting in the driver's seat, he fired up his laptop once more and moved the phone-number hosting service from Maracay to an outfit in Pakistan's Khyber Pakhtunkhwa province.

Paranoia was an Orphan's best friend.

He rubbed his eyes, trying to take in the turn of events that had for once proved fortuitous.

An informal pardon from the president of the United States. A quiet life tending his living wall, sipping chilled vodka, and meditating. Maybe at some point, he could even see about rehabilitating his relationship with Mia. And Peter.

He was all clear. Nothing ahead but the unbroken horizon, the faintest outline of shapes to be colored in. Nothing between him and freedom but wrapping up the mission with Max and bringing his old life to a close.

The truck bounced across the cracked earth of the desert for a time before rumbling onto a paved road. Several kilometers later he merged onto the freeway and blended into the river of lights flowing toward Los Angeles, just another guy in another truck beneath the endless night sky.

50

Contingency Plans to Our Contingency Plans

Even though the meeting took place in the dead center of the night, the Steel Woman had prepared juice and bagels. They were closer to breakfast than dinner, and besides, there were scant etiquette guidelines on what to offer at this hour.

She waited for the small talk of golf handicaps and country-club gossip to die down. "Tea?" she asked. "Coffee?"

The public-works director and the city administrative officer indicated their preferences, and a few others followed suit. She served them, as always enjoying the confusion elicited by her mixed role—hostess and iron-fisted leader. Men preferred their women to be more readily categorized. But she'd learned that power lay in contradiction.

She gave her best smile to those who had demurred. "Water? Sparkling or flat?"

"Flat," the city comptroller said. "No garnish." And then, quickly, "Please. Thank you, Stella."

She obliged him and then proffered the silver plate of bagels.

"Oh, God, no, Stella," Councilman Edwards said, patting his belly. "I'm off carbs again."

This sparked a volley of workout talk.

She sat quietly and watched them. The boys rimmed the table, hands resting on the walnut slab, gamblers tucked into a high-stakes poker game.

Which—in a manner—this was.

Now they were at it with the usual banter.

"I can pull three hundo out of Child-Protective Services," one of them said. "Bury it in the overhead assessment."

"I'll see your three hundred," the man across from him said, "and raise you a cool mil from Veterans' Affairs."

They were frustratingly myopic, yes, but that was why she had selected them. They kept their heads down, squirreling away in their little domains. She alone was able to stand back and assess the whole playing board.

The trick was to target line items so vast and shapeless that they verged on being unknowable. One hundred and forty-five million for a building and safety-enterprise fund. Twenty-three and change for a sidewalk-repair allocation. Six for a neighborhood-empowerment reserve. If you put Aging and Animal Services together, you had nearly thirty million. Street lighting came in a tick higher at thirty-one. Police Services tipped the scales at nearly one and a half billion.

That's how you did it.

You nibbled.

Building inspections would be less stringent by 3 percent. The cupboards of battered-women's shelters would grow a touch more bare. Police officers would patrol with last year's model of Kevlar vest. Everyone would still get by.

But she and her team would get by a little easier than everyone else.

Unfortunately, the time for business as usual had passed. The game had changed.

"Gentlemen," she said.

The men muted as if she'd punched a button on a remote.

"Benjamin Bedrosov was killed earlier tonight," she said.

They sagged in their chairs, dread tugging them downward. After they caught their breath, speculation erupted. "What's that mean about our holdings?"

"How are we gonna keep the operation together?"

"Did the same guy off him?"

"Not inside Twin Towers."

"Must've paid someone off."

"What's this guy's fucking reach?"

The Steel Woman lifted a manicured hand. The boys silenced once more.

"Our contingency plans?" she asked, eyeing the heavyset gentleman in his usual seat halfway down the left side of the table.

Fitz registered her look. She'd anticipated as much. As an assistant officer in charge at LAPD's Criminal Investigation Division, he would have attuned himself to nonverbal signals.

He also had access to all order of disgraced former operators and off-the-books weaponry.

He nodded, tugged at the sallow folds of his jowls. "I have a new team in place," he said, sounding a bit ragged. "And we're moving on it."

"And the contingency plans to our contingency plans?"

At the mention of this, nervousness stirred the room.

Fitz said, "I wanted to talk to you about that—"

"We don't have to *do* anything," she said soothingly. "Not now and probably not ever. It's a last resort. We just need to lay the theoretical groundwork."

Like so many, he required encouragement to do what was difficult but necessary.

He rubbed his forehead, clearly agitated. "Fine," he said at last. "I'll look into it myself."

"We're decided, then." She clapped her hands together, a rare show of cheer. Now she had to refocus their lizard brains from risk to reward. "I've begun the process of making inquiries for Bedrosov's replacement," she said, moving breezily to the next action item. "Which means that our affairs call for a bit of restructuring." She reached for the blocky phone and tapped the intercom button to the side of the keypad. "Rolando. We're ready."

Contingency Plans to Our Contingency Plans

Rolando entered in a waft of cologne, a steel briefcase handcuffed to his wrist.

The handcuff was of course absurd, a bit of testosterone-intensive stage direction she included for the men.

She'd assembled the papers herself as always and locked them into the briefcase prior to the meeting. For all Rolando knew, they were take-out menus.

She extracted a set of keys from her pocket, freed her daft assistant from the manacles, and waited for him to exit. The door sucked closed behind him with a certain heft, completing the soundproof seal.

Only then did she unlock the briefcase and click open the titanium snaps. She distributed the latest operating agreements to the appropriate parties around the table.

They sipped coffee, tea, and sparkling water.

And they signed.

51

A Troubled Son of a Bitch

Evan drove through the thin light of earliest dawn back to Max Merriweather. As he drew up on the Lincoln Heights house, he noted a creamy white Jaguar parked in the driveway and a dose of adrenaline hit his weary bloodstream. The car's door was open, and as Evan eased past to park out of sight, he noted a silver-haired man in a Fila velour tracksuit prowling across the front lawn, lifting his tennis shoes high with each step to free them from the sucking mud.

In the man's other hand was a gun.

Leaving the truck, Evan jogged up behind the man, who stood scraping the bottoms of his shoes on the lip of the cracked concrete porch. He held the gun uncomfortably away from his body, as if concerned it might nip him. He smelled powerfully of Bengay and gave off no aggressive energy that Evan could discern.

Before Evan could address him, the man rapped on the door and shouted, "Whoever's in there, I'm giving you fair warning to desert the premises."

Evan said, "Excuse me."

The man swung around, an uncocked Smith & Wesson .44 Special flopping in his loose grip. Evan could see through the frame into the empty chambers of the cylinder. An orange tint of surface rust on the decades-old revolver said it was a sock-drawer gun.

"Don't point that at me." Evan's headache was gnawing on his skull with a vengeance, and it was all he could do to keep the undercurrent of rage from his voice.

"This is my property," the man said. He had a Bluetooth wireless bud in his right ear, turned off.

"I understand," Evan said. "But you don't want to point a gun at me. Even if it is unloaded."

The man looked at the gun, sighed, and lowered it. "I hate this thing anyway."

"What are you doing here?"

The man drew himself upright. "That's the precise question I'll need you to answer. I'm the owner of this property."

Behind him the front door hinged open unevenly. The early-morning light hit Max's face at a diagonal, splitting it in half. "Oh," he said. "Damn."

The man took him in. "Well, this just keeps getting better."

When Max looked at Evan, his face wore the weight of years of exhaustion. "Meet Clark McKenna." Max shifted the bag on his shoulder. "Violet's dad."

"Max Merriweather," Clark said. "It was my understanding that I'd never have to see you again." He scratched the side of his nose with the hand holding the Smith & Wesson.

"Why don't you put the gun away?" Evan said.

Sheepishly Clark complied. "I saw that the water meter was moving. And it shouldn't be. We set up alerts for all the properties. We get a lot of squatters." He said the last word pointedly, hoisting one shaggy eyebrow.

"Violet helped me out," Max said. "I was in a bit of trouble."

"Now, why don't I find that shocking?" Clark said.

Max looked down at the porch stair and stepped around his ex-father-in-law.

Clark grabbed him by the arm as he passed. "I'll need to inspect inside," he said. "If there's any damage, you'll be held account-able."

"Damage?" Max laughed, shaking his arm free. "You'll have to inspect for anything that's *not* damaged."

Evan said, "Why don't I handle the walk-through?"

As Max moved away, Clark grimaced. "You can't acquire a sense of honor," he proclaimed, stepping inside. "You either have it or you don't."

Evan followed him through the dank interior. The revolver hung weightily in Clark's sweatpants pocket, flapping around.

"—racked up twenty dollars on the water bill," Clark was say-ing. "Who's supposed to pay for that? It's not the money. It's the *entitlement*." He shook his head. "Six in the morning, and I'm out here overseeing my own business personally."

He looked fit and healthy, a vibrant seventy-something. The kind of man who was superb at caring for himself. Organic food and facial peels and a weekly massage at the racket club. The kind of man who marveled at why others couldn't just keep their heads above water like he did, who didn't understand that if you don't have any boots, you can't pull yourself up by your bootstraps.

Evan found few things more grating than a man who believed he had the answers to life.

Clark kept on. "Do you think I *need* to be here? No. But do you think if I wasn't the type of person willing to drive from my house in Pasadena to Lincoln Heights to make sure things are right, I'd be where I am in life?"

Evan asked, "Where *are* you in life?"

Clark came up short, blinked a few times. It was as though he'd never considered the question. "Who are you to Max again? You're a . . . ?"

"Friend."

Clark frowned at that, toed a patch of rotting floorboard. "Doesn't surprise me he landed in a mess. He's a troubled son of a bitch. I'll give him this, though. He keeps his word. Never thought he'd honor the deal." He moved to the trash bag taped over the window. "Was this like this before?"

"Yes," Evan said. "Wait. What deal?"

Clark just looked at him. Then headed out. "Have a good day, Mr. . . ."

Evan let the ellipses ride.

Clark high-stomped across the muddy front yard, removed his shoes, and put them in the trunk of his Jaguar. As he got in the driver's seat, Evan tugged open the passenger door and sat beside him.

"I beg your pardon—"

Evan said, *"Talk."*

Clark pulled back his head, clearly unaccustomed to receiving a directive. He started to object, then seemed to notice something in Evan's stare. Something unsettling.

"Do you have a daughter?" Clark asked.

Evan thought of Joey sitting next to him in the car, spinning through radio stations at warp speed in search of a favorite song. Her endearing aggravation over fine points of arcane hacker etiquette or the incivility of texting "kay" with a lowercase *k*. How she'd wept against him once when a dam of memories had broken loose, her frail body shuddering as if trying to come apart. The smell of her soap, lilac and vanilla. She owned a piece of Evan as Evan owned a piece of her, and there was no undoing that, not now or ever.

He said, "No."

"If you did, what would you be willing to do for her? To protect her?"

Evan pictured the faulty latch on the flimsy, single-pane window at Joey's apartment. The broken light above the call box downstairs. The loose guard plate on the front door. The feeling it engendered inside him, an unease inching up his spinal cord toward imagined scenarios.

"This doesn't interest me," Evan said.

"Then I'll tell you," Clark said. "You'd do anything. If you thought something wasn't right for your daughter, that she was going down the wrong path." He wet his lips, his eyes glassy with some memory. "She was *failing*. My baby girl. And if you had resources, you'd do anything to—" He caught himself.

"To what?"

"To get her the help she needed. To save her." Clark's shoulders broadened with self-righteousness. "With this guy. Max. He could hardly . . . I mean, just look what happened."

"Have you ever lost a child?" Evan said.

Clark pulled at his mouth with the cup of his hand. "No."

Evan's head throbbed, and he was tired and nauseous and had been in jail not eight hours ago. He wondered why he cared to have this argument, and then an image flickered through his mind— Mia with her bulging satchel briefcase, Batman lunch box, and her travel coffee mug. Her wild hair and the insistent sharpness behind her eyes. Peter at her side, vibrating with energy and the undying optimism of youth, because every moment held an adventure if you weren't old enough to look past it.

Because of who Evan was, there was so much he'd never have, but that didn't mean that Max couldn't have it. Or Violet.

"He was a hardworking guy," Evan said. "And he saw something in your daughter. Who he wanted to be for her. Something better. Isn't that what we're supposed to see in each other?"

"He saw *money*." At this, Clark's lips tightened in a snarl.

"When he agreed to your terms, did you offer a payout?"

"Of course. Of course we did."

"Did he take it?"

Clark didn't answer.

"Does your daughter know?" Evan asked. "Or did you not show her that respect?"

Clark pawed his mouth once more and gazed through the windshield at the sagging garage door ahead. "Her mother was adamant," he said.

"You mean your wife."

"Yes."

"That absolves you of the decision?"

"Of course not," Clark snapped. "That's not what I'm implying."

"People who proselytize about accountability are usually blind to the circumstances that exempt them from it."

"So you don't believe in accountability."

From beneath his thumbnail, Evan dug out a fleck of ash remaining from the jailhouse fire. "Oh, I wouldn't say that."

A Troubled Son of a Bitch

"You might think your friend is some kind of saint—"

"I don't think anyone's a saint," Evan said. "But I've seen his apartment. I've seen how he was willing to live to see that she got whatever the hell you could offer her. Maybe you need to rethink your assumptions."

Clark set his hands on the padded leather steering wheel. A $120,000 car going nowhere. "This is why I prefer business," he said. "It's so . . . *transactional*." For a moment he looked unguarded, even vulnerable. His blue eyes watery, his clean-shaven cheeks chapped. "Relationships—real relationships—are a goddamned mess. What you want. What they want. What you want for them. What you want them to see."

"What's right," Evan said.

Clark laughed.

"What?" Evan said.

"It's cute," Clark said. "That you think that's a thing."

Evan took his money clip from his pocket, peeled off a hundred, and dropped it in Clark's lap. "For the water bill," he said. "You can keep the change."

He left Clark behind the wheel staring at the wrecked house.

52

Last Resort

First thing in the morning and here Fitz was, sitting in his Lexus in a school parking lot, sipping coffee laced with Jack Daniel's. He didn't like to drink this early, but he needed something to work up his nerve.

What had the Steel Woman called it? *Contingency plans to our contingency plans.*

Just a last resort. Theoretical groundwork.

Stella Hardwick deserved her nickname, that was for sure. She was more like a robot than a woman. The bitch probably skipped breakfast every morning, poured motor oil in her ear instead.

A few parent volunteers in orange reflective vests worked the drop-off line, waving the vehicles in, unclogging the lanes, shepherding the children from car to curb. The kids streamed into the elementary school with their massive backpacks. Kindergartners held hands with their mommies and the occasional stubbled dad in a hoodie. Boys threw footballs and jumped from benches, doing their best to show off. The girls paid them no mind, clustered in groups, bent over their iPhone screens.

He thought of Jimmy and Danica, now lost to college and grad school, respectively. When they were young, their mother usually drove them to school, but he'd made a point of dropping them off once a week, even early in his career when he was still working his way up.

What would his young self—fit, trim, and fresh out of the academy—think of him now? Slouched over his expanding gut in the front seat, slurping coffee-flavored bourbon, the air-conditioning on high to blow the panic sweat off his forehead. Preparing to—

To nothing, he reminded himself, taking another long pull.

Last resort.

Theoretical groundwork.

The first contingency plan was in full effect already, and if that worked, there'd be no need for this. No one would ever have to know that he'd considered it. Maybe after a time, even he could forget.

He climbed out, nodding affably at the parents as he passed. There were plenty of older dads around, so he fit right in.

The familiar scene in the front office gave him a bittersweet twinge in his chest. Kids and parents milling around, turning in field-trip paperwork, nursing twisted ankles, organizing group projects. The secretary was being pulled in a half dozen directions, so distracted that she barely noticed when he flashed his creds.

"Just following up on the security protocols," he said. "Someone should've called last week."

She waved him past onto school grounds.

He cut through the quad, dodging kids and teachers as he searched out the best intrusion points. The playground fences were too high, protected by privacy slats. The vehicle gate by the handball courts was locked and in full view of a wing of class-rooms. He reversed course past the cafeteria.

A small alley led to a chain-link service gate.

Promising.

Heaving a sigh, he walked up to the gate. Twined his fingers through it. It let out onto the side of the school, hidden from the drop-off lanes and most of the cars. A van could back right up to it. The rear doors could swing open, blocking everyone and everything from sight.

Then it was just a few strides up the alley to the nearest row of classrooms. Stealth in, stealth out, and no one would be the wiser.

Not that it would ever need to happen.

He reached down and tugged at the padlock securing the gate.

He'd tell the men to bring bolt cutters.

"Hey!" A high-pitched voice from behind him. "What're you doing?"

He turned to see a slender black kid standing at the mouth of the alley, a soccer ball tucked under his arm as if he'd just retrieved it. Fourth grade, or maybe he was in third and big for his size the way Jimmy had been.

Fitz released the padlock, did his best to look unsuspicious, though he knew it was already too late. "C'mere and I'll tell you." He started walking toward the boy, but the boy took a step back. Smart kid.

"You look sneaky," the boy said. "All hiding back here."

Fitz held up his hands. "No, it's okay," he said, feeling as low as he'd ever felt in his fifty-seven years on the planet. "I'm a police officer."

He reached for his creds out of habit before thinking to flip his leather billfold over to show off the more impressive badge. Holding it out, he approached.

The kid didn't retreat any further. But he didn't come closer either.

"What are you doing back here?" he asked.

"Can you keep a secret?" Just asking the question made Fitz's stomach roil. In his long and distinguished career, he'd learned how pedophiles groomed their victims, how abusive parents inculcated loyalty in their kids. That he was employing these tactics now made him want to puke.

"Depends."

"What's your name, son?"

"Miles."

"I'm doing a super-secret security check on the school." Fitz crouched to bring himself to eye level, another predatory trick. "To keep you safe. And to keep all your classmates safe."

Nothing could be further from the truth.

"And I need to know you're on my team, Miles. That you have my back." He kept the shiny badge visible, glinting in the morning light. "Are you willing to help? To be an honorary junior police officer?"

Miles studied him, and Fitz worked to keep his face relaxed, the situation threatening to tilt either way. His lower back ached from squatting, but he made no move to rise.

"Sure," Miles finally said. "What do I gotta do?"

"This security check is top secret. Because if the bad guys find out, they'll know I was already here. So they'll figure that it's safe to come now."

"Come and do what?"

"You never know." Fitz pocketed the badge and offered his hand. "Can I count on you?"

Miles reached out and took his hand. It was a limp shake, but Fitz firmed it and looked the kid in the eye. "I'm counting on you." He was dismayed to hear the edge of a threat beneath his words.

Miles slipped his hand free, stepped away a few paces, then turned and ran back to the kids on the playground.

Fitz rose with a groan, threaded past the picnic tables, and cut through the front office. It was so busy that the secretary didn't even look up to see him go.

Back in his Lexus, he gulped the last of his laced coffee and pulled out into traffic.

Last resort, he told himself.

Last resort.

53

Fallout

The morning sun wrapped the pickup in brightness. Evan and Max drove toward Culver City. Evan had promised to search Max's apartment and then shadow him for a few days until it was evident that there'd be no fallout from Bedrosov's death, that the way ahead was clear. They'd had a terse exchange about Clark as they left Lincoln Heights and had driven in silence ever since.

Finally Max said, "Eighteen thousand dollars a week."

Evan keep driving. He could tell that the words were hard for Max to coax out and that he needed room to arrive at them on his own time.

"That's how much it cost. Some treatment facility in Malibu. It had a name like a spa, Fresh Journey or Recovery Road or something." Max gave a bitter laugh. "It took me six months to make that kind of money. And they recommended a ten-week inpatient plan. Clark and Gwendolyn said if she didn't go, she'd try'n kill herself again. And she'd be successful the next time." He chewed his lower lip, bit down as if holding back a flood. "They said they'd only pay for it if I left her. And that I could never tell her why."

The run-flat self-sealing tires hammered across potholes, jostling the two of them in their seats. Max wiped roughly at his cheeks, and again Evan admired how freely he could express emotion.

"I made a choice to protect her. At any cost." Max cleared his throat. "At any cost to me, I guess. It wasn't what she would've wanted, but I think it saved her life. People talk about love, write poems, songs. But they never say how totally fucked up it is. The positions it can put you in. Doing the one thing a person would least want you to do. Because you can't bear to not do it."

Evan exited the freeway. They waited at the stoplight, the click of the turning signal pronounced. The left side of Evan's head prickled where it had smacked the wall of Cell 24, and he resisted the urge to rub it. The contact in his right eye felt like a disk of sawdust.

"It was my fault," Max said. "It was my fault. I didn't make enough money." He looked away, out the window. "I should've chosen a better career. I should've done better in school and had enough money to take care of my own wife."

"'Should have' is the enemy," Evan said.

"Of what?"

"The future."

"I look at my family," Max said. "Like Grant, who—sure—could be an asshole. But he took care of himself well enough to take care of everyone around him."

"He didn't take care of you."

"I don't count."

"If you believe that," Evan said, "then it's true."

"It *is* true. It's how I feel. Broken. I don't know how to fix myself so I can live an ordinary life like everyone else. Do you know how that feels?"

Yes.

As they neared Max's street, he straightened up in his seat. "God, listen to me whining. I'm sorry. You told me to figure out

329

what I want to do with my life when you get it back for me. Well, you delivered on your end. And I'm not gonna waste what you've done for me. I'll honor you by being . . . I don't know, better than I am. I don't know how, but I will."

This was the part where Evan told them that he had one thing to ask of them. To find someone else who needed him. Someone in just as impossible a situation as they were. And to pass along his number: 1-855-2-NOWHERE.

The words pressed at the back of his throat, fighting to come out. The old impulse twitching like a missing limb. But he said nothing, looked dead ahead at the road. It was over for Max. And it was over for the Nowhere Man. How different this was, a new pathway being carved through his gray matter.

"Hang on," Max said. "Stop."

Evan screeched the truck to a halt.

They were in the middle of the street a half block from Max's building. Exhaust from the tailpipe floated past their window, giving the effect that they were drifting backward.

Evan said, "What?"

"That white van," Max said. "It's in Mr. Omar's spot. But that's not Mr. Omar's car."

Evan examined the worker's van in the front spot. No one in the driver's seat or the passenger seat. There wasn't any smog leaking from the tailpipe. But as he looked more closely at the rear of the van, he could make out a visual distortion from the exhaust heat, the pavement giving the faintest mirage wobble.

The van was running. Which meant one of two things.

A worker had run inside to make a delivery.

Or a team was sitting stakeout, keeping the engine on so they could use the heater.

Evan squinted, bringing the license plate into focus. The frame sported yellow lettering: HERTZ RENTAL.

He dropped the truck into reverse.

Before he could stomp the gas pedal, the side door of the van flew open and a dozen operators exploded out, wielding magazine-fed carbines.

They opened fire.

54

Urgent

Evan thought of his Ford F-150 as a war machine.

Kevlar armor reinforced the door panels. Laminated armor glass composed the windows. He'd disarmed the safety systems, removed the air bags, and knocked out the inertia-sensing switches that shut down power to the fuel pump in a collision. A built-to-spec push-bumper assembly up front shielded the vulnerable radiator and intercooler. A special adhesive compound in the tires sealed most bullet holes, a support-ring "second tire" waiting inside the core as a backup.

All these contingencies were required now.

As Evan peeled backward, the tires smoking, divots spiderwebbed the windshield. Max was shouting hoarsely as lead dented the body of the Ford, a deafening series of clangs.

Over the din Evan noted the cadence of the bullets, the muzzle flash, the operators' SWAT-light attire—golf shirts and khakis.

The bullet-resistant glass would last only so long when confronted with an onslaught of 5.56 rounds, so Evan locked the wheel to the left and fishtailed around in a J-turn, barely slowing momentum.

The rear window went opaque beneath the bursts of rounds. Evan cut right hard and then right again, gunning up an alley and screeching through a red light, slewing for the on-ramp.

He ran the freeway a few exits, Max white-knuckling the passenger seat and breathing hard. And then Evan exited, burying the truck in traffic.

The Ford F-150 was the most common truck on the road, as well as the most stolen. People tended to look past it—when it wasn't riddled with bullet holes. It drew a few stares now, but not as many as it might in another city, one that didn't host countless film and TV shoots that required countless stunt vehicles. Even so, he'd have to get it off the street soon if he didn't want to tempt fate. Pulling up an alley, he coasted to the curb and killed the engine.

Max had finally caught his breath. "Who the hell are *they* now?"

"My guess?" Evan said. "Dirty cops or contract washouts. Former operators, probably SWAT."

"Sent by?"

Seven endless days ago, Max had come to Evan with one problem. It had turned into two problems, which had turned into three. The fourth problem—Bedrosov—had now led to a fifth. At this point, despite Joey's assurances, it was barely worth getting surprised over.

Before Evan answered, Max said, "What's to say the guys who just shot at us weren't *real* SWAT?"

"The carbines," Evan said, rubbing his head. "The muzzle flash looked to be from a sixteen-inch barrel. That's an M-forgery, designed to have the look of an M4 without all the features. The legit select-buyer models have fourteen-inch barrels. Plus, the forgeries have only two positions—safe and semi. They were firing at us a round at a time. Federal- or state-acquired weaponry go to full auto, which, if they'd had, believe me, they'd have used."

"You noticed all that? In the middle of everything?"

But Evan was already dialing his RoamZone.

Tommy answered immediately. "I knew you'd come to your senses about that Ballista."

"It's not about the rifle."

"Well, fuck a duck," Tommy said. "Why do I get the sense you're about to do that thing you do? An urgent need followed by an urgent request followed by an urgent timeline."

"You said you're in L.A. today. I need to see you."

Tommy sighed, cigarette smoke blowing across the phone on the other end. "I'll text you times."

"Oh. And I might need to swap out trucks."

Evan disconnected before Tommy's cursing could pick up steam.

He texted Joey: NEED ADDRESS FOR BENJAMIN BEDROSOV.

He hopped out, dropped the bullet-scarred tailgate, and retrieved another set of license plates from one of the flat rectangular vaults overlaying the bed. After swapping out the plates, he climbed back into the driver's seat.

Max was leaning forward onto the dashboard, resting his forehead against his hands. He seemed to be catching his breath. He looked over and noticed that Evan was in the same posture—face to his knuckles, hands gripping the steering wheel, trying to breathe. The adrenaline spike had receded, the headache returning angrier than before.

"What's wrong with you?" Max sounded genuinely worried.

"I'm okay. Just need to close my eyes for a sec."

"Bull*shit*."

When Evan let his eyelids fall, it felt so good he thought it might be nice to never be awake again. "Concussion," he finally said. "Just . . . haven't slept in a while. So."

"Let's get you somewhere you can rest."

"No time." Evan used his arms to shove himself back in his seat.

"Why?" Max said. "What are we doing now?"

Evan forced his eyes open. "Going fishing."

55

An Elaborate Piece of Business

Benjamin Bedrosov's house, a nothing-to-see-here single-story perched on a steep hillside in Beachwood Canyon, squatted beneath a riot of bushy magnolias. No guard booths, no security fence, no locked gate—from the outside it looked as innocuous as Bedrosov himself. The relative privacy that he no doubt relished worked to Evan's advantage now as he took on the Medeco dead bolt of the front door. The alarm system had been disabled, the wires beneath the main panel inside cleanly snipped and bypassed.

"Someone beat us here," Evan said.

Max looked around warily. "Who?"

"Let's find out."

Splitting up, he and Max moved swiftly through the house, their search streamlined by the sterile modern interior. Bedrosov, it seemed, was no more a fan of decor and clutter than Evan was, which had no doubt made matters easy for the search team who'd moved through ahead of them. The plentiful windows, shaded by encroaching boughs, threw blocky light across bare tile floors.

A metal swoop intended for logs sat empty by the hearth. On the marble counter, an acrylic pasta holder contained a silo of red fusilli. The pantry held four cans of vegetarian beans, the refrigerator a jug of salsa and a half-drunk bottle of Chianti. In the garage a Tesla slumbered beneath a car cover. A small workbench backed by a pegboard held a few basic tools and a partially finished model of a World War II Flettner helicopter.

"Hey!" Max called out from somewhere deep in the house.

Evan stepped back into the house proper and walked down a bare corridor to the bedroom. Small monitors paneled one wall. They provided security views all around the property, another of Bedrosov's precautions that would serve them well now in case unexpected visitors showed up.

Max stood across the room before an open wardrobe, hanging suits raked aside to reveal a wall safe.

"It was hidden behind this." Max pointed to a panel of drywall he'd pried off and set to the side. "Almost seamless. But the cut was nonstandard, so I poked around some."

"Nicely done," Evan said.

"Yeah, well. Don't know how far it'll get us. The safe has a fingerprint reader."

Evan drew close and examined it. The safe was an elaborate piece of business—Israeli make, hingeless outer frame, no combination dial to drill through. He tapped the steel-plate door with his knuckles, judged it to be a half inch.

"Check this," Max said, and hovered his thumb over the black square of the fingerprint reader. A green laser scan started up with a calming hum, mapping his print. The light blinked red. "You don't touch it. It uses the laser to read your print in midair."

"That can be more precise," Evan said. "Sometimes when you press a print, it distorts the ridges."

"Great. So there's no way we can get in there."

Evan said, "How do you know it reads your right thumb?"

"You can see finger smudges where he gripped the side of the safe to position his thumb. Look."

The steel edge featured four dapples of oil corresponding to the four fingers of Bedrosov's right hand. Evan looked at Max, impressed.

Max knocked the wall around the safe. "Sounds like it's concreted in there between the slabs. I'd need a whole lotta gear and a whole lotta time to pry it out if we want to work on it in another location. Even then, I've never cracked a safe before."

Evan scanned the room. A single nightstand with a single drawer. He opened it, hoping for a remote control. He got something better.

An iPad mini.

Touching only the edges, he lifted it carefully and set it on the bedspread. Then he crouched to eye the screen at a slant.

The alkali-aluminosilicate glass, expressly designed to capture touch, was marred by a beautiful thumbprint.

Evan turned to Max and said, "Don't touch that."

He walked back to the garage and retrieved wood glue from the cabinet beneath the workbench. Next to the telephone in the kitchen, he located a pencil. Back in the master bathroom, he found a shampoo heavy in glycerin and grabbed a few Q-tips. He returned to the bedroom where Max waited. Using the iPad as a palette, Evan squeezed a dab of wood glue onto the surface well north of the print. Then he stirred in a drop of shampoo to moisten and putty up the glue.

He smashed the pencil and used his fingernail to scrape graphite dust from the core, sprinkling it onto Bedrosov's fingerprint. He blew the excess away, a layer of raised graphite clinging to the print.

Max said, "You are an insane person."

Evan said, "Thank you."

Scooping up a lump of the glue mixture with the Q-tip, he smeared a thin layer carefully over the print.

"Certifiable," Max said. "Stark raving."

The concoction dried quickly, and Evan peeled free the hardened slug of glue. The underside held an impression of Bedrosov's print.

"Now you can just hold it up to the laser," Max said.

"Not yet," Evan said. "It's reversed. A mirror image."

He laid the dried glue on the floor with the print side up. Then he turned on the iPad. Bedrosov had turned off the password feature, a stroke of luck that meant Evan wouldn't have to hack it.

Using the iPad camera, he took several close-up photographs of the fingerprint impression. Then he went to the app store and downloaded high-end photo-editing software. Using the program, he flipped the print from left to right, then reversed the color so the print was white and the background black. Using a digital enhancer, he brought the image to 2400 dpi, then sat back and admired his work.

"No way," Max said. "No. Way."

Evan crossed to the wardrobe, held up the iPad image before the safe's scanner, and waited for it to initiate. The green laser scanned the digital print top to bottom, and then the door clicked open.

Evan and Max exhaled simultaneously.

Inside rested a single thumb drive. And nothing else.

Evan withdrew it. He and Max looked at each other.

The mission had begun with a thumb drive. Looked like it would end with one, too.

Evan jogged out to the truck, checked up and down the street, then retrieved his laptop. Back inside, he fired up the computer and plugged in the thumb drive.

He sat at the deco letter desk in the corner, Max hovering at his shoulder.

A profusion of spreadsheets invaded the screen.

The figures on these dwarfed the numbers they'd seen in Grant's files.

Evan scanned the documents. Wires, dates, withdrawals, bank statements, multiple sets of doctored books, meeting minutes, shell-corp formation papers, LLC articles of organization and operating agreements.

And this time: names of the players at the top.

As Evan google-searched the names, Max made a dry noise in his throat.

Bedrosov and everyone who'd come before were nothing compared to this.

A city councilman. The city treasurer and the finance director. The economic-development director and a leading city-admin officer. The public-works director and the comptroller. An assistant officer in charge at LAPD's Criminal Investigation Division. An LLC manager by the name of Stella Hardwick.

All stakeholders in a fund with the impressively forgettable name of the Los Angeles City Reserve Fund. Its balance, held in Bedrosov's captured bank in Singapore, was two hundred and twelve million.

Evan read until the throbbing in his head grew almost unbearable, then leaned back in the chair and pressed his fingers to his eyes. He thought of the potholed city streets, the film of pollution wrapped around downtown, the ragged metropolitan facilities crumbling where they stood, desperate for cash allocations that never seemed to come.

A perennial shortfall.

City budgets had checks and balances to safeguard against embezzlement by segregating duties across a variety of departments. But it seemed Stella Hardwick had found a way around those safeguards.

"Looks like all the big players were in on it," Max said.

"You don't need all the players." Evan pointed at a scanned PDF of the signature page of the LLC's operating agreement. "Just one in each division."

The scheme required a perfectly placed set of men able to verify a fake spending cut. To corroborate a supposed budget shortfall. To create fictitious invoices. To nudge investigations into the circular file.

A dozen men, with Stella Hardwick at the helm, had victimized an entire city.

At the end of the trail, there wasn't a face but a committee. Not a head to the monster or even nine heads but a mini-bureaucracy. The more legitimate the veneer, the less anyone would question what lay beneath.

By plugging into Bedrosov's existing criminal enterprises, Stella and her men had established an infrastructure beneath them to wash the money they skimmed off the city's $9.2-billion budget. After routing their embezzled cash through his bank, Bedrosov fed it out through multiple franchises beneath him, like Petro's. The money was cleaned and delivered in nonreportable, nonsourceable chunks to the men's—and Stella's—respective accounts. Bedrosov had kept the principals sealed off completely, insulated from the process. Which explained why Joey had been unable to pierce the veil of his enterprise.

Stella and her men had used the authority of their offices to cover up their corruption.

They had used dirty cops to further their abuses of power.

They had used contract killers, crime bosses, and psychopathic businessmen to neutralize their opponents.

And in the process they had gotten help from a very surprising source.

The awareness sat heavily in Evan. How awful for him and Max to have come all this way only to realize that the truth had been right there the whole time, right beneath their noses.

He waited a moment for the flush of the revelation to subside and then refocused. He returned to the laptop, studying the meeting minutes. They were aggressively specific, listing attendees and detailing procedures and the precise order of events. An ironclad assurance against an associate's developing a sudden fit of conscience. If anyone went down, they'd all go down.

"God," Max said. "Grant barely scratched the surface. I mean, he was still deciphering code names way at the bottom of the scheme."

Chagrin washed through Evan, prickling his skin. He'd assumed that Max had put it together as well.

"Max," he said, "Grant wasn't investigating this case for the cops. He was cooking the books for Stella Hardwick."

He could feel the heat of Max at his back, searching the screen. Could practically sense the wheels turning in his head, searching for traction.

"Wait," Max said. "No."

Evan's head ached from the prolonged focus, so he reminded

himself to speak clearly and with the same kindness he'd want to be shown if he were in Max's shoes. "There were two sets of spreadsheets on the thumb drive Grant gave you," he said. "We assumed he was working to unearth the real transactions. But he was actually the one burying them."

Just before Evan had killed him, Bedrosov had referred to Max as Grant Merriweather's cousin. In hindsight it seemed telling; Bedrosov knew Grant well enough to make him the point of reference. Grant had been hired into the operation to clean the books. Right away he must have sensed he was in over his head. Given the power players behind the scheme, he'd have figured he needed insurance for when he finished the job. He needed to be able to threaten mutually assured destruction to anyone thinking of taking him out.

So two months ago, shortly after he started the job for Stella Hardwick's band of brothers, Grant had pulled some preliminary spreadsheets onto a thumb drive to be delivered into the hands of a *Los Angeles Times* reporter in the event of his death. Lorraine Lennox was an expert in L.A.'s crime networks. Evan recalled scanning over one of her articles that had made insinuations about a secret cabal of unidentified city leaders. Lennox had been sniffing around the bigger story, which was likely why Grant had chosen her once he realized he'd gotten himself in too deep. And why Stella's hit men had wiped her off the board as soon as Grant fled with the damning thumb drive and they feared they might lose control of the narrative.

"Why would you say that?" Max's voice was hoarse now, the truth dawning.

"What Grant gave you was only his rough work at the beginning of the job. Pieced-together files, partially encoded, even hidden. In case it fell into the wrong hands, he couldn't trust you with something that had the explosive details—the names of the higher-ups—spelled out overtly." Evan pointed at the screen. "But *these* books are dated fifteen days after the first set—right before Bedrosov got arrested. And they're complete. Every last payment that's been moved out of the city budget to the Singapore bank, laundered, and delivered to the principals has been codified by legitimate bookkeeping. That requires the skill level of a superb accountant."

"Maybe they hired someone else," Max said. "You don't know that it was Grant. How could you know that?"

"Because," Evan said, "Grant gave this thumb drive to Bedrosov."

Evan slid the thumb drive out of the laptop and tilted it to the light. He hadn't checked yet, but his gut told him it would be there.

Etched onto the metal plug of the USB connector was a nifty little logo, the right downstroke of the *M* merged with the rising slant of the *A*.

Merriweather Accountancy.

Max retreated until the bed struck the backs of his knees. He sat down abruptly, wrinkling the smooth duvet.

As Evan had anticipated, two thumb drives bookended the mission. Before and after.

He snapped the laptop shut and rose.

Max was still gazing blankly at the far wall, his eyes unfocused.

"I'm sorry," Evan said. "But we've gotta go."

56

The Fucking Mary Kay Lady

Tommy rattled up in his dually to meet them beneath a freeway underpass where the 10 met the 405. A traffic cacophony roared overhead, endless streams of cars tracing the cloverleaf's ramps and exits.

Evan's bullet-riddled F-150 was parked beneath the cramped rise of the overpass. Spots of black mold clung to the concrete above. Aside from a few overturned shopping carts and a ragged army of smashed beer cans, the spot was deserted. That's why Evan had chosen it, sunken here beneath the city, a stone's throw from a thousand Angelenos up in the real world moving too fast to pay any notice.

Tommy parked nose to nose and stared at Evan and Max through the facing windshields. Evan gestured for him to come over.

Tommy looked none too pleased about that.

He thumbed a wedge of tobacco into his lower lip, lit up a cigarette, took a help-me-Jesus drag, and then threw up his hands and kicked open his door. He slid out, landing hard on his boots, and took a moment to set his warhorse joints in order and straighten up.

Then he strode over to Evan in the driver's seat and knocked twice on the door panel. "You may have noticed, I'm not the fucking Mary Kay lady."

"Yes," Evan said. "That's evident."

"You can't just call me up when you're outta mascara and I roll up in a pink Cadillac."

"No. But that would be awesome."

Tommy glared at him, but already his hound-dog eyes had softened. "Hell," he said, "it's my own damn fault. If I didn't keep failing retirement, I wouldn't have to deal with the likes of you."

"Listen," Max said, leaning over. "I just want to say I really appreciate——"

"Don't talk to me," Tommy said. "I don't know you." He looked at Evan. "I don't know him."

He sucked a good half inch off his Camel Wide with a single inhale, shot the smoke up at the underpass, walked back to his dually, and got in. The *passenger* side.

"Uh," Max said. "You sure about this?"

Evan said, "No," and got out.

He walked over and hoisted himself up into Tommy's driver's seat. The two men sat side by side a moment. Evan lifted his boots, sunk to the ankles in discarded Starbucks cups, Red Bull cans, and empty ammunition boxes that clustered around the base of the seat.

"Sorry 'bout the truck mulch," Tommy said. "But that's how you get a vehicle, you know. You grow it from the ground up."

"I'll take good care of it," Evan said.

Tommy flicked his chin at the lead-bitten Ford F-150. "Yeah, you seem to really baby your gear."

"Look, with my truck, I need you to——"

"I know. I'll deliver it back to you good as new. With all the fixings." Tommy winked, the crinkle at the edge of his eye fanning down across his cheek. "It'll cost you."

"How much?"

"An arm. A leg."

Evan nodded at Tommy's tattered Strider Knives T-shirt, the breast pocket torn clean off. "Get you some new duds."

"Shit," Tommy said. "My version of dress for success is two extra mags." He jerked a thumb to the backseat. "Your FN Ballista's back there in the Hardigg Storm Case. Take good care of her. She's a Tommy special. The mall warriors ain't getting their mitts on a beauty like that."

Evan started to protest again that he didn't need a rifle, but then he recalled the dozen men he'd seen spill out of that van, SWAT-ready and armed to the teeth, and kept his mouth shut.

Tommy flicked his cigarette out the window, sucked a stray bit of tobacco through the gap in his front teeth. "You put metal on meat with that baby, fuckers'll be DRT." A wicked grin. "Dead Right There." He reached for the door. "All right, get your boy outta your truck and we'll be on our respective ways."

"He's gotta go with the truck, Tommy."

Tommy did a pronounced double take that for anyone else would have seemed theatrical. "I know my ears are shot to shit, but I could swear you just said you want me to take that Strange Ranger over there with me."

"The group that's after him, they've got their tentacles sunk deep throughout the city. I need you to stash him somewhere out in the desert."

Given the reach of Stella Hardwick's group, the last thing Evan could afford was having Max near anybody who could be connected to him—especially after his contact with Violet and Clark. He needed to clear out way beyond city limits and let Evan do what had to be done.

The Ninth Commandment: *Always play offense.*

"I hope you have a lotta money," Tommy said, "'cuz babysitting's not on the list of services any more than mascara delivery is."

"I do have a lot of money," Evan said.

He thought of the meeting minutes from Stella Hardwick's power summits in her conference room on the seventh floor. And then of Tommy tripping over gear and ordnance in his lair.

"I need one more thing," he said.

"Shocking," Tommy said.

Evan told him the last item he required.

"Fine," Tommy said. "Let me get less fucking annoyed before I draw you up an invoice. If I did it now, you wouldn't like what you'd be looking at."

He shouldered the door open, braced his ankles and knees for the slide out, and hit the dirt with a grunt.

"Tommy," Evan said. "I knew I could count on you."

"Well, shit," Tommy said. "It's getting so saccharine in here I might hafta self-administer insulin."

He slammed the door and ambled over to Evan's truck.

57

Taking Steps

Evan had lost track of how long he'd gone without sleep.

Walking through the Castle Heights lobby, he felt faintly intoxicated, his feet like foreign objects he had to operate with every step.

Ida Rosenbaum, with the aid of a walker and a physical therapist, moved at a snail's pace around the love seats, working on regaining her balance. The bruises on her face had faded to a sickly yellow. She wore a brick-red sweat suit with reflective stripes down the sleeves and legs, high-visibility precautions in case any traffic came blazing through the lobby.

"It's good to see you up on your feet again," Evan said.

"If that's what you call this," Ida snapped.

The physical therapist, a young Hispanic woman, said, "Would you mind watching her for a moment so I can use the restroom?"

"I don't need *watching*," Ida said.

Evan wanted nothing more than to get upstairs and lie down,

but he paused and rested a steadying hand on the walker. "No problem."

An awkward silence ensued after the woman departed.

"I heard you got your necklace back," Evan said.

"I did. And they arrested the crook who took it."

"But you're not wearing it."

"No." Ida waved a dismissive hand. "I'm done with that nonsense. Acting like I'm something to look at." She shook her head. "At my age."

"Don't give him that."

"Oh, please." She shoved the walker at him, the tennis-ball sliders squeaking on the marble floor, and he had to skip back. Firming her shoulders with pride, she took a surprisingly strong step. "Spare me your bumper-sticker aphorisms."

"Yes, ma'am."

"You don't know what it's like. To have *real* concerns."

"No, ma'am."

The physical therapist returned, thanked Evan, and took over. As he walked away, he heard her say, "You're really improving, Mrs. Rosenbaum."

"Sure," Ida said. "I'll be ready for the hundred-yard dash in no time."

Evan had just closed the penthouse door behind him when his phone rang. He clicked to answer and held it to his face.

Joey said, "Hang on," with great annoyance, as if he'd called and interrupted her. A rustle as she slid the phone aside and then muffled shouting. "Get *off* that! You chew my Das Keyboard one more time, I'll get you fixed."

"He's already fixed," Evan said, heading down the hall toward the master suite. The nausea was back, creeping beneath his skin, turning his flesh clammy.

"Well, I bet it's just as unpleasant the second time," Joey said. And then, "I spent all morning scrubbing the jail footage, which would've been way easier if you weren't so incompetent."

The sheets remained, a dirty swirl atop the floating mattress, fuzzed with dog hair. He had to squint against the sight of it.

He stepped through the bathroom and into the shower stall. "How am I incompetent?"

"Where do I start? I told you in advance where the cameras were."

"I thought I avoided them pretty well."

"Perhaps by your low standards."

His hand swiped at the hot-water lever and missed. He reached for it again. A quick turn and he was through into the Vault. "I was busy trying to not get killed."

"You should be used to that by now."

"Fair enough," Evan said, dropping into his chair with relief. His jaw started watering, a warning signal.

"Have you been resting?"

"Sure."

"How's the concussion?" Joey asked.

Evan hit MUTE, slid over the trash can, and threw up into it violently enough to strain his intercostals. He wiped his mouth, unmuted the phone. "Okay," he said.

"Sure," she said. "You sound fresh as a daisy."

He gripped the edge of the table to try to stop the room from spinning. Vera II looked on with moral support.

"I just wanted you to know you're free to retire now. Your tracks are completely covered. Once again I swing to your rescue. You're such a damsel in distress. I mean, if I hadn't found the hidden files on Grant's thumb drive, you'd still be—"

His Gmail account, projected onto the wall before him, showed an e-mail message.

No sender. No subject line.

"Joey," he said. "I have to go."

He hung up on her while she was still mid-insult.

With a trembling hand, he clicked to open the e-mail.

A single sentence: *Have you considered my offer?*

The president, checking in on the status of the informal pardon.

Beneath the single sentence was a familiar phone number, a code word, and an extension.

(202) 456-1414. Dark Road. 32.

The informal pardon would put an end to the race he'd been running since the age of twelve, when he'd stepped off that rest-stop curb and into Jack's car. No more knife wounds and concussions. No more dogfighting pits and shooters in shadowy parking lots. No more police-station raids and voluntary jail stints.

No more missions.

He'd always thought that being the Nowhere Man was his way of paying penance. But maybe it was more than that. Maybe risking his life for others again and again and again gave him the only sense of purpose he could find.

Would he be able to find another purpose as true as that?

He looked at Vera II. "What do you think?"

She seemed skeptical.

This wasn't the time for debate. He still had a makeshift SWAT command on his ass and a cabal of city leaders to exterminate.

He returned Vera II's haughty glare. "I know, I know. 'Miles to go before I sleep.' I just need a sec to lie down."

Vera II gave him more passive-aggressive silence.

"Fine," he said. "I'll have a quick peek. But that's it."

As he plugged Bedrosov's thumb drive into his computer, he felt a pang of guilt for hanging up on Joey. Despite that, he didn't regret cutting off her bragging about discovering the hidden files on Grant's thumb drive.

He froze, hands a few inches above the keyboard. He looked at Bedrosov's thumb drive, protruding from the computer tower like a stubby arrow.

Given the cascade of discoveries, he hadn't checked it for hidden files.

He right-clicked on the icon, selected the option to run as administrator. Then he typed in *"attrib-s-h-r /s /d."*

A single cloaked folder came into view.

Police and court documents with highest classification markings. Of course they'd been hidden behind one more layer of protection for Bedrosov; they pertained to his investigation alone. They had likely been fed to Grant so he could know more specifically what charges he needed to play defense against as he shell-gamed Bedrosov's money.

The documents didn't merely detail the case against Bedrosov. They also showed a flurry of activity surrounding the simple wire-fraud charges that had been leveled. Filed motions. Internal memos from the district attorney's office. Annotated interview transcripts. Copies of court orders. Interview requests for the DA investigator. Demands for Lorraine Lennox to reveal her confidential sources. And a host of search- and electronic-surveillance warrants looking to expand the investigation. A few even targeted the players at the edge of Stella Hardwick's empire—David Terzian, Alexan Petro, Detectives Ignacio Nuñez and Paul Brust.

Someone was looking to expand the case.

Evan's muscles had locked up, his shoulders a sheet of stress pulling at the tendons of his neck. He knew in his gut who that someone was even before he found the matching signature at the bottom of each and every warrant.

In her conference room alone, gazing out at the mediocre view of downtown with her Turing Phone pressed to her ear, Stella Hardwick received the update with a ramrod spine and a stiff upper lip. She permitted no change of her expression or rise in the volume of her voice.

"So they failed," she said. "You failed."

There was a pause as Fitz seemingly gathered himself. "The man helping Grant's cousin had a truck with discreet armoring."

"An armored truck."

"That's right. Yes. Look—I'm sorry. We've been scouring the streets. We'll get him."

"Yes. You will. But now we can't afford to hold off anymore."

"On what?"

"We can't take any risks. Clean up the rest of it."

Another long pause, interrupted only by the crackle of static over the line. "I know we've taken steps before," Fitz said. "But this is a whole other level. We're talking about a Los Angeles County district attorney. To be clear—"

"I am being clear," Stella said, and severed the connection.

All the signs had been there.

And Evan had missed them.

Every time he'd seen her, she'd been on the phone with her office, pushing for search warrants, forging into blowback, fighting to keep her investigation on track—the investigation he'd unknowingly collided with at every turn. She'd been up late and up early, cycling through court suits and spending most of her waking hours trying her long-cause trials downtown.

Stella Hardwick and her cabal had proved they were willing to kill to protect what they'd built. It seemed certain that with the walls closing in on them now, they'd be willing to assassinate a DA as well.

Agitated, Evan stood up. His vision filled with snow, and he reached for the desk, missed it, and fell over. He lay on the cold floor a moment, his head buzzing, and then he pulled himself back up into his chair.

He brought up the folder containing the files he maintained on every resident of Castle Heights. Mia's was just as invasive as the rest of them, with zero-day exploits granting him access to her iPhone, her work calendar, the DA databases, and virtually everything else.

He hovered the cursor over her name.

Hesitated.

He could only imagine the ire Mia would unleash if she knew he was about to illegally pry into her life.

He recalled Max's anguish at walking away from Violet to save her. How he'd done the one thing she would have least wanted him to do.

Because he couldn't bear not to.

Evan opened Mia's file.

58

Beautiful, Furtive Choreography

Mia jammed her thumb into the crosswalk button at South Grand and 6th, the downtown traffic so solid it looked like a wall before her. She'd donned sneakers for the long walk over from her office, stuffing her ankle-strap flats into her overburdened purse.

A last-minute mystery witness had stepped forth, e-mailing her from an anonymous account and promising to reveal incriminating evidence about a pay trail leading to the dirty detectives who'd been killed at Hollywood Station last week. The witness had claimed that she was flying out first thing in the morning for her own safety and requested that Mia take her statement in the privacy of her room at the Standard Hotel.

Mia checked her watch. Five minutes to 4:00 P.M., which meant Peter would be at language lab. Another late evening for the case that stubbornly refused to break open.

The light changed, and she crossed the street.

She did not notice the white van idling at the crosswalk. The two large men occupying the front seats. Or the bulkhead partition hiding the others in the rear.

The driver signaled to two SUVs parked across the street.

They pulled out after Mia, shadowing her as she stepped up onto the opposing curb, her satchel briefcase swinging. She weaved along the sidewalk, the van and the SUVs rotating in the background, enfolding her in expert surveillance.

As she made her way toward the hotel, the SUVs accelerated past her and parked on parallel cross streets. Two operators emerged from each, leaving the vehicles behind. They wore bone-conduction headsets wrapped around their left ears. The inconspicuous units conveyed sound waves as auditory vibrations that passed through the bone behind the ear into the cochlea. The men shuffled into the various streams of pedestrians, riding the currents in a swirl around Mia. The lead operator peeled off, slipping through a side door into the Standard Hotel.

The van slithered through traffic, coasting past her. Oblivious, Mia neared the hotel entrance. A man glided up on her heels. Two more approached from opposite directions, splitting and overlapping.

A beautiful, furtive choreography.

The dance continued through the lobby as she headed for the elevator, men rotating around her, menacingly close and somehow inconspicuous. One paused to linger by a pillar. Two more vectored to the stairwell, blending into foot traffic, merging with the bustle of an average evening.

Mia stepped onto the elevator, knuckled the button for the twelfth floor. One of the operators was waiting inside, shouldered to the rear behind a cluster of women with oversize shopping bags.

The doors closed.

As they rose silently, Mia checked her e-mail, confirming the meet in Room 1202. A screen embedded above the buttons flashed glammed-up images of the restaurant, the gym, the spa-blue swimming pool on the rooftop.

She watched her screen. The man watched her.

When the doors opened on the twelfth floor, Mia exited, head down, reviewing notes on her phone.

The operator sidled out weightlessly behind her.

They walked up the corridor. The stairwell door opened silently behind them, and another operator eased out. A third emerged from an intersecting hall. Seconds later the neighboring elevator car delivered a fourth.

Mia padded down the hall, her footfalls soft on the carpet, scrolling through e-mails with her thumb. The men swept in from various directions, gathering behind her.

A graceful convergence on 1202.

The door was—oddly—open.

Through the gap she could see that it was a huge corner room.

Mia palmed the door open and gasped.

Evan Smoak stood in a Weaver stance, pistol raised, aiming at her face.

59

Guardian Angel

Mia froze in the doorway, staring at Evan and his drawn pistol, seemingly pointed at her. Their eyes locked. Her pupils were constricted with shock, and he read in them equal parts terror and confusion.

He fired over her shoulders—literally through her hair on either side. It swayed with the velocity of the rounds.

The sound, even suppressed, caused her shoulders to jump upward.

Two bodies fell behind her.

Before she could look, he grabbed her around the small of her back and pulled her close, shooting even as he spun her, cheek to cheek, a violent waltz. Her chest was pressed to his, her palms flattened against his ribs. His body blocked her from incoming fire.

She clung to him, spinning, disoriented, as the men flashed across the threshold and jerked back and down. The clank of gunmetal on carpet. Wet gasps. A deep-voiced grunt.

And then Evan stopped, still holding her tight enough that he could feel her heartbeat through her blouse, the heat of her skin. Her hand was curled against his chest, half shielding her eyes.

She was untouched. All four operators lay heaped in the doorway.

He released her, and she staggered to the side, one knee buckling, her face blank, stunned. The spilled contents of her briefcase littered the floor at her feet. She stared at the bodies.

"I'm the one they . . ." Her voice went husky and guttered out. "They were going to kill me."

Two of the men's pistols lay on the floor. One operator hadn't yet cleared leather, and the fourth had died with his gun in his hand.

Evan dragged them in, kneed the door shut behind them, and took a moment to steady his breathing.

He had counted a straight dozen men spilling from the van outside Max's apartment. That left eight more out there. He'd brought plenty of extra mags as well as the FN Ballista in case the clash went rangy, but right now he needed to figure out where the other operators were positioned.

He crouched over a body, reached behind the still-warm ear, and clicked the bone-phone to speaker.

"*—repeat: Confirm target is neutralized. I'm eastbound on Grand, circling around for pickup. I have Little Bird in hand if we need to shift to B plan.*"

A charge went through Evan, snapping him upright.

Mia's shock evaporated as it hit her, too. "'Little Bird'? Is that . . . Do they mean Peter?"

Evan recovered and sprinted to the giant windows, looking down on the traffic grid of the surrounding streets.

He spotted the white van in motion below.

It blurred, and he grabbed his face hard, squeezing his eyes, and then let go.

"What are you doing?" Mia asked. "Are you okay?"

He ignored her, his focus on the road below. He calculated.

Then turned. Mia wobbled on her feet, her back to the wall, using it to prop her up.

"White cleaning van," he said. "It'll be at the corner of Seventh and Grand. You'll be clear."

Her lips firmed as if to fight down panic. "How do you know?"

He said, "I know."

"I'm unarmed," she said. "What am I supposed to do?"

Evan was already on his knees before the Hardigg Storm Case, pulling the twenty-six-inch fluted barrel from the foam lining, mounting it on the receiver, and quick-locking the suppressor. He looked up at her, a wisp of hair falling across his eyes. "Go to your son. Draw them out. Everything else is on me."

She stared at him. Swallowed down her terror.

And bolted out the door.

Evan finished assembling the Ballista, configuring it for the .338 Lapua chambering and slotting in the ten-round box mag. Then he cycled the bolt, flung open the balcony door, and set up on the railing. His right pupil was still blown, but he could use his preferred eye—a bit of luck on this endlessly luckless mission.

Behind him the bone-phone squawked. *"Team One, come in, over. Team One? Team Two, come in."*

Way below, the white van coasted out of view. It would emerge any second onto Grand.

He didn't have a range card for the new rifle, but it had been zeroed at four hundred yards. He needed to range the target, so he swung the scope, looking for a standard-dimension object. A half second later, he locked on to a stop sign near the kill zone.

City stop signs are standard anywhere in the United States. Thirty inches across the red octagon. White border just shy of an inch. Five feet from the bottom of the sign to the pavement. Using the stop sign as a measurement reference point, Evan calculated his hold-under and cosign compensation and focused in on the scope. At three hundred yards, if he held under ten minutes of angle, he'd be right on.

The white van emerged beneath him, a dot in the stream of traffic driving directly away. An optical illusion made it appear to be rising before him, an air bubble in an IV tube. It disappeared behind a high-rise. Materialized on the other side.

An image rushed him—Peter in the back of the van, his charcoal eyes flat with shock. Maybe they'd knocked him out for ease of transport.

Had they taken him from his school? Removed him with a show of false authority and the flash of a badge? Or simply snatched him from a sidewalk?

They'd taken him as a contingency plan to control Mia if the execution didn't go smoothly in the hotel. And once Peter was no longer necessary, they would handle him the way they'd handled Grant Merriweather and Lorraine Lennox and anyone else who'd gotten tangled in their web.

At the thought Evan's heart rate quickened, a thumping in his neck. A headache spread its steel fingers through the back of his skull.

And then—all at once—the view through the scope got soupy.

He pulled his head away, his face washed with sweat. *Not now.*

He blinked hard and put his face back onto the stock, in line with the scope. The van was a blur, moving among other blurs. The road was full, and as his vision doubled, it grew fuller yet, phantom vehicles appearing and blending into one another. It was hard to tell which were real and which were illusory.

Five minutes of clarity. That's all he required.

He ripped two autoinjectors of epinephrine out of his cargo pocket. Gripping them side by side in one fist, he popped the blue safety caps off with his thumbnail. Then he rammed the needles straight through the fabric of his pants into his outer thigh, holding them in place until a double click announced that the doses had administered.

Warmth surged through him, rolling up his stomach and chest, setting his mouth tingling. His vision snapped into focus with a sudden heightened lucidity.

He'd pay for it later.

Gladly.

For the first time since he'd smacked his head on that parking lot, he felt entirely clear-minded. Better than clear-minded. Like the rifle was a part of his body and he was a part of it and together they would operate like a single piece of weaponry.

Through the scope Evan zeroed in on the van once more. Aimed at the rear right tire. Tracked it as it flickered in and out of sight behind other vehicles.

Guardian Angel

He exhaled. Waited for the space between heartbeats.
And readied to apply 2.75 pounds of trigger pressure.

Mia spilled from the elevator and sprinted across the lobby, knocking over a businessman. She slammed out through the hefty front door and bulled through pedestrians, ignoring the shouts and protests.

The white van strobed into view a full block away, turning onto Grand Street.

She forged into traffic, darting up 6th Street through blaring horns and screeching brakes. Tears streaked her face.

She ran to her son.

Even over the city bustle, the crack of the round was audible.

The van's rear tire blew. The vehicle reared up on its front tires and smashed through the picture window of Bottega Louie. Glass waterfalled, tumbling onto the sidewalk. Inside the upscale patisserie, patrons screamed and ran. One of the take-out counters shattered, spilling a rainbow of macaroons across the marble floor.

Directly above the wreckage, street signs announced the intersection of 7th and Grand.

The package, delivered right on the mark.

The driver drew his gun, stepped out, and immediately lost half his skull.

The man in the passenger seat peered into the side mirror an instant before it was sheared off by the next sniper round. Panicking, he flung open the door and dove for the restaurant. Another round whined in.

He was dead before he struck the ground.

The sidewalks erupted with panic. Commuters left their cars in the middle of the street. Pedestrians shouted and headed for cover, washing through the abandoned vehicles to the safety of the surrounding buildings.

Inside the van the six remaining operators kicked through the damaged bulkhead partition, crawled to the front, and spilled from the doors. They fanned out, carbines at the ready, a strike team unleashed.

Evan cycled the rifle, ejecting the brass. He eased out a breath through his teeth. Heart rate—normal. Body temperature—normal. Hands—steady.

Eye back to the scope. A breeze riffled his hair. Cries carried up to him from the street. Mia came into view below, running into the chaos.

His view was blocked by panicked civilians. But there were slivers between the rush of bodies that let him see through to the operators readying for battle.

No margin for error.

He would have to be perfect.

He emptied his lungs once more. At moments like this, the voice inside his head was Jack's.

Don't think about Mia.

Don't think about Peter.

Don't think about anything that matters.

A simple process.

Track. Exhale. Squeeze.

Repeat.

Mia sprinted toward the crash, sobbing with fear, dread, rage. People were surging away from the van, banging into her, knocking her back against the tide.

She tripped, bloodying a knee, but kept on.

She emerged from a clot between abandoned cars and saw—finally—what everyone was running from.

A formation of heavily armed men, spread in a V-formation, advancing directly at her. They were a half block away, the van that held her son at their backs. It was shoved crookedly through the restaurant's window, hoisted higher on one side from the impact. One of the men rolled his neck, another shook out an injured arm. They readied their rifles.

Mia braced herself.

And sprinted directly into their midst.

There was no way she wouldn't be killed.

And yet.

She floated through the fray untouched.

A man spun to aim at her and was ripped out of sight as cleanly as if he'd been lassoed by a passing truck, his dome cracked from a V split of a round.

The operator behind him caught a faceful of bone fragment, pounding him into the asphalt.

A third lunged as she neared and took a bullet to the neck.

She sprinted through the blood and death to her son.

Invisibly protected by a guardian angel.

Ten yards ahead two operators closed ranks, sighting on her. They were afraid now; she could see that in their rolling eyes. But even as their ranks thinned, felled by an invisible hand, they kept coming at her. She was the only thread they had to follow, the sole target for their desperation. Two barrels rose and aimed at her critical mass.

She closed her eyes. Did not slow.

She heard the crack of the gunshots and knew herself to be dead. A double clap of corpses struck the ground. Neither was hers.

She opened her eyes. Warm syrup on her cheeks, her shirt. Flecked with blood, she never slowed. Breath burning. Lungs on fire. A panic heat lighting her skin, flushing her face. Running past the fallen men.

Running to her son.

She was almost there.

The last operator lifted his rifle to aim at her. Her legs had gone numb, sprinting of their own accord, carrying her forward. The world turned to slow motion, every detail rendered with hyperclarity—the single furrow of his brow on the right side, the glisten of sweat at his hairline, the whiteness of his hand on the grip. She sensed that her mouth was open, that she was screaming.

Fifteen yards out. Now ten.

She saw the bore come full circle. Stared down the throat of the rifle. Every muscle clenched, a razor edge of rage slicing through her fear, cutting her to ribbons.

And then he was gone, a blood spray painting the van's rear door.

She halted before the bumper, panting, terrified. Glanced back, sweaty hair whipping across her eyes. A trail of dropped bodies charted her wake. She turned back to the van.

The rear door gleamed in the late-afternoon sun.

She reached with a trembling hand and opened it.

It creaked on ungreased hinges.

A boy was balled up in the corner of the cargo hold, face tucked behind the tops of his knees. Through a fall of golden hair, Peter peered up.

The tiniest of voices. "Mommy?"

He scrambled forward and fell into her arms.

Sobbing, she held him.

60

Fly Away

The sound of sirens drifted up to the twelfth-floor balcony.

Evan scooped up the kill brass and hustled across the hotel room, leaving behind the empty Hardigg Storm Case. Stepping over the bodies, he cracked the door and peered down the corridor.

Empty save for an overturned housekeeping cart, probably up-ended by a fleeing employee when gunfire had broken out.

He jogged to the cart, fluffed out a transparent trash liner, and slid the FN Ballista inside. Tommy had been right. It was an excellent rifle, and if Evan had been the type to grow attached to tools, he wouldn't have been so quick to discard it.

He grabbed a jug of bleach and emptied it inside the bag as he moved swiftly down the hall. Knotting the bag, he dumped it in a trash chute and then stepped onto the elevator.

A Muzak rendering of Lenny Kravitz's "Fly Away," heavy on woodwinds, accompanied him down. His heart rate started to slow, the epinephrine easing off to a more gentle glow in his veins.

Though the lobby was largely cleared out, a few workers and guests huddled behind the front desk.

Evan stepped out into the street and hustled up 6th to the intersection. The intensity of holding perfect focus had cost him, as he knew it would, the concussion symptoms seeping back, messing with his perception. Squad cars were pulling up on Grand Avenue from all points of the compass, clogging the side streets, corralling the damage zone. He misjudged a step and banged into the fender of an abandoned car hard enough to knock himself into a quarter turn. Straightening himself up, he progressed more cautiously, ignoring the mounting pressure at his temples, concentrating to keep his vision clear.

Looking up the block, he spotted Mia.

She was holding Peter.

Relief tore through Evan, something giving way under a strain he hadn't let himself acknowledge.

Peter was clamped onto his mother, his face buried in her shoulder. Mia spoke to first responders, gesturing at the bodies around the van with her one free hand.

Evan had no idea what she was telling them.

For the first time, it struck him that the life he had built in Castle Heights was now over. As an officer of the court, Mia would be obliged to implicate him. She'd made her position clear. And he'd be on the run once again.

He thought of the informal pardon that President Donahue-Carr had dangled before him, the different life so tantalizingly close.

But staring at Mia and Peter now, he knew he'd make the same choice a thousand times out of a thousand.

She turned slightly and—way across the mob of cops and civilians—spotted him.

For a suspended instant, they locked eyes.

The officers speaking to her noted her shift in position and started to pivot. They were just about to spot Evan when Mia turned and stepped in front of them.

Fly Away

Blocking their view.

She squared to them, hoisting Peter higher to wall out their vantage.

When she turned back around, Evan was gone.

61

Speechless Terror

The boys assembled around the conference table on the seventh floor. The meeting had been hastily called. It was 11:00 P.M., and they were off their usual crisp standards in appearance and demeanor. Crooked ties, untucked shirts, patches of stubble.

The Steel Woman, however, was seamless. Pressed suit jacket and slacks. A perfect veneer of makeup. Her bun as tightly wound as ever, a water-smooth stone at her nape.

With a smudge of dried ketchup on his cheek, Fitz shakily finished his update. "So that's it. My entire contingent wiped out. I don't know what the next steps are."

"Fortunately, I do," Stella said. "You boys—all of you—will use your considerable resources and reach to hunt down Max Merriweather and the man responsible for this, eliminate them, and retrieve the thumb drive."

There was no sound save the rush of the air conditioner, blowing an even sixty-five degrees.

"Additionally," she said, "we are dissolving the LLC until further notice."

A few of the men leaned forward as if to object, but she stilled them with a single look.

The city treasurer mustered his voice. "I don't know that that's entirely fair."

"I did my job perfectly," Stella said. "For *years* I worked to set up this arrangement. Never so much as a misplaced comma. You boys were given a single task, and you fucked it all up. So I share your assessment, Neil. It isn't fair."

With a manicured finger, she compressed the intercom button on the hefty telephone before her. "Rolando," she said. "We're ready."

Her assistant coasted in on a breeze of cologne, steel briefcase in hand. She'd dispensed with the handcuff. After the boys' failure, there was no longer a need to indulge their egos.

Rolando delivered the briefcase and exited as crisply as he'd entered, the soundproofed door suctioning closed with a finality that seemed baldly symbolic. The room had a deflated feel, the men leaning back in their chairs bonelessly. The fun was over, and now there was nothing left except paranoia and the fear of exposure.

But if Stella was good at one thing, it was minimizing risk. She would cover their tracks. They would hibernate. And when the threat had been dispatched, they would reconstitute themselves, perhaps in a new iteration that had shed the deadweight. Once more they'd lodge themselves into the underbelly of the city like a tick. And they'd gorge.

The titanium latches snapped open with a robust click.

She lifted the briefcase lid.

At first she did not register what she was looking at.

How could she?

She lacked the expertise to identify blocks of C-4. More precisely, untraceable Detasheet devoid of coded microparticles.

Nor could she understand that the soundproofed conference-room door and commercial-grade Sheetrock designed for maximum privacy would also maximize the overpressure from the coming explosion.

Sitting in the chill conference room, feeling her flesh firm around her with a kind of inborn protectiveness, she found herself unable to formulate words for the first time in memory. Her left eyelid twitched, a ticklish flutter.

"What?" Fitz was shouting at her. "What is it?"

One of the boys knocked the briefcase. It swung around, on full display.

The comptroller lurched up from his chair, tangled in his neighbor, and fell over.

The act of opening the briefcase had initiated a five-second timer.

The digitally rendered numeral had already reached 2.

Now 1.

Bound together by a speechless terror, they watched the final second of their lives vanish off the board.

62

God or Fate or Whoever Runs the Universe

At midnight Evan's doorbell rang.

He'd been lying on the floating bed, a cool washcloth resting across his eyes, the first hours of actual relief from the concussion pain he'd been able to get since Petro's man had introduced the back of his skull to the asphalt.

There were no sheets, just the bare mattress. When he'd arrived home, he'd stared at them helplessly, overwhelmed by the muddy dog prints and stray hairs. Dispensing with any notion of cleaning them, he'd stripped them off the bed and launched them down the trash chute. He had more work to do mopping the floors and scrubbing the counters, but it would have to wait until he could stand for longer than five minutes without getting nauseated.

Besides, he had more important concerns. President Donahue-Carr's pardon offer was still floating out there, and he had to claim his reward before it vanished.

He descended out of his breath meditation, eased off his floating bed, and walked down the hall, pleased to note that—for the moment—he felt normal.

Even before checking the security monitor, he knew it would be Mia.

What he didn't know was what she'd say.

He opened the door, and they faced each other across the threshold. She wore an oversize sweater, her hands lost to the sleeves, arms crossed low on her stomach. He couldn't read her face.

He sensed a new appreciation for how clear his head felt after his brief rest and how crisply he could see her. He wondered what life might feel like moving forward, injury-free and able to indulge simple pleasures. His right pupil remained slightly enlarged, but it was nowhere near as noteworthy as before, and it seemed to evade even Mia's sharp attention.

"How's Peter?" he asked.

"Shockingly good," she said. "He asked me to pray with him tonight. And he said . . ." A quicksilver glimmer filled her eyes, and she tilted her head back and blinked several times. "He said, 'Dear God or fate or whoever runs the universe. Thanks for sending help to me.'" She stared at Evan, her chin quivering. "What am I supposed to say to that?"

"I don't know."

"I didn't tell anyone. That you were there. Who you are. I said they lured me to the hotel room and someone grabbed me and then gunfire broke out and I escaped."

"All true," he said. "Except *I* lured you to the room."

She gazed at him, her eyes as large and vulnerable as he'd ever seen them. "As a DA you have to think in black and white. Or at least you get hammered into it. But it's all a mess." She shook her head, her chestnut curls swaying. "Either I'm wiser now or I'm a hypocrite. I'm not sure which."

"Maybe they're the same."

"They had Peter," she said. "They had Peter, and there were laws and oaths and procedures, and I didn't care about any of them." Now her cheeks were wet. "They had my son. And that made it different. What I wanted to happen. What I would have been willing to do. It was different."

"Yeah, it is," Evan said. "Every time."

"It doesn't make any sense."

"What doesn't?"

"*Anything.*"

She went up on her toes and kissed him. Deeply. She tugged at his lower lip with her mouth, then let it go and stayed close, her forehead pressed to his. They were both breathing hard. She was curled into him, her hands on the sides of his face, and he was inhaling her, the scent of her, and one of his hands cupped the back of her neck, and it was so warm, so fragile.

She pulled herself away.

"I have to get back to Peter," she said.

She took another reluctant step up the hall, and it was as though she were fighting herself away from him, fighting gravity. He felt the same pull but stayed in the doorway. He could still feel the wetness of her mouth on his lips.

"I know you now," she said. "I really know you."

He watched her walk away.

63

Tipping Point

In the dead of night, Evan waited in Tommy's truck beneath the freeway overpass. A half hour passed before Tommy drifted up in Evan's F-150. The windows had been replaced, and the bullet holes were gone. The body work was superb, the truck as good as new—a whole lot of ordinary wrapped around an exceptional core.

Evan could see Max sitting in the passenger seat, but Tommy mumbled something to him before he got out and Max stayed put.

Tommy ambled over to Evan and opened the door of his dually. "Scoot yer ass over," he said, and Evan climbed over the center console into the passenger seat. Tommy hoisted himself up with a groan. "Got my money?"

Evan handed him a wad of hundreds, which Tommy thumbed through. He smelled strongly of cigarette smoke and wintergreen tobacco. He gave a nod. "Taggant-free Detasheet ain't cheap," he said. "Hope it was worth it."

"It was worth it."

"How do you like your Ballista?"

"It was great."

Tommy cocked his head. "Why the past tense?"

Evan told him.

"Come again, motherfucker?" Tommy said. "You did *what* to my gun? Bleach? In a garbage bag? Down a trash chute?" He shook his head. "What'd I expect from a mouth-breathing trigger-puller like you. Pearls before swine." He rubbed his eyes. "Aw, hell. I think I need a drink."

Evan said, "I could use one, too."

"There's a flask of Smirnoff in the glove box."

Evan laughed and then saw Tommy was serious.

Evan's head felt significantly better, the worst of the concussion behind him. It seemed that taking a respite from crushing life-or-death stakes hastened one's recovery. After everything he'd been through, he figured he could risk a sip or two.

He retrieved the bottle, unscrewed it, and took a sniff, doing his best not to recoil. Tommy dug two paper coffee cups out of the console and slapped one against Evan's chest.

Evan shrugged. "What the hell."

He poured two shots.

They drank.

Clark McKenna couldn't doze off.

He hadn't slept for shit since his run-in with Max Merriweather at the house. Or—to put a finer point on it—his run-in with Max Merriweather's friend. A holier-than-thou roughneck brimming with swagger and moral sanctimony.

Who was that guy to question Clark's choices?

Clark shifted around in bed until Gwendolyn gave a rumble of displeasure, and then he slid from the sheets, wrapped a bathrobe around himself, and headed into the kitchen. It was a cavernous affair, with vaulted ceilings and oversize doorways. The counter space alone was sufficient to seat a basketball team.

The help wasn't around and the night was past the tipping point to morning, so he brewed up a pot of coffee and sat alone at the island. The room seemed to dwarf him even more than usual. The under-cabinet lights were on, the windows throwing back his reflection.

If there was one thing he didn't want to look at right now, it was himself.

He'd raised the issue to Gwendolyn already twice, and twice she'd shot it down.

She was a stubborn woman, and that had made him a stubborn man. He supposed she would have argued the reverse.

He sipped his coffee and glared at himself.

For nearly three years he and Gwenny had clutched the secret close to their chests, content in the knowledge that they'd saved their daughter's life. After the miscarriage he'd gone over to that hovel of an apartment and found his girl curled up on the kitchen linoleum, shuddering. Though it was nearly noon, she was still in her nightshirt and a pair of boxer shorts, her flesh as pale and cold as marble.

His paternal instincts had risen up, fierce as a cornered beast, and he'd vowed then that he would do anything to save her. Gwendolyn had found the treatment home. And later that night, privately in their bedroom, Gwendolyn had set the terms.

Violet was alive. But over these past years when Clark caught her in an unguarded moment gazing blankly out a window or drifting off in a meeting, he understood that a part of her was still lying on that kitchen floor, shuddering and alone, trapped in the knowledge that her husband had left her there.

That he'd found her no longer worth being with.

That was the kind of thing that could kill someone even if they were still breathing.

The coffee was cold now, the mug cool within his hands.

He'd known what he was going to do all along. He'd just been pretending that he didn't. And he knew he had to do it before Gwenny's alarm roused her for her morning yoga in the back garden.

He picked up the phone and dialed. It wasn't as hard as he thought it might be. After all, he'd practiced countless times over the past two years and seven months.

When Violet picked up, her voice hoarse with sleep, a surge of emotion ambushed him. "Hullo?" she said.

"Sweet girl." He had to fight out the words. "I have to tell you something."

And then he'd lowered his eyes into his hand and wept.

Parking tickets sheeted the windshield of Max's TrailBlazer. It felt like a lifetime ago when Evan had directed him to meet here in the lot by Universal Studios.

One problem had led to the second, the third to a fourth and then a fifth. When Evan had blown out Stella Hardwick's conference room and everyone inside, he'd put down the sixth and final problem.

Now there was nothing left to do but watch the shrapnel settle.

Evan had given Max a thousand dollars to get back on his feet, along with Grant's thumb drive and a cover story that they'd worked and reworked until it was more real to Max than what had really gone down.

Max was ready to walk into a police station and lay out a version of events that protected him fully and disclosed nothing about his relationship with Evan. Max had simply been a guy in the wrong place at the wrong time. Like most successful fabrications, this was an extension of the truth. The criminal networks Stella Hardwick had assembled around her scheme had collapsed due to internecine warfare, or so the story would go. Greed and turf disputes had turned the parties against one another until they'd brought themselves down, sinking into a morass of blood.

Max hesitated by his TrailBlazer, keys in hand, and looked back at Evan. There was always this moment when they tried to say the unsayable. The bond forged over the course of a mission was unlike anything else.

Evan wondered how much he'd miss it.

This was the part where Evan empowered them to find the next client. To pass on his phone number and, in doing so, to help them move from victim to savior.

Evan cleared his throat. "Good-bye, then."

"Okay." Max bobbed his head. "Okay." He tugged open his door.

"Write your own story," Evan said. "Or someone else'll write it for you."

Max looked down at his shoes and smiled shyly. "I like that."

"And one more thing," Evan said. "Pick your damn head up."

The past twelve hours had been among the most exhausting of Max's life. He'd been interrogated by rotating sets of detectives, DAs, and even briefly by *the* district attorney, until he'd literally fallen asleep in the chair. But he hadn't cracked and he hadn't slipped up. The past week—and his time with the Nowhere Man— had introduced him to a new part of himself.

He drove straight from the police station to a 7-Eleven, where he bought a disposable razor and shaved in the restroom. After he splashed cold water on his face, he stared at himself in the rust-spotted mirror. It took a moment, like an image slowly pulling into focus, but he recognized himself again.

Next stop was the big Spanish-style house in Beverly Hills, the site of the Merriweather clan's Taco Tuesdays. News of Grant's corruption had leaked to Jill already—he'd gleaned as much from his time at the station—and he felt a need to show his face. He wanted them to know what Golden Boy Grant had done to him and what Max had gone through to protect them all. He pictured Grant with his overpriced suit and that easy, swallowed-the-canary grin. *C'mon, Mighty Max. For once in your life, maybe step up, shoulder some responsibility.*

A member of the staff let Max in, and he found the family in the kitchen, the trays of carne asada and al pastor sitting untouched. Jill's face was pink from sobbing, the rest of the family fanned out around her in support or deference.

All eyes shifted to him.

He felt an overpowering urge to do what he always did—to slink away and nurse his self-loathing. But this time he didn't. He stood his ground.

For a moment he didn't know which way it would go.

The chef came in wielding a tray of corn tortillas and read the mood of the kitchen. "Maybe this isn't the best time, sir," he said to Max.

Jill wiped at her eyes. The family was silent. And then Max's father found his feet. "It's *not* the best time," he said. "Which is why we should all be together."

He pulled out an empty chair for his son, and Max blinked at it.

"Thanks," he said. "But I can't stay. I just finished at the police station."

Jill rose, crumpling a tissue in her hand, her swollen face heavy with remorse.

The words were right there at the back of his throat, a lifetime of resentment and vitriol fired with newfound righteousness. He was ready to unleash, to set her straight.

But instead he heard himself say, "I'm so sorry, Jill. I wish it wasn't true."

She collapsed into him, sobbing against his chest. And he held her.

Michelle came in from the backyard with a plate of food and hugged them both from the side. Then she took Max's hand and moved to press it to her stomach. He hesitated.

And then let her.

The baby bumped against his palm. A charge moved through him intense enough to bring moisture to his eyes. Wonder, yes. And grief for the baby he'd lost, as sharp as a fresh wound. But he noticed one feeling that was outshining them all.

Joy.

He kissed Michelle's forehead. And then he left.

The drive to South Pasadena took the better part of an hour.

The cottage peeked out from behind the ivy-covered brick wall. Air crisp. The porch enveloped in the scent of roses.

His hand shook when he rang the bell.

But for a second time he stood firm.

Footsteps.

And then she was there.

Dark eyes and red lips and a long-sleeved sweater to cover her arms.

They both had so many scars to hide.

He held up the key to the Lincoln Heights house. "I promised to return this to you. But it's really just an excuse to look at you one more time."

He set the key in her hand. His fingertips brushed her palm. The smell of her perfume—orange blossom and vanilla—hit a spot in his brain that turned present into past and rolled them together.

She closed her fist around the key. Stared down at her knuckles. She looked like she needed to say something, so he waited and then waited some more.

"My dad called me last night," she finally said. "He told me what you agreed to. The deal you struck. And why you did it."

Her eyes were shut, and he couldn't tell if she was going to cry or scream at him.

He said, "If you ever forgive me . . ." And then he lost the words.

She kept her eyes closed. She was breathing hard, her chest rising and falling, rising and falling.

He turned to walk off.

Her voice caught him halfway to the brick wall.

"I'm just—" She broke off in a sob. And then, "I'm just having an unlucky run. If you're smart, you'll get as far from me as possible."

He looked down, and the grass got blurry and the walkway and the roses and the street beyond.

"Don't worry," he said. "I'm not that smart."

He turned around.

And he lifted his gaze.

64

A Forever Fall

After loading up the truck vaults with the required gear, Evan stopped by Joey's on his way to the desert. Construction trucks lined the block, and workers busied themselves installing a premium steel-front door and replacing the broken light fixtures.

Evan stepped past them, heading for the stairs, and climbed to the second floor. Joey's door was open, and she was ushering a repairman out, holding Dog the dog by the collar so he wouldn't scramble to freedom. His stitches had come out, the horseshoe scar marking his chest proudly.

Evan entered, and Dog rammed his nose into his crotch until Evan crouched and scratched behind his ears. A big fluffy red dog bed lay beneath the pull-up bar, a new addition.

"God," Joey said. "All the construction's been a friggin' nightmare. They're putting in new security windows on every floor."

"Yeah," Evan said. "I saw a notice downstairs."

He sensed Joey's attention sharpen and kept his gaze on the dog.

"Right," she said. "From the new owner."

Evan examined a hangnail.

"Do you know where this new owner's from?" she said. "I mean, that's the sort of thing you'd research, right?"

"I guess a consortium out of Abu Dhabi."

"A consortium," she said. "Out of Abu Dhabi."

He could feel her eyes lasering through him.

"I can just move up the block, you know," she said.

Evan kept petting Dog. "I can buy that building, too."

She let her hands slap to her sides. "You're *beyond* impossible."

Evan said, "I'm thinking that things might change soon—"

"What does that mean?"

"For the better. That my life might get . . . more peaceful."

"Peaceful?" Joey said. "Who wants peaceful?"

"And I want to know you're safe, too."

"What are you talking about, X? What are you gonna do?"

"I'll tell you once it's done."

He headed out, and she yelled after him, "Given your peaceful new life, maybe you could take the stupid dog!"

He shut the door behind him.

Outside, he hesitated and listened. Through the door panels, he heard Joey's footsteps creak the floorboards. The crack of her knees as she knelt.

And then she spoke in a baby voice he'd never have imagined she was capable of. "Who's a good boy?" He heard the jingle of Dog's collar as she petted him. "Who's the best, best, most lovey-faced puppy in the *whole wide world*? Yes, you are! Yes, *you* are!"

Grinning, he descended the stairs.

As he climbed into his truck, the RoamZone dinged with a text from Joey.

It said, I CAN'T BELIEVE YOU BOUGHT THE BUILDING. U'D BETTER CHILLAX.

Evan typed his one-word response. Before sending, he stared at the screen, a smirk curling his lips. Then he deleted the message, took off the caps lock, and typed again.

KAY.

As Evan rode the 60 Freeway east into the Mojave, the sun set with blistering beauty. By the time he pulled off into the arid scrubland, the earth was lit with oranges and pinks. He drove until there was not a road or building in sight and then another twenty minutes after that.

When he finally stopped, the sun had freshly vanished, the sky backlit with an ambient glow. From the truck vault, he grabbed a three-man tent, popped it up on the dirt, and then lowered shades over the mesh windows to seal them tightly.

If there was to be a live video feed, he couldn't afford to have anything in the background. No star positions, no distinctive geographic features in the landscape, no sourceable plant life indigenous to the region.

He went back to the truck, hauled out a Pelican case, and brought it inside the dark nylon dome. He pulled up the yagi directional antenna and then set up the SMA connector and the omni stubby antenna. Within seconds the tiny makeshift GSM base station had stealthily hooked into the network.

Teasing the RoamZone from his pocket, he turned it on and enabled the Wi-Fi hot spot, joining the LTE network. Before leaving Castle Heights, he'd slotted in a brand-new SIM card and moved the phone service from Khyber Pakhtunkhwa to Istanbul.

It was full dark outside, the tent lit only by the phone. The cicadas were going at it aggressively, and he played with audio filters until he'd dampened all background noise.

He dialed the number and told the switchboard operator, "Dark Road."

After the click he punched in the extension.

It rang a half dozen times.

And then President Victoria Donahue-Carr answered. "I'm glad you reestablished contact," she said. "I'm going to give you another number enabled for video feed."

Evan did not answer.

She read off a number.

He hung up.

He dialed the second phone number through an encoded video-telephony software program.

The line gave a spritely trill, and then the president appeared.

She was sitting on a high-backed couch in the Oval with a Secret Service agent at her side. Having been broken up into digital packets and bounced around the world, the connection was grainy, and when Evan leaned closer, he saw that the agent was not rank-and-file but Special Agent in Charge Naomi Templeton.

Broad shoulders, tough bearing, bluntly cut blond hair.

She was one of the few people to have seen Orphan X in the flesh.

"We can't make anything out," the president said. "It's just black."

Evan moved the RoamZone closer to his face, showing only the strip of his eyes and the bridge of his nose.

Naomi looked over at Donahue-Carr. "That's him, Madam President."

Donahue-Carr straightened on the couch. Her hands were resting open on one knee. A practiced pose to disguise her tension. "Thank you," she said to Naomi. "That's enough."

She and Evan waited while Naomi exited the Oval through a panel door that disappeared seamlessly as it shut.

The president said, "Have you considered my offer?"

"What are the conditions?" Evan said.

It was the first time he'd spoken, and his words had an impact. Donahue-Carr's hands flared up from her knee, but then she remembered herself and settled her posture once more.

"We can't pardon you, not officially, since you don't exist," she said. "But we'll stop coming after you if you stop coming after us."

Evan said nothing.

"Think about it, Orphan X. You could have a normal life. Live like a human being."

Evan thought about Mia in his doorway last night. Her hands on his cheeks. The taste of her mouth.

A Forever Fall

"Are you still there? I'm seeing only blackness."

Evan said, "I'm here."

"There is one more condition," she said. "There can be no more extracurricular activities. Of any kind. You've been rumored to run missions of a . . . personal nature."

She waited for Evan to respond, but he gave nothing up.

"We cannot have a former government asset with your training operating in *any* capacity," she added. "Understand?"

"Yes," he said, and hung up.

When he arrived back at Castle Heights, a late-night get-together was in full swing in the so-called social environment. A number of residents slurped Nespresso and gabbed on the armless love seats.

Johnny Middleton told an animated story, and at the punch line Hugh Walters threw back his head and slapped his knee. Even the Honorable Pat Johnson from 12F had made a rare appearance, throwing some ham-handed flirting in the direction of Lorilee Smithson.

Mia wasn't among them. But Evan figured that given his newly minted status, they'd have time enough to resume the conversation they'd begun in his doorway.

Johnny shifted, and Evan caught a glance of Ida Rosenbaum sitting in the center with queen-bee aplomb. Her feet were up on the synthetic leather ottoman, her hands folded across her purse. Her vintage marcasite-and-amethyst necklace was on proud display against her white cable-knit sweater. Now and then her fingertips crept up to find assurance that it was still there.

Bathed in the sounds of laughter and conversation, Evan walked from the garage to the elevators.

None of them noticed him.

Once home he headed straight for the kitchen and liberated the bottle of CLIX from its horizontal recline in the freezer drawer. He shook it over ice until his palms stuck to the stainless steel. Then he wrapped a towel around the cocktail shaker and gave it another trouncing.

He poured the vodka into a martini glass frosted opaque from the freezer and plucked a single basil leaf from the living wall for garnish.

He sipped.

White pepper, a hint of cinnamon, and something else bordering on sweet. Vanilla? It was as clean a finish as he could remember, competitive with Kauffman, which was high praise indeed.

He'd kept the lights off, the workout pods looming in the darkness of the great room like slumbering beasts. He wondered what exactly he would do with all his newfound time.

He drifted over to the floor-to-ceiling windows. For once the Los Angeles night seemed not expansive and filled with opportunity but vertiginous, a forever fall into a chasm.

If he wasn't the Nowhere Man, who was he?

He supposed he was going to have to start finding out.

He stood there at the wall of glass, staring through the heart of Beverly Hills to the jagged teeth of the downtown skyline as he finished his drink.

It was almost sufficient, twenty hours later, to clear the aftertaste of Smirnoff from his palate.

When he was done, he washed the glass and cocktail shaker, dried them, and put them away. He looked around.

It was as though no one lived here.

He wandered through the darkness back to his bedroom, once more giving the heavy bag a spin kick that jounced it on its chain.

In the bedroom he pulled his shirt off with a groan. As he looked at his floating mattress, exhaustion hit him in the face like a shovelful of wet cement.

The pocket of his cargo pants vibrated.

The RoamZone.

Odd.

Before driving home, he'd already shattered the SIM card he'd used to contact the president and replaced it. He hadn't tasked Max with finding the next client. Which meant that no one should be making use of this phone number.

Now or ever again.

Orphan X had received a pardon. The Nowhere Man was retired.

Caller ID showed a familiar international number with Argentina's country code. The missed call from earlier.

Puzzled, Evan thumbed to pick up. The line was thick with static.

He was accustomed to answering as he always did: *Do you need my help?* He paused, momentarily speechless. How did ordinary people answer the phone?

He said, "Hello?"

"Evan?"

It was the same voice he'd heard on the voice-mail recording, feminine and slightly throaty. As the shock of hearing his name reverberated, he didn't say anything, and for a moment she didn't either.

"Evan," she said again. "It's your mother."

Acknowledgments

This year I lost a dear friend, my attorney, Marc H. Glick, who was the first person to sign me as a writer when I was a mere twenty-one years of age. François Mauriac observed, "Each of us is like a desert, and a literary work is like a cry from the desert, or like a pigeon let loose with a message in its claws, or like a bottle thrown into the sea. The point is: to be heard—even if by one single person." For me, Marc was that single person, that first single person. The meaning of that to me is inexpressible. May we all live up to his example; may we all try to be the one who hears a new voice and, in joining our voice to it, gives it the strength and courage to speak alone.

I also wish to express my thanks to the squad of operators who backed X in his latest mission:

—Keith Kahla, Andrew Martin, Sally Richardson, Don Weisberg, Jennifer Enderlin, Alice Pfeifer, Hector DeJean, Paul Hochman, Kelley Ragland, and Martin Quinn at Minotaur Books

Acknowledgments

—Rowland White, my superb editor, as well as Louise Moore, Laura Nicol, Ariel Pakier, Jon Kennedy, Christina Ellicott, Bethan Moore (spirits consultant), and the rest of my fine team at Michael Joseph/Penguin Group UK

—Maureen Sugden, my world-class copyeditor in the west

—Lisa Erbach Vance and Aaron Priest of the Aaron Priest Agency

—Caspian Dennis at the Abner Stein Agency

—Trevor Astbury, Rob Kenneally, Steve Lafferty, Joel Begleiter, and Michelle Weiner of Creative Artists Agency

—Stephen F. Breimer of Bloom, Hergott, Diemer et al.

—James Bennett, my federal-deputy friend, who was instrumental in helping me get X behind bars

—Lauren Crais, who weighed in with legal counsel and aided me in getting everyone into an exceeding amount of trouble

—Billy Stojack, who lives on in Tommy

—Kurata Tadashi, for always covering X's six o'clock

—Geoff Baehr, Philip Eisner, Dr. Melissa Hurwitz, Dana Kaye, and Dr. Bret Nelson

—Simba and Cairo, 225 pounds of menace and delight

—RLSBH, know that you are loved

—NCH, the Best in the West

—Delinah Raya, endless grit, endless heart

And to my readers:_____ _ __ ___ _____. (To receive the cipher to read this message, sign up for the Orphan X comms newsletter at www.gregghurwitz.net.)